Beside The Still Waters

JACQUELINE T. LYNCH

Published by Jacqueline T. Lynch
P.O. Box 1394, Chicopee, Massachusetts 01021

In memory of Mrs. Eleanor Griswold Schmidt, Mr. Walter Johnston King, and the last generation of Swift River Valley kids.

Four towns…dismantled as an entire valley is prepared to be flooded. The past is being wiped clean, the present threatens, the future belongs to the fearless.

Three generations weave a tapestry of isolation and stubborn independence, battling the forces of nature, the Commonwealth, and each other in this family saga. A courageous girl becomes the guardian of her family's heritage, and ultimately, the one to determine what happens next.

Beside the Still Waters is based on actual events that displaced four entire towns in central Massachusetts in the 1920s and 1930s for the construction of the Quabbin Reservoir. Families are torn apart, divided between those who protest the construction, those who give up and leave while they can, and those who help to build the dam that will flood the towns.

Return to the Swift River Valley, its charm and its pain, its mysteries and its lessons—to a community, a family, and a young woman in a race against time.

ACKNOWLEDGMENTS

Cover by Carl Graves. Back cover map of the Swift River Valley towns from *Atlas of the Boundaries of the Towns of Amherst, Enfield, Greenwich, Hadley, Pelham, Prescott, Hampshire County : Leverett, Shutesbury, Sunderland, New Salem, Franklin County : Barre, Dana, Hardwick, New Braintree, Petersham, Worcester County,* published by the Board of Harbor and Land Commissioners of Massachusetts (1912). Special thanks to John Hayes for one more proofread, and to Sharon M. McConnell, editor and publisher of the former *Chickuppy & Friends Magazine* for which I was first privileged to interview former residents of the Swift River Valley towns.

PART I

CHAPTER 1

Dana, Massachusetts, was gone.

Enfield, Massachusetts, was gone.

Greenwich, Massachusetts, was gone.

Prescott, Massachusetts, was gone.

Hand shaking, eyes suddenly blurry with unexpected tears, Eli tugged his grandfather's watch and chain from his vest pocket. His family pulled closer to him to watch over his arm as the second hand swept past midnight.

At 12:01 a.m., April 28, 1938, small children in the town hall looked around at the walls, at the adults, at each other, incredulous at the miracle. They had believed they would all evaporate at midnight. It wasn't true. Life went on.

Then the grownups, in an unusual, rather grotesque display of open grief, sang "Auld Lang Syne" and wept, and then the children knew the world was over after all.

Eli closed the watch, gathered the chain and fob, and pressed it, warm from his hand, into his son's hand.

"This was meant for you." It had been unfinished business. He capped it off by kissing his wife, as if that were also a matter of unfinished business.

Jenny watched her parents, and all the old folks, and the children. Day laborers and farmers dressed in the suits they would one day be buried in; wives and daughters dressed each in her plain, simple, one good dress. Bearing witness to the last time most of them would ever feel a sense of belonging and of community; Jenny, with her documentarian's eye, knew that's what it was.

Roger Lewis shook hands, cast his eye around the crowded room, hugging his wife and shaking hands with as many people as he could reach, like a candidate seeking votes.

Mary turned to her daughter Ella, whispering something into her hair, with arms around each other's waists like girlfriends. It struck Jenny that Ella did not need her.

Jenny blew a kiss to her that was free and with no obligations or debts. Then Cousin George and Cousin Eliza stumbled through the crowd. Eliza, tear-streaked and pitiful, nodded to Mary and twisted her gloves. Mary, in a frenzy rarely seen in the Valley except at infrequent religious revivals, not that she ever partook of them, threw her arms around Eliza and bawled.

George and Eli shook hands quietly, and George smiled to see all of Eli's children here. Of George's boys, only Calvin came with his two kids. They did not speak of Alonzo, but each privately thought of him. Without realizing they were doing it, they searched for a sight of his face in the crowd. The rumors about him were obviously rather foolish, but those who liked romances and fantasy stories enjoyed them and made up more. Alonzo Vaughn, the great, brooding giant of a man, like a pioneer man, like rebel Dan Shays, and like Shays was chased off his land. He would wander in hiding, ever sorrowing for his lost home and his lost love, some said, like an old New England ballad of ghosts and hardship.

Jenny believed they must have been secretly glad he wasn't here. That would ruin the scenario. If he had suddenly come through the door in a new suit announcing that he had a swell job somewhere, that would just ruin the romance. She had seen the darker side of the romance. But she looked for him, too.

Other missing faces were recounted less romantically: Miss Rebecca, who used to run the Prescott Hill store; the Sullivans; Miss Murphy the Greenwich Village teacher...only his family remembered John Vaughn.

Jenny stepped out into the cool, damp night air that still smelled of dust from their long auto convoy earlier in the day. Wandering people coming and going searched for their cars or smoked, and drank beer under moonlight, and the massive collection of stars which seemed within arm's reach; and the hanging lanterns, less enticing because they were within reach. Dick followed behind, dreading what she thought as she searched the black, shaggy Prescott Hill with her eyes.

"This isn't the end, Jenny," he said.

"As long as someone makes a buck?"

"No, I don't mean that," he said, pained that she used his words against him.

"This place, it's got a life of its own. And what was here...you'll always carry that around inside you. Somebody like you would."

"Then you believe in redemption? And eternal life?" she asked, turning to face him, with more acceptance, even humor, than he expected. "I'm glad. I think I do, too."

Just as though stating a matter of fact, she gently pulled herself against him, and kissed his lips. She looked into his eyes for confirmation, brushed his jaw with her cheek, slowly nuzzled and kissed him again.

Over his shoulder, her eyes searched the dark sky over where Prescott used to be until an hour ago.

"I can't ever remember not knowing this day would come."

He smiled, holding her closer against him, then realizing with disappointment that she was talking not about him, but about the destruction of the Valley, and the coming of the reservoir.

***

1904 - 1910

Massachusetts harbors diminutive mysteries, thin sagas of emotionally close people. There has never been enough room for grand epics.

It is not a large state, yet within its borders are distinctive and unique divisions. These places are set apart not always by legal boundaries but delineated by how their inhabitants choose to be known, how they see themselves. The very essence of individuality is isolation. People on the shore. People of the mountains. City folk.

Nantucket is an island. Cape Cod is an arm of sand jutting out to meet the sea. Boston is the capitol, an historic American metropolis, the grand dame of American history, but to New Englanders for whom the rest of America does not exist, Boston is sometimes regarded as the center of the universe, the so-called Hub. The Berkshires are western mountains, behind them is where the sun sets, unseen by the Hub until tomorrow. Massachusetts is a small place, settled for the most part by Europeans from small countries, whose sense of space is perhaps by now genetic.

Hitching the wagon. Backing out the horses and hitching the wagon. Saying goodbye to Mother at the window, with a nod, and going to the barn. One last look at Mother, not meaning to, but catching her dismal expression, her disapproval and her sense of loneliness, the attention she felt was due her. Jerusha Vaughn had never left Prescott in all her life, not even to go to a community picnic in the next town. Her sons John and Elijah, and her husband, Walter, tried to leave for their outing with light hearts, but she wouldn't let them.

Some people from Massachusetts had left New England and settled the American West as pioneers. They became different people from the ones who stayed. The ones who stayed became like a hybrid plant, truer and truer to itself with every generation, but hybrid, lacking the new and different, becomes weaker, and extremely sensitive to exposure.

"You're for the parade and the war vets, Pa?" John smirked, giving a sidelong glance to Eli that mimicked his father.

"The latest war with Spain, that's T.R.'s war and he can have it."

"Can't compare to the War Between the States, hey, Pa?" Eli returned John's glance, and Walter huffed.

"Different sort of men. Why, my father..."

"Who fought with the 31st Mass.," John and Eli echoed.

"That's enough out of you boys." Walter smiled.

In the central part of the state lies the Swift River Valley, whose small mountains form the rim of a bowl. The Swift River flows in three separate branches through the valley called the East, the Middle, and the West Branch. They join in the town of Enfield, the southernmost town in the Valley. The united streams make a river that leaves the Valley, continuing southward where it empties into the Chicopee River, which flows westward to the Connecticut River, which dumps itself into Long Island Sound and the Atlantic Ocean. Swift River Valley children have made the journey in their minds when dropping a leaf into one of the branches, trying to follow its course. The hopeful leaf is their message to posterity.

The children know that the Swift River Valley is not near the ocean, which none of them have ever seen though barely eighty-odd miles away. It is not near an equally mythical sounding place called Boston, and the western Berkshires can just be seen if one climbs the Great Quabbin Hill on a clear day. The small, affable, almost cartoon-like train locally called the "Rabbit Run" rumbles through the Valley like a fourth river branch. It links the small manufacturing town of Athol to the north with the large commercial city of Springfield to the southwest on the Connecticut River, and stops so often on the whim of its conductor, Mr. Doane, that it takes pretty nearly three hours to make the fifty-mile trip. Despite these links, the towns of the Swift River Valley: Greenwich, Dana, Prescott, and Enfield were as isolated from the rest of Nineteenth Century Massachusetts as the old Bay Colony was from the Crown. Just as distant psychologically, just as different, just as vulnerable to outside edicts, and just as contemptuous of them.

At nineteen, John Vaughn came specifically to chase girls and mainly to take a day off from the farm, which was unusual for a Tuesday. Sunday was the day for rest, which meant after chores and church. Chores always came, no matter which day one chose to rest. John quickly lost his brother and father in the huge tent staked on the common.

These communities' divergence began with the colonists' defeat of the Pequots of King Philip's War when the ancestors of the current populace settled the Valley, then part of Narragansett Township 4. They worked it into Quabbin Parish and were left quite alone for generations. There had been that furor between the Commonwealth and local man Daniel Shays, to be sure, whose tax-ridden, poverty-stricken post-Revolutionary War rebels were hunted down by Governor Bowdoin's militia in the surrounding hills. Shays' Rebellion was only an historical footnote now, an anecdote told by firelight, even though it helped lead to the creation of the United States Constitution.

It had been many years since Shays' Rebellion, since the last local settler was captured by Indians, and since the Commonwealth, i.e. Boston, had anything to do with them, which was fine.

At eighteen, Elijah, or Eli as he was called, came to the town picnic for reasons which were not as clearly defined as his father's or his brother's. He guessed he was interested in seeing the parade, and to hear the band concert given by the Mount L Band of North Dana and eat at the formal noon dinner. Mostly, he wanted to be part of something and start the lessons he knew were out in the world waiting especially for him.

In Industrial Massachusetts of the late nineteenth century, the Swift River Valley was still teaching its children by the primer, still arguing Whig and Federalist, while the great social causes of the day like child labor, women's suffrage, Emancipation swept by them, though enough Valley men had fought for the Union on principle and for something to do.

They were the direct descendants of Revolutionaries and Rebels. However, by the early twentieth century, they were neither. Their Swift River Valley was just managing to enter the late nineteenth century, which had found the Valley at its zenith. The arrival of the railroad, of the motorcar, and of the miracle of leisure time for some people, had opened the Valley to industry, to summer residents whose rustic camps along the lakes dotting the Valley's floor swelled the population in Enfield alone to 1,036 in 1906. Distance in Massachusetts was always more a state of mind than of fact, but lately the mind was playing tricks. Some gloomily predicted a day when the Valley might actually become crowded. They would lose their isolation, which despite its inconvenience had made them just what they were.

Eli wanted, he thought, at least to be part of things, not just a bystander. Eli's problem, so he felt, was that he was always too ready to see things at a distance, a quality which removed its possessor from those very things which interested him most.

Greenwich (pronounced by its inhabitants as Green-witch and not "Gren-itch" as with other more sophisticated or affluent communities with the same name) celebrated its Sesquicentennial in August of 1904 with these feelings of rapturous self-identity, expressed not so much in words as in banners and bunting. Situated smack in the middle of the Swift River Valley, the little town on the Valley floor formed a community core for all the towns and lonesome villages in the area.

Red, white, and blue drapery billowed halfway up the steeple of the Congregational Church at Greenwich Plains. One entered the road along the common through a kind of triumphal arch made of wood, ropes of greens, and a little more bunting. The banner read "Greenwich 1754 - 1904."

Teams of horses filed along the converging roads in a makeshift parking lot. The train brought more visitors from Springfield and Athol. It would be the largest crowd ever gathered in the town's history, the biggest celebration in the Valley. The crowd, especially the organizing committee, summoned strength from resurrecting the glories of the past. The future was bothersome and suspect.

At one of the nooning parties, into which the crowd had broken up for dinner, Eli paid for his meal with money he'd gotten for helping cut ice from Quabbin Lake last winter. Holding it had made him feel rich for months, but he graciously let it go now. Since he did not see his father or John for company, he sat by himself, and carefully began work on the suspiciously dainty chicken salad sandwich, but he made up for its lack of substance with the customary wedge of mince pie, heavy with lard. A good pie was a meal unto itself. Surely the chicken salad was only for esthetics.

Eli knew about esthetics. That was what separated his father's rough hilltop farm in Prescott from the doilied, credenzaed parlors of Enfield, from the shops and hotels of Dana which had electricity, sometimes, in some parts of town, for some people. Eli knew about the better things, even if he'd only heard about them second or third-hand. Like the chicken salad sandwich, he was not sure about the worth of all of them. What he most wanted in life was to be able to judge for himself. He distrusted the opinions of just about everybody else.

The speaker on the platform intoned a litany of their God-given rights of self-preservation, fussing at the end of every glorious paragraph to pull his celluloid collar away from his Adam's apple. His wife listened distractedly and caught deft snatches of gossip over the back of her chair while pretending to publicly adore her husband.

Eli listened, fighting drowsiness, pondering the self-congratulatory tone of the speech, which defended the Declaration of Independence as a darned good idea. The whole day was a tribute to Greenwich and to themselves for being themselves. The women's choir sang songs of home and hearth, ballads of the honest farmer and the glories of battle and being Christian. Such self-absorption gave Eli a gloomy moment and he glanced to the north at Mount Pomeroy, and south to Mount Lizzie, and west to his own Prescott ridge for comfort. Each round, shaggy peak decorated the Valley with precision, like points on a compass. It made a person certain of where he stood.

In a moment Eli heard the clash of voices, cacophonous against the backdrop of the well-meaning ladies' choir, and he turned to catch the tail part of his brother being hustled away from the parked carriages. John had evidently gotten too friendly with a girl whose father was one of the celebration's "Special Police," deputized for the day to locate missing youngsters and remove heavy drinkers, though if a man could find a drink here he was nothing if not resourceful, an admirable quality.

Eli walked over but watched from a distance. Making sure John was all right was one thing, sharing his disgrace was another.

John brushed indignity off his made-over suit and angled his hat to its former tilt. John had started a mustache of late and though it had begun slowly as a dirty shadow under his nose, one could see the promising future in his so handsome face.

A girl standing near him caught the smile of Eli's self-imposed distance. "My uncle don't find it so funny."

Eli then noticed her beside him. She was a child, rebuking him with the scornful dignity of a matron, but a child still in her white pinafore. She held her straw sailor hat in her hand because she thought it made her look like a child, not dreaming it was not the hat.

"Watch you don't get no freckles." He refrained from pulling at one of her braids.

"My uncle will settle him. That's my cousin he's being fresh with."

"Don't tell me you wish it was you?" John said as he passed her. John grinned down at her and actually grabbed a fistful of black braid, but she only jerked her head back and crossed her arms, standing her ground. She smiled a little as well. Eli noticed, because he was likely to, and John did not.

"Eli, I'll find my own way back."

Eli nodded. John walked away, lost in the crowd again. Eli stood with his hands in the pockets of his new long pants, with the girl at his side, both watching after John.

"So, he's y'friend," she said in mock contempt, as if it did not surprise her at all.

"He's my brother, if it's any of your business. Well, I'm goin' to watch the baseball now, if you wanna follow me."

"Who'd want to follow you?" she pulled apart her folded arms, slamming them down at her sides. "You're just like y'brother." She stomped away as much as anyone can in hobnailed boots on damp grass. It had been drizzling since dessert.

Eli watched her go, smiling at what she had said. He was not like John and everybody knew it.

Eli looked around for his father, knowing he would want to be going home soon, as being away from Prescott too long made him anxious. He found Walter standing by the carriage, running his hands through his graying beard, wiping the mist off his cheeks with his handkerchief. He had known Eli would come to find him there, he knew that John would come home when he wanted.

"Had enough, Eli?" his father said to cover his relief.

"Yes, Pa." Eli freed the horses and backed them up into the road. Walter Vaughn watched, knowing from experience some jobs were for four hands, some were for two. He climbed up beside Eli. Eli grasped the reins.

"Rain doesn't seem to be spoiling their fun." Walter Vaughn said, "We ought to get back to your mother."

"How'd y'like the old vets, Pa?"

"Old is right. We lose a few each time. They are the times past, Eli. Past dies slowly around here, but it surely does die."

Eli and Walter Vaughn turned up the Prescott-Greenwich road, crossed the Middle Branch of the Swift River which flowed nervously under the wooden bridge, and returned home to the hill town of Prescott.

The Valley was comprised of several villages, "hollows" and minute communities which did not appear on the state atlas. The four incorporated towns a person could actually find on the map were called Prescott, Greenwich, Enfield, and Dana. Prescott, where the Vaughns lived was the smallest and most agricultural of the Valley towns. It was the most remote on its high, stony ridge where people lived as they had lived for three hundred years, without running water, without electricity, without paved roads, or without help from anybody.

Some eighty miles east of here, Boston, the Hub, formed that center of the universe from which rippled rings of travel, trade, culture, and history. From its earliest days, it attracted a large population, larger than that appendage of soil could sustain. Parts of its so-called Back Bay were filled in to create more land. As early as the colonial days the Charles River was both its main source of water and its main repository for sewage. It was overworked and polluted. The search for a supply of clean, fresh water began.

It ended three centuries later in the Swift River Valley.

CHAPTER 2

A web-like mist rose from the eastern hills in an eerie display. The cooling earth, reflecting solemnly on its wantonness in summer, prepared to repent and settle down come autumn. There is a time in late summer when the light is golden, the air clear and still, and a visual epiphany occurs, possibly having to do with the equinox, which is to say there is a scientific explanation for everything. The mystical qualities of the land had vanished with the Algonquin, or else he was the last to interpret them.

Eli drove the cows to water. They were just as present-minded as he was. He finished his morning chores and now looked forward to the haying. Eli loved farming, the hard work, and the idea that he himself could literally reap the benefits of his work. The first sight he remembered from childhood was watching his father pulling a load of hay to the barn and then toss it into the loft with the long fork, the wagon pulled by enormous draft horses. His father had stood upon the wagon with the shaggy mountain of sweet hay behind him, beneath him, spilling abundant fragments from the rolling rick, as if his father were the god of hay.

Walter Vaughn wore a sagging, wide-brimmed hat, his beard longer then, like a prophet's. His gray shirtsleeves were rolled up to expose muscular, brown forearms. He laughed at his little son and waved to him from atop the wagon like a man who loved his work, a man who felt truly blessed and questioned none of it.

Independence was the point of it all. Do for yourself. Your ancestors died for independence. It was the secular salvation in his Calvinist upbringing.

Today they slashed the hay down with a mechanical thresher. Walter Vaughn left the machinery to Eli, as he had never trusted anything beyond his old scythe, which hung in the barn as a curiosity. John was also handy when it came to machines, but only really useful when something was broken. The repetition of farming tasks bored him and standing out in the hot sun left him irritable and more in the mood to set fire to the hay than harvest it.

Fortunately for John, the thresher broke, which lifted him from near-homicidal boredom by the opportunity to make something move. By silent agreement, Eli and Walter left the job to him. They walked together back to the house for noon dinner.

Eli waited a moment for his eyes to adjust to the cool dimness of the kitchen. His mother stood at the table in the kitchen, carefully laying down plates. She moved deliberately, as if thinking about every move, telegraphing by her silence that her moves cost her effort and she was sick of the burden. Eli went to the sink and impatiently cranked the pump. When the cold water finally regurgitated from the earth, deep beneath the house, he caught it in the palm of his hand and smeared it around his sticky face and neck.

His mother seemed to scan through him with an expression of deliberate irritation.

"Hoo-aryes your father?"

"Out back." Eli replied, meeting her tension with calculated calmness. His mother already knew that his father was in the outhouse, always referred to in vague terms such as "out back" because the outhouse and such natural functions as were performed there were too rude to mention. Hypnotically familiar with the small circle of her family's activities, yet she demanded constant verification of her constant suspicions as the only stimulant to her own unvarying life.

Eli's eyes lifted across to his mother's face. Her former countrywoman's ruddiness had turned sallow. The muscles and skin of her face had fallen with her expression in these past years. She was a few years older than his father, but now she looked very old.

She would always wear a house-bonnet, as they did when she was a girl, though younger people and even some of her generation had drifted away from what was once considered sensible, even morally correct clothing. Jerusha still wore sober, dim colors, high-waisted day dresses that billowed down to her ankles. No modern shirtwaists for her, no corset or girdle. She was what she was and defied anyone to change her: a seventeenth century Puritan in nineteenth century form, living to her regret into the twentieth century.

"Careful with that," she said. He held the cast iron pot in mid air, while she painstakingly spread a small braided potholder on the table. The potholder, braided from colorful rags, was a wedding present given to her years ago. Jerusha Vaughn knew the history of everything she owned and called each story to mind if she did not always speak it aloud. Eli knew this, and he automatically shared her thought of the potholder as a wedding present while he set the pot upon it.

She remained an Old Testament, self-styled Congregationalist, which is to say she took her scripture without milk or honey. Her proper church was the church of Jonathan Edwards, New England's foremost visionary and fearmonger. It was a church mostly of her own mind and making. She had no idea the Great Awakening was over. She believed in torment and release from torment; that was the depth of her faith. She knew she was saved but grew less satisfied in the knowledge. She wanted only to prove it before she stopped caring altogether.

Walter Vaughn stepped in briskly and went to the pump at the sink.

"You've been a time." Jerusha said.

"What've you got for us?" Walter said, peeking down into the iron pot as he wiped his hands. He sidestepped his wife's mood truncheons deftly, like a polished, gallant, if unsuccessful showman. Eli set down cups of milk and planted a hard pillow of bread on the table for something to do to hurry the meal. He flinched in preparation when his mother scanned the room, unnecessarily, for John.

"Hooware's your brother?" she addressed Eli.

"Mending the mower, Mother." Eli hardened himself to the penance of self-control.

Jerusha looked at him as if he were crazy.

"Don't he know to eat?" she looked down in harassed attitude at the four plates on the dark table.

Jerusha Vaughn, only forty-four, had aged herself to an emotional invalid after the death four years ago of her youngest son Nathaniel, who, at ten years old, was killed playing with fireworks on the 1900 Fourth of July. Jerusha mourned both her son and the Nineteenth Century.

"Leave him." Walter said, sitting down with exaggerated anticipation, "We all got our work to do. Mother, sit down now."

Bewildered, Jerusha dropped herself in her chair and wiped her hands on her apron in disgust.

They were in the Last Days, she predicted, reading her Bible. Iron battleships and men trying to fly. They were in the last days. Nathaniel had been taken as the century turned, and Jerusha knew nothing would be the same.

"This is no way to live," she muttered, and resignedly bowed her head. Walter watched her nod and followed her example. Eli's head had been rigidly bowed for some time.

"Loward, thank you for our share of your bounty, and our place on your land." Walter said in a soft, lilting tenor voice he reserved for prayer.

Eli had heard the prayer a thousand times and not understood its meaning, or at least had not agreed with it. The bounty was theirs, the land was theirs. The risk was theirs. He kept it to himself.

They ate the boiled vegetables they grew and the thick slices of bread smattered with their own butter. Gratitude may have been due the Lord, but they bore the responsibility.

They picked out the smells of the dusty hay and the barnyard on their clothes, of the wet Fels-Naptha soap by the pump, of the warm, comforting steam from the potatoes and cabbage and carrots, boiled to near-extinction.

They could hear the tinny clock in the front room, and the afternoon rustle in the oak trees.

Eli equated the workings of his soul to his moods and how he felt inside, instead of a separate part of himself that he would relinquish like a claim check on Judgment Day. Eli found his soul in their land on Prescott ridge, while his mother kept her soul in the cupboard where the family Bible lay.

Walter and Eli cleared the table while Jerusha studied the remnants in the pot.

"Don't mind," Walter said gently, "He'll have 'em cold when he gets in soon." He filled the washbasin for her and searched for his old straw hat. In many ways Walter was just as set as she was. He would not go over to the denim overalls that John and Eli found comfortable. He lived in his homemade corduroy trousers and his loose, homemade cambric shirt that billowed from underneath his suspenders.

"George is here." Eli called, "And Eliza."

George's father was Walter's brother Asa, who lay dying in bed of cancer, though nobody spoke of it. They lived on the next farm over, slightly down the slope of the ridge. The land had been all one property once, but as is the custom among heirs, the land had been divided and divided again. George had come to help with the haying, and his wife came to visit. Pregnant and well beginning to show, for that reason Eliza needed to excuse herself from the world before her confinement.

This was the custom, though there was no real need to confess her pregnancy. Jerusha could see even from the window that Eliza was pregnant, and so could Walter and Eli. No one would of course make notice or comment, even if she were to deliver in blood and anguish on their doorstep, if she had not cleared her throat in the middle of a contraction and brought the subject up first.

Jerusha welcomed her with competence and with no more notice than was necessary.

"Let me take y'things." Jerusha said, "Sit down first, child, and tell me how your people are."

Jerusha knew Eliza had something to say and so gave her leave to say it.

"Well, Miz Vaughn, looks like I'm gon'ta have a baby." She grinned as if it were a grand joke that went well. She looked into Jerusha's tired, but not unsympathetic gray eyes and saw only a mirror of her own happiness, and none of the irony or skepticism that lingered there as well.

"Well, that's fine, Eliza," Jerusha said at last, patting Eliza's soft, plump hand as a matter of course. "I know Hester n' Asa must be pleased."

"Oh yes, though it's not the first grandchild for them, and George..." she smiled deeper, carving spectacular dimples in her round, ruddy face.

"Well, that's fine." Jerusha said, "I'm only up the hill, here, if you need anything, but you might consider the *huspital* in Ware...."

"Oh, I hate the thought of it," Eliza shuddered, "I'm not fond'a hospitals...."

"You've never been near one."

"And I don't intend t'be caught dead in one. I'll have Doc Wendell, and that's enough." She did not notice Jerusha's wry smile.

***

Two large draft horses pulled the wagon. The thresher preceded, gleaning the ancient crop which had been cut for centuries with a scythe cradled in a man's arm.

Other crops were Indian corn, rye, buckwheat. The corn grew in straight, firm stalks, dark green soldiers standing in line patterns that matched the ornery contours of the uneven land. George had started an apple and pear orchard since taking over his father's farm. He said small fruit orchards for hereabouts was the future, the only way Massachusetts farmers could get a cash crop. Eli did not know if he agreed about that but envied him his independence. Because his father was sick, George could run their farm his own way.

Despite the few cash enterprises that developed, most family farms still grew small varieties of truck, raised only the cows, pigs and fowl they needed for their own use. Whatever they happened to have sold for cash was whatever happened to be left over.

Little profit flowed into their kitchen counter coffee cans, let alone bank accounts, but no one in the Valley went hungry. They were cash-poor, but they owned their land outright, their birthright for generations.

Eli thought of the fortune he would make if he could run the farm. His father was too easily satisfied.

"I know, I know, George, but mind, your father and I were in the same way, and then your brother moved to Hadley." Walter Vaughn said, "How can I turn the farm over to that John, and he not ready to settle yet? It seems like nothin' ever works out the way you think it will...."

Eli started, but only inside himself, careful not to show it outwardly. He had been daydreaming, but heard his father declare in his offhand manner that he intended to leave the farm only to John.

Eli looked at Walter out of the corner of his eye, and Walter noticed. Walter had wanted to make himself clear for a long time. He found his opportunity, determined not to feel guilty about it. Eli looked away and took a drink from the dipper that rolled in the wooden bucket. Walter knew his son's feelings were hurt. Well, there was no help for it. Better to be plain about it.

The ricks stood like strangers in the field. Eli looked at them with contempt, like someone whose passions are denied him, who then in turn denies his own passion. Eli looked down towards the Valley in search of equity somewhere. The legal rights of property were what made Valley men citizens of the Commonwealth, responsibility for that property made them men. Here he thought he was a man, and his father said he was not. If he were five years younger he might cry. He made a decision instead, because any decision was relief. He decided he would get his own land. It would be better than this hopeless chunk of sorry hillside.

"Set to go, Eli?" his father said to him, his only apology.

"Let's get it done." Eli sneered back at him.

***

Darkness consumed the land and sky by the time Eli came in from the field, and only lanterns and stars braved it. The haying had been finished long before and the equipment left idle by the barn. Eli glanced at the blades, which he had rinsed clean with buckets of water, thinking they must be as bone-weary as he.

Eli stumbled upon John in the barn.

"Eli, what d'ya think? I'm going to the mills this winter."

Eli did not answer. He regarded John a moment, then hung his buckets on their nails.

"Well, you don't have much to say. What's the matter now?" John asked, slapping his hands on his knees.

"Never figured you for factory work."

"Lot of fellows do the mills in the winter. There's nothing doing here, and it's good money."

"You're getting the farm, John."

"What? What do you mean?"

"Pa says so."

"Hell, Eli. You can have it."

"No, I can't." Eli walked out of the barn with nothing else to say, though John called him once.

***

The small local mills were not the urban coke-belching giants that made the Industrial Revolution money-wise, power-driven and ugly. These Enfield buildings were really only the legacy of colonial mills. Planted along the Swift River that cut through town, the Enfield mills included woolen and cotton mills, sawmills, and the box factory located at the upper village, called Smith's Village. Powered by the river, they were ramshackle buildings and for some years had become the winter workplace of many farmers.

A new generation joined them now, young men who found that a trade as a machinist could be just as respectable, and more profitable, than farming. These men were called *ambitious,* rather than *industrious.* It was no longer fashionable to be industrious.

Eli decided to work in the mills this winter, too. If John could do it, he could. He made the trip daily from Prescott when the weather permitted and would board over in Enfield when winter came. John was right about the mills. Eli could earn money for his future farm here.

Coming into Enfield, he drove past the Swift River Hotel, a grand three-story wooden structure with an attic level under its peaked roof. Double verandahs wound along the building, one on the first floor and one on the second. Yellow stagecoaches once barreled along the turnpike roads, sounding distant horns, dropping travelers here with their gossip of the outside world.

Summer tourists came these days, people with money and time to spend it, people who came to the Valley on purpose, not as a stop on the way to someplace else. They arrived in Enfield with relief and recognition to the summer cottages they owned on the lakes, not with the old dull surprise and scornful amusement of those long-ago travelers who may have thought the driver had gotten them lost.

Eli began his day at the carding machine. His mind did not wander much because he was still new enough to the work to be afraid for his fingers.

When the dead of winter at last arrived Eli looked forward to it and how it would set him totally free from the farm, and he found himself a room with a family in Enfield called Pratt. Mr. Pratt was part owner of a mill in Ware. Too ill from a weak heart to work now, he lived in genteel semi-retirement in his fine Enfield home. He intended his three daughters to be well educated, as he had been to Amherst College. The eldest had already started her first term at Mt. Holyoke College in South Hadley, still called the Ladies' Seminary by a nostalgic few.

Mrs. Pratt, a self-disciplined and self-designed mistress whose sense of duty fueled itself mainly by her fidgety need for something to do, was equal in her supervision of Eli as she was of her girls. He paid a small fee for his room and board, and also took care of firewood and other men's jobs in exchange for his laundry, his noon meal with the Pratts and sometimes Sunday dinner, when he was not taking Sunday dinner home or with his cousin Sam's family in Greenwich. Mrs. Pratt saw that he was well fed and that he went to church. Eli did not mind the supervision; he had been under his parents' supervision all his life, and rather enjoyed the larger and more polished choir of the Enfield Congregational Church. Across the road stood

Enfield's fine two-story brick Town Hall, where Eli sometimes stood flat against the wall at a country dance, without Mrs. Pratt to observe him. Eli settled himself safely into the Pratts' routine, convincing himself of his independence.

He met the eldest daughter on her term break. Jane was tall, wore cologne, and smiled squarely, barely parting her lips, and wore the appearance, at least to Eli, of being modern.

The middle girl, called Hattie, was a heavier version of Jane, a little less fine in that Eli sensed she was not as smart or ambitious. He could not see Miss Harriet going to the ladies' seminary. Likely, she would marry soon. He wrote her off as a younger version of her brusquely capable mother.

The youngest girl was going on fifteen, changing her pinafore for a house apron when she had to, hunting wildflowers along the Swift River when it suited her, and making the daily trip to Belchertown for high school with resignation. Her name was Mary, but she was dallying with the idea of calling herself Mae because "Mary" was too old-fashioned. She smiled at Elijah Vaughn's Old Testament name.

It was the girl at the Greenwich Sesquicentennial, who had criticized John.

"Knew you'd get freckles if you didn't wear your hat."

"Welcome to our home, Mr. Vaughn." She dismissed Eli as she was in turn dismissed by her mother.

Eli's room had dark, large floral print paper. The bed was oak with a feather mattress under a patchwork quilt, not a crunchy cornstalk mattress as he had at home. A small table by the bed, a small oval mirror above, washbasin and pitcher, and a wide oak wardrobe that entirely swallowed his two sets of overalls and three white shirts. He was wearing his Sunday suit.

Here, Eli realized the inferior quality of his life in Prescott, yet he knew that he was not inferior to the Pratts. Like them, he was Puritan descended, and his yeoman ancestry, his independence, made him an equal to Mr. Pratt and his property and his floral wallpaper. And his brand new indoor plumbing. A real wonder. Not a corncob or mail order catalogue in sight. That indoor privy, created from an upstairs closet, was a wonder.

Eli felt quite happy with himself. He wondered if John was, too.

John had left the farm for winter work in the box factory at nearby Smith's Village, but grew bored and decided to go to Springfield, instead. That was a bigger step.

Springfield, about twenty miles to the southwest, a real city of concrete, stone and steel, with streetcars and motorcars, held all races of people and all manner of foreign born. Living with the Pratts was adventure enough for Eli.

"Dear Mother and Father,

I send this by mail, even though I know if I sent it by Henry the Fishman it would get to you sooner. I thought perhaps you might like to see the stamp. We did not get mail often at home and I can tell you it is for certain a change to send a letter as much to get one. Mother, you must not mind John going for Springfield is not so far. The Rabbit will bring John back as easy as it took him. I will see him off tomorrow and remind him of his home and property here. I know the Good Lord will mind your cares. I will close now, and remain Your Devoted Son,

Elijah."

Eli prided himself for a very devoted son, and as such wanted his parents to feel his spite. Eli sealed the envelope, carried it to the Post Office in Mr. Howe's store, took the little square, pink, two-cent stamp with Washington's picture on it and stuck it to the envelope after wiping it across his tongue. He enjoyed that. Not as much as the indoor privy, but he enjoyed it.

Indoor plumbing had long been commonplace in the cities like Springfield. In Boston, whose population had expanded rapidly in the 1800s, the urgent need for a stable water supply led to the search for new sources of water beyond the great city itself.

While John and Eli lived away from the Prescott farm for the first time in their lives, many miles east of the Valley, the Wachusett Reservoir was being constructed. Fed by the Nashua River, parts of the towns of Boylston, West Boylston and Clinton were taken by eminent domain. Completed in 1908, the Wachusett Reservoir would be the largest manmade reservoir in the world, but only for a while.

It was a subject that fascinated Walter Vaughn, who read everything he could about it in the newspapers he got a few days after they were published.

CHAPTER 3

For Walter and Jerusha Vaughn the winter's ordinary stillness cut deep into their dread and depression, and the sharp, crystal land seemed to dominate them right through the windows. He overworked himself doing nothing, and she felt crazed. As spring came closer their anxiety grew. John sent them no word of returning home. They were reluctant to admit the impossible.

They had never been alone together before, even from the first days of their marriage. Being alone seemed unnatural now and they grew self-conscious in each other's presence, found relief in irritation.

"Can't we ask Eli to bring him back?" she asked, aborting the pretense.

"We can't ask Eli anything now. Let's see what kind of men they are."

John spent the following planting season in Springfield, where he met Greeks, Poles, European Jews of various nationalities, Negroes, a crush of humanity. Fascinated by them all, he rode the noisy, anarchic trolleys up and down Main Street.

He took a job as an assistant to a photographer. In the studio he met whole immigrant families whose gray rags or native costume worn during the week would be shed for one American outfit to wear for pictures to send back to Europe.

An Italian family came in and John saw that the lady, who might have covered herself in dark clothing for work during the week, walked into the studio in a skirt and white shirtwaist, a feathered straw hat nestled on a pompadour that would match the style of any elegant American lady. She made his mother look like a hag.

She would send the picture of her smiling self in her American attire, her husband with his proud countenance from under the straw boater and show her family how well they were doing. They worked in sweatshops and lived in a fourth-floor cold water flat, but even though the streets were not paved with gold, they would not tell this to their family in Italy. They were too proud. Besides, they were in fact, successful and success is almost always subjective.

Had they known the handsome young assistant to the photographer was heir to twenty acres of hilltop farmland they would have considered him royalty. It gave John a greater appreciation of his inheritance, but he still did not want to go home to that empire. Not just yet.

A harvest had come and gone since he had been away. Eli worked the land, as usual with competence but with a new deference and distance that was on purpose and calculated to affect his father. It did. It made Walter more stubborn in his decision and irritable that his sons should be so contrary. Walter wrote to John to come home and take his place, that were it not for Eli, he could not work the land by himself and take care of Mother. Eli wrote to John as well, but his letters were almost in the form of reports on the progress of the farm, a servile, solicitous correspondence that puzzled John as much as his father's frustrated, petulant epistles annoyed him. John postponed his visits. He realized he should tell them directly that he did not want the farm, but inside he was pleased to be propertied.

Greuber, the photographer for whom he worked, had plans to open another studio in New York City.

John decided to come home for one last visit to say goodbye, inside himself if not aloud. Walter and Jerusha did not know this was John's goodbye, and having pinned their hopes on Eli for bringing John home for good, were pleased with Eli for his success.

Eli shrugged off their sudden warmth, and though he thought he forgave John for being John years ago, there was a part of him which felt a lifetime on that farm with his parents was just what John deserved.

Eli had other plans for himself, still being cautiously formed. In 1906 he was twenty years old. It was time he courted seriously and decided this as mechanically as glancing at the calendar to decide when to plant. He wrote in Mary's school autograph book at her invitation,

'May you through life be happy,
And your friends prove kind & true.
May the bitter cup of sorrow,
Never be for you.'

... right after the place where her grandmother wrote:

'May Angels guard you with particular care,
And every Blessing fall to Mary's share—'

Her grandmother possessed beautiful Spencerian handwriting, much more suitable to the calico-covered autograph book than his grammar school penmanship, though his verse was similar to the others written by her friends and therefore measured up.

Mary was sixteen. Her face was losing its baby-roundness. Her figure had formed, what he could see of it, and she was putting up her dark hair behind her mother's back.

A junior Gibson Girl, Mary was slim and graceful, with deep blue eyes and a charming attitude of being aware of these things. She had brought Eli his dinner to the mill a few times, and he had sometimes met her at the train from school and walked her home. He became her servant in her search for lady's-slippers and hazelnuts, and in turn she gave him the assumption of being courted.

No lovemaking occurred between them, no flirtation and no expectation, but in a small town it is convenient to find a proxy lover. It allows one the privilege of company at dances and hay rides and sugaring-off parties without being called bold, and yet allows the freedom of marrying someone else if desired.

As part of this arrangement, Mary went with Eli, and Eli's cousin George and his wife Eliza and their year-old son Alonzo to meet John at the Enfield station.

Eli took charge of the assembly on the station platform. Eli took Alonzo in his arms, and Mary reached up to pat Alonzo's bottom in a grown-up, motherly way. There was a psychological instant they played father and mother and baby. They smiled at each other when the Rabbit train came into view through the woods at the bottom of Great Quabbin Hill. They all began to clap for the Rabbit, and for John.

John climbed into the carriage sheepishly; he did not expect a welcoming committee. Little Alonzo cried most of the way home in his mother's arms. John smiled briefly at the baby out of courtesy, then dismissed him and listened absently to George's description of his laying out of a new apple orchard on his land next to theirs. John looked up at the two wooded hills in Enfield that both bore the name of Quabbin. He knew he was home. They were sentries to this place. Eli followed John's gaze to the hills. They had found arrowheads there as boys.

Great Quabbin Hill and Little Quabbin Hill in the town of Enfield were names left from the first owners of the land. In the language of the Nipmucs of the long-dispossessed Algonquin nation, the word "Quabbin" was said to mean "land of many waters" and referred to the convergence of the three branches of the Swift River.

Mount Pomeroy and Mount Lizzie in Greenwich were both named for early victims of Indian attacks. Mr. Pomeroy was put to death on the hill that later took his name, and Mrs. Elizabeth Rowlandson was executed on the hill later named for her. Arrowheads and stories gave the Valley children scant clues about their home, but not of how it compared to other parts of the American nation.

Mount Pomeroy stood a little over 930 feet in height, and Mount Lizzie was just under 900 feet. Even heights on the Prescott ridge, the highest point in the Swift River Valley hovered only just over 1200 feet. Since the highest point in Massachusetts is only just under 3500 feet, height is relative. Perspective is subjective; it was to the colonists who settled a wild Massachusetts, and it was to their progeny coping with another kind of survival.

***

John scanned the choppy furrows of his father's newly plowed field for a fresh perspective. The turning of the cold earth had released that deep, rich scent. All around him the soft rain tickled the distant trees, the small rock garden, his own back.

His father sat in the parlor reading a week-old *Athol Transcript*. His mother churned butter with self-absorbed rhythm. John knew this without seeing it. He found Eli in the barn.

Eli sat on a milking stool, a harness draped over his lap. He looked up as John pushed aside the barn door.

"You should have been born a girl." John said. Eli looked up, gripping the awl and setting his legs farther apart.

"And why is that?"

"Then there wouldn't be this thing between us. Y'could have your own life apart from the farm, not just a copy of Father's."

"Better not tell people what's good for them."

"What has this place ever done for him?"

Eli looked up. "Do not now or ever tell me what to do or tell me what you think. I don't care."

John pushed himself off the wall. He put his hands on his hips. "Why don't you stop being such a damned priss ...." Before he could finish, Eli was up. He threw himself with such force at John, tripping over the harness that fell from his lap, that John stumbled back against the barn wall. The old wall shuddered, dust sprinkled down upon them from the hayloft, the lantern mounted by John's head jumped from the spot, and their father's scythe dropped from the pegs that held it. John grappled for the lantern by his face to push it away from Eli. Eli thrust his arm out and knocked the scythe away to protect John. They stepped away from each other, breathless.

"Blade cut you?" John asked.

Eli shook his head. John settled his hat and walked out of the barn. Eli wished he had asked John if the lantern burned him. It was too late now.

The rain poured suddenly harder and dropped a curtain of water down upon Prescott Hill, and John pulled his old hat firmer upon his head. He had taken off his city clothes his first day home. They made him conspicuous, and it embarrassed him. He was angry at having to be embarrassed.

He dug his heels into the soft ground and ran across the field towards the house, but he passed the house, and ran instead to the muddy road, pitted, and full of ruts and holes of rain. He ran until his legs felt the strain of dodging ruts and clumps of mud, until his lungs hurt, sick of hearing the rhythmic thud of the rain on his hat brim, feeling the cold trickle on his cheeks, feeling the weight of his wet clothes dragging on his shivering body. He leapt onto the porch of Berry's store and stomped up and down to shake off the wet, the mud, and his feelings. He took off his hat and slapped it against a porch beam and caught his breath before stepping into the store.

Miss Rebecca looked at him from behind the counter, with a strange expression, as if she expected him. Her hands folded neatly on the dark, worn wood, her chin lifted slightly and she seemed to smile from behind her round spectacles. She breathed neat slices of air through her small nose as if excited and trying not to show it. Her eyes did not dart over him. No sir, Miss Rebecca did not scrutinize people, for that would be rude. She looked a person in the eye, or else stared just over his shoulder.

Everything about her was muted and curtailed. She had operated the store with her married brother for years, since John was a child, and also cared for her ailing mother in a back room where ailing people belonged. Her brother, Mr. Berry, meandered in the storeroom, arranging his springtime stock of plow blades and hayseed, axes and shovels. He left notions and yard goods to his sister Rebecca. He loved shiny metal. He almost wished he were a farmer, but the store had been left to him by their father, and that had spared him from making an agonizing choice.

His sister had been called Old Miss Rebecca by children since she was in her late twenties. Her maturity, a daunting thing for suitors but convenient to a proprietress, came upon her early. Now at thirty-five, she seemed much younger, in an ironic twist of hormones, or attitude, for the first time in her life, than her actual age. The first gray streaks in her hair seemed only to spotlight that which was left of its natural chestnut color. The tiny lines around her eyes gave attention to them, accenting their brilliance, their expression of what might have been mirth held in reserve. Her pale, clear-skinned face suddenly began to mirror her vast personal feelings and she had achieved beauty in her maturity that she never had as a sallow, near-sighted child.

John scratched the stubble on his cold, wet cheek, and stepped towards the counter. He rested his hands upon the counter near hers. He smiled in the middle of a shiver. She stepped smoothly, carefully around the counter, and placed her thin, warm hand gently on his wet sleeve.

"Come you." She spoke softly, barely audibly, and led him to the old Windsor chair by the stove. There was the old black coffeepot on the stove.

Miss Rebecca poured in the mixture of browned bread crusts, eggshells, and a little actual coffee, into the pot. She poured the brew into a china cup and saucer with a delicate rose pattern. Such fine china tea sets were unusual in Prescott, but everyone living in the Valley towns had something pretty to complement or to defy the daily reality of their lives. They were not sure that daily reality could be called poverty, in a word, but there was room for speculation. Still, hardly a home did not have a "good" tablecloth, or a "good" pitcher, or a "good" highboy or other piece of furniture. Miss Rebecca's cups and saucers were her "good" thing, her pretty trifle.

She put the cup and saucer into John's hands, folding his cold fingers over the china, passing him an opened tin of Uneeda biscuits.

"Sit, young man." she murmured and went to get the crocheted afghan from her parlor.

The rain had slowed to a steady drizzle. Miss Rebecca had made more coffee, and John removed his boots and placed them near the stove with his coat and shirt. He sat nestled in Miss Rebecca's afghan. He guessed that it had been an item for her hope chest. That interested him. He would have liked to have a peek inside her, as one would peek into a hope chest.

They talked a little in slow, quiet words, interrupted only a few times by her brother Mr. Berry, who whispered to her,

"Why can't John Vaughn just go home and take his clothes off there instead of in the middle of my store?" Miss Rebecca shushed him.

A group of three children stumbled in for molasses. As it dripped from the container into the pail they brought for that purpose, the children voted on which penny candy they would choose.

John sipped his coffee, slouched in his chair, and watched the children, ragged from the rain, but bright with unused energy and fun.

"Thank you, Miss Rebecca," they called as they clutched a chocolate drop each, and sharing the carrying of the molasses as an important job between them, slammed the battered screen door as they stepped out onto the porch.

"How many chocolate drops you sold in your life, Rebecca?" John broke the silence after they left. She smiled at him from behind the counter, amused that he had omitted the "Miss." No one ever did, except her brother and sister-in-law and her mother, and they demanded much of her. She had no close women friends. Other women melted under her quiet interest, believing her to be judgmental when she was actually fairly unassuming. Unaware of this, she naively accepted people's distance as a display of awkward respect.

"How is it you never married?" he demanded, foolishly and rudely, he knew. Still, he smiled. He knew she would not be offended.

"There's probably a reason," she said, "I don't look too hard for it."

He looked at her hands neatly folded on the counter.

"I'm going to New York City." It felt good to confess it to someone.

"Don't forget us."

"You've never been more than five miles from here, hey?"

She fingered the fabric of her sleeve. She shook her head.

He wanted to share the Windsor chair by the stove with her, both of them folded into the afghan. Mr. Berry came in again to sift the bucket of nails and look out the window and straighten a bolt of cloth. He disappeared into the storeroom upstairs again.

John jerked his head towards him.

"He want me to buy something?"

Rebecca grinned. She did not act like he was committing blasphemy by going to New York City. Why couldn't Eli understand him like this? His own brother for God's sake.

He pulled on his boots and slipped into his shirt, not buttoning it but pulling his coat on over it. He stepped up to the counter, folding the warm afghan in his hands. He placed it on the counter and placed his hand on Rebecca's.

"In that case, I'll take some chocolate drops." He gave her a penny, rubbing the profile of the Indian before he placed it into her palm. She gave him a little fold of parcel paper with the candy tucked inside.

"I'll keep 'em forever."

Then he leaned across the dark counter and the afghan and softly kissed her cheek.

"G'bye Rebecca," he said at the door, "Thank you for keeping me warm."

***

"Come Thou Almighty King
Help us Thy name to sing
Help us to praise,
Father all glorious,
O'er all victorious
Come and reign over us...."

The lilac bloomed fresh and sweet outside the open window, on the other side of the stained glass.

Reverend Holland smoothed the Bible page underneath his white hand and let the small congregation settle a moment before he began his sermon.

He had only been to the Prescott Hill Congregational Church for three months, and had an idea from the still, ghastly stoic congregation that he would be on probation for another twenty years. He had only just graduated from the seminary. He waited another moment and began another sermon on brotherhood.

Jerusha Vaughn stiffened and audibly sighed. Changes in the Congregational church occurring coincidentally during her lifetime led away from Jonathan Edwards and his splendid horror tales of endless torment. They left Jerusha Vaughn and her revered Nineteenth Century struggling for survival. The twentieth century seemed not to be about a quest for salvation, but only for peacefulness.

Peacefulness had its boundaries. For Jerusha, and for most of her congregation, 1906 was still too early for ecumenical services between faiths. It was not even quite time yet for tolerance among Protestants for other Protestants. In the Valley, unions and separations occurred regularly among sects. For the most part Methodists were merely tolerated as competitors and Baptists still looked upon as exhibitionists. The New England Congregationalists, the church of Edwards and of the Mathers and Jerusha Vaughn was holding itself in reserve, though perhaps they were not as bigoted as they were baffled. The Protestant church since its beginnings had been a movement of intellect, of reasoning, of debate over man's proper place and his significance, if any, among the Mysteries. Mysteries in fact, were disdained. Jerusha personally had about as much respect for them as dust bunnies under the furniture.

Jerusha glanced briefly at Walter, and at Eli. John was not with them.

While the Roman Catholic faith, Judaism and the faiths of the Near and Far East born across the ocean and brought to America in trunks and satchels had thrived on the rituals of their carriers and not a few miracles, the Protestant Christian became the doubtful child of the Western world, paradoxically just as full of faith and yet demanding to know the logic behind his own salvation, and reason for others' failing to be saved. There was a constant redefining of his faith, of his expressions of his faith, of his very soul.

Their Cousin Sam Vaughn, his wife Agnes, and their young son Tyler shared their pew today. They had come up from Greenwich specially to visit because John had come home.

In every New England town, it seems there is a hill, even if only metaphorically. At the top of this hill, there is a plain, white Congregational church. Pristine and quiet, painted and photographed, emblazoned upon Christmas cards and revered in the hearts of even New England Catholics, this architecture stands for New England the way cranberries and autumn foliage does. It has become a symbol. The gospel according to Currier and Ives.

Eli leaned wearily on the minister's words, on the lilac, and his own thoughts, and searched for a comfortable position for his tailbone. He was close to sleep.

In Prescott as in the other Swift River Valley towns, the day of Edwards was slowly ending. Their God still the God of the Old Testament, jealous and punishing.

Walter Vaughn had been peacefully unconscious for some time, as he was most Sundays from boredom, the soft warm breeze, and a week of hard work. It was not easy for a hard-working man to be suddenly idle one day of the week even if it was decreed in Scripture. Instead of relaxing it made him fall apart.

When around the turn of the century a thing called "brotherhood" sold in a way ascension robes were sold some sixty years before, it came to the Swift River Valley in a furtive way. Young ministers, like Reverend Holland, were bringing it in the way children sneak a stray dog into the house, apologetically, trying to prove its usefulness, hoping it will win the folks over.

Jerusha Vaughn was not to be won over easily. She preferred religion straight up, with the vigorous scrubbing of hours-long sermons she heard as a girl. Tolerance among different peoples seemed a watered-down religion to her. It did not seem to have anything to do with saving her own soul. Her soul was her business, other people's souls were theirs. Even heathens had the divine right to be left alone.

In service of the Lord she attended monthly missionary meetings which through middlemen sent God's Word out of her hilltop church into the dirty wilds of Africa with a demure but off-key chorus of "From Greenland's Icy Mountains" and a clothing drive, but her heart wasn't in it. She still felt it was none of their business.

Jerusha noticed Tyler's straight posture that seemed to indicate he was paying attention and contriving to benefit from this sermon. Actually, he was mentally trying to assuage an itch.

Tyler was ten years old. He was a good boy. He did his chores and studied hard at school. There was talk even now that he might be fit for more than farming. Once the noble occupation of the yeoman class, farming slipped in consequence, considered by some to be the repository of young men with no ambition and little other talent.

Eli glanced at his mother and as usual, knew what she was thinking, saw her approval of Tyler. He looked at Tyler, mistrustful and slightly disgusted. Eli believed farming to be noble. This kid shouldn't set himself above it, or his elders shouldn't.

Eli scuffed his boots on the pine board floor. Mary was not with him now. Their friendship had not advanced so far as for her to visit with his family in Prescott. He felt alone and wished her here. He felt like a stranger in his family. He had always thought amusedly that John was the odd one, the black sheep of the parable.

I guess it's really me, he thought.

John had left last night. He took his bundle and himself out his bedroom window, right after coming home from Miss Rebecca's store, leaving a note for Eli.

His father had not spoken to Eli since Eli read the note to him. The last time a Vaughn ran away from Prescott was during Shays' Rebellion. At least *he* had a good excuse.

In 1795, eight years after Daniel Shays plotted his Rebellion against the Commonwealth at Conkey's Tavern in what would later become the town of Prescott, Boston's need for water forced it to become creative, or die, so water was taken from Jamaica Pond in nearby Roxbury, the first step westward of many.

In 1822, Boston had grown large enough to become a city. That same year, many miles westward, Prescott became a town. The rebellion born there by the previous generation had been thoroughly crushed. The people in Prescott took their water from backyard wells, streams, and a river. The rebellion may have been crushed, but the water was still left to make them independent.

CHAPTER 4

Walter shouted at Eli, "Your brother is a lazy, irresponsible fool...."

"Agreed."

"I'm not asking you what you think. I know what you think. You're so greedy for this farm, you'd push me and your mother aside in a minute if I let you. Well I'm not letting you. Don't you look astonished. I know what you're about."

Eli looked back at his mother, who gave no confirmation of her feelings. She was working too hard at looking stricken.

"I don't deserve that," Eli answered, his cold, flinty eyes the mirror of his father's, but the self-satisfied master of the smooth, quiet hatred in his own voice, "but I'm glad you said it. Now I know." He turned from the room.

"Where are you going?" Jerusha called.

"Enfield."

"Walter, stop him."

"Let him go. Who needs him?"

"Eli...?"

Eli called from his room.

"I'll be back for your planting. Like a good son."

***

Eli put his bundle of clothes down on the porch and smoothed his hair under his hat.

"Everything all right at home?" Mary asked, sitting there as if she'd expected him.

"Everything's cut, winnowed, stored, hung, jellied, smoked, or canned. Or dead."

"That's a tidy report. Come into the house."

"Your parents will take me again?"

"Need you ask?"

Mr. Pratt enjoyed treating Eli like a son at his disposal. When his bad spell came in the middle of January, Eli went for the doctor, Eli helped him to bed, Eli amused him with checkers.

"They must truly appreciate you at home, Eli," Mr. Pratt said, again and again. Eli's stoic male company soothed him. Eli only smiled and read to him from the newspaper. He did not want to talk of home.

Eli drove Mrs. Pratt in the buggy and maintained with her the delicate position of family friend, boarder, and servant in such a gallant and privately self-superior way that even she was impressed. She uncharacteristically allowed herself to be taken care of, which alarmed the girls. It showed she was somehow slipping. Their father had been slipping for as long as they could remember; it no longer had an effect upon them. They were not ready to let their mother become dependent as well.

"Eli, you'll be here for our Quabbin Club Guest Night, won't you?" Mrs. Pratt poked her head from the kitchen.

"Yes, ma'am. Thank you."

Mary snorted an unmaidenly chortle.

The Quabbin Club was similar to many ladies' clubs across the nation, formed by community pillars and run exclusively to add to the social sphere in town, to aid the community with good works, to better themselves by improving their minds with study, and to discuss those not present. The annual Guest Night was to be held in Mrs. Pratt's parlor this year.

Men were allowed at this occasion. Men were decorative if they were quiet. Tonight, the speaker was a professor of Ornithology from Amherst College, who Jane's beau Mr. Davis, late of Amherst College himself, had hunted up for them. Robert Davis' Bachelor's Degree paled beside Eli's indispensability, and he wanted to be in like Eli.

Mr. Pratt, gratefully too weak for company, spent the evening in his bedroom with a large, water-damaged volume of Tennyson. Since it always irritated his wife when he behaved in a vague manner to her guests, which he always did, it was just as well. He could be as vague as he wanted in his room. Eli was the only one who said goodnight to him. Then he set up the borrowed chairs.

He arranged them in what he imagined was an audience-formation, while Mary bounced out of the kitchen with a tray of deviled eggs.

"Hey, you'll drop that!" Eli smiled and took the tray from her, setting it upon the sideboard. Then he took a step back from her and folded his arms. She touched him with a sidelong glance, then nodded to the chairs.

"You must have done this before in somebody else's parlor. We'll just leave everything to you, Mr. Vaughn, and I shall go make myself pretty."

"You're pretty enough."

"I'm pretty enough for you, but what about the Amherst fellows? I think they have higher standards. But no, I think nobody has higher standards than you, do they Eli?"

"Your mother know you got your hair up?"

"I'm seventeen years old. Here, look what else I can do." She rushed to the Victrola and began the business of setting up a disk. She searched among a set of paper envelopes for something to dance to, but her father had acquired too many ballads of John McCormack and beautiful but complex Slavic violin pieces of Fritz Kreisler, listening music to Mary and not dancing music. Dancing music did not require one to think, only to move.

"Why don't you at least wind it up for me?" she mumbled into the cabinet, and Eli quietly set a chair down and put a hand on her shoulder.

"Forget that," he said, "It's too much bother for a minute of dancing, and there's no room. Sometime I'll take you to one a' High Harry Smith's do's."

"Dancing on the mountain? Is there still carrying on up there?"

"What do you know about it? You're not old enough to remember anything. There was a time, little girl, when the hill people would have parties and games, contests. Now they're just as proper as you, more so. They don't dance at all anymore, being a sin, you know, while you here in Enfield got church halls done up for all kinds of parties. Scandalous."

"That where High Harry plays?"

"When they can find him fairly sober." Eli had removed his hand from her shoulder. The novelty of being in a room alone together, despite the clattering of Mrs. Pratt and the older girls in the kitchen, gave Eli and Mary the kind of subtle adventure one finds when looking in the mirror. Self-knowledge in a stolen glance of intimacy.

Jane bumped through the door. They each took a quick step back from one another, noticed with superior amusement by Jane who was too vain herself to be a chaperone for anyone else. She set a tray of freshly washed punch glasses on the sideboard.

"Has Mary recited her piece for you, Eli?" Jane asked while Eli followed with his eyes the slender tapering made by her corset.

"Jane, you would bring that up!" Mary said, annoyed, leaning on the Victrola cabinet. "I'm giving the infernal 'Hadley Weathercock' again."

Eli laughed, "I never heard it called 'The Infernal Hadley Weathercock.' Are you speaking as well, Miss Pratt?"

"My young man has snared the speaker, so I am blessedly free of any other obligation to this evening," she rolled her eyes and resumed her fine, jaw-uplifted pose.

"Neither of you sound like you'll be enjoying this at all." Eli's brows converged with hasty befuddlement, which Mary loved.

"Oh," Mary said, "It's nice...I suppose."

"Yes, but more so if you happen to have talent, which Mary and I do not. But, we have to do right by Mother." Jane winked at Mary, "What can you offer towards the evening, Mr. Vaughn?"

"Leave him alone, Jane," Mary said irritably and moved to leave but would not leave Jane and Eli alone, not exactly for the same reason Jane would not leave Eli and Mary alone. She wondered why Eli did not think of leaving, and then of course it would be all right. He seemed to have no notion of leaving, instead he put his right hand in his pocket, seemed to think for a moment, then tapped a finger lightly on Jane's arm. He began:

"In good King Charlie's golden days,
When loyalty no harm meant,
A zealous high-churchman was I,
And so I got preferment.
To teach my flock I never missed:
Kings were by God appointed,
And lost are those who dare resist
Or touch the Lord's anointed.
And this is law that I'll maintain
Until my dying day, sir,
That whosoever king shall reign,
Still I'll be Vicar of Bray, sir.

When royal James possessed the crown,
And popery grew in fashion,
The penal laws I hooted down,
And read the declaration:
The Church of Rome I found would fit
Full well my constitution:
And I had been a Jesuit
But for the revolution."

Eli ran through a couple more verses, then stopped to see if he was being laughed at.

"Go on." Jane urged.

"How much longer is it?" Mary asked. Her sigh was meant to hurry him along.

"Mary chooses her verses by the line. Go on please."

Eli felt brave and continued.

"When royal Anne became our queen,
The Church of England's glory,
Another face of things was seen,
And I became a Tory:
Occasional conformists base,
I blamed their moderation:

And thought the Church in danger was
By such prevarication."

He took another breath, racing with the mantel clock and ran through a few more verses, ending confidently with the immortal lines,

"That whatsoever king shall reign,
Still I'll be Vicar of Bray, sir."

"You recite very nicely," Jane said, covering her smile, but also discovering that though the heavier hill accent might sound comic in comparison to the carefully intoned speech of the college men at Amherst, it was ideally suited for poetry and seemed to render even the chestnuts rugged and firm, and full of irony. The poem was rough. It suited Eli. This would have disappointed him. He thought the poem refined and so bothered to learn it.

The "Vicar of Bray," a lesson in how hypocrisy helps people individually and collectively to survive in changing times, was so old nobody knew who wrote it. It had gone by the way of more fashionable poets like Longfellow and Whittier. Unknown to the Valley elocutionists, Longfellow and Whittier were now also passé, in favor of Carl Sandburg and Robert Frost, who in their way reflected back to the earthiness of those colonial bards. But nobody told them in the Valley.

Mr. Pratt, who enjoyed his library mainly because he enjoyed collecting things, would have been appalled that his superior collection of Longfellow and similar stupefyingly rhythmic works, triumphantly New England, were considered in some circles to be sweet, sentimental, laughable.

Eli's appreciation of poetry was based on the coveted ability to memorize.

"Fifty-six lines," he answered Mary's question.

"Well, that's something, Eli," Jane shook her head behind a smile and retreated to the kitchen whether proper or not.

That evening after Mrs. Atchinson presented her paper on the feeding habits of migratory songbirds, and after little Agnes Pierce sang "... softly, softly, Jesus is calling..." in a teeth-clenching piano duet with her cousin Emily, Mary doggedly delivered her poem to the parlor audience of attentive ladies and their decorative husbands or beaus or whoever they could get to come with them.

"The wind blew south, the wind blew north;
I saw an army marching forth;
And when the wind was hushed and still,
I heard them talk of Bunker Hill."

She tried to sound like Eli.

At least, she comforted herself, neither she nor her audience had to suffer through "Curfew Must Not Ring Tonight."

Eli watched from the back of the crowded room. He held a punch glass, which he rolled back and forth in his grip to feel the rough-cut design rub his rough palm.

As Mary finished, Eli waved her to the porch, then set his glass down on the highboy without turning to see if she had acknowledged him.

In a moment she joined him.

With his hands held in a knot behind his back, he rolled his gaze through the dark yard, and the night sky beyond the porch roof, until her small figure stood beside him. He leaned over quickly and kissed her.

"Eli!" She was careful not to pull away too fast.

"We won't be alone in another minute. I had to make a quick decision."

Mary stepped back, frowned at her shoes a moment, then looked back up at him. He was inconveniently tall.

"Don't get ahead of yourself," she said for something to say.

"No, I think it's time I got on with this. I want to marry. Shall I ask your father?"

"Father's already married."

He threw his head back and blew a short, red-faced laugh to the porch roof, and she was relieved.

"All right for him, but what about you?" He recovered much more quickly than she did.

"Eli," Mary tried to laugh again, but her sudden embarrassment choked her, "'Course I like you. I'm not prissy enough to pretend I don't. I...just don't think you should talk about this. Not tonight. I don't know what my mother would say. I'm only seventeen. You know that. I think we should go inside now."

He caught her hand.

"I know all that, but I hate games, and I won't play them. I love you, please marry me. You won't regret it, but I won't ask you again. Of course, it's got to be all right with your parents, and to wait and all, that's fine, but you'd better make up your own mind as to how you feel because I will ask them."

"Eli ...."

"I think we both know they'll approve, so it's really up to you."

"Well, who are you suddenly?!" Mary pulled her arm away and he let her. He considered her calmly behind his suddenly resentful glare and stepped to the door. His large hand covering the glass knob, he leaned on the door a moment.

"I'm the best man that's ever going to go into your father's room and ask him for your hand."

"You leave my father alone. I mean it. You're taking advantage, Eli."

He did not see the tears form behind her eyes because of the dark, but he heard them in her voice. The doorknob rattled as someone tried to come out onto the porch, but Eli held it shut.

"Your father is letting go his share of the Ware mill to pay all the bills that cropped up from his illness. Hattie's not going to the ladies' college not just because she doesn't want to. Your folks have got enough on their minds, and I think they'd be glad to see you settled. Mary, I'm not forcing this on you if you don't want it, and I'm sure not going to kidnap you away to Prescott tonight. We don't have to marry until you're ready. I just want you and your parents to know how it is. Now I'm going up to your father so he can throw me out if he wants to. You have to make up your own mind. This isn't sudden, but I won't ask you again."

"No, it's probably not sudden, just to me. You've probably been brooding about this for months and no word to me. You sure know how to court a girl. You didn't learn from John, did you?"

Eli yanked open the door, and a couple stumbled out. He pushed past them.

***

The moon had sailed halfway through the deep black sky by the time Eli arrived back in Prescott. It had kept him company on the ride up. He said goodbye to it regretfully at the door.

Jerusha Vaughn's spells were more frequent now, and her psychological misery apparently so acute, though it had seldom wavered for as long as Eli could remember, that he wondered how his father managed to live with her. Ashamed, Eli realized his own relief in being away from home with the flush of renewed irritation upon returning. It grew upon him as he came up the ridge. It was complete when he heard his mother's hard voice from her room.

"Which one is that at the doaer?"

"Eli." His father nodded to him, and absently turned the pages of a three-day-old *Hampshire Gazette*. He scanned an article on the building of that reservoir in the eastward towns of Clinton and Boylston. He tried not to notice Eli.

"'Lo, Father." Eli said, putting down his bundle of clothes.

"Back are you?"

"Mother well?"

"'Course not, what'd you expect?"

"Get the doctor?" Eli asked.

"Think I'll know when to get the doctor."

"I'll just say hello then."

The room was gray and brown from the dim splash of dusty yellow light on the wall raised by Jerusha Vaughn's bedside oil lamp.

"How are you, Mother?"

"I can't catch my breath," she whispered from the pillow, "I know this will be my last winter, Eli. Know it."

"No, don't talk that way, Mother." Eli mumbled immediately, scratching under his chin and glancing, as if interested, at her opened Bible.

They were quiet a moment, Eli waiting to be dismissed, Jerusha watching her son.

"You have a big do, t'noight?" she asked curiously, weakly nodding to his plain good suit.

"Ladies' club a'Mrs. Pratt's. Quabbin Club. Had their Guest Night."

"Oh yes. Yes. Mrs. Pratt's big with that, init she?" Jerusha asked softly, "What did you do?"

"Oh, not much. I set up some chairs. Ate cake."

"What kind?"

"Had fruit and nuts in it. Good."

"Did you talk to anybody?"

"Friends a' the girls."

"You're stepping up, Eli," Jerusha murmured softly, with what sounded like wonder. He sat down on her bed stiffly, as if he were also bold tired and bewildered by life. He wished now he had thought to bring her a piece of cake.

"Mary had to say a piece," he offered. "She wasn't much good."

"We were mostly takin' pieces from the Bible, but there used to be a lot of good pieces when I was a girl. The men would have contests at the tavern. My father used to meet the stage at the tavern to catch the mail. They stopped at taverns then, didn't have post offices," Jerusha took a breath. "They'd pass out the mail, hands would be flyin'. They'd go into the tavern. My father grew up on rum, same as water. Even little children drank it. Sinful now, I suppose. Funny how things change. I wonder why."

"What did Grandfather do for a piece?" he asked, finding politeness surprisingly less difficult than he thought it would be.

"Well, your grandfather, he was known for a fine speakin' voice. Here, I bet I know somethin' you don't."

She cleared the phlegm from her throat with an effort that made Eli's stomach turn, and then took a deep breath.

"On Springfield Mountain there did dwell
a likely youth It was known full well
Leftenant Merrick's only Son
A likely youth near twenty-one

One Friday Morning he did go

41

down to the Meadow for to mow
Hee moved around and he did feel
a poisoning Serpent at his heel
When he received this dead Wound
he dropped his Scythe upon the ground
and straight for Home was his intent
calling aloud Still as he went
At length his careful Father went
to Seek his Son in discontent
and there his only Son he found
Dead as a Stone lay on the ground

T'was the Seventh of August year '61
This fatal accident was done
may this a warning be to all
to be prepared when God shall call."

Eli smiled. It was the sort of poem his mother would know.

She closed her eyes and swallowed hard after her effort. An eighteenth-century poem of local settlers, the Meadow was now the towns of Longmeadow and East Longmeadow, and Springfield Mountain now the region of Wilbraham, another town south of the Valley. The poem had gone the way of "The Vicar of Bray," and "Wolfe's Adieu," and the Valley did not know it yet.

His mother closed her eyes. She would be dead in another month. Two strikes of the church bell would announce her passing. By custom, it was one for a man, two for a woman, three for a child.

By 1848, when Jerusha's father was a boy in Prescott, Boston had outgrown Jamaica Pond, and its polluted state led to epidemics. A new aqueduct then linked the city to Lake Cochituate in Natick, a little farther west. From this pipe water flowed out from a fountain on Boston Common. In 1870, Lake Cochituate required augmentation from the Sudbury River, as the supply was not enough, not even enough to put out Boston's Great Fire of 1872. By 1878, when Jerusha was a girl in Prescott, the aqueduct from Sudbury Reservoir to Lake Cochituate was completed.

It wasn't enough. Boston desperately required more. A new water source then tapped into the Nashua River, a little farther west.

The Wachusett Reservoir, still a little farther west, whose progress Walter followed in the newspapers, neared completion a year after Jerusha's death. Only a few people, a handful of politicians and engineers, realized even at the time it still wasn't going to be enough to serve the needs of Boston.

Shortly afterwards, state engineers visited the Swift River Valley towns of Enfield, Prescott, Greenwich, and Dana. They scouted for a new reservoir site

End of Part I

PART II
1918 - 1926

CHAPTER 5

Now, everything was Before the War or After the War.

Names of the boys who had joined the service were painted on wooden Rolls of Honor, planted on the town commons. Memorials to the dead were planted in the town graveyards, while the dead were planted mostly in France.

Eli Vaughn brought his wife Mary back to his family's Prescott farm. His father lived alone there now, for his mother had died Before the War.

Mrs. Pratt relinquished her turn as Quabbin Club president in autumn, 1918. Her husband had been dead since Before the War and much of her sense of responsibility went with him.

Jane married her Robert Davis, now a professor permanently ensconced in Amherst, the only life he would ever know. Mrs. Pratt gave her approval to the less distinguished match between Mary and Eli Vaughn though her opinion of her new son-in-law was the same as when he was her boarder/servant. She still regarded him rather benignly with her social superior's condescension. She could not help it. It was the natural order of things.

Harriet remained the unmarried daughter and her place in the natural order of things fell to being her mother's companion, a lady-in-waiting, eventually a nurse. So it is with remaining unmarried children. Nobody questioned it.

Since Jerusha Vaughn's death, Walter Vaughn found himself searching for his place in the natural order of things. He suffered agonizing indecision about turning the land over to Eli instead of John, whom he had not seen since Before the War.

John was still in New York City, at least he had been since his last letter over a year ago. He had joked of the photographic portraits he took of dandy privates and colonels.

"S'pose he's eating in a fancy nightclub?" she smiled one evening into the dishwater.

Mary had learned to manipulate the pump. She learned to cut up chickens, snapping their joints with savage skill, and to cook on a wood stove with cast iron pans as her mother had done. She also learned what her mother did not teach her: how to milk cows, how to manage a home as if it were a subsidiary of the farm, which was a business as much as a way of life. She learned to cope with the life that awaited her on the Prescott ridge: the plain church, the crude store, the quiet, private townsfolk, seldom seen except at church. While growing up she had known that Enfield was not a bustling city like Springfield, but Enfield was still a proper little town with sidewalks and ice cream socials and piano-playing little girls. Tame and smooth, it invited company.

Prescott was none of these. Its hilltop, postage-stamp farms had been carved from forest and rock ledge. If New England's rolling landscape is gentle compared to the Rockies, then Enfield's well-behaved lanes and picket fences were gentle compared to the hill town of Prescott.

Population had been slipping since pre-Civil War days when pioneers had planned their futures on the frontier, still at that time east of the Alleghenies. After the Civil War Swift River Valley men, particularly it seemed Prescott men, sensed greater opportunities farther west, beyond even Pittsfield. There was a wider world to grasp, beyond their reach here. Their bear hug on little craggy Prescott no longer satisfied them. They came to realize Prescott would always be what it was: difficult to traverse, difficult to farm, and its simple, wild beauty no longer in fashion. Farms were big out West. The land there lay flat, fertile and grand in its proportions. The railroad out west was a stupendous and formidable magic carpet, not the bunny-hopping trolley it became when it entered the tiny valley, like an insignificant mucky brook off a great river. Prescott would never change.

By 1918 the population of Prescott was about 230, a drop of about 600 since the 1840s. This new figure included Eli's and Mary's children. Ida was six years old, Doris was four, Jenny was two, and Harrison was almost six months old. His birth made them both think of the future as they had not before.

Eli would not accept his father's farm. He could not make himself accept this land by forfeit any more than Walter could offer it by forfeit.

Mary came into their bedroom, stepping carefully in the semi-darkness with the baby cuddled against her chest. His legs kicked ripples against the outline of her robe. She lowered herself to the edge of the bed and nursed him.

Eli looked at her round-shouldered back. When the girls were babies, especially with Ida the oldest, Mary had climbed in bed with the baby, turned the lantern up to an almost daylight glare and chattered to Eli, to the baby with a giddy alertness remarkable for the middle of the night. She had wanted Eli to see her breastfeed, her figure, and her importance.

Now she wanted to keep this baby to herself. She was not in a hurry to plan his future, or even to see the day when he would begin to walk. She wanted to keep him little for a long time.

Eli's cousin Sam Vaughn in Greenwich had a fine little farm on the rich Valley bottomland. It would be Eli's, because he would pay for it, which did not entail the dark encumbrance of his father's favor. He could get another loan now that the old loan for the tedder and hay rake was nearly paid off. And Mr. Pratt left a small inheritance to Mary.

And Tyler was dead.

Sam's son Tyler, who had been a good boy in church, got shot through the face in the Argonne a year ago. He had been Sam's and Agnes' only child. Heartbroken, yet they somehow were able to believe they had made a great sacrifice for their country and managed to get through the horrific process of placing a memorial to Tyler in an empty grave in the Greenwich Plains cemetery.

"Greater love hath no man than this, that a man lay down his life for his friends." The verse from the Gospel of St. John had gotten much use After the War.

It was a good farm, the more Eli thought about it. He had not mentioned his idea to Sam for fear of being indelicate. He had not mentioned it to Mary or his father.

Mary hated the Prescott farm. She was quiet, distant around his stony father, but cooked her father-in-law's meals and washed his soiled shirts with dull thoroughness. She worked the plain clothing and soaking diapers of her children up and down the board, until Eli bought her a second-hand washing machine as a birthday present. It had a crank that moved the agitator, and another for the ringer. Turning the crank one hundred times would clean a load of wash. She was twenty-nine years old. Her delicate face grew ruddy, her hands red and veined. She hated the Prescott farm.

They were going to visit Sam in Greenwich tomorrow. He glanced again at Mary. She began to rock Harrison, her back to Eli.

***

Eli harnessed the draft horses to the wagon and noticed a distant dark figure over the back of the animal. He looked up and smiled at George's fourteen-year-old son. Alonzo trudged back through the corn stubble with his rifle over his shoulder, a rabbit in his hand. Eli recognized something of himself in Alonzo but marveled with amusement at that something else in Alonzo's personality that he did not share, a wildness to the boy, a quality that seemed vulnerable and yet fearless. He grew to manhood with confidence, but completely without direction.

They noticed each other from across the field. They nodded to each other. Alonzo continued home and Eli turned his attentions back to loading the wagon with blankets and rugs.

On the short, but bumpy ride to Greenwich, Mary could hold only so many on her lap. Eli had thought of asking one of George's other boys to come along and hang on to the children. Calvin was a year younger than Alonzo, a quieter version but too manly even at thirteen to want to mind children. Daniel was only eight, but he might have done. James at five would have been no help at all of course; he was a year younger than Ida.

At six years old, Ida was learning to mother the younger children. She would boss them into behaving, or if they were noisy and naughty, Ida would sternly waddle over to the offender and shove her into the dirt. Usually worked.

Except with Jenny. She would mind her Daddy and usually her Mama, but she would have none of Ida as if she knew even with a toddler's perspective that Ida was neither parent nor boss, only Ida.

"We're goin' to GREEN-wich, aren't we Daddy?" Ida skipped over to him, trying to peer into the wagon.

"Yes, we are."

"See?" Ida said to Doris, slapping the corner of the blanket out of Doris' mouth, "We're going in the wagon on a trip to Greenwich. It's very far away."

"Do you remember my cousins Sam and Agnes?" Eli muttered as he pulled Jenny away from the horses' twitching legs.

"Yes." Ida announced with extreme confidence, though she did not.

"We're going to church services with Cousin Sam and Cousin Agnes in Greenwich Village."

"Are we going to OUR church?"

"Not today. Jenny you come away from there. I mean now."

"Will they miss us?" Ida crossed her arms over her belly.

"I doubt it. Don't you be steppin' on your dolly, now, you pick that up. Dolly's all dirty now."

Mary watched from the screen door, Harrison in her arms. Eli put up with the girls so well, yet there was so much he did not understand.

George's wife Eliza had tried in her enthusiastic way to make friends with Mary, but Mary thought Eliza homely, forward, and stupid. Eli made attempts to defend Eliza. He thought Eliza honest, simple, and good-hearted.

"If that's the best your Prescott can offer...."

Eli folded his mother's dishtowel over the sink carefully and faced Mary.

"I didn't bring you t'Prescott to punish you." he began calmly, "I brought y'here because it's my home. If it's such a prison, maybe you'd better think again."

He held her stare for a moment, then he walked out the back door and stayed in the fields until evening. Eli had learned courtliness from his father, but there were limits. Walter had been sensitive to his mother's brittle feelings until she died. Eli had keenly felt his mother's subtle tyranny. He would have none of it from his wife.

The facade of his New England stoicism, quiet and charming in her mother's Enfield parlor seemed a mask up here. If Eli was courtly and amused, he could also be inscrutable, aloof, and reserved to the point of being self-involved. Mary, with her scorn for unfashionable neighbors and resentment at an outhouse supplied with old corncobs, pasted with old Sunday comics, still was not as covetous as Eli. He was possessive in a grand way.

She learned it the first night of their marriage. Mrs. Pratt had made up Jane's old room for them, and there in her sister's old room in her parents' Enfield home the boarder Eli made himself at home.

He acted methodical, to the point of being strange, Mary thought. With his boots under the bed and his vest draped over the chair, he stood fingering the sheers at the window, glancing with a kind of princely satisfaction at the quiet street below in casual preparation to sleep with his new wife.

"Expectin' a chivaree?" she asked a little doubtfully, testing a bride's humor on the stranger by the window.

He looked back at her and smiled, a wide, slow, all encompassing smile that enveloped her with queasy vagueness. For a moment she noticed in his eyes the look with which he held her, that of a winner with a prize. A satisfied customer. She stood awkwardly, forlornly still, until he came and hugged her carefully as if she were a child but kissed her softly, deeply, over and over because she was really a woman, and a beautiful one, as he had told her. Then she was relieved, convinced that his desire was greater than his sense of ownership.

The thin squeal from outside distracted Mary's attention and she noticed once more the dark kitchen around her. She settled her felt hat quickly and nodded briefly to her father-in-law, who read a chapter from the Bible in the shabby parlor in deference to his dead wife.

Mary grasped Ida's arm and yanked her back from Jenny, on whom she was sitting. Four-year-old Doris recovered from the surprise of a kick from Jenny and began to cry softly now that her mother had flown out from the house and they were sure to be in trouble.

"What's wrong? Don't y'be sitting on your little sister, Ida." Mary said, lifting indignant Jenny from the ground and yanking up her sagging underdrawers.

"She kicked Doris, an' Doris was only keepin' her from the chickens, Mama." Ida explained in accurate, authoritative fashion. Doris, in an effort to be taken as seriously as her big sister, tended to dramatize her explanations, and Jenny never explained anything at all.

They rolled away, their voices growing louder to compete with rumbling, down the Kelly Hill Road, down the West Road. Soon the land leveled off, all of it parceled in small farms, tucked in and around small, thickly wooded hills of ancient timber. Around Parker Hill the Vaughn wagon came abreast of a handful of neat houses. This was Greenwich Village.

"Want t'visit Eleanor Holt on the way back?"

"Eleanor Holt?" Mary turned to him in surprise. "Y'know I was thinking of her on the way down. Yes, I'd like to stop if we have time."

Eli nodded. That would be another plus. Mary would like to live close to one of her old school friends.

Sam's farm lay before the broad, gentle western slope of Mount Zion. It was a two-story white frame house, with a porch, and a white glider swing in the yard. They pulled into the yard and Sam Vaughn stepped out of the screen door.

He greeted them with equal parts warmth and shyness in his white shirtsleeves and lifted the little girls from the back of the wagon. Doris squealed with delight, while Ida assumed dignity for her father's cousin, and Jenny did not know where she was or who Sam was. She consented to being lifted, and patiently endured Sam's quiet nuzzling when he did not put her down. Eli watched him with a pang. Sam was a childless man now.

"Children, whyn't y'take your Mother to see Cous'n Agnes in the house, whilst y'Father n' I take care a' the horses." Sam said. Mary shook his hand in greeting with a weak smile and took her children up to the porch.

Sam and Eli unhitched the horses from the old wagon and walked them to the barn. They watered and fed the animals, enjoying quiet men's work in a man's place.

Well then, at it.

"Beautiful property, Sam. I know I've said it before."

Sam breathed in deeply for a moment, as if testing the manure-scented air. He examined the palms of his hands and rubbed them together.

"Been happy here."

"Well, y'worked hard."

"Y'got some nice kids." Sam smiled, Eli smiled back, taking care not to show much pride.

"They're a handful."

"Your missus does a fine job, Eli."

"She has a time. But, it's not easy on the farm for her. None a' her family or friends close by. She wants to stop by, see Mrs. Eleanor Holt before we leave."

"Oh yes," Sam scratched his cheek, "Holt's shifted almost entirely to poultry now."

Well, well, another cash farmer.

Sam sighed, and Eli's chest tightened in anticipation.

"You know, Eli, it was a good life for us. But…farm is for the family."

Dropping like a brick in the dirt, the truth made them both catch their breath. Eli bled for Sam through his anticipation.

"No point to it now."

Eli courteously met Sam's glance, then swished the dipper of water and baptized a struggling Black-eyed Susan near the well.

"You know how sorry we are, Sam."

"Yes. Well. There y'are. I was thinking. Lot a' factory work in Athol. Pay plenty well. Be nice to have a small place, just enough for us. Buy things for ourselves. Radio set, automobile possibly. My wife an' I would like that."

Eli assumed a thinking stance, as if he were carefully considering Sam's position, and found himself seeing the attraction of it.

"Well, factory's hard work, Sam. I can tell you. Still, it'd be a change for you both."

"Sakes, can't be any harder than this. Anyway, can't stand to see her moving about so, as though she were still waitin' for him to come across the field. Too much remembering here. Always will be, s'long as we stay."

"Suppose."

"Tyler's buried in France. Nothin's gon'ta bring my boy back, and there's nothing for me and Agnes in the Valley. We could have a new life somewhere else."

"Talk this over with Agnes?"

"Yup. We're just about set to look for a buyer."

"I might be interested myself." There. Sam raised his eyebrows. Eli shrugged. "Might do for Mary."

"Leave y'father alone?"

"No, course not. George's got an army a'young boys. Vaughn's gon'ta need room up there."

"Will we ever see that rascal John again, d'y'think?"

Eli stiffened. "I wouldn't know."

"That young fellow may have had the right idea all along. Leaving all this behind him. Well, I'll have to talk with my wife. Maybe it's for the best, Eli."

"Hope so, Sam."

They stepped up to the porch and prepared to visit with their wives, flushed and anxious, full of greeting as if they had not seen them in years. The children scooped mouthfuls of applesauce into their cheeks, and a suddenly chilly breeze forced them into the house.

***

Walter Vaughn snorted when Eli mentioned Sam's plan of moving to Athol but went coldly silent over Eli's plan of taking over Sam's farm in Greenwich. The haying was done, Eli had thought it appropriate to wait for that, at least.

"Your Enfield girl too fine for a hill farm?" Walter sneered, and Eli glared at his father, too shocked at his bad manners to defend her.

"My wife and I," Eli said, summoning dignity as a weapon, "will decide what's best for us and our children."

Walter looked away.

"Well, children's what it's all abowoot, init?" Walter said. His pause only gave a chance for his bitterness to gel. "This farm came to us through fathers an' sons. Huh. My sons. Nathaniel ... died a child. John's not a farmer, and you're too much of a farmer. You want to own bottomland. You want to own every piece you see. You want to own the whole gol-darned Valley. Go ahead, mortgage yourself to blazes. Fool! What abowoot the orchard you've been always pestering me for?"

"That orchard was never going t'be, not so long as you like to have things your own way. Keep your land. You get y'boy John to look after it, if you can find him. He's the landowner in the family. You sure made that clear enough."

Eli walked briskly back to the barn, dragging the horses with him. Walter stood alone in his mowed field, his pockets, his hair full of chaff. He wiped the brim of his wide rumpled hat, his eyes filled.

***

State engineers came to the Valley again. They repeated the survey that was done Before the War.

Nothing had come of that one. The Valley folk understood now that the survey was for a new site for an even bigger reservoir for Boston, but such a proposal was a pipedream. They did not spot the pun anymore than they were able to see into the future.

***

"The farm was all that ever mattered to my father." Eli said slowly, at last. "It's his heritage, his whole life. I always figured it was my heritage, too. But maybe I'm more of a businessman after all. I can separate myself from it."

Mary answered, "I'm not sure that's entirely true, dear."

"Sameness is security to him. I want more than that. I'm trying to get it with as little fuss as possible."

"I always knew you were more than a ploughboy, Eli. Did you and your father ever discuss the survey?"

"Good lord, Mary. Forget about the state."

"What does your father think?"

"He doesn't say what he thinks, he just reads out loud when he sees something about it in the paper, like my mother reciting from The Book of Armageddon. Don't worry about it. It's not going to happen."

***

Calvin and Daniel called for Ida at the back door. Mary tugged at the pleats in Ida's new white dress for the last time. The little girl was perfectly composed for her first day of school and the honor of a new dress made by her mother seemed to reflect her importance, at least to Doris who wistfully watched her from behind her breakfast. Jenny was more excited to see her boy cousins, inconsolable when Mary pushed her aside to let only Ida out.

"You're looking very nice t'day, boys. Ready for y'first day of school? Ida, you walk with your cousins," Mary said, and patted Ida's shoulders as the little girl primly stepped into the damp dirt and flashed her younger sisters a farewell smile laced with self-knowledge of her superiority, like a pudgy miniature opera diva. Jenny peeped out the screen door and Mary held her back with her leg.

"Get back in, now," Mary said to her absently, and watched her eldest march out to her future with her two cousins. Mary tried to keep the scene in her mind, because it was important, because Mary felt she was already letting too many important things fly by her. With any luck, perhaps her children would be going to the Greenwich Village school next year.

In the meanwhile, she bided her time, as Eli asked her to do. Fall comes, children must go to school, the wash must be done, the baby must be fed, though you want to sit at the table and think of next year's plans.

Walter cleaned the cider press in the barn. Eli rode off in the wagon on the milk run to Enfield where he brought the milk from their small herd to the Rabbit, for transport to the dairy, the funds from which were deposited in a Springfield bank.

The first Wednesday in September, fresh with sunshine and cool breezes, Mary took Harrison outside, placed him on a blanket near her washing machine. Doris obediently plopped down near him and teased him with his little stuffed lamb, ragged and chewed. Jenny stood on sturdy, pudgy legs and stared distractedly into the dark ceiling of the trees over the side yard. Mary dumped the overalls and work shirts, the long knitted socks into the drum, added soap. She did not think about what she was doing, always of other things. Her hands knew enough to keep working.

With a rustle from the trees and the light tread of worn high-button shoes, Eliza strolled around the corner and waited respectfully for Mary to conclude the wringer's revolution before good morning.

Mary's eyes followed absently from the children on the blanket, to Jenny in the yard, to Eliza's large frame in its cotton dress. Her blonde hair as severely tied back as ever, giving emphasis to her small ears, her round, ruddy face and the beginnings of a double chin. Her warm brown eyes made her oddly beautiful though, even Mary would acknowledge that were she not very tired of Eliza and pained with the thought of becoming like her.

"You've got a good start on the day." Eliza nodded brightly, then wiggled her fingers in a wave to Jenny's abrupt grin.

"Don't tell me your work's done, Eliza, I'll despair."

"I had t'find Alonzo and get him to the bus for high school in Belchertown."

"I thought Alonzo was determined to leave school this year." Mary mumbled, lugging the heavy wet clothes to the basket.

"Oh, he's determined to leave and we're determined he shall stay."

Eliza took the other handle and they carried it together to the clothesline, strung from three trees in the sunniest part of the yard.

Like the ancient peoples who had been doing the same thing at Stonehenge, Mary's calendar was the telling sunlight as it progressed over the eastern hills, through strategic marker trees, on this side of the barn in summer, on the other side of it in winter and early spring. It set on this corner of house in summer, over that corner in winter. She tracked the sunlight on her clothes, from the stolen fingers of light through the trees in the summer, to the full pale sun through the bare trees in winter.

Eliza began to clip the shirts onto the line in stoic rhythm, and though the two women might complain about the work, they secretly would agree perhaps that there was nothing so satisfying as the sun on the wash, flapping in the breeze, the wind making sheets into clean, white sails.

"You must have y'own chores, Eliza." Mary suggested. Eliza continued hanging, a slight smile playing on her lips, oblivious to hints, content in Mary's company, lonely for the companionship of another woman.

"Well, I'm going t'wash the dishes, now Eliza," Mary said, "Think I can manage. Thanks for your help. Say hello t'George and the boys." Mary lifted Harrison onto her hip and thrust out her hand for Jenny to come, but Jenny was busy hopping all over the ground. Eliza picked her up.

"I miss babies." Eliza said, kissing Jenny's stomach and rocking her in a pretend waltz. "James is six years old. Makes me feel old. I'd like another one."

Eliza reluctantly set Jenny back on her feet and handed her small arm like a leash to her mother. Mary stooped for the little hand and Eliza opened the door for her.

"Maybe you will yet, Eliza," Mary said as amends, and went inside.

Mary was pregnant but said nothing to Eliza. She did not want to talk about it.

She boiled water on the stove for the dishes and reached for the bar of strong-smelling Fels-Naphtha soap, a new one from the mottled orange wrapper. Doris sat at the table with a rag doll, and Jenny stared contentedly through the lower part of the screen door at the oblivious blue jay in the dirt. She heard the clomping of horses' hooves and the hollow rattle of empty milk canisters and waited impatiently for her Daddy to reappear.

The sound of men's voices from the yard caused Jenny to pick herself up from the braided rug and walk over to the back-screen door. She did not toddle, even at this age, but moved with an animal's sense of balance on legs that were slow, but strong. The man who was her grandfather took a small note tablet from the man who was her daddy. She smiled and wrinkled her nose, lifting her knees one at a time and contorting her face for pleasure and the hope of being noticed. She was not.

Eli lifted the empty tin canisters from the wagon, and he and his father brought them to the shed. Walter Vaughn peered at the tablet and patted his chest for his reading spectacles.

"Let's eat first," Eli said, "We can look at it all later."

"I'll look at it now." Walter took the tablet into the shed.

Eli turned toward the house and spotted Jenny, her moist palms planted upon the dusty screen, her expression fallen to calm uncertainty, a kind of infant worry. Eli gave her a smile and opened the door carefully so she would not fall out.

"Jenny been a good girl?" he asked, looking at her sideways, "Let Daddy wash his hands now."

Eli pounded the kitchen pump and sloshed water upon his face and neck. Doris slyly waddled in, tired of baby Harrison, and began to plié around her father.

Mary lugged Harrison on her hip, Eli chucked his chin and kissed his waving, pudgy hand.

"Go all right?" Mary mumbled the same question, while doing a mother's deft double take to check if Jenny had more than her fingers in her mouth. She dropped Harrison into his high-chair, while Eli lifted Jenny to her place and patted Doris' chair for her to sit.

"Yes."

"Where's Ida?" Doris asked.

"Ida's at school. Ida's having her lunch at school. Stop wiggling," Eli said. Mary hoisted the cast-iron pot of boiled potatoes, carrots, onion and cabbage down onto Jerusha Vaughn's wedding pot holder. Eli watched it land with precision and thought about a prayer.

"Where's Grandfather Vaughn?" Mary asked lowly, peering out the back door.

"He'll be along," Eli mumbled, "He's settling the milk accounts."

Mary lowered her ladle in a farmwife's dull surprise.

"This family never eats all at once. This is no way to live."

Eli looked at her with such stunned curiosity, reminded of his mother, that Mary felt foolish.

"Hope Ida's eating her cheese sandwich and not dropping it on the ground or giving it to someone else," she muttered, "And I hope he comes in soon. It'll get cold."

"Sit down," he said, "We'll start without him, if that's what he wants."

Eli assumed solemnity as a cover for his irritation and bowed his head. Mary sat down, bowed her head, albeit with an eyeball on her children. Doris dutifully bowed, Jenny's eyes wandered about the oil lamp on the wall, Harrison stared at the ceiling and began to tip over.

"Lord ...." Eli began in his father's voice, suddenly he could think of nothing else.

"... thank You," he said, and raised his face to his wife's, then directed his attention to the stew pot.

"Well, that was moving." Mary's mouth twitched.

"Quiet. Eat y'dinner." Eli smiled.

"He think there's something wrong with the accounts?"

Eli looked up at her, his eyes stern, his brown cheek bulging with potatoes.

"Time to cut the apron strings." she said simply.

"Enough. No matter," Eli said, "I can't leave the farm to an old man...."

"Alonzo's ...."

"... and a half-grown boy. Cut ties? Yes. Well. How can I cut ties? That's all I've got. No money, no land, but plenty of gol-darned stupid ties. Plenty of ties enough to choke me. John was the smart one after all. He knew what he was doing. Sakes, all our digging brings us poverty and rocks."

"Hush, Eli, just eat," Mary answered, afraid of what she'd started. It was never easy to fight with Eli, he never let it go.

"Except for Sam and his wife. Happy to buy a radio and an automobile. And eat in restaurants. Restaurant food'll probably kill you anyway...."

"Eli!" Mary startled her children and herself by the shrillness in her voice, as well as the old man stomping his boots at the back door. Walter Vaughn high-beamed a disapproving glance about the corners of the room and proceeded to prod the kitchen pump.

Eli breathed in tight breaths through the steam on his plate and watched his father to his chair.

"I'm taking Mary to Springfield on the Rabbit," Eli said. Walter looked up at him, glassy-eyed, and Mary looked surprised.

"Time to collect the dairy money, and time she saw some of the city. Kids can stay with George and Eliza. Alonzo can help out."

"Fine," Walter said, and ignored his son's family as though to exercise his own prerogative.

"Grandfather Vaughn..." Mary said into her plate.

Because he was Walter Vaughn, he stopped at the sound of a woman's voice, as Mary knew he would. He took off his hat and turned to face her with a wooden posture of pride.

"We haven't started yet; won't you please say the grace?"

"I shall." he said, rigidly gracious, and took his old chair. Eli looked at his wife because he could not look at his father.

***

While Mary and Eli were in Springfield for the day, their children stayed with George and Eliza. Walter, to exercise his own prerogative of independence, went to Athol for the day, to window shop, brood, kill time, buy an adze, and purchase a copy of the *Athol Transcript* on the same day it was printed, for the first time in his life.

Walter returned home that evening. He climbed down from the rig, already out of breath for thinking of what he had to say to them.

"Eli!" he shouted into the dark barn. There was no answer.

The house was dark as well, no oil lamps had been lit. Walter stood by the door, reached shakily for the sconce on the wall near him and lit the lamp. He rolled his eyes slowly over the clean but vacant kitchen. He stepped slowly, cautiously to where he could peer into the front room, by now fully expecting ghosts or murder. There was nothing. They should have returned by now.

He backed away through the kitchen, out into the yard. He glanced all around, and to his relief saw lighted windows at George's house through the trees and across the field. He took the lamp with him.

"Uncle Walter," George opened the door for him, "We were wondering where you were. I was about to drive the roads to Athol searching for you."

"Don't be ridiculous, there's nothing wrong," Walter said, "But you might send Lon out to take care of the horses, I left them with the wagon."

Alonzo wordlessly slipped past them to attend to it.

George pushed Walter to a chair and Eliza produced his supper as immediately as a magic trick. Momentarily at a loss to be casual or comforted, Walter cleared his throat.

"Something's happened," Walter said, but even after his long rehearsal on the ride home, suddenly did not know where to begin.

"Oh, no, Sir, don't worry. Eli said if they were running late, they'd stop the night at Mary's mother's house in Enfield. That's where they probably are."

"Those rumors, all the past year, about men from the State? About surveying the Valley for a reservoir? Well, they're true. By God, they're true. It's not just a study. They mean to do it. They want to flood us out."

He put down his fork. He was too tired to eat.

CHAPTER 6

The Metropolitan District Water Supply Commission of Boston desperately needed to find a new source of water.

In 1898, a year after the first subway in America was built in Boston, the Wachusett Reservoir underwent construction, farther west beyond the city. Some three hundred sixty homes, four churches, eight schools, six mills were removed. Completed in 1908, the Wachusett Reservoir was the largest manmade reservoir in the world.

But still not large enough.

Soon the MDWSC was formed to make studies on the diversion of the Millers, Swift, and Ware rivers even farther west in central Massachusetts. By 1921, when a second survey of the Swift River Valley was concluded, Boston's population had grown to about 748,000.

As a response to the suggestion that a new reservoir should be created in the Swift River Valley, the *Athol Transcript* published an editorial poem which Walter Vaughn read aloud.

"Prescott is my home, though rough and poor she be.
The home of many a noble soul, the birthplace of the free.
I love her rock-bound woods and hills, they are good enough for me;
I love her brooklets and her rills, But couldn't, wouldn't and shouldn't
Love a man-made sea."

It was only the first in a long line of written protests, tributes, and memorials that the subject would inspire over many decades.

"That ought to show them how things are."

"S'pose anyone in the statehouse subscribes to the *Athol Transcript*?" Eli meant to needle his father, but his own sarcastic words gave him an uneasy feeling.

***

58

In late April, Massachusetts shook the snow from its hair and the cold mud from its feet. The timid branches sprouted tender, glowing green. The damp hills grew luminescent, rejuvenating in the tepid spring sunshine. In another few weeks, there would be lilacs.

Jenny did not know this. At five, every day came as such a wonder to her that she forgot the day before and could not imagine tomorrow. She patted her gray oatmeal with the bowl of her spoon, with a delicate touch and an eye for detail, until her mother snatched the spoon away.

"You'll get no more if y'haven't got sense to eat it." Jenny, startled for an instant, then happy to discover her problem solved, jumped from her chair and ran out the back door. She waited by the wagon for her father, who would take her on his milk run.

Ida and Doris glanced enviously after their younger sister. She did not have to go to school yet or eat her breakfast.

Three-year old Harrison was too young for school or the milk run, so he ate methodically and with purpose. Baby Ella made whimpering sounds from her high chair. Sickly the first ambivalent year of her life, Ella was fussy and her pasty face stamped with what seemed a permanent expression of distress. Her thin, uneven tufts of blonde hair on an otherwise bald and blotchy head were so ridiculous as to be funny and kept her mother from pitying her too much. Mary choked on the fear this baby would not live, and she dealt with her fear by unconsciously treating her youngest child with stoic indifference.

She wondered what connection her fear had with the premonition of the view of a giant sea that came to her when the child was born. She felt now it was a premonition, and until now, had not said anything about it.

"Eli," Mary said to him at bedtime, "Nature is violent, sometimes."

He untied his boots.

"What are you on about now?"

"Try producing a baby sometime and you'll know what I mean."

He turned after removing his shirt and gave her his attention.

"Are you all right? D'you not feel well?"

"No, that's not what I mean. I'm not talking about me. Well, I am. When Ella was born, just after she was born...I had this thought come into my head. Your mother would have called it a premonition."

"Well, Mary, I'd like to get ready for bed, but I somehow don't feel it's right for a man to take off his pants while discussing otherworldly matters."

She smiled. "I don't know exactly what I want to say, Eli, except that I don't want to keep it from you. I think that even when nature is violent, it doesn't have to be...apocalyptic. Like when a baby is born. When it comes into the world, it comes with a ripping kind of pain, a force that no woman can stop, but she can still withstand it even if she can't stop it. It's terrible, but then it's not. It's just the way things are. Maybe death is like that too. We'll all find out someday."

"You are getting most frighteningly like my mother. I have to get you out of here. Must be the house."

"Eli, I saw a sea here in the valley, with the land all gone, flooded, and the hilltops like islands...."

"Stop listening to my father. He's obsessed."

"I can't explain it. But it didn't seem terrible. It was as if nature was going to take care of things."

"Nature isn't threatening to flood the Valley. Men are. That's the difference. And they've got another thing coming if they think they can get away with that."

"Eli, what happens if the state...."

"Don't worry about it. What can they do? Evict us? Like we were rent payers? We own this land. Owned it for two hundred years. Owned it when we were still a colony of Great Britain. Granted to us by the king."

"Yes, but they've taken homes before. Your father read to me about it."

"Yes, pieces of neighborhoods. But whole towns? Hundreds of people, farms? Ridiculous."

"I wish I was as sure as you."

He slipped his arm under her head and yawned, "The old Republic is backsliding. Late war hasn't done anybody any good. People are dissatisfied and greedy, especially politicians. Newspaper full of automobile ads, toaster ads, Arrow collars and life insurance. World's going to perdition."

He suddenly thought of his mother again and smiled. She would have loved to be present when the world went to Perdition.

Early in their marriage she would have playfully questioned him about that grin, wanted to know what he was thinking and wanting to be a part of it. Now she accepted the frank need for a man and woman to occasionally be apart psychologically if they were to continue to live together physically.

***

Jenny kicked the wagon wheel rhythmically with her boot, waiting for her father. Walter Vaughn stepped out from the milk shed and patted the wagon with his dry, flat palms, as momentarily bored and yet captivated by the morning as his granddaughter.

Walter Vaughn brought up some phlegm and spat in the dirt, Jenny watched him admiringly.

"Dairy'n round with y'father?" Walter asked.

Jenny nodded. They stood a moment in the quiet sun until Eli emerged from the house.

"All set, Jenny-girl?" he called. He lifted her to the seat, nodded to his father, and they rolled out of the yard.

"Y'haven't much to speak of this day, Jenny-girl." Eli bellowed over a rocky bump.

"Ida says we're goin' t'be drowned."

Eli lost his breath for a moment. *My God,* he recalled much later, *I knew it then.*

"Ida's schoolmates been listening to silly stories?" Eli asked, "What do you know of it?"

"Lon says he'll shoot anybody that tries to bring water."

"Boy better mind himself with that talk. Get himself into trouble."

"How'er they goin' t'bring water?"

"You're too young to worry about such silly things, Jenny. You never mind."

"But how do they bring water? Will they have pails?"

They pulled over the side of the road by Berry's store. He anchored his team and lifted Jenny down. She ran ahead of him and jumped onto the porch, clomping up and down the weak and weathered boards with her boots. The store was wonderful, a very special place. He father took the box of eggs from the wagon. She opened the door for him.

Cool and dark inside, the close air smelled like coffee and those things in the tins, and Jenny immediately became still and awed, like some people who unthinkingly hold more reverence for the shelves of baking powder and constipation cures than for less convincing evidence of miracles from the church pulpit.

He set the eggs on the counter and Miss Rebecca reckoned them up to his account.

"Warmer today," she greeted him.

"Think so."

"How'r y'keeping, Miss Jenny?" Miss Rebecca shifted her intelligent eyes for a moment down to the ruddy-faced child just level with the counter, then returned her gaze to the worn, paint-chipped counting beads.

"Fine, thank you Miss Rebecca." Jenny answered the jar of lemon drops.

"Ever hear from John lately?"

"Oh, why, no. Well, not much lately." Eli answered, surprised at the question from her.

"That's two dollars and forty-two cents, Eli."

"Right, thank you, Miss Rebecca." He replaced his hat and took Jenny's hand to leave but stopped abruptly.

"Almost forgot. Could I have a penny's wortha lemon drops, Miss Rebecca?"

Back in the wagon, her round straw hat fell away from Jenny's face and threatened to choke her with its ties, but she was busy sucking the sugar out of a lemon drop.

"You catch freckles, you don't wear your hat, young girl. Won't catch no fellow that way."

"I gotta fellow now." Jenny mumbled, nearly losing the lemon drop but quickly pushing it back into her mouth with a dirty finger.

"Who's your fellow?" Eli smiled, knowing she would say that it was him.

"Lon," Jenny answered and Eli looked at her from the corner of his eye a moment, with a suddenly, foolish pang of jealousy, and something else.

"He is, huh?" Eli muttered, bringing his eyes back to the dusty road, squinting from beneath his hat brim into the glare of sunlight.

"Uh-huh." Jenny slurped. "Daddy, you still got the other candy in y'pockets?"

"Yes, I'm holding it for the other children."

"But not Ella, 'cause she's only a baby. She can't have candy."

"Well now, how about your Mama, don't y'want her to have a candy?"

"Yes."

"Well, all right then. Y've had yours. Be still, now. You slip off this wagon, y'could end up dead."

They drove down the shaggy hill to Enfield. Eli, like an emperor returning with a kind of naïve affection to a land he has conquered, did not acknowledge the conquered land has changed and the conqueror remains unnoticed in it. Still, Eli felt he had left his mark, though nobody could see it but him.

"Why's Lon your fellow?"

"'Cause he is."

Enfield was the biggest town in the world to Jenny, if there was such a thing as "the world." She half doubted this, not quite able to understand Eli's explanations that they would put the large milk canisters onto the Rabbit train, and the train would follow the tracks all the way around that curve behind the Great Quabbin there until it disappeared. It would be gone to Springfield, a real city Eli said, not like Enfield at all. Enfield wasn't a city at all, he said. They had buildings and trolleys and automobiles and Negroes and Chinese people and electricity in Springfield. Enfield had some electricity, Eli noted, but there was none in Prescott, and Jenny liked to visit her Grandmother Pratt who now had electricity in her house. And the indoor privy.

"Daddy, how come we don't have electricity and an indoor privy?"

"Quiet now, we will sometime. Gonna take you to visit Grandmother Pratt now. Be good, and don't shame us."

Jenny felt almost as much as awestruck in her grandmother's house as in Miss Rebecca's store, too timid to touch things, though she did use the indoor privy twice. Even Eli did once for old time's sake.

Grandmother Pratt had made gingerbread. Eli watched Jenny drink her lemonade and passionately savor her gingerbread in a way that was indecent.

"We do occasionally feed the child," he joked, but felt embarrassed. The Pratt girls were always playing at cooking, not trained in survival the way dutiful hill girls were. They had played in the making of fudge, of blanc-mange, and small, jam-topped cookies. They had probably never seen plain food, not like the kind he knew from boyhood. Not like the kind Mary now cooked every day.

How did Mary do it? She had adapted to his home better than he had.

He looked at Jenny and forgot to smile as Mrs. Pratt did.

"How come don't we have any Negroes?" Jenny suddenly asked, her eyebrows knitting. "What are they? Why can't *we* have some? And Chinese people."

Mrs. Pratt colored in a proper Enfield-lady way and chuckled and patted her son-in-law's hand.

"Mr. Pratt would have loved to have a sit-down conversation with this child."

"Hush, now, Jenny," Eli said, and threw a rueful smile over the top of her head to his mother-in-law.

"That reminds me," Mrs. Pratt said, rising from her chair at the kitchen table, she stepped in the parlor, her low, skipping voice dimming and rising as she returned.

"Here are some books I know Mr. Pratt would like you to have, Eli. Maybe now that your children are growing, they'd like to read them. I know you used to be fond of reading."

They were a volume of Shakespeare's plays, the battered copy of Tennyson, and Charles Dickens' *Great Expectations.*

"I gave some to the other girls, but I sold the bulk of Mr. Pratt's library."

"I remember. Mr. Pratt was a great reader. Thank you, Mother Pratt. I'm sure the children'll come to like these as much as I did." Eli held the books and felt suddenly embarrassed.

"I ... did Mary ever mention we're planning to move to Greenwich?"

"Oh, yes, she mentioned it. Are you settled on it?"

"Yes, well, I hope this'll be the year. Close to after harvest, I think we'll be set."

"Has your cousin, Mr. Vaughn, settled in Athol yet?"

"Yes, he's been there a month. He's rented an apartment. Different way to live, I guess."

Mrs. Pratt said, "I know there'll be a day I won't be able to manage this old house of mine."

"That'll be a long time to come, I'm sure, Mother Pratt."

"I hope you like Greenwich. I guess you pay no attention to the talk about the state taking us over."

My word, he thought, *she just says it so easily.*

"Well, now, I doubt that will ever happen."

She gave him an odd look and turned her back to him.

***

He lifted Jenny into the wagon. They drove back across town and up the hill to Prescott.

"We're on a hill, we won't get drowned!" Jenny said, her brightened expression beaming at him with a look of triumph.

CHAPTER 7

Moving day arrived. Walter Vaughn and Eli communicated as eloquently as possible with mute hostility. They justified it as the most practical course. Nothing said was nothing lost.

Mary finally found her voice in the matter.

"It's a fact that a coldness, a wooden courtesy between two New Englanders might mean they like each other, or else they intend to kill each other very soon. It's hard to tell unless they make some sort of move for the ice pick."

Eli sat on the top step and took the glass of lemonade his wife handed him.

"I don't care for your humor, Missus," he grumbled into his drink.

She smiled, wiped her wet hands and stepped around him, and jumped to the dusty ground. She put her hands on her hips and peered over to the dark barn.

"You look set to dance," he said, wiping his mouth on the back of his hand.

"You never did take me to one 'a High Harry's do's, did you?"

"Did I ever mention him?"

"Yes, you did. A long time ago."

"I don't remember. I forgot about all that myself."

"You're a busy farmer now. Like y'father."

"Please don't say I'm like my father." He laughed, "Oh, but he's a stubborn old barn owl, isn't he?"

"He likes it in there. It's his place. This is his place." She turned to see the dark expression. "I'm sorry Eli. You men are so territorial, always vying to see who's top dog."

He stood abruptly and handed her the empty glass. "I wish that's all it were. For to tell you the truth I'm sick of all of it."

"You're not enjoying this day as much as you thought you would."

He stiffened. He put his work gloves back on and went back to loading the wagon.

No, I'm not enjoying this, he thought. That meant his father had won.

"Aren't you going to talk to him?" Mary shattered his thoughts, wanting to and knowing how.

"I'll say goodbye when the time comes. Just glad we'd already discussed the stock, these stupid chickens beforehand." He tapped the wire of the makeshift traveling chicken cage as a hen tried to snap at the tip of his glove.

"He'll depend on Alonzo for much of the work. I hope that boy's reliable. He could spend less time hunting." Mary said.

"Lon'll settle himself down now. He's got a purpose. Got a farm."

"He'll inherit, y'think?"

"Why not?"

"What about John?"

"Yes. What about him?" John sure didn't torment himself with what was his duty when he left. Just left. Didn't worry about leaving an old man.

"I'll take this load down to Sam's, then I'll be back. He'll have the milk ready for me by then, and I'll take some of the furniture after the milk run."

She nodded and watched him climb over the wheel.

She went back to her packing, but there wasn't much to pack. She filled a wooden box with a few pots and pans, and some linens. She lingered too long over her schoolgirl's autograph book and tossed it scornfully into an old potato sack with their clothes. She couldn't lift the large cast-iron kettle she used for soaking whites and making stew. She thought suddenly of Eliza. Alonzo and Walter would depend upon Eliza for their laundry, and some baking.

Well, she'll thrive on it, Mary thought, feeling as sardonically sinful as Eli. Walter and Eliza were good, honest, hardworking people, and Eli and Mary wanted to run away from them.

The last possessions to go in the wagon were their children. They had been waiting for their turn all day. When they rolled at last out of the yard, they were too excited by the thought of going somewhere that they did not realize they were leaving their Prescott farm for good.

None of them took a look back.

When they clattered at last into Cousin Sam's yard in Greenwich Village the children, and their parents, were hit with a strange feeling of lost and found, a surge of proud wealth and humble confusion when they understood the neat, white frame house was home.

Jenny gazed with wonder at the new vista of Mt. Zion behind them and noticed that here the view of the horizon from the ridge top was absent. Eli ached for the wide, pink Eastern view as well but would never admit it for the rest of his life.

Eli immediately got the stock settled and organized his new barn in such a way that was completely unoriginal and typical of any Valley barn. He self-consciously climbed to the hayloft and scuffed his boots on the worn gray board floor.

Mary felt far happier organizing her kitchen just as typically as other Valley kitchens. She truly felt organized, where Eli felt momentarily out of control.

Soon Mary would realize that the drudgery of her routine was the same here as it would be anyplace else, for now it was enough to know that she was part of a new community.

Greenwich Village lay on the Valley floor spare and simple, like a clean sheet in the breeze to Mary, but still bore the comfort of familiarity. Though baseball, courting, and spelling rivalries sometimes occurred at picnics between the people of Dana and Enfield and Greenwich and Prescott enough to make town pride a reason for sliding into second a bit too high, these communities shared so much in terms of ancestors and heritage that moving from one town to another did not make one an outsider. Eli and Mary were spared this. They were, eventually, as much at home in Greenwich Village as Mary had been in Enfield or Eli in Prescott. Their children would feel connections to all the Valley towns, and because these towns shared one more important aspect of geographic peculiarity, the Vaughn children and all the Valley children would consider the area of the four towns as something whole, complete, and indivisible.

They lived now near the East Branch of the Swift River, which left its headwaters in Petersham. It erupted into the fat and lazy Pottapaug Pond hidden on the other side of Pottapaug Hill, then drifted neatly through Greenwich Village and Walker's Mill Pond, to Quabbin Lake, and then demurely linked hands with the Middle Branch before continuing to Enfield. Their farm was near a crossroads, shadowed by the long and shaggy Mt. Zion and the little Parker Hill. The tracks of the Boston and Albany Railroad on which the Rabbit train made its run was not far away, and Greenwich Village had its own depot.

They would not need to go to Miss Rebecca's store any more, for Greenwich Village and Greenwich Plains had their own stores with Post Offices in them. There were churches and schools and a few mills.

There were new neighbors, but no close family. But, journeys were not so arduous as they once were, and time could be found to visit. That was something to think about later, once all the jars and tins were neatly lined up on freshly papered shelves, and tools were hung on new rusty hooks, and the different demands of farming a new terrain could be figured out.

Family was not so vital for survival now. Family could be put away and returned to in moments of leisure much like mementos in a scrapbook. A little distance would bring novelty to old relations.

"Y'know," Eli's face flushed as he laughed, trotting Harrison around the yard, "I recall how my father, my brother John and I would cut ice on

Greenwich Lake. The ice would be sent down the Rabbit to companies, stores, and restaurants as far away as New York City. A lot of it stayed in the local icehouse, of course, but some got sent away on the train. Ice harvesting had once been a big thing hereabouts.

"It was a project, though. The men marked off a grid on the frozen lake, see? Like this." He dug a few lines in the dirt with his heel. "And cut a channel through to the icehouse so as to float the blocks they would cut and chop out blocks of ice by hand with saws. Big, jagged saws. It was raw work."

Eli's children were not as impressed with the description of how hard it was to cut ice, how men had gotten hurt. They had been witness to hard work and struggle from an early age and it bored them. They were more amazed, and a little doubtful, of the existence of either New York City or their Uncle John, whom they had never seen.

Greenwich. Eli felt they would have a finer life here. Whist parties at the Grange. Oyster suppers on the common. Well, there was not so much of that now as there once was, but as least there were more people here. Prescott was draining dry of its people. Its heyday had been when his father was a young man, and there were visiting ministers and town picnics...enough. *Enough of your father's life,* Eli thought.

The future was here. Was it? Yes, it was. Damn his father and damn the Commonwealth. His children could skate on nearby Walker's Mill Pond in winter. He imagined Harrison playing hockey with new friends. His children would attend the Greenwich Village school, the two-room schoolhouse near the Walker's Mill dam. His children would play in the yard and collect lady's-slippers and mayflowers here. They would go to high school in Belchertown, all the way through to graduation, and maybe beyond. Their Grandfather Pratt had been a college man and even their Aunt Jane had been well educated. His children should know what was possible.

Eli trod about the farm, walking carefully, thinking as he stepped over the cool autumn fields. It did not look like his ideal farm, not yet. There drifted a cool shadow of some unfamiliar reality hanging about the place that affected him to uneasiness. He shook it off. Probably it was only the diminishing color of the land and the first hint of winter on the shifting wind.

He wondered if it was too late in life for him to start an orchard. But that was not really what he was thinking.

***

Younger children sat in the front row desks. This was where Jenny was directed by the teacher, Miss Murphy, on her first day of school. Doris and Ida sat with their age group. Being older and already used to a different, though very similar schoolhouse in Prescott, Doris and Ida were more self-conscious than Jenny was. They knew the cliques awaiting them. Jenny had no notion of belonging, or not belonging, to anything.

Jenny, quietly observant, stifled her nervousness with active fingers that touched the ironwork on the side of her small desk, that probed the edge of the inkwell cut into the top right-hand corner of the desktop, that plucked at her school dress, and scratched her mosquito-bitten arms.

There were nearly fifty children in the school, large by Prescott standards. Back up there with the Vaughn family gone, plus or minus the average Prescott mortality/moving figures, there were now two hundred and twenty-four people living in the town.

Greenwich and Greenwich Village were different from Prescott indeed, but not only because the town was in the Valley lowland, surrounded by hills rather than being perched among them. The antebellum liveliness and livelihood which Eli's grandparents enjoyed had slipped away up there somehow, even by the time Eli was a boy.

Greenwich had not reached the commercial and social heights of Dana or of Enfield, but it was the oldest town in the Valley. It had been settled first, and other towns broke off from it. Greenwich had a kind of permanence, and just the fact of being at the bottom of the Valley, in the geographic center of the Valley, there was a kind of special focus in the sunny schoolroom window that morning for Jenny.

Miss Murphy settled the children expertly, with very little actual effort but maximum authority. She had been a teacher first in her home town of Palmer, but with the death of her parents and the breaking up of their home when her brother moved west, Miss Murphy decided to live more cheaply and more quietly in the Valley and boarded at the home of a selectman. Unlike many enthusiastic teachers, she did not look for genius in her pupils, or for a prodigy to push. She found excellence in simple things, like trying hard, manners, pleasantness, and the inner strength it takes for a real genius to teach himself.

A short, heavy woman, with straight, thin black hair tied severely into a knot at the back of her head, her plain dark dresses were clean, her plump hands were expressive, and her smile was constant. The big boys did not bother to tease her because they knew she would not cry or get flustered.

She had been teaching since she was sixteen. At thirty-eight, her patience was boundless, and she laughed at what she could not change.

Despite her concerted efforts to blend in, Jenny possessed that weird combination of refined intelligence planted in a raw and rough appearance. Nothing in Jenny could be called soft; even at five years old she had lost her babyishness. She did not have the round, soft face of other little girls, the pudgy, clumsy fingers, the slow pace of enjoying a shared apple, the crushing depression of a hard arithmetic problem, the easy distraction. She seemed beyond that, and dead serious.

Jenny stood taller than her grade, lanky but not awkward. Her face had the usual ruddiness of the Prescott child who spends a lot of time outdoors. Her deep-set eyes were a most startling blue. She looked older than she was, and she unknowingly masked her young age further with a cautious demeanor that swallowed fear with stubborn will.

They lived only just down the road from the schoolhouse. Behind their new farm, to the northeast, was Mount Zion, a long green hill, feathery with oaks and maples and pines. Her father quoted, "...the joy of the whole earth, is mount Zion...." and laughed and said it was from the Bible, which gave Jenny the notion early on that the Bible was prophesying about them.

Mary found herself missing the queer colors of light that made up her Stonehenge-like calendar at the Prescott farm. There were different landmarks here and she was not yet used to them. Parker Hill and Greenwich Plains loomed beyond to the southwest, Mount Zion to the northeast, the East Branch of the Swift River to the southeast, with its pearl-necklace effect of linking pond upon pond. She recalled that "Quabbin" was the land's original name in Indian days, as in nearby Quabbin Lake.

Massachusetts' relations with Indians was story-like, and events which occurred had occurred so long ago, when the recording of history was usually relegated to weather notations in a minister's diary. Hard historical fact passed all too quickly into murky legend.

By the 1920s New England was already some three hundred years old, yet before this New World chunk of time the unknown decades and lives lived were blandly referred to as "pre-history." It was not history because it had not been written down. That was the rule, somebody's rule, and those who might have perpetuated knowledge of that misty era died swiftly from diseases strangers brought from the Old World.

Perhaps the northeast Indians were not so very different in temperament from their European heirs, who could say now? Native tribes who hunted and roamed the area's dense woodlands, its rolling hills were small factions compared to the larger Indian nations out in the Midwest plains. Perhaps they were also insular like Swift River Valley neighbors today and kept to themselves, jealous of their privacy. The Indians in what would one day be a Commonwealth labeled with an Indian name, were comprised of small groups. The Pequots, the Nipmucs, the many other tribes of the Algonquin nation were more like extended families, which came together for common survival and fought bitterly with each other over insult. Perhaps they were just as resistant to change and being bullied by the weather and each other as the Europeans in after times. Perhaps the land hereabouts made them, too, what they were.

Real information on these people vanished when they did. Fables replaced them. Squanto saved the Pilgrims. The children had learned that from Miss Murphy. King Philip came later, massacring settlers in small towns along the Connecticut and the western Massachusetts river towns. Knowledge of the ancient native civilization was confined mainly to the two incidents.

The Swift River Valley had its own legends. Mt. Liz or Lizzie, named for Mrs. Elizabeth Rowlandson, a captive and victim of the Indians, was a small mound of earth below the East Branch in the south of Greenwich. Mr. Pomeroy was burned at the stake by Indians on the hill west of Greenwich Village that later took his name, though these small hills were no Montmartre, no "hill of martyrs," for the spare, sunny hillsides of grass held no markers dedicated to the past.

Mrs. Rowlandson, and Mr. Pomeroy, and the Indians might as well not have lived at all.

There were tales of Indian kidnapping of white settlers during the French and Indian wars, of these captives taken to Canada. One family came back to Greenwich to live after their ransom, it was said, but the older son went back to his adopted Indian family.

Mary stepped out onto her the porch and put her hands in her apron pockets. Her father had once said that around the turn of the century there were tribal meetings on Mt. Quabbin, a kind of feast day celebrations. The Indians came one day, and then left, mysteriously, like gypsies, to who knows where. Mary searched the hills for the Little Quabbin. Perhaps the Great and Little Quabbin hills with their Indian name, not named after people, or from the Bible, held some mystery into the past.

Sam Vaughn used to tell a story of seeing an old Indian man down near the Greenwich Cemetery. The old man would come one day in the spring, and just sit there in the cemetery all day long, still and quiet, until the sun had set behind the Prescott ridge. Then he would leave, to return the next spring. This last was nearly twenty years ago. The old Indian was probably dead now.

Why did he come to the Greenwich Cemetery? Did he have family buried nearby, was it really an old Indian burying place? Mary never considered Indians as anything but characters out of boys' adventure books, those colorful wild Indians of the west who mostly lived on reservations now. Standing on the porch, Mary began to sense something melancholy about the sunny yard.

"He gave me the shivers," Sam had said, rubbing his hands together, "like he was saying, my people are gone. We thought we would be here forever, but now we are gone. So, don't be too sure of yourselves, you can go this way too."

Mary jerked as Eli suddenly gave a whoop from the side of the house. Mary watched Jenny run like the devil was chasing her. She jumped into her laughing father's arms for protection.

CHAPTER 8

The heritage that remained was their own heritage. Unlike the unfortunate Indians, they determined to keep it.

Eli slowed the wagon to a crawl as they approached the common in Greenwich Plains, and Mary lifted her gaze over baby Ella's bonnet to question him. He sat stiffly erect and a slight smile played around his lips. The girls and Harrison stopped chattering in the wagon bed and at once looked over the side.

"Are we here?" they called out.

"Something wrong?" Mary asked, squinting under her new hat, a new style called a cloche hat. She was faintly annoyed with Eli for wearing his ragged farmer's broad-brimmed felt hat with his suit. Eli had grown less concerned with style in their years of marriage and leaned towards dowdy comfort.

He turned his tanned face toward her. Age had hardened, defined his face and made her admit he was handsome; a new hat couldn't make him more so. "Queer feeling of something gone." he said, "Reminds me of nineteen-four and driving my father and John to the Sesquicentennial. Remember? You were there, with your braids and pinafore, sassy young girl too big for her britches."

Mary gave a wry smile out of the corner of her mouth.

"I remember John, and the Special Police...." she glanced back at her children and said no more.

Eli shook off the shackles of memory and drove the team to the parking area.

The July 4th town celebration this year of 1922 was the second largest town observance in Greenwich's history, second only to the Sesquicentennial of 1904. Over two thousand people arrived, many by automobile. This was a change from 1904 that Eli noticed immediately. Some cars drove in the parade, decorated with banners and crepe paper. There were brass bands, marching veterans. Eli thought of his father and the Civil War vets who impressed him. There were only a few Civil War boys here now, riding in a car because they were old. A happy group of World War vets strolled behind.

Eli saw his cousin Sam Vaughn park a black flivver by the carriages. He tugged at Mary's arm. "Look, Sam's got an automobile."

Mary peered around him and admired the dusty vehicle rolling over the burned grass. "Children, we're going t'say hello to Cousin Sam and Agnes. See, they've got an automobile."

The children were torn between the parade and the sight of a relative in a car. Their parents made the decision and brought them to the parking area where Sam Vaughn was struggling with a picnic basket.

The children scrambled into the automobile, and Harrison pretended to drive while the girls squealed at imaginary obstacles in their path.

Sam Vaughn held Ella against his chest and murmured soothingly into her bonnet. Agnes, his wife, watched blankly, and nervously tugged at Mary's dress, muttering soft compliments.

"Athol's fine," Sam said, making the baby cross-eyed by tapping her nose, "In fact, Athol's home to more and more of us Valley folk, Eli. Men finding work in the mills. Ever since the State matter, well, people'd just rather not live with that uncertainty."

Eli scratched his cheek. "Guess it'll be all the talk today. I suppose half the speakers they've got for us'll talk on the State's doings, the other half'll go on about George Washington. I just want to hear the band and eat my wife's dinner."

Both families gathered with the audience to listen to the speeches. To do otherwise would have been impolite, moreover, impractical. There was no getting away from it.

The speakers were urgent, argumentative, frustrated and futile. Eli stared at the podium bunting. Where was the old bombastic, safe and comforting Americanism they knew from childhood picnics? It was missing today. These speeches did not dwell on recalling glories of the past, but treaded uncertainly, uncomforting, into the arena of the present.

***

The Commonwealth concluded its findings. The administrators of the Boston water project, the Metropolitan District Water Supply Commission, or MDWSC, proposed eliminating the towns of Enfield, Greenwich, and Prescott, and parts of other villages to create something like a thirty-nine-square mile reservoir to serve Boston.

"State think we're just going to get out of their way?" Eli murmured out of the side of his mouth.

"Just like Boston to be greedy. And worse, impractical. Wouldn't do. Wouldn't work." Sam answered him.

Commissioners from the four counties of western Massachusetts had declared their opposition to the project, and Connecticut officials joined them, as they also had an interest. The three branches of the Swift River which when dammed would create the mythical reservoir, were important tributaries of the Chicopee River, which was an important tributary to the Connecticut River. The Swift River Valley may have been a fairly isolated farming community, but it was still linked tenuously to the rest of Massachusetts and an industrial Connecticut River Valley.

Beyond its protective hills were other cities and towns which had not missed the Industrial Revolution as they had, and which were devoted, some cities like Chicopee almost entirely, to manufacturing. Industrial New England relied upon rivers. Rivers were responsible for the factories' existence. If the water flow from the tributaries affected by the damming of the Swift River was decreased, then important manufacturing would be destroyed.

In Chicopee several companies including Dwight Manufacturing, A.G. Spalding sporting goods manufactory, the Fisk Rubber Company and the Ames Sword Company all put together their legal counsel and filed complaints.

"Boston should look closer to home to solve its own problems." Sam said.

Eli replied in a low voice, "I guess everyone feels the same way. They can't do it after all this. There's clearly too much opposition."

A month later, the town of Prescott celebrated its centennial. Eli was prepared again to enjoy the sweet sadness of boyhood nostalgia in the town he still considered home despite his adjustment to Greenwich. Despite the huge banner strung over the road across from the Grange Hall which said "Welcome - Old Home Day - 1822-1922," there was even here mingled with the forced sentiment, a subtle, urgent warning.

The Petersham band played to its audience seated in chairs under the trees in Atkinson Hollow. Dinner was served in the Grange Hall. Reverend Holland gave an address, and a town boy, Barre Hurst, who had been a classmate of Eli's and had gone on to made a success of himself as a lawyer, was an honored guest. He made a speech to his former townsmen, telling them as the *Athol Transcript* later reported, to "take up the torch of the men who had fallen in war, to rebuild the stone walls of their grandfathers, to till the soil and make the town prosper, despite this…issue of the Swift River project."

Contrasting this shaft of modern day peril to the town's very existence, the ladies' historical society gave a short piece on the history of Prescott. The lady speaker told of the rough-hewn taverns where men like Dan Shays defied the Boston aristocracy, of the Conkey brothers who settled near Bobbinville, of the great names of Prescott like the Atkinsons, the Mellens, the Vaughns, of the Berrys who arrived in 1755 from Deerfield, just barely escaping the Indian massacres there. Most of the old families were Ulster descended, Scots-Irish and English fellows. She spoke of the little isolated schools and churches, the old cheese factory and the charcoal kiln. *Charcoal kiln?*

"She's digging rather deep looking for things to be proud of," Eli whispered to Mary.

She also recited that verse written by a local man and published in the *Athol Transcript*, that declared the poet
"couldn't, wouldn't and shouldn't
Love a man-made sea."

"Next they're gon'ta have you do "The Hadley Weathercock," Eli teased Mary.

Walter Vaughn stepped up next to Eli, and they shook hands.

"Not gon'ta be any reservoirs around here s'long as people say what they think." Walter said, "My own father…."

"Who fought with the 31st Mass.," Eli finished, suddenly wondering what John was doing right now.

"I was going to say, to keep this country together in the Civil War." Walter smiled, "I should think we could save our small piece of it." Walter waved his hand, "All this is utter nonsense. Oh, there's Eliza wandering around looking for your lady," Walter took his hat off briefly in Mary's general direction, "An' George is havin' a time finding a place for his rig by all them automobiles."

"Must be a hundred of them!" Little James danced toward them. Eli shook hands gravely with George's youngest and tousled his blond hair.

"S'pose you're all set t'buy one them flivvers yourself soon?" Walter winked at his son in an overly friendly way. It made Eli suspicious and uncomfortable. Both he and his father felt he had deserted him; there was no need to be coy about it.

"No Pa, I don't think I'd know what to do with one." Eli replied, "How are you and Lon getting by?"

"I lost Lon somewhere back by where they're settin' up for the dancin'. Boy reminds me a' your brother John."

"Then you got y'hands full. Hear from John?"

"No," Walter said quietly, squinting at the crowd and the brassy oomphing of the band.

Barre Hurst caught Eli's eye from the podium and came over to shake hands all around.

"What say, Barre?" Eli asked, "Keep fixing the stone walls, then?"

"Just a bit of rhetoric, chum. I haven't a crystal ball."

"You know the law, though."

"It's not written in stone." Barre said, with an attitude more jovial than he felt, "Except of course, when it is."

***

To Jenny, who was six, the summer of 1922 would always be of celebrations because of these two town picnics. Ribbons, and the sounds of Sousa, and the grave, measured voices in righteous speeches clustered in her mind. They were momentous, awesome, and the feeling of permanence they gave her uplifted even her six-year-old's soul. She rejoined heartily in words and sentiments she did not understand. She enjoyed herself immensely with a sticky watermelon face. It seemed as if the summer would go on forever and the deepening blues of the twilight sky creating a canopy over Prescott did not signal the end of an era to her, but only the beginning of the evening's dancing under the lanterns in the trees.

She found Alonzo at last. Searching for him since suppertime when her family, and Cousin George's, and Grandfather had eaten in the Grange Hall, Jenny wanted to ride on Alonzo's shoulders once more around the picnic grounds.

She watched him climb into the back seat of someone's big black automobile. She was not afraid of cars; she had played in Cousin Sam's automobile.

A girl named Nancy from New Salem, belle of the junior class at the New Salem Academy, was not surprised to find Alonzo so tender and gentle. The other girls had giggled at his lean strength, his awkward country stiffness, his secret smile all of which they found attractive and would have been aghast to think of as sexual. They were nice girls, who were not above flirting, who wanted handsome men for husbands and who knew little about romance otherwise. Nancy was bold only in that she stood apart from her number and wanted to prove to them and herself, and to this appealing stranger that true love, pure and holy, was possible even in these brassy days.

That was why she agreed to meet him in the back of the automobile at the end of the lot.

That Alonzo Vaughn held her with passion, and not lust, that he kissed her not with the zeal of a vaudeville villain, but with the slow firmness of sincerity was proof to Nancy that Alonzo was good, that she herself was correct in thought and perfectly in the right to seek her destiny in love the way others sought their destiny at secretarial school, and that there was nothing wrong in making love to a young man she met only five hours ago.

But then, making love had different meaning to Nancy than it would to later generations. She had meant to keep Alonzo on a narrow path, not letting him go too far, as a young lady should. She was not quite sure where too far was. Didn't seem important just now.

As his large brown hand began to grope the bodice of her shirtwaist, she noticed the nose of a little girl pressed against the side window, half-rolled up against the evening breeze. Nancy gave a short, perfunctory shriek.

Alonzo turned in the seat and looked at Jenny.

"Jenny-girl, you go on back t'y'mother. You're too little t'be out here in the dark by yourself." he said patiently.

Nancy scrambled out of the car before Alonzo could stop her. She fled between the cars and disappeared in the darkness.

Alonzo took another deep breath and climbed out of the car. He sat down on the running board and pulled Jenny down beside him. "Don't y'know not t'folla me?" he said. Jenny sat very stiff and still, a frown working on her expressive face.

"What're you doin' here?"

"What I'm doin' here is none a'your business. That young lady was a friend a mine and we were talking. Now don't y'go telling anybody about her, or I'll give you a spanking, yes I will."

"Why not?" she demanded, and he growled at her like a bear, then he grabbed her sash and slid her into his lap.

"Because, Miss Jenny, her Daddy doesn't think she should stay out this late in the dark. It wouldn't be right to tell on her. How'd y'like it if somebody were to always tell on you?"

"Ida does that."

"You don't want'a be like Ida, do you?" He made a face.

"No."

"Then you promise me y'won't tell that she was here, not to anybody?"

"All right." She answered into his ear, comforted by sharing a secret with Alonzo, happy to be sitting in his lap with his strong arms draped playfully around her as the last orange glow from the Berkshires sank out of sight and Prescott became dark.

"You still my girl?" he said to the sunset, his chin on her head.

"Yes," she said, satisfied.

CHAPTER 9

The summer did end, and the Commonwealth "came to bide," as Walter Vaughn said.

They moved in, the surveyors and engineers labeled collectively by the Swift River Valley residents as "State People," to study them some more. They took measurements and made drawings. They lifted soil samples and charted logging roads. They tried not to disrupt life in the towns and to be unobtrusive. They took rooms at the Swift River Hotel and boarded with local families who found the income a wonderful thing.

One assistant engineer, a recent graduate, found he stood out more than he realized, more than he would have liked. Roger Lewis had grown up in Scituate, south of Boston, and carried in his voice the mark of an easterner. When he requested cigarettes in the Phillips grocery, he unwittingly became the center of attention. He carried no surveyor's charts or implements, and there was no sign on his back, though his suit was new. When the man behind the counter answered him in a different voice, he suddenly realized why he was marked.

The New England Accent as imitated by bad actors is more vague than false. There are actually several different accents in New England, even within Massachusetts. The Boston Accent commonly thought the New England Accent is limited only to certain areas of the eastern counties. Worcester (pronounced Wuh-ster by New Englanders all and Wusta by people who live there) has a slightly differing speech, and western Massachusetts is like an orphaned child, separated from its eastern half by a string of blue hills, a broad river valley, and a completely different arsenal of vowels. The Swift River Valley accent, in the middle of them all, is still different from either. With its reminiscent throaty gag of working class Olde England, one may imagine the first settlers of the Bay Colony spoke as such. It had an old sound, resonant and particular. It stood apart from the flatter, open-wide vowel yawn of the east, that much caricatured Hahvud Yahd Accent and the sing-song drawl of the west where lips barely move, skipping over syllables. In the Swift River Valley, consonants like double d's or t's in the middle of a word are both pronounced clearly as if they hadn't been introduced to each other. One-syllable words are often stretched to two syllables where "house" becomes "howoos" with a dipping inflection.

Roger listened as the man repeated himself, staring at his lips like a deaf person trained to interpret their movement.

"No," Roger said at last, "I'm nawt from around heah."

The man behind the counter would have asked Roger if he were with the State, but it seemed redundant at this point.

Soon the suspicion was irrelevant and the uncertainty over.

***

The Valley came alive with the spring once more in June of 1926, but to people who attended Dana's 125th anniversary, the sweet festive season seemed more like a wake.

Eli Vaughn and his family did not go to Dana for the celebrations. Instead, they rode in the old wagon up Prescott to bury his father.

Walter Vaughn died of a heart attack. Pulling on a tin dairy canister, he slipped into the mud in front of the shed and lay there until Alonzo found him.

It had rained that morning, and like the adage "Rain before seven, clear before eleven," the sky cleared and the sun was shining off the puddles in the yard. Alonzo strode around the house and started in surprise when he found Walter. He looked towards Walter's crumpled body in front of the open shed door as if not believing, then suddenly accepting.

Walter lay curled like a sleeping child, his arms pulled to his chest as if to reach for the pain. His face was gray and mud spattered. The milk canister stood next to him, impregnable, waiting. Alonzo stepped over the body and lifted the dairy canisters into the back of the wagon, one by one. Then he dragged the body into the shed. Then he went on the milk run.

They buried Walter Vaughn in the Prescott hill cemetery, a small shingle of land where determined headstones made shade for dandelions, where the sunny ground was guarded from a distance by a clump of trees, a dirt road, and its isolation.

"'The Lord is my light and my salvation; whom shall I fear?" Reverend Holland said. Eli looked up at him. Reverend Holland had gone mostly gray.

Eli rubbed his forehead. He had suffered a headache since dawn. He prepared the wagon for the trip as competently, as mechanically as ever he had done, but to Mary it seemed he moved as though physically burdened. He snapped at the children, was silent to her. He seemed totally, frightfully within himself.

"The Lord is my shepherd," Reverend Holland began, and the bereaved joined in, "I shall not want. He maketh me to lie beside green pastures. Beside the still waters, He leads me...."

It became generally accepted in town that Walter Vaughn had died of a broken heart over the Reservoir. It made good telling.

A month earlier, the Massachusetts Legislature passed the Ware River Act, which appropriated funds for the construction of an aqueduct from the Ware River to the Wachusett Reservoir. It would be the first link through a long tunnel to the Valley, the first real link the Valley and Boston ever really had. It was the first trickle that would lead to the flood.

George and Eliza received the mourners with dignity in their home. Alonzo resumed the spring plowing.

The neighbors in their good print dresses and their good store suits sat in the parlor and on the back steps and spoke respectfully of the dead or not at all.

"He couldn't bear to leave, like the rest of us must. Perhaps he's better off."

"Certainly couldn'ta timed it better. Or the State did."

"Shh, don't be so grim."

"It's funeral, by God. Supposed t'be grim."

"True, when better to be mindful of our own mortality...."

"We should all think of our souls...."

"Y'take care of y'own soul, I was talking about the reservoir."

"Oh."

"They'll have to drag me off. I won't go." Alonzo said. He appeared suddenly around the side of the house and his words were carried inside the house by others.

Eli stepped out the screened back door, intending to walk a while by himself when Alonzo's words hit him in the face. Eli reprimanded him with a glare and turned toward his old home, but Alonzo, insensitive to reproof jumped to his side and offered to show him around the place. There had been few improvements, but what there were, were Alonzo's and he was proud of all of it.

Eli cut him off, "I know the way, boy."

Eliza and Mary exchanged brief glances of embarrassment from their discreet position inside the huddled, humid parlor, and it occurred to both of them that somehow Walter Vaughn was missing a chief mourner. Was it to be Alonzo or Eli? Being properly mourned was every man's due, so Eliza and Mary shared the duty between them and wordlessly accepted the wordless sympathy around them.

Jenny made a feeble attempt to follow Alonzo and her father outside, but Mary caught her wrist as she stepped by the settle.

Miss Rebecca watched her.

"Thank you for coming, Miss Rebecca," Mary said as an afterthought, "Is there still much to do, now?"

Rebecca smiled her sweet ironic expression.

"Not as much since the government had us close down our Post Office. All the mail goes through Greenwich now. I admit, we miss the extra money. Still, there are a few families left. For how long I don't know."

Eliza studied the print of her good dress and worried that the State would leave them stranded, as stranded and helpless as she had felt by her ignorance on this and on many things.

Alonzo caught up with Eli. He stood apart from him, his hands in his pockets. For the first time Eli stopped and noticed him, noticed that he had his farm boots on with his "good" suit, which was really George's old one cut down.

"I'd like to know what you're thinking." Alonzo said. "Uncle Walter left the farm to me."

"He did, huh? I guess he didn't leave the farm to you, Lon, I did. Me an' John, by unspoken agreement. Wherever he is. I wrote to the last address we had for him. Sent him my father's watch. Guess John left you the farm."

"I don't mean to speak outa place. Especially not today. But, I want to stay here."

"It's for John to say. I don't care."

Alonzo's brief smile of triumph and reassurance faded as he noted the cynicism in Eli's voice.

"You're thinking a' that damned reservoir. They might move you off, but they won't move me."

Eli looked off towards the dim, blue-purple east. That sweet, heartbreaking view.

"Y'think we can't fight them?"

Eli said nothing.

"Well, I ain't goin' to be chased off."

Eli suddenly gave him his hand, which Alonzo at first was prepared to dodge. He took it and shook it foolishly.

"Good luck," Eli said, "It's nothing to me anymore."

Eli left Alonzo the master of his own land and went back to his cousin George's to collect his family.

Later that evening when the house was quiet and dark, Eli was still awake in bed. The moist air hung heavy with the scent of lilacs, the golden moon rose over Den Hill within his view at the window. The old world had never seemed more vital and alive.

He rubbed his forehead with the sleeve of his nightshirt, and Mary gently moved his hand away to see his tears. He made as though to ignore her, but she recovered her surprise and silently stretched her arm across him. She pulled herself closer against his body and tried to wrap herself around him.

***

The next morning Roger Lewis left his room at the Swift River Hotel in Enfield and stopped at the store before going to the office. He loved going to work. His interest in the reservoir project was almost passionate. The intriguing figures in their calculations, formed on slide-rules and sprinkled about blueprints and carbon copy reports dared them to go on.

There had never been a reservoir project of this size. The hills, the three river branches of this isolated valley would all be exploited to the best advantage. Nature was surely a partner in this work. To call the project the largest *man-made* drinking water reservoir in the world was not precisely correct, for it was not entirely man-made.

Roger Lewis knew this, and he grudgingly gave credit to the shaggy green hills out the store window. They were to be his true partners in this adventure, much more than the eager college men like himself on the staff. Much more than the older engineers on the crew who had gained confidence, experience, and weight since their army days, more than the many skilled construction workers, and especially the hordes of unskilled laborers that would one day crawl around these green hills like ants.

This poor section of earth, it could be so beautifully improved. As a small-town boy who grew up with that slow, sullen resentment small town boys sometimes have for small towns, Roger Lewis felt that his own tragically phlegmatic boyhood could be redeemed in this one outstanding feat of engineering. Having grown up in Scituate, he always felt that was his biggest problem. That coastal town, one of the many that lie south and north of Boston, seemed so desperately to feed on the energy of that great city without being sucked up into the helpless vortex of its darker side. Lewis drew his steeping thoughts back to this place called Enfield.

This valley, these towns of utter loneliness straggling on the edges of the modern world, could be saved. In its very destruction, the land could all be saved.

He never dwelled on the word destruction. Yes, it fit, and he was not one to turn his head from truth. In the case of this project he was to be not only a builder but a destroyer. It had to be done. He would have liked to have done the same for Scituate, over in the vague place these people from western Massachusetts referred to blankly as "the East." While directionally correct, the term seemed to infer that "the East," i.e. eastern Massachusetts, was as unknown and mysterious a place as the Orient. Well, perhaps to them it was.

Roger smiled as he tied up his satchel, his college graduation present to himself. There was nothing to do about Scituate except leave it. There were no dams against the unrelenting ocean, and no destruction would save it, since the shoreline altered itself regularly from storms and wind. It always came back. The idea that the town's vulnerable existence always proved impregnable at last haunted him.

He bought his M.I.T. degree with odd jobs. He supported his sickly widowed mother and his younger brother with gentle, patrician disgust. They were back in Scituate, where his mother would not leave her home and his young brother was probably safer. What he knew of Dickie, ten years his junior, was enough to make Roger prefer to take his responsibility to his family from a distance. It seemed that Dickie found his hometown just as hopeless, but with an inventive nature, he had found himself on the wrong side of the police. His mother wanted Roger to take Dickie because she could not manage him.

He could not imagine a tough like Dickie skipping rocks on a lake for amusement. Roger looked out the window at the green valley and wondered if Dickie's need for destruction was the same as his own.

Roger Lewis stepped out into the dusty street and picked out his window over at the Swift River Hotel. He wanted to get his bearings of the place as quickly as possible. He planned to walk around quite a bit, make notes, sketches and diagrams. He wanted to be as familiar as he could with the terrain. He wanted to be able to see the reservoir, as it would be, in his mind's eye as soon as possible. It gave him, he thought, an edge.

Already he looked at the clear line of the horizon made by the distant Mt. Zion, almost as if all of the town of Greenwich were not still in the way.

Proud of his ability to manage details, he had omitted one detail that would be a factor in the project. That was the fact that he, and most of the others, would not be able to study the valley incognito. Because he was from "the East," because he was a stranger they would watch him, point to him. He would soon find out that their curiosity would slow his work, their rudeness would burn him, their kindness would embarrass him. One day it would be a struggle to regard them in the same way he looked at the trees, slated for cutting down.

Roger Lewis tugged at the front of his vest in a nervous habit and continually smoothed his slicked blond hair. He often cleared his throat before speaking, as if he were continually speaking before a crowd. He thought of people that way.

Soon more engineers and construction men would arrive. The townspeople only knew that some surveyors from the State had opened an office in Enfield, at the old A.H. Philips chain grocery.

Elaine Coffey had not known this. She came prepared to buy groceries and was surprised to see a young man with a briefcase loitering in front of the building.

"What is it?" her husband asked from the back seat of the car.

"Nothing," she said, "The store is closed. We'll find another."

"Shall I ask this man?" said the woman beside her in the front seat.

"I will, Emily. I'll just get his attention. Hey, excuse me...." she called to Roger Lewis, "You!"

Lewis started and glared at the woman.

"Could you help us here?"

Roger looked the car over quickly and stepped over.

"What?"

"I thought this was still the store. It's been a while since I've been in Enfield. I think I've forgotten my way. Look, I need to get some supplies, get this car over to my cottage on Quabbin Lake and I need a man to help me lift my husband from the car to the house. If you could *please* help me I'll be happy to pay you ten dollars."

It was a tough decision to be insulted, irritated or amused, so Roger Lewis gave up the decision and climbed into the back seat with her husband.

Lewis would wonder later what made him do it, and he came to several conclusions but preferred to always believe it was because she had said "please" so endearingly.

There was not much else that seemed endearing about Elaine Coffey. She was a loud, impatient woman whose conversation seemed forced and who spoke too freely about personal matters. Lewis quickly realized his mistake and would have shared amused and embarrassed glances with her colored servant Emily there in the front seat with her, if he had not felt that was also beneath him because she was a servant.

He could not share companionable glances with her husband seated next to him. Roland Coffey was blind. He sat in the back seat as though deposited there, his head was bandaged almost completely and he was slumped against a barricade of suitcases and pillows and linens from home.

Home was Newton, near Boston, but since her husband's unsuccessful operation on a brain tumor, Elaine Coffey thought it was a good time to bring him back to her beloved childhood summer home to die.

Was it not indelicate to speak of his death so freely with him here in the car? Lewis looked purposefully out the car window at a clump of weeds by the road.

Roland Coffey gave no reaction. Perhaps he could not hear. Perhaps he was unconscious. For the first time Lewis noticed Emily also staring hard out her window as well and for the first time felt a kinship with her.

"My grandfather took us out to the camp every summer. I haven't seen the place since I was married, I thought it was about time I did. I know I won't have a chance to ever again once the reservoir is built." Elaine said. Suddenly she stopped talking and the car swerved into a gravel drive. Roger was not sure where they were. Greenwich? She never said where they were going. They could not still be in Enfield. He tried to think of his maps.

"What do you think of this?" Elaine asked, but Lewis didn't know if she were talking to him or to Emily.

"Grandfather Forbes went to the bother of carting in gravel and planting boxwoods and carving a sign for the old post there with his name on it. What a little laird he was," she laughed. In a moment she was crying, that was evident even to Lewis who had been trying with propriety to ignore her.

"Mrs. Coffey? Are you all right?" Emily asked.

Mrs. Coffey began to hiccup violently while still crying.

"Mrs. Coffey, ma'am, is there anything I can do for you?"

Mrs. Coffey slipped her white gloves off and began to wipe her eyes with them. Emily bit her lip and slid out of the car. Lewis took this as his cue and also climbed out. He walked around to the other side and opened the door for Mr. Coffey.

"Ma'am, I'll need the key to open the door." Emily said into driver's side window. Elaine handed Emily her purse. Emily shot an exasperated, companionable glance to Lewis, and he pushed aside some of the gear holding up Mr. Coffey.

"How do I move him?" Lewis called to no one in particular.

"Just get me to my feet and let me lean on you." Coffey responded in a guttural voice. Roger jumped.

Blushing at the intimacy with an ill man who was not unconscious after all, Roger awkwardly put his arms around Roland Coffey and half-dragged him to the cottage porch and into the small parlor. It was dank with age and absence.

"Sir, you can leave him here in this chair." Emily said to him, "Thank you so much for helping. I think Mrs. Coffey would like me to pay you...."

"No, I don't want it," Lewis said, "I'll just be going."

"Do you know someone we could hire to help with some heavy work around here, a boy or young man?"

"No, I'm new here myself." He nodded goodbye and retrieved his satchel from the car, barely glancing at the woman still crying softly behind the wheel.

Dismayed that he now had to find his way back to Enfield and his hotel, Roger Lewis became grudgingly acquainted with the terrain on which he would be working for some time. He started the walk down Route 21.

A paved road, he was sure they had been driving along the same paved road since Enfield. Route 21 was paved, and so was the old turnpike road to Monson, but most other roads around here were not. They were just old country dirt roads. It suddenly occurred to Roger that they had not seen much traffic, and he would likely have to walk all the way back to Enfield.

Roger noticed a river through the trees on his right. It was a small river, undoubtedly one of the three branches that would one day fill his reservoir. Which one? If they had driven to Greenwich it was either the Middle or the

East branch. That lake behind Mrs. Coffey's cottage, that was probably Greenwich Lake. Or did she say Quabbin Lake? Flighty woman. What was wrong with her? She had been through a lot, of course.

Wait a minute, Roger thought. A few houses lined the road now, and he came to a crossroads. A dirt road intersected the paved one. A mountain stood ahead of him, some small wooden mills by the river.

"Where the hell am I?" Roger said aloud to himself. Crossing the intersection on the dirt road at that moment was a wagon driven by Eli Vaughn.

"Hey!" Roger called, suddenly blanching at the thought of sounding like Mrs. Coffey.

Eli reigned in his draft horses and shot a glare at the man in the suit who shouted at him.

Roger walked quickly over, "Sorry, look I need some directions. Can you tell me how to get back to Enfield?"

"Could take you to the station, but the Rabbit won't be along for a bit. I could take you there myself, I suppose."

What was he talking about? Rabbits? Roger already had gotten a cramp in his side from the unaccustomed exertion.

"Thanks," Roger said and hauled himself with difficulty up the seat. It had been his first time on a wagon and he thought about making a remark about riding shotgun but figured the farmer would be humorless.

They continued down the dirt road. Roger felt uneasy. He was sure he should have stayed on the paved road.

"Is this the way to Enfield?"

"One way. You were headed north by the way, not south to Enfield."

"I was going north? Toward Dana? I'm new around here. Lost my bearings a little."

Eli glanced at him, then back at the road ahead. They rounded a curve and there was the typical white church with the high, piercing steeple.

"Nice town." Roger said only as a matter of course, which Eli knew.

"Are you one of the state men, come to build that reservoir?"

Roger had dreaded the direct question, but only Eli was surprised he had asked it. He did not expect it would come out of his mouth like that.

"Yes."

It occurred to Roger that he might be at this man's mercy but waved the thought away as they crossed the railroad tracks and soon turned onto another paved road heading south to Enfield. Roger swallowed his pride.

"Would'ja mind telling me where we are?"

"You were in Greenwich Village, up ahead's Greenwich Plains. After that is Enfield."

They came to another convergence of roads, with the tall white church on one corner and the colonial cemetery on the other, a scene repeated in any town in New England.

Roger wondered, did the man know they would be under one hundred feet of water when the reservoir was finished, if they stood in this spot? He probably would not like to think about it, just as Roger did not like to think about the little town at the crossroads.

They picked up Route 21 again, cutting across the juncture of the Middle and East branches that would one day fill his reservoir. They rolled into Enfield.

"This is fine," Roger motioned to the bridge over the Swift River. He knew where he was now.

Eli put out the brake and did not watch as the young man stumbled down.

"Thank you, sir." Roger called, and even removed his hat. Eli nodded.

All the way home, Eli thought about Mary's talk of nature, and healing, and creating. That young man was not a force of nature. A full of himself dandy with education and the power to destroy people's lives. How could that be natural?

End of Part II

PART III
1930 - 1934

CHAPTER 10

Forty-eight people lived in Prescott.

Chapter 321 of the Commonwealth of Massachusetts Acts of 1927 was for the towns of Prescott, Enfield and Greenwich, a disaster unlike any war, storm or ill luck they ever knew. Its simply being unique to their collective experience seemed especially frightening. The Commonwealth called the Act simply a "provision for the water supply needs of the Metropolitan Water District and for communities which now or hereafter may require water there from, by the development of an adequate future water supply for the Swift River."

Legal language left, they suspected, intentional murkiness, but that did not alone distress the people of Prescott and the other towns. Far more disturbing was the simple language they could understand. How casual it sounded, how vague. Did the Commonwealth really understand that they were destroying entire communities? These towns had been founded before the Commonwealth existed.

"...The commission on behalf of the commonwealth may, at any time and from time to time, take by eminent domain or acquire by purchase or otherwise, such lands, waters, water rights, easements and other property...as it may deem necessary or desirable...."

The people living in the Swift River Valley had no idea any one small group of people (they wondered how many a "commission" was) could wield so much blank power. For a construction project of such magnitude and undertaking, the legislation that first brought it to life was only a simple document. That bothered them the most. The point of it sounded so simple, and the very simplicity of the language made them feel even more inconsequential. A more flowery verbiage, such as they heard at Home Day orations, would have at least impressed them.

But this thing was law. They did not treat the law lightly.

Those forty-eight souls left in the Town of Prescott carefully considered the options left to them.

Two of these people were George and Eliza Vaughn, who farmed their land with effort but without hope for the future. They did not like to think about settling elsewhere, they spoke little about it.

Daniel was nineteen and pursued a business degree at Amherst College on a scholarship and a summer factory job in Holyoke. The stock market crash that occurred shortly thereafter seemed awesome and interesting in the papers, but as remote as a storm on the other side of the continent. Those living in the Valley did not see how it could affect them much; it was a rich man's problem. They did not personally know anyone who had become poor who had not already been poor.

James was sixteen. The recent closings of the public schools in Prescott was all right with him, and he didn't intend to go on to Belchertown High to continue his education. He wanted to farm with Calvin. He and Calvin got along well. They never discussed who would inherit their father's farm. They knew the state was heir apparent.

Both were of a mind to sell soon. The State was paying around a hundred dollars an acre, a fortune. Appraisers were visiting their neighbors. If they sold now, perhaps they could get much better property further west along the Connecticut River. There was some wide fertile land there, wide by New England standards. They could buy a large enough property for the both of them and run it together. If only their father would sell.

To actually discuss selling out right now was disloyal. They would not be so crude as to broach the subject. They watched their father for signs of change, not knowing George Vaughn had been quietly thinking about it for a long time.

Alonzo was firm. He would not sell for anything. He said he would sell his soul to the devil before he would sell his land to the State, and his helpless parents replied by pitying him from a distance. Here he was twenty-four years old now, well old enough to marry and start a family. But who would he marry? Prescott was losing population like water through a sieve and selling out was starting to occur in the other Valley towns. People in Enfield and in Greenwich were becoming anxious as well, even in Dana, which was not included in the Reservoir project perimeters so far as anyone was sure. The men from the State were surveying all over, up close now, not from a respectful distance as before. The state bought properties and took photographs of the houses and land, tested soil, made drawings, made maps, made adjustments to maps like men cruelly dissecting a creature that had not yet died.

Alonzo had lived alone in the farmhouse since the death of his great uncle Walter. He cooked simply and when he felt like it, cleaned intermittently, but tended his fields with the vigor of a soldier. He had ceased to make too many cosmetic appearances on the farm as he had tried to do when he first moved in; it took all his energy now just to keep it going.

He cut down on the dairy stock and concentrated on eggs and garden truck. The people who were left in Prescott and the other towns, people who said they'd never leave, needed to buy food and were happy to barter like the olden days.

Miss Rebecca still ran the store, the only store left in Prescott. The town was now being officially run by the Commonwealth of Massachusetts, one of the provisions of Chapter 321 of the Acts of 1927, because the decline in the population had been so sharp. Prescott could no longer sustain its own town government without help. Like a hospital patient on a respirator, it had to be kept alive artificially until the proper time for its scheduled demise.

Miss Rebecca mused that she must be a State employee and wondered comically if she would be up for a pension. Her brother worried more vividly and planned their move to Amherst. They would fare better there. He might even leave the general mercantile business and take up with his brother-in-law's real estate business. He had his responsibility to his spinster sister to consider, he told his wife repeatedly. She was a weight around his neck, always.

Miss Rebecca, aware of this, knew she would never be on equal and easy terms with her brother unless she married, impossible now that she was fifty-six, but perhaps just as impossible when she was twenty-six. She would never be off his brittle conscience. Miss Rebecca sorted the stick candy and listened hard for the jingling of the bell on top of the door. Some days it never rang at all.

Roger Lewis sat in the white wicker chair on the porch of the Swift River Hotel, glaring towards a curtained window at a Lusterware hurricane lamp. His appointment had been due fifteen minutes ago, and he had lost the pose of the distinguished but impatient professional he had practiced. Now he felt only impatient, and irritably fatigued. The MDWSC office had been moved to a new building near the Enfield - Belchertown line, coincidentally situated so as to actually stand like a marker on the site of the future dam at the foot of the great reservoir. The water would one day stretch from its parking area towards the north, a mighty vista. It took a lot of imagination to envision this, but Roger imagined it often.

At last, the fellow arrived. It must be him, this fellow with the satchel.

He noticed Roger upon the porch, smiled somewhat to himself, and approached. Roger sat up straighter, meaning to give him his full dissatisfaction. The fellow looked older than Roger had expected. The haggard weight that hung on his shoulders, and his belly, as a mirror of his own fatalistic surrender to life's misfortunes somehow did not lessen the effect of the man's charm. The old fellow had an animal swagger to him still, an air of confidence that fought vainly to suppress his vulnerability.

He set the satchel firmly on the bottom step and looked up at Roger as if the steps were a mountain too high for him to climb. He looked Roger swiftly up and down and nodded to him.

"Mr. Lewis?"

"Yes. Mr. Vaughn, is it?"

"John Vaughn."

"You're late...." Roger said, waiting to be interrupted with an explanation, but John Vaughn only continued to smile pleasantly, and took a moment to light a cigar.

"Well, would you like to sit down?"

"How long is this going to take?"

"Do you want the job, or don't you?"

"I'm sorry, Mr. Lewis, it's just that I have some relatives in this area, and I'm anxious to see them again."

"Oh? Here in Enfield?"

"Mostly in Prescott, and Greenwich. I understand both are falling under the ax."

"Mr. Vaughn, I have your résumé here. I know you've been a photographer for a number of years."

"I've shot happy families, World War heroes, governors, film stars, and not a few hydroelectric dams when the money was low."

"Well, you know what you'll be shooting here, don't you?"

"More dams? To hold back the course of nature? To bring relief to suffering city dwellers? To stand as a monument to twentieth century engineering? I'd be honored. Hell, I'd even be grateful."

"No, Mr. Vaughn, not the construction. The destruction."

"Fine. Suits my mood."

"You'll be working under Carter North, he's our project photographer, as well an engineer. He'll do the construction, the aerial shots, etcetera. You'll be taking pictures of houses."

"With families and dogs in front of them?"

"With a diagram to illustrate their location on the grid map, noting any pertinent landmarks. You'll be taking pictures of houses and farmsteads that will be evacuated for the construction of the reservoir. If you work out, you could have work for four or five years. It won't be exciting, but it'll be steady."

"Four or five years?" Vaughn exhaled his cigar smoke and squinting a moment into the sun over the depot across the river, decided not to make a remark about pertinent landmarks. "How big is this thing going to be?"

"The reservoir and the watershed land around it will encompass the towns of Greenwich, Prescott, and Enfield, as well as some fringe villages in Belchertown, New Salem, Hardwick, Petersham, oh ... Dana of course, Barre ... uh, let's see... Pelham...."

"Lord." Vaughn looked at him, "You left out Springfield and Worcester."

"It will amount to about a thousand buildings. Barns, houses, etcetera. Do you think you can do this?"

"Of course. Outhouses too?"

"I mean... since you are from Prescott and have relatives here...well, if you feel ... awkwardness...."

"Evidently less than you do. I left Prescott nearly twenty years ago. If I didn't need the work, I wouldn't be back now. I am a victim of that impressive stock crash last autumn. Left my business, what was left of it. Mr. Lewis, do I get the job?"

Roger Lewis slapped his folder shut and regarded John Vaughn with the kind of showdown which young men who think they are successful like to have with older men whom they think are failures. "Yes, Mr. Vaughn, I'll recommend you. Do you have lodgings yet?"

"I will."

"Then report to the office on Monday. You've been there already, you know where it is? They'll set you up with equipment and your assignment sheet."

"These homes I'll be shooting, will they already be empty?"

"Yes of course, you don't have to worry about that. We've already bought up several hundred acres so far. Many of the Dana Center population are helping us by voluntarily selling their property, though to what extent Dana will fit into the watershed plans isn't determined yet. At the moment, of course, they still have the highest population of all the towns to be involved. I'm sure you'll have no trouble beginning there. We'll get you a vehicle and a driver...."

"What is the population of the towns now, roughly, do you know off-hand? Have people all over been selling out for you?"

"Here in Enfield there's almost five hundred, there are around two hundred thirty left in Greenwich, and there are forty-eight left in Prescott."

"Forty-eight?" Vaughn's incredulous expression, its inferred heartsickness at the news agitated Lewis again.

"You're sure this is the job for you, Mr. Vaughn?"

"Yes." Vaughn looked up at him suddenly. He noted for the first time Lewis' familiarity with his notes, with his studied air of possession. And numbers. Vaughn took off his hat.

"Thank you for the job, Mr. Lewis. I won't let you down."

"Good afternoon, Mr. Vaughn." Lewis nodded to him and stepped back across the porch to the door. He thought that would look best.

Then a huge, dusty open touring car pulled up in front of the hotel. The driver left it running and stepped out quickly as if he had no business driving it.

"Mr. Lewis?"

"Yes. My car?"

"Yut. Leave it here?"

"My Gawd, what a battleship. Yes, leave it I guess. Well you can turn it off, can't you?" Lewis turned sharply and went inside.

John Vaughn looked at the car and the young man, who jerked his head toward the porch.

"Big shot." he muttered and Vaughn smiled wearily in return. The young man whistled as he walked away and Roger came out with his briefcase.

"Are you going to Greenwich?" John Vaughn asked. It sounded like an accusation. Roger bristled.

"Why?"

John smiled. "I need a lift. As close to Greenwich Village as you can make it. It's near Quabbin Lake there on your grid map."

Roger stared at him, relenting.

"Get in."

John tucked his satchel in the back seat and took out a fine, gold pocket watch. He saw that Lewis noticed.

"My grandfather's. It's easier to get rid of watches if they are not engraved. Remember that."

When they had pulled away from town and the long road ahead lay bare before them, Lewis relaxed his grip on the wheel. He hated company, but perhaps this was a good time to improve himself.

"Your family will be glad to see you, I'm sure." Lewis coughed out the jagged pleasantry.

John Vaughn smiled at him. "I'm not expected. I haven't written to my brother, that's where we're going, to my brother's, in over six years."

Lewis thought of his own brother.

"Greenwich is a nice town."

"No, we lived in Prescott. Young cousin of mine, second cousin, now runs the old place."

John laughed thinking of the irony that if he had stayed in this dump he would be a richer man.

No, Prescott wasn't what I wanted, he thought to himself. At least my life's work isn't going up in smoke because of some decision made in Boston.

My problems are of my own making, he thought, satisfied.

They passed Quabbin Lake, but Roger did not turn his eyes from the road to look when John pointed to it. Below Mt. Zion John directed him to his Cousin Sam's old farm.

"Thanks."

Outside the white farmhouse he saw some children racing and shouting, tagging each other, dodging each other, squealing and falling to the ground. A girl about ten years old, with blonde hair and pale blue eyes, giggled, bubbling with explosive anticipation over the little boy attempting to tag her. The two other girls, a little older than the blonde girl, tried to escape around the side of the house. Then a taller girl, with brown hair and sharp blue eyes jumped down from the maple tree in the front yard and lifted the boy onto her hip with strong brown arms. She was older than all of them, in her early teens. She cuddled the boy because she felt sorry for him. He had been "it" for so long, his frustration reached her warm heart way up in the tree. She came down to rescue him.

"You're welcome," Roger sighed, and pulled away.

Another boy raced around the house. He was about twelve, and he immediately halted and charged back around the house when he saw the older girl was "it." He knew she could catch him easily, so he retreated with all his might and an excited shiver up his spine.

The girl let the squealing little boy go, happy in his freedom, and she set about to catch her victims when she noticed John Vaughn in the dusty road.

He stood still, watching her with pleasure. She was lean, with a straight back and a strong, intelligent face in which shone the deep-set hungry eyes. He had seen evidence of her kindliness and he waited for her to push the dark hair out of her eyes once more before he spoke.

"Is this the house of Eli Vaughn?"

She tilted her face in a question. The blonde girl and the other two girls tripped back to see what was keeping her. Their presence made the girl bolder, and she lifted her gaze from off the ground and into his eyes.

"Yut." she nodded briefly, "Are y'looking for my father?"

"Is Eli your father?" He gave her a broad smile, which she thought made him seem wolfish.

Could he be from the state, sent to clear them off?

"Yes, sir." she said squarely, her pulse quickening, "Shall I call him?"

"What's your name, child?" he set down his satchel in the dirt and placed his hands on his hips.

Then the skinny little blonde girl stepped over to the tall girl and slipped her thin hands upon the girl's arm.

"Let's go inside, Jen," she mumbled anxiously into her sister's sleeve.

"Are y'from the State?" piped up the older boy.

John Vaughn smiled. These were smart, careful children, wild, but somehow less free than he remembered being. Their shackles were not the same as his had been.

"My name is John. I'm Eli Vaughn's brother. I come from New York City, among other places. If any of you are my nieces and nephews, I'd sure like to meet you."

"Sakes," muttered the tall girl under her breath, "Harry, go get y'father." The boy about twelve nodded and bolted around the house.

"And what's your name?" John asked her.

She met his eyes evenly.

"Jenny."

"That's a pretty name."

She did not acknowledge the compliment, but gently extricated her arm from the clutches of the little blonde girl. "This is my sister Ella, that was my brother Harrison. Eli Vaughn is our father. This is Nance, Charlie, and Jane Holt, our neighbors from next door."

John Vaughn removed his hat and bowed ceremoniously to them. "I'm please to know all of you."

They stared at him, sure there must be a proper protocol for such an occasion, but not sure what it was.

Eli strode around the side of the house, Harrison at his heels. Eli looked skeptically at the red-faced man with the salt-and-pepper hair and was amazed at how it was still John, despite how much he had changed.

"John." Eli nodded to him, extending his strong brown hand.

"Hello, Eli." John wavered, just slightly, as he stooped for his suitcase.

CHAPTER 11

John Vaughn sat back in his chair and smiled at Mary, looking as though just eating the meal had worn him out. He lit a cigarette and used his plate for an ashtray. He brushed his two hands through the graying hair at his temples.

Mary nodded to the girls, who began to clear the plates.

"Well, John. What're you up to these days?" Eli had not taken his eyes off him the entire meal.

"I am now an employee of the Commonwealth. I think. I'll have to look at the bottom of the paperwork I signed."

"That's good," Mary called from the kitchen. "Lot of people would like to have a secure job with the state in times like these."

"Times like these?" John pulled a small hip flask out of his coat pocket and took a drink. "What do you mean?"

"I mean the, the bad times, of course." Mary stepped in from the kitchen and started at the flask. She looked to Eli, who was calmly taking it all in.

"That's nothing," John said, "Every day is bad times if you don't have a job. Oh God, it's quiet here."

"What brings you this way, John?" Eli asked, sounding to Mary like he already knew the answer.

"The reservoir."

The children looked at each other. Ida and Doris did the dishes, as quietly as possible so they could listen. Jenny, Ella and Harrison went to their rooms but left the doors open.

"I'm still a photographer, as I wrote you last time, Eli...."

"That was a while ago. Years, in fact."

"Well, here I am. I'm shooting Valley buildings for the state."

"They want pictures of the properties? Why?"

"I don't care why. They're paying me. So, when are you selling this place, Eli?"

Eli flushed with anger and the effort to hide it, which John did not notice.

"Don't take any pictures of this place anytime soon, John. I'm not selling to nobody."

John looked in confusion to Mary. She dropped her glance and went back into the kitchen.

"We got an uncle working on the reservoir." Harrison came into the girls' room whispering.

"Wish he'd go away." Ella whispered back. Jenny said nothing. She was thinking about her father. He had never before said what he would do about his land. Their parents did not speak of the reservoir at all. Now she knew the reservoir was not an imaginary boogeyman. It was real.

***

Roger Lewis squinted into the highway of moonlight on the dark lake, mesmerized by the sound of evening crickets. A nice, peaceful place and he felt glad to be finally alone a moment with his thoughts, yet anticipated Elaine Coffey's footsteps from the kitchen.

In a moment, she bumped the screen door open with her hip and held two brandy snifters aloft like lanterns. Roger roused himself and reached for one, not waiting for her to offer it.

Elaine plopped herself without regard to safety on a dangerous old porch swing, but Roger stayed where he was, backside embedded into the peeling porch rail.

He had asked himself a hundred times why he accepted her offer of supper that night months ago, why he still did. No, "a home-cooked meal," was how she put it, but it was not the idea of a home cooked meal that appealed to Roger. He was a fussy eater who liked the convenience of dining out quickly and alone. He concluded once again it was the way she said, *"Please."*

Something about someone asking for help undid Roger, though he was only dimly aware of it. He liked to give, to be in control, to be in a position to bestow favor. He did not grant wishes with good-natured beneficence as the arch-Samaritan does. His harried, annoyed facade never revealed the ego boost.

Elaine Coffey had already apologized for her inconsiderate breakdown on their first meeting, thanked him profusely for his aid.

"I love responsible men," she'd said long afterwards, even before her husband had died.

Emily Pete, Elaine's housemaid entered and folded her hands before her, pulling herself erect.

"If that's all Mrs. Coffey, I'll say goodnight."

"Yes, that's all, thank you. Goodnight, Emily." Elaine smiled up at Emily with what Roger thought might be amusement.

Emily nodded, wordlessly dismissed herself and left them.

"I don't think she likes me." Elaine said in a stage whisper.

"I thought she was a maid, not a companion." Roger downed the last of his drink. He held onto the glass because he did not know what else to do with it.

"Well, I can't separate jobs, and people, and feelings into different pockets the way you and Emily can. It's all one pot of soup to me. My husband was like you, too. He could keep his business and his personal life separate, and then he could divide his personal life according to his home, his club, his friends from business, his friends from college, and me. Emily hails from Maine, you know."

"I could tell by her accent."

"She's divorced and said so with no explanations. I like that. I have a lot of admiration for divorced women. It must be especially difficult for people of her race. If she were rich and famous I like to think she could make a career of being divorced the way some rich and famous white women do."

"You talk too much." Roger broke in. Elaine tilted her head and looked at him now. She took a step closer to him to retrieve his glass and to see if he would step back.

He did, and she smiled, reaching for his glass. He gave it to her with both hands and shuffled closer to her because he did not like to be dared. Just as he was vulnerable to the word "please," he was a sucker for a dare.

"Well," she said, "I'm glad you came tonight. I know I talk too much, and I guess I can't even pay people to listen."

"Maybe if you paid her more. Why don't you get to the point, and then I can go home?"

"If that was an attempt at being witty, I'll ignore it. This time," she said. "I'm sentimental. I like to reminisce and Emily won't have it. She starts doing the dishes the minute I mention my childhood. I have very clean dishes."

"So, you grew up around here, and you resent the reservoir. You know, I hired a new man today. He grew up around here, but the project seems okay with him. He left his childhood behind. I think that's best."

"And you resent people resenting the reservoir." She smiled, "No, I didn't grow up around here. I grew up elsewhere, both literally and figuratively. My family lived in Longmeadow, and my Grandfather Forbes bought this cottage as a summer camp way back in the 1880s when the whole town used to have oyster suppers on the common. My father spent his boyhood summers here, until military school, and so did I. Because I was a girl, and Grandfather's favorite besides, I never went to military school. I never grew up, either. Not here, anyway. I was allowed to play and laze around even when I was big girl of seventeen while my mother planned my coming out in Longmeadow. God, I love this place."

"So you've said a couple of hundred times."

"Well I liked coming out after a fashion, but I was married so soon afterwards that there was little time to enjoy it. Roland Coffey was there waiting. He was a junior executive and used to be an athlete at school. They called him Dash, and he insisted I call him Dash. He had everything but a sense of humor."

Roger did not reply. She pressed on.

"I have to say this to someone just once. I'm sorry I ever married. I thought I was looking for a husband. I was really looking for a home like this."

Roger put his hand on her back, tentatively. She slipped herself against him so it was necessary for him to complete the embrace.

"If your heart isn't in this, let me know," she said into his lapel, and he grimaced for a smile.

"Very little of what I do seems to involve my heart. According to my family."

"Your mother still wants you to take your little brother in? Forget him. Let's not think about him right now."

"No, let's not. Or the reservoir, or the Valley."

"I'm thirty-two." she said. He felt her clutch him harder. He kissed her, and found his way, anticipating her quiet responses. She lifted her face and he looked into her eyes briefly before they kissed. He remembered their strained expression long afterward.

Later that night he wanted to joke that he finally found a way to make her keep quiet, but he did not. He also wanted to tell her it had been his first experience, but he did not do that either. Why give her that superiority over him?

Instead, he lay quietly against her while she clung to him but did not sleep. Softly she murmured into his chest, "I love this place. I could stay here forever."

He glared at her in the dark, humiliated that her sleepy, satisfied remark had been about this place and not about him, angered that he let it bother him. Long after she had fallen asleep, he argued semantics with her in his mind the rest of the night, about the word "forever." He might have said that neither of them really belonged here. Still, the Valley was full of strangers these days. Each had a different purpose and all collided with each other. But for now, for this moment, all of them belonged here.

It was as if this was the only place to be.

***

The construction project, like the Valley, formed its own all-encompassing universe.

The undertaking of it involved the talents of many people, who otherwise had nothing in common: engineers, whose vision bordered on science fiction. To the Valley residents they were like a secret society with slide rules and specifications, wizards, their technical knowledge aided and abetted by gifted imagination.

There were politicians. Men in the Boston statehouse who looked to the present, rather than to the future. They knew that the reservoir would solve metropolitan Boston's water problems at last. This big hole in the center of the state would feed them forever, but they did not really think about forever. They thought about this year, next year. They thought about elections, and jobs, and prosperity. They were not nearly so visionary as they proclaimed to their constituents, but they knew how to use the visions of others, like the engineers.

There were the politicians of western Massachusetts, too. Not many of them entirely approved the reservoir project, some were even vehemently against it. But they rowed in little circles in a large pond, controlling only their wards, their friends, like ancient petty barons. Their towns really belonged to the Commonwealth, and the Commonwealth was the property of the Boston power-brokers. So it was since the time of Daniel Shays, so it was now. Geography was their betrayer.

The construction on the reservoir would be accomplished through many stages and many years. Separate contractors handled only bits of a large puzzle. A dike wall, a pipe tunnel, an abutment, a spillway. It was small surgery at first, seemingly unconnected with the total picture.

Part of the construction dealt with the removal of current landmarks. Rock ledges blasted, streams diverted, fences and farms were surveyed, and then marked, and then bought after their contents were auctioned off in the front yard while the family watched through parted curtains, and then the families left and the houses and barns were bulldozed. A few homes were removed by their owners. Soon a house could be seen on a flatbed trailer, lurching down the road to some other place. Parts of houses were lifted away, pieces of houses were pried off. Mantels went into moving trucks like so many pieces of china, a doorknob was as prized as a photograph.

It started in small ways, in dislocated areas, and the people got word and fluttered like birds jarred from their rest. They looked into each other's eyes nervously for a moment, silently asking, should we go? Should we go now?

Others kept their heads down, to the plow.

Some were angry, hostile, ready to arm themselves with axes and lawyers. Some were bitter, resigned, willing to leave only when there was nothing left, as if to see if this all were really true, who remained mainly for spite. They demanded too high a price for their land and dared the Commonwealth to remove them in the end. Some were anxious, wanting to leave before the price of the land went down, excited to start life over elsewhere. Many young people felt this way. After all, the Valley was so old-time, they said. There were no proper restaurants, no movie houses. Life was different in Athol, in Palmer, in many of the surrounding towns that had tenuously in the past thirty or so years shaken hands with the twentieth century.

Or Springfield, even. Imagine going to Springfield, or Chicopee, to one of those huge smoke-belching factories, settling down in a nice little house companionably set within ten feet in a row of other nice little houses. That might be something. One could save for a car, or anything.

Then there were those who could not think at all. The past was tugging at them, begging them heartrendingly not to let it go, and the future frightened them.

All these groups, from engineers to politicians, to Valley folk, sought signs of this impending reservoir like changing weather on the horizon. They looked for progress, or evidence of money well spent, or success, or disaster, or doom, or just of what to do next. One of the first tasks in creating the reservoir came as a surprise. Nobody had thought of it, except the engineers. Nobody realized, though it had been done before during construction of the Wachusett Reservoir some thirty years ago.

Corpses must be exhumed.

All the dead in every town cemetery or church graveyard were exhumed, and there were more people dead than alive. Skeletal remains were pulled from hillside tombs with everything from heavy machinery, to hand trowels.

They would be relocated, the project coordinators said, to a new, well-planned and orderly cemetery for all the Valley people in Ware, or to any cemetery of their family's choice.

The Ware cemetery would be a special place apart. It would be their own cemetery, they told the living, a place for them as well when their time came. This was meant to ease their anxiety, after all, these people were funny about tradition. Knowing where they were going to be buried was awfully important to them. One disgruntled State gravedigger replied that other people in the world worried about where their next meal was coming from, but not these Valley folk, all they cared about was where they were going to be buried. His supervisor warned him about not talking about it too much. The project coordinators did not want trouble. Well, neither did he. Only he didn't want to be stared at like he was some ghoul.

So, the ragged colonial graveyards were unearthed, headstones were carted away to be reset in the new, orderly cemetery in a new town. Remains of bodies were scratched up and carefully replanted in new soil. People who had never left the Valley in their lifetimes were at last leaving now.

The crumbling remains of Revolutionary soldiers, of soldiers from the Civil War honored with solemn ceremony each Decoration Day, were pried away from their centuries-old graves and put onto the trucks. They would be honored again, in another place not their own.

"Sacrilege," some people said and wept for their mother's memory. Some only felt sick. Sam and Agnes Vaughn could not bring themselves to go see Tyler's untenanted memorial planted all over again. Once was enough.

The Men from the State need not have worried about the anxiety of house moving and land buying. The shifting of the graves was what really demoralized the Valley residents. Nothing else shocked them after that.

***

John Vaughn marveled a moment at the simplicity of the office in such a grand room. Only a battered wooden desk, two file cabinets, two wooden chairs, no carpet. He shook hands with Carter North, a man twenty years his junior whose department this was, and said aloud, "This house used to belong to my brother's mother-in-law. Mrs. Pratt."

It sounded cheerful. It was what he was thinking. He felt silly to find himself saying it out loud. Carter North gave him a quizzical glance. John mused that he must be careful. These men did not want to know the history of the land they were destroying and were suspicious of their workers' links to the land.

Some of the sympathetic engineers sincerely regarded the morose feelings of loss as something they must eradicate for the better good. Eradicating the valley was not enough; indeed, the difficult work was to eradicate the mourning over it. To this end, as many local men as possible were hired, as long as quotas of unemployed men from the metropolitan Boston area were met. Such involvement by locals would prove productive for everyone.

John loaded his issued equipment into the old touring car with the help of his driver, one of the chosen locals, given a job in exchange for his home. He was a young man named George something and he came from Dana but moved in with cousins in Smith's Village last year to work on the Reservoir. He needed a job; his sister was sick. He was a good driver, and he was quiet.

"I am also glad to be working," John said to him in the car. In recent months, he had begun to enjoy talking to himself, and talking to George was almost the same thing.

"The thought of earning enough money to stay in Enfield, in a rooming house close enough to shops and to Bondsville so I can get something to drink once in a while. Yeah, I'll be all right now. I can't live with my brother Eli forever. Depresses me. He's got a nice family, though. Nice kids."

Mary had made him a lunch and put it in a shoebox. John put it on the back seat and finally picked up his assignment sheet.

They were already at the site, to which George proudly gestured as he stopped the car near the new construction of Shaft 12 by Quabbin Lake. He stepped out of the car and began to haul out the tripod and camera so John could shoot the vacant cottage near the one still occupied by Elaine Coffey.

***

Elaine raised the shade and leaned towards the screen-sifted breeze. The diffused mid-morning light sprayed delicately on the old floral print wallpaper, on her old floral print robe, and on her puffy face. She left Roger lying in the darkness to appreciate it or not.

He snuffed out his cigarette and lit another and checked his watch. He did that a lot, she had thought it ceased to bother her. He ran his hand through his thick light hair and blew a decided stream of smoke across the bed.

"What don't you leave here?" He'd been thinking of saying it for some time.

She pulled herself up off the weathered windowsill and let her loose, unfastened robe fall, cover her where it would or would not. The effect was less artistic than she imagined.

"Why? I don't want to. There's plenty of time, isn't there? I don't want to think about it. Listen, why don't you ever use my name? My name is Elaine. Call me Elaine just once, just to show you know who I am."

"Elaine, why don't you pack up Emily, and your things, and get into your car and get away from here?"

"There's no use."

"Don't stay for me." He had a moral obligation, he felt, to say that.

"You arrogant little man." She gave a short laugh to demonstrate she found herself amusing, or else a demonstration of superior mind.

He snuffed out his cigarette and began to dress.

"Oh Roger, don't be hurt. You're such a boy sometimes. Let me try to explain. You know, you've never understood, Roger. This place is just too comfortable to leave, like an old couch and you want to...."

"Or bed ...."

"Don't be vulgar," she smiled.

"I mean a sick bed. Or a deathbed."

"You're getting worse. Morbid. I just want to be warm for a while. That's all. And happy. And quiet, safe. There's nothing out there, Roger. There really isn't. I know. After the funeral all I could think of, accepting condolences like a fool, was that I had to get back here. Everything would be all right if I could just get back to Grandfather's cottage on the shining lake."

"That's all you talk about. At dinner, in bed. In your sleep, practically. I don't think we should be with each other anymore. I don't think it's good for either of us."

"Now, have you found another healthy young widow in the village?"

"You wouldn't care if I had." He watched her close her robe. "All the while…there's no … intimacy. You're out on that lake all the while, not with me, here in this room…."

"You're one to talk," she said, smiling, "Mr. Distant…unapproachable…."

"Why play the lady of the manor when the manor is an ugly, run-down little shack in a town that's not going to be here in a few years? Who the hell are you trying to impress? They could give a damn. Emily's not impressed and I'm not. In fact, I'm kind of repulsed."

"So much for intimacy. Are we talking about you, or are we talking about that reservoir? Make up your mind."

"I am the reservoir."

She turned her back to him if only not to let him dare her. In a moment, she realized she was not going to feel his thin hands on her shoulders.

"I think you'd better leave now," she said.

"*You'd* better leave now, Elaine. I have a reason to be here, you don't. You've watched your husband die, you buried him in the family plot, your biggest mistake was to come back here afterwards. You should have started over right then. Comforting place. That's a lot of garbage. This is a lousy place. It's short on money, roads, and toilets. It's got plenty of memories for you and everybody else living here, sure, I don't dispute that. But you can't live on memories. You can't."

"Roger, go away, I mean it." She refused to let him see her cry.

He rushed towards her with a sudden inspiration and spun her around, gripping her arms and shaking her body furiously to make her cry. When she did, it was an ugly eruption of violent tears, leaking nose and spewed resentment. He would not comfort her but shook her once or twice more for effect and to express his own control, and denial of desire. "I'm not your grandfather and you're not safe!"

"Why don't you just walk away from this," she said wearily, "I won't chase you, I promise."

"Because you'll still be here, and I'll feel tempted."

"I thought so." she lifted her chin. "I knew it."

"But you will leave, eventually. You have no choice. If you leave now it will be much better."

She smiled. "I don't think you want the responsibility of me."

"That's right. I don't want responsibility for anyone."

Completely dressed, satchel in hand, he stood there like the day she first met him, but only for a moment. Then he left the room.

Outside he took deep breaths. As he drove down Route 21 he noticed John Vaughn and his young assistant setting up for a shot. From his peripheral vision he saw John wave, but he refused to look at him. John's smile was like a sneer, as if he knew what Roger had been doing.

CHAPTER 12

"Oh God, why hast thou cast us off forever?
Why doth thine anger smoke
Against the sheep of Thy pasture?
Remember Thy congregation,
Which thou has purchased of old,
the rod of Thine inheritance,
which Thou hast redeemed;
This mount Zion, wherein Thou has dwelt."

Miss Atkinson lifted her head. She and Jenny regarded each other for a moment. Then Miss Atkinson nodded, and Jenny sat down. The younger children in the Sunday school class squirmed with boredom and with sick wondering who would be called next. Memorizing psalms did not require deep understanding of the Gospels; it was thought that familiarity with the syllables would be profound enough.

"Speaking pieces" was as old a New England custom as church suppers or excommunication into the wilderness.

Miss Atkinson had quietly marveled how many of the psalms had to do with the sorrow of an exodus. The children were equally thrilled by the coincidence of so many references to Mount Zion, as if their Mount Zion in Greenwich was the one mentioned in the Bible.

Jenny used to think so too, but her mother had corrected her once, laughingly, and yet though she now knew better, Jenny still pricked up at the Thresher boy's recitation of:

"They that trust in the Lord
shall be as mount Zion,
which cannot be removed,
but abideth forever....."

Miss Atkinson glanced doubtfully at Tommy Thresher. They would not abideth here forever. Adults would not speak of it offhandedly lest they upset the children, but they knew. Would Mount Zion itself abideth forever? She did not know.

Though the reservoir construction was publicized and well under way, there were still many ignorant rumors about it. Some Valley people believed that if they did not sell their land, the State would flood them out. Even fifty years later rumors would pervade to the effect that if one looked deep into the clear water of the reservoir during a period of drought when the water level was low, one could see whole houses standing there like bitter ghosts. It was not true. Only the ghosts were there.

Jenny was as ignorant as Miss Atkinson about the exact nature of the construction. Would the reservoir flood all the way up to the top of Prescott Hill, the highest spot in the Valley? Would their old farm be flooded, even that high?

Alonzo said nothing would happen. He'd said it over and over to her.

Prescott had not been her home for years, but she thought of it more often now, romantically drawn to it. Too young for nostalgia, yet she always remembered Prescott as 'the olden times' when there had been no reservoir and people were happy. Alonzo kept it alive for her. He did not seem burdened like her father and all the other adult men she knew. He was funny and careless, and played with her. They ran races through the cornfield. He put dandelions under her chin. She told him stories from books she read. Prescott was too high. Alonzo would be safe up there. He said he would keep her safe as well. Sometimes he cuddled her, as they sat with their backs against the stone wall, when they finished the sandwiches she'd brought him.

Greenwich Village would be deep under water.

Ella froze. Experiencing slow death, she could not remember her psalm. She waited for the roof to fall in on her, somewhat disappointed when it did not, and sat down at Miss Atkinson's frown. Jenny was no help, only stared out the window. Miss Atkinson rapped the top of her desk briskly. All eyes focused on the tiny watch pinned to Miss Atkinson's breast, which she peered at upside down.

The test was over. They could relax and forget everything.

"Y'wanna go by the cemetery?" Harrison asked Tom Pierce as they walked home.

"No!" Ella cried

"They wouldn't be working on Sundays, anyway." Tom said. "Would they?"

"My father says they don't care about the Sabbath," Nance said, "They'd work just the same."

"I guess we can see enough dead bodies passing by there on weekdays without making a Sunday picnic of it, Tom," Jenny said.

Ella said, "Jen, tell them not to go. Let's go home."

"Don't be a baby, Ella," Harrison frowned, "We're not doing anything. I'd just like to see what they're doing. Don't you wanta see?"

"Be quiet, Harry, stop teasing her," Jenny said, glancing at Ella. "There's nothing to look at. Anything y'want to know about this reservoir, y'can ask our father."

There, she said it. She said *reservoir* out loud. They looked at her with admiration, and discomfiting superstition, feeling as if there should be some touching of wood, some salt to throw, some type of action to remove the hex. But Jenny somehow knew they could not ask their father.

They passed Roger Lewis' automobile parked by the church. The stranger in the parked car could be anybody and was probably somebody.

***

Roger Lewis glanced at the children walking in the middle of the road, kicking dirt and rocks.

Miss Atkinson was the last to leave. She walked right up to his car.

"Are you all right?" she asked, hitching her satchel under her arm.

Roger had been slumped in the driver's seat; he pulled himself up.

"Huh? Yes. Yes."

"You've been here all through services. I could see you out the window. You didn't join us."

"I'm sorry, I didn't realize I'd been parked here so long."

"Are you all right?"

"Yes. Of course. It's very quiet here. Except when the children came out. Are you the teacher?"

"I teach Sunday school. And I play the organ in church. That was me playing." She smiled self-consciously and touched the car's side view mirror. "My brother is Reverend Atkinson. I keep house for him. I'm Martha." She looked away as if suddenly realizing she said too much.

"I'm Roger Lewis," he said, awkwardly taking his hat off in the car. "I'm with the MDWSC. I'm an engineer."

"Oh. You work on the reservoir."

"Yes." The word was beginning to make him flinch.

"Would you like to take Sunday dinner with us?"

"Why?" he asked, in a tone that was close to sounding horrified.

"Because if you don't eat you're liable to drop down dead sooner or later. Food is a good thing, generally. My brother and I, we'd like to have you. You're right, it is very quiet here." She noticed that his hands on the steering wheel shook a little, and his tired eyes were bloodshot. "Yes, come for dinner. My brother's not the only one who can minister to people."

"Are you ministering to me?" He smiled a little wearily.

"That was impertinent of me. But, you are parked in front of the manse. You might as well come inside."

He looked down the road and watched the children getting smaller.

He surprised himself by popping the door handle.

***

Jenny Vaughn, like Roger Lewis, was uncompromising in her lack of forgiveness, and like Lewis was an egotist who enjoyed responsibility, who found strength in acting strong. In small and mostly unconscious ways, her parents added to her responsibility, lately in not explaining the reservoir to them.

Ella held Jenny's hand and watched her withdraw again. In many ways, Ella was her child, more than their mother's. It was an arrangement that suited both of them, yet Ella also demanded of Jenny the superhuman interest in her that mothers are supposed to have for their children. She became hurt and angry when Jenny failed her, which happened a lot lately.

Like any egotist, and most mothers, Jenny believed she was doing her best. When she had experienced menstruation for the first time she tried to learn as much about the process from her busy and embarrassed mother, from even more ignorant school friends, from an old medical book of her grandfather's, and would have asked Doctor Wendell except he was so hard to get a hold of unless you were bleeding from something much worse, like a tractor on top of you. She was not sure he knew either. It was a female state, her mother had told her. A man probably could not tell her much about it, even if he was a doctor.

Her intention was not so much to find out about her own body but to be able to explain to Ella about hers. She wanted to prepare her for menstruation and math tests and moving away. It was Jenny's way of believing she had some control. Like explorers in a snowy wilderness, Jenny made careful footprints for her sister to follow. She consciously forced herself from going too far ahead.

Mary felt the years between her youngest child and her eldest were stretching her out, pulling in opposite directions. Ida would soon marry a Belchertown boy. Here Ella was still a little girl.

As if that were not strain enough, the reservoir, not even in existence yet, cast a long shadow. Only Uncle John seemed to bring a smile to her too-lined face.

They talked of the old days now, the two of them, though they did not share those days. It did not matter; each knew their different memories were as interchangeable as old stereopticon illustrations.

They only talked of nutting, and sleigh rides, and the children they used to know, and the children they used to be.

John sipped a tumbler of murky apple cider and wiped tart moisture from his trembling upper lip.

"Mary," he said, and started to laugh, "do you remember the old story about Silas Vaughn? Did Eli ever tell you?"

She smiled with closed lips on the rim of her glass and looked up at him, expectantly, eager.

"Eli, what's the matter with you?" John scoffed and waved him away, chuckling still. "He never was a story-teller. Well, our grandfather, Silas Vaughn...." both he and Mary laughed prematurely and laughed the more because of it.

"Silas Vaughn was a stern, old, skinflint. He was a God-fearing, church-going, hymn-singing miser of a gentleman. A gentleman, I believe, is what he would wish to be called. Well, Grandfather was particularly fond of cider. Loved it. Ever since the day his doctor and his wife told him another drop of rum would kill him. Because his wife would kill him if he ever took another drop. So..." John waved his tumbler across the room as if proposing a toast or giving benediction, "He became fond of apple cider, not the hard kind, having no other choice. The only thing he loved more than apple cider was saving time, work, money, and bits of string. What ever happened to his three-foot wide string ball, Eli?" Mary chortled out loud now, and John was flushed with his success.

Getting no answer from Eli, John continued, "Well, he hated wasting anything. Including his own steps. So, when Grandmother asked him to re-fill the cider pitcher from the keg in the root cellar, because he had drunk most of it himself, he was very much annoyed. But being a gentleman, he stood, and did as was asked. There went old Silas, down the cold, dark cellar steps to brave the spiders for his cider, and refilled this old, earthenware pitcher that must have been in the family since Vaughns were living in caves. Nobody in this family has ever learned to throw anything away.

"As he climbed back up the stairs, Grandfather Silas slipped, and fell head over heels down the stairs! He made such a racket that Grandmother, after she finished her tea in due course, rushed to the cellar door. There was he, lying in a heap. For a moment, there was a deathly quiet. She listened and heard nothing. Then Grandmother hollered down the dark stairs, 'I hope ya didn't drop the pitcha, Silas!'"

Mary laughed now.

"Grandfather answered, 'No, by Gawd, but I will now!' And he jumped up and smashed that old pitcher against the farthest wall."

John took the time now to laugh at his own story, but then found himself tired.

Eli watched his brother's aged, florid alcoholic's face. He had shaved his mustache. John moved slower, as if burdened.

He could see it in the way John lumbered about fussily while preparing to take photographs of the children, of him and Mary and the children. John's hands shook and he swore under his breath at the film plates.

He let John take the photos, as long as they were family mementos and not for the state archives. Perhaps it was John's manner of paying his way. Still, Eli silently feared the materials were stolen from John's reservoir work. Well, who does one blame if eating a gift of stolen bread? Eli thought about the gospels, but he had been so accustomed to memorizing certain useful passages in order that they failed to materialize when he needed them randomly.

There was a formal shot of Eli and Mary sitting on wooden kitchen chairs outside on the lawn, with the kids all around them. One of Eli and Mary together in front of the house and Mary was wearing a hat but he was not. It left him squinting. A photo of the children sitting on the grass with a slope of hay behind them, which had spilled out from the loft. One of Ella and Harrison with Jenny between them, though all dressed in their best clothes they perched on the top of the hay, laughing. Jenny's arms were around them, and they leaned into her, mouths open, eyes rolled to the heavens in hysteria. Only she looked squarely into the camera. A wide, clean, knowing smile that made her look somehow tragically older.

Eli realized the pictures were a moment in time they could never have back. The pictures John took of the doomed houses and shops were a moment frozen. They said nothing of the future or their past.

The sound of the platter clattering slightly as Ida placed it on the table made Eli think for a moment he was watching the Pratt girls playing at cooking. He looked up into their faces. It was his own daughters, Ida and Doris.

They were preparing for Ida's young man to come to Sunday dinner. Mary left the men again to have another look at her chicken. Only because the hen had stopped laying and because this young man might be her future son-in-law did the Vaughns have chicken. Eli put the photos down and went to put on a tie.

Ella said good morning to Uncle John. She warmed up to him, and no longer wished he would go away. He had charmed the little girl, there was just enough left in him for that, and he was flattered Ella had a crush on him.

Jenny and Harrison were sent to the old Prescott farm to bring back Alonzo for Sunday dinner. He had not been in a while, and they were to keep an eye on him since Eliza and George moved to North Amherst last winter. Their new farm was not the large Connecticut River Valley farm Calvin and James wished for, but it was new ground all the same. It would be theirs one day.

Alonzo lived alone on the ridge now.

A slow, lovely ride up the ridge. For once, she and Harrison did not discuss the house movings or land buyings, or store closings. The springtime air fairly burst with tender wild smells, so poignantly sweet and fresh, and the pines on the hill greeted them like old friends.

Then the hulk lurched around the bend in the muddy road, and Harrison pulled the horses to a stop near a meandering line of stone fence. The Prescott Congregational Church rocked a bit as the flatbed trailer carefully changed direction around the curve.

"Guess *they* work on the Sabbath," Harrison said. Jenny gripped the seat, dizzy at the sight.

"I didn't know anybody could do that, move a whole building." she replied, "I wonder how they do that?"

The church was on its way to South Hadley. It had been bought by a Holyoke manufacturer as a kind of trophy, but he did not bring it home to Holyoke, it did not fit in there.

Holyoke, an industrial city over on the western side of the Connecticut River, seemed to drip from its green agricultural highlands down to the murky canals at its feet. Founded by manufacturers, it was a planned city, an orderly grid of avenues and canals, an Eden of right angles where Yankee planners sought to preserve the Christian work ethic by creating a proper universe for their industry. The paper and cotton and silk mills were down by the river, fed by the canals, dumping wastes in the river which a hundred years later would be some cause for environmental concern.

At the moment, nobody was concerned. The rowhouses were close by where the immigrant, mostly Irish and French-Canadian workers were kept by their masters, who themselves lived in grand Victorian houses atop the heights from which they could observe their work and call it good.

Some of these masters were born of simple yeoman stock, who grew into their gilt and mahogany lifestyles as surely as they grew into men's clothes from boyhood knickers. They never forgot their simple roots and strove to illustrate their present success by gifts of charities, foundations, and museums. This Holyoke manufacturer bought the Prescott Church because it reminded him of a similar church of his boyhood. It was a symbol of Yankee integrity, and to leave it to destruction was heartless. He could not save its congregation, but he saved the building. It was not the only thing from the Valley he had saved.

Months ago, touring the area to inspect his new purchase, the manufacturer came upon a soapstone in the yard of the George Vaughn farmhouse. The soapstone, despite its Indian innovation, was also to him a symbol of all that was Yankee and good, dug from the very soil of this uncooperative land when the sod was first broken. It, too, was a symbol of Yankee nobility and therefore a reminder of his own nobility. He offered the round, ruddy farmwife a ten-dollar bill for the chunk of rock, provided she throw in the two chickens she had been dressing to sell to someone else. He prided himself for a mean bargainer. All real Yankees did.

The deal done, it was not until after the stone was loaded by the cussing chauffeur, along with the chickens, and she had crinkled the clean note in her hand that she had begun to feel resentful.

Eliza Vaughn handed the bill with disgust to her husband George and went to bring in the wash.

She and the manufacturer were of different social plateaus, but they both lived according to the strict rules of their shared heritage.

The past, their history, was their heritage, an etiquette of conformity where comfort was sought through balance and control.

Eliza's marriage to George could stand as one of thousands of small examples of heritage, etiquette, conformity, and balance. Eliza suddenly realized this when they left the Valley and moved from Prescott to North Amherst.

North Amherst at that time was not so very different from Prescott, a small community based mainly upon small agriculture. That one fact should have been sound and simple, but all the many other differences, glaring to George and Eliza, stood in the way of their ever feeling completely at home.

For one thing, North Amherst was part of Amherst, and that hallowed town of Dickinson, Frost, and enlightenment of a more belligerent variety than Brook Farm but still enlightenment, was a member of mainstream New England if not mainstream America. Admittedly, they lived in a New England for which mainstream America was still outside and therefore irrelevant.

Amherst had a town center whose fledgling commerce catered to the colleges, those two bastions of identity.

It did not seem incongruous for Amherst College, a private school for gentlemen, and for the Massachusetts State Agricultural College, a school for anybody else, to coexist not a few streets from each other. It was part of Amherst's heritage to be egalitarian and exclusive, therefore perfectly in keeping with the town's history and personality. Heritage was everything in New England then, whether for a town or a family, or a single person. Heritage was all. New England's reputation for progressiveness in certain areas is a contradiction.

George and Eliza felt lost in Amherst. So close to Prescott, yet its dual heritage was not their heritage. Both grew up in Prescott, he on a windswept hilltop and she in a sunny hollow. George married Eliza after having seen her three times, twice at prayer meetings and once at a sleigh ride. He told his parents he wanted to marry her before she knew anything about it, and his parents nodded. When he proposed to her it was the first time she had been alone with him, the second time was on their wedding night.

George brought her home to his parents' house and took as much care as he could to make her feel at home there because that was what Eliza expected of him. Eliza was a respectful daughter to his parents because they expected it of her, and they welcomed her as the daughter they never had when she met them for the first time on her wedding day. Everyone knew what his place was, and when Asa Vaughn called her "Daughter" instead of her name, which he did until the end of his life, he meant it. It showed that he took responsibility for her as a member of his family and that she would take responsibility for him when he was too feeble to take care of himself. When he died she grieved more than anyone.

Now Eliza stood on the very real and solid threshold of her own farmhouse in North Amherst and felt more lost and alone than she did that day she approached George's father and mother with a carpetbag and a shy nod. She told herself she should feel a freedom and carefree way about moving in with her husband of many years, her nearly grown sons, and a fresh start. She felt horribly, sadly lost.

They all bumped into each other. Where to put the box of apple corers and nutmeg graters? Why, in the kitchen of course, now move. How to choose the rooms? It was uncomfortable for everyone to be new to the place all at once with no one to make them welcome and show them what to do. It was unsettling that there was no heritage here to which they could at least conform if they had no ideas of their own.

George was thinking much the same as his wife and tried to think of the best way to ease her mind and make her feel comfortable. But it was not his home, so how could he do that? He could not welcome her here, and his parents were gone. What would they have thought of this?

Of all the generations of Vaughns that had ever lived in Prescott, only Alonzo remained. There were two other families in the northern part of town left, and one down by Atkinson Hollow, and Miss Rebecca and her brother and sister-in-law. These scattered households were like separate kingdoms now for they scarcely saw much of each other.

***

Alonzo's farm was overgrown, but he refused to wear the look of a doomed man the way his sullen neighbors did. He was confident that this was his land and always would be.

Jenny and her brother rolled into the yard of their old home. While Harrison watered the horses, she stood in the tall grass near her mother's old garden and studied an orphan morning glory vine that had snaked up a linden tree. Alonzo walked around from the barn and smiled at them. He slapped a rough hand on the back of Harrison's neck and made him jump. Harrison giggled, squirmed, but held back from poking Alonzo back. Growing up with four sisters and no brothers, he never learned the expressly male knack of roughing a man up to show his affection. Alonzo considered the boy's offer of a handshake effeminate and grabbed him, lifting him off the ground. While Harrison struggled against Alonzo's chest, feeling both enthralled and embarrassed, Alonzo called over his shoulder to Jenny and tossed her brother into their wagon headfirst. Harrison scrambled to his knees with as much dignity as he could but grinned like a fool.

Alonzo was gentler with Jenny. He stood a yard away from her with his large, dirty hands behind his back. "Do you miss us?" he asked smiling, "Me and the tree here, and the house and that hen over there?"

Jenny smiled so suddenly and magnificently that Alonzo's face fell. Harrison felt invisible. "Still think of it as the old home."

"My home is still yours, little girl."

"Ho, not so little," she objected and pried his right hand off his right hip so she could hold it. She took a giant step towards him and looked up for his reaction. At five feet ten inches, she was almost as tall as he. "Who do you think you're calling little?"

"Glad to see y'got your father's height and your mother's looks."

"Do I look like my mother?" she asked, surprised for she had never heard anyone say that.

"I think you look like me."

"Second cousins supposed to look like each other?"

"Well, you and I have dark hair and this one," he grabbed Harrison by the seat of his pants and made the boy shriek, "has got light hair like your father. Harry, you're the odd-man-out today. You stay back there and get your rest, I'll drive back."

He handed Jenny up to the seat and walked around the horses to check the bridles. Harrison had been the man on the trip up and was now the boy, a son-figure to Jenny and Alonzo and he glanced up in annoyance to his sister's face. She did not see him, she watched only Alonzo. When Alonzo at last climbed onto the hard seat next to her, he briskly turned and kissed her cheek. She returned it.

***

Ida and her beau, Walter, observed over roast chicken by the family for signs of their devotion, were startlingly eclipsed by Jenny and Alonzo. Mary gaped at their smiles, Eli frowned over their teasing at the table, John Vaughn smiled secretly.

Ida could not shove her sister in the dirt from where she was sitting, so she patted Walter's fork hand and beamed a confident signal of her superiority. Hers was a done deal.

Alonzo occasionally pulled his attention from Jenny and shot a glance over at John. John surveyed the table, chewed slowly, brought his napkin from his lap up to his mouth to dab at his lips as he looked over at Alonzo.

Ida had already planned out her life with Walter Doubleday, a Belchertown boy with an automobile, as if it were the beginning of life itself for her. Walter had an uncle who owned a trucking firm in Athol. Trucking was the future as far as Doubleday was concerned. Gasoline was plentiful and cheap. Peddlers were on the out. Walter Doubleday's time had come. They could rent an apartment in town until they could afford to buy a home.

Alonzo could not remember John, as he had left when Alonzo was still very small. He had painted a huge image of him in his mind over the years, as a mystery and a possible rival for his land.

That Ida would be the first Vaughn ever to marry and not live with either her parents or in-laws was amazing to Eli and Mary. Young people today seemed to get what they wanted much faster, they were much less willing to wait for things. It made Eli and Mary slightly distrustful of modern times, but mostly envious. Silently, each wondered what they had to show for their life together.

"What does he want here? Why did he come back?" Alonzo pulled Jenny aside in the kitchen when she was washing dishes.

"Just to come home, I guess."

"He wants his father's farm back, I'll bet. He's not getting it. It's mine."

Jenny slowly wiped her hands on the worn, threadbare dishtowel. "I have no idea, Lon. I didn't think of that. But look at him. He's no farmer."

Alonzo had been looking at John through the entire visit, and that had not occurred to him.

"He sure ain't." He said it with relief, and made sure no one was watching, and kissed Jenny full on the lips.

Soon Ida and Walter were married in the Greenwich Plains Congregational Church, because Ida, like many nineteen-year-old girls in 1931, demanded a modern wedding. She did not want to be married in the front parlor of her parents' home, or in the backyard standing in the grass under a rose trellis. That was old-fashioned. It made an ugly picture compared with the majesty of a real church wedding, with cake and punch served afterwards in the church hall.

John Vaughn set up an elaborate wedding picture outside the church of the happy couple and their wedding party, and a stray dog which wandered by to urinate on a shrub at the critical moment of exposure.

"Damn," he giggled under the cloth.

Sam Vaughn from Athol came with his wife Agnes. They arrived in their new used 1927 Hudson, not the old flivver he drove at the Prescott Centennial some six years ago.

Alonzo, like Eli and his family, came in a wagon. Mr. and Mrs. Berry and Miss Rebecca came from Prescott. Grandmother Pratt came on the arm of her unmarried daughter Hattie, with whom she lived in a rented cottage in Belchertown. All eyes on the church hall turned to her in deference and quiet sympathy. She seemed to draw the strength to take each step from her daughter Hattie. All eyes seated her, then turned away when she wonderingly searched the room, and panting, dismissed them all with a sigh that said everything.

Hattie moved with boredom suggesting confidence and impatience. The middle girl Eli thought would marry one day like a consolation prize rewarding all patient womankind, was a career woman. This is what she considered herself though the term was not in vogue. She was a clerk in the Belchertown town offices.

Her older sister, Jane arrived with her professor husband, the former and forever college man, but minus her college student sons. She was still stylish, but it was with the self-knowledge that this was all she was ever going to be. She watched her sister Hattie nanny their mother and was irritated that Hattie showed more mettle than anyone thought she had.

Jane looked again to her husband to give her distinction. They also arrived in a car, which was mainly what everyone noticed if they noticed anything about her.

George and Eliza Vaughn came from North Amherst in a second-hand truck. Daniel, Calvin, and James climbed out of the truck bed, brushing off their best suits.

"I can see you're doing fine, George." Eli shook hands with the boys. Eliza tugged self-consciously at her brown cloche hat. She searched the faces of the crowd as they filed into the white church.

"You're looking very pretty today, Eliza." Eli said as he pecked her cheek. She grinned and looked down at her shoes a moment. She felt awkward out of her old high buttons, but she had come to the point everyone else had in the Valley. Was her duty to the old ways, or was her duty to the new? In good Christian faith and stern conscience, she gave herself over to the new. She believed the meaning of life would be shown to her in time.

John Vaughn stood by the refreshments table, watching the happy couple at the other end, lifting his cup of pink liquid with sad amusement.

Miss Rebecca regarded him from a corner of the hall where she clutched her cake and napkin and listened to the monologue on illnesses of the groom's mother. She knew John Vaughn was home from his travels, but she would not have recognized him had he not been reintroduced to her on the steps by Mary. Heavy, in body as well as spirit, and his eyes were rheumy with his alcoholism, and insomnia. Without his mustache, his face seemed naked. Without his former charm and the youthful angst behind it, his face was certainly naked, and vague.

He stood alone because he was a bachelor and that was his privilege. Where people naturally paired off, he was allowed to be by himself with no social repercussions. Miss Rebecca, however, being a spinster was not allowed to be alone. Though she had not sought society she was continually escorted by her brother and his wife, by various married ladies and single girls in twos and threes by turns. She was used to it, and it amused her as much as it annoyed her.

Quite suddenly, she put down her cake and napkin and walked easily up to John Vaughn, before the next subtle changing of the guard could occur. John Vaughn caught her eye, lifted his head, and smiled.

"The men of the Valley," he nodded in their direction, "sturdy, haggard, strong men who hardly swear, except to mutter gol-darn if the thresher breaks, hardly drink except a companionable snort behind the barn from some old bottle when male guests arrive. If a man drinks at all, it is always a social, self-conscious pastime. I'll tell you Rebecca, I prefer to drink in private. Oh, not that I haven't heard axioms about people who drink 'alone,' but I've found nothing perverted in the practice. So far."

"You've made a study." So, she was still Miss Rebecca, aging, with fine lines around her knowing eyes, but never so old as she was when Ida's age. She was growing beautiful, to whom age was more than kind, it was a blessing. She was still growing into herself.

"The Valley is upside down, Miss. Like Alice's world in the mirror, everything is contrary and backwards. You know the Outsiders, my last contact with them, were a cynical self-advertised 'Lost Generation.' They bedizened themselves in pearl lassos, rolled-down stockings and flasks, wavering in their ideas between cruel, careless but always witty humor and an ugly self-pity. Meanwhile, curious thing, the Swift River Valley learns what it is to be truly doomed. The outside world has grown cold and old, but here we're near extinction. Oh well. Do you still sell chocolate drops?"

She smiled, putting her gloved hand over his clasped ones. "Inventory is a curious thing these days. I don't know just what's left."

"Your brother hasn't decided what he wants?"

"He wants a safe place in a small business, on a quiet street in a town like Prescott. Why have you come back here, John, when there's precious little left?"

He looked into her teasing, gentle eyes.

For a moment he forgot his train of thought.

"And how is it, John, you never married? You asked me that once, do you remember?"

"Something about the permanence of it all."

He smiled when she did and looked up to find Mr. Berry and his wife approaching them. It was time to be social again.

Mary Vaughn sat down a minute by the window, with the customary sick fatigue of the mother of the bride. Eli asked if she was all right, and she nodded, saying that she was only tired from rising so early, and with the planning and everything.

"Doesn't everything look nice? Isn't Ida beautiful? Something to be proud of? I suppose Doris won't be far behind."

Eli smiled and patted her shoulder. He went outside to the street so Mr. Doubleday, the father of his new son-in-law, could show him his truck. Eli was not much interested, but knew it was what he was supposed to do.

Mary looked at Ida, chatting happily with her bridesmaid, whom she knew from school. Her new husband looked deserted by male companionship in this thoroughly female event. Ida was happy, hopeful. Ida looked to the future and saw something nice there.

Mary thought about being a grandmother and threw a searching glance at her own mother. Mrs. Pratt sat in her wooden folding chair with dim eyes riveted to the face of the neighbor speaking to her, straining her ears to hear the conversation. Bless her, something in her still cared.

What would be her mother's place in the community when there was no community left?

Jenny tugged at her gloves for the fourth time and Harrison's face erupted in an ugly yawn. She frowned at him.

Doris, the maid of honor, tried to attach herself to the best man. The wedding party laughed over fruitcake and the excitement of being somehow in charge over their elders.

Alonzo, another bachelor in the crowd like John, stood apart from the joy of the occasion to lend an aura of something more dignified and lonely.

He walked over to the younger Vaughn children after a perfunctory hello to his parents and younger brothers. He did not want to be questioned on his well-being or hear of their success at their new farm and decided suddenly he did not want to be anyone's long lost son. It occurred to him that being a loner had more glamour to it, especially after exchanging hot, if distant glances with the groom's laughing sister.

Jenny noticed, was jealous, and turned cheerful attentions toward him much as her sister Doris did at the uncooperative Best Man. Alonzo dusted her off with a secret smile and a quick appraisal. He nodded to her family and held Harrison off with a turn of his dark expression when the boy tried to make up for his shyness the last time Alonzo tumbled with him. Harrison jumped at him, tried to put his thin arms around Alonzo's waist in a guess at a wrestling hold, but Alonzo knocked him down with a look of his instant dignity that was austere and unforgiving. Embarrassed once more, the boy looked around briefly to see if anyone noticed his rebuff.

"She's not half as lovely as you are," John Vaughn sidled up to Jenny.

"Who?"

"That girl with the Marcel wave. Lon's a fool for being distracted."

"Excuse me," Jenny said, annoyed and about to leave him, but John clutched her hand at his side and sipped his drink with the other.

"Before you win his attention back, as I'm sure you will, I wonder if you could handle a delicate matter for me, Jenny."

"What is it?"

"Has Lon mentioned his future plans?"

"We're not that serious." Her own embarrassment surprised her.

"No, child," he said, "I mean about moving away from the Valley. I mean about selling my farm."

Alonzo stood in a half-shadow by the window into which the sun was most glaring, and clasped his large, rough hands tightly in front of him, like an usher protecting his groin.

"Ask him, won't you?" John asked, lifted her hand to his lips, kissed it, and then released her, walking away to join a group in a discussion about which he cared nothing.

Jenny lightly stepped around Harrison and stood next to Alonzo without looking at him.

"Are you ever going t'get married?" she asked in her low, surprising voice.

Alonzo turned his face to her and lowered his glance to the top of her head, where the sun was dancing through the lost and forgotten wisps of her dark brown hair, exploring what no one before had seen.

Captivated, he clasped his hands tighter against himself.

Outside Eli watched them together through the rain-spotted window. His heart seemed to stop. He could not explain why.

***

Meanwhile, Roger Lewis was also at a loss to explain why. On the pretense of inspecting the Shaft 12 area, he parked his car and looked beyond Quabbin Lake to the cottage once owned by Elaine Coffey's grandfather.

She said she couldn't just leap on the next outbound train like some fugitive. Even though she could hear trucks passing and distant booms like a dull headache in the morning.

Roger sat in a car at a distance he hoped was too far to be seen, but it was close enough to make him ashamed.

He gasped when a sudden face blew soft breath behind his ear.

"Y'seem to do more parking than driving." Miss Atkinson said, with no smile to expose her latent sense of humor.

Roger glanced at her, his annoyance gaining the upper hand on his surprise.

"Oh, hello."

"I'm just returning from my aunt's house."

"Oh," he nodded.

"Do you know where you're going?" She jerked her head simultaneously at the car, at the road, and at him.

"Yes," he said, clearly irritated.

"Good. Just hope you do."

"Miss Atkinson!" he hollered as she continued her march down the road.

"Yes?" she asked from where she now was, blinking expectantly, about to look at the watch on her breast from habit.

"Get in the car. Please. I'd be happy to drive you home. Are you going home?"

"I expect so."

They headed back towards Greenwich Plains and Roger resolved never to come back to Quabbin Lake again.

"Thanks again for that Sunday dinner." Roger muttered over the steering wheel.

"That's all right."

"Your brother off fishing today?"

"He's performing a marriage ceremony today. Ida Vaughn to Walter Doubleday," she answered out the passenger window.

"Why aren't you there? Don't you have to play the organ or sing or something?"

"We've got someone from the Enfield Congregational to fill in today. I had to stay with Aunt. She's sick."

"That's too bad."

"I don't really like weddings that much anyway."

"Isn't that your main line of work?"

"It's my brother's work. I just play the organ and teach Sunday school. I'm an appendage, Mr. Lewis."

Roger would have made a cheerful remark in a moment but he lost too much time thinking of one.

"Weddings only remind me that I'm not married."

Roger began to whistle.

"I know I'm making you uncomfortable. Sorry. I'm in an uncomfortable mood. Never discuss marriage with a bachelor, my mother used to say. Might scare him off. Just show up at the minister's one day and let him think the idea was his."

He stopped the car in front of the manse. Children ran around the church, and in between the parked cars. They could see people through the windows of the hall.

"Here we are." she said, looking at her watch.

"What time is it?" he regarded the breast chronometer with a smile and looked at his own wristwatch. "Yikes, I've got to meet the train in Enfield. My brother's coming."

"That's nice. I hope your brother will like it here. Is he an engineer too?"

"No, he's just a kid. A smart-mouthed kid. I'm hoping he'll be safer here than he was in the city."

"None of us are safe here, Mr. Lewis." she said, slipping out of the car, "and some of us have smart mouths, too."

"Like you," he said, and waved. Then he caught Eli's eye across the street. They nodded to each other.

***

He had arrived early at the depot after all. Only a few hand trucks with crates on them, a shipment of milk, a few passengers with suitcases.

Emily Pete sat on the bench on the platform, one suitcase at her knee, her purse in her lap, her hat screwed onto her head and skewered with a long hatpin. She was going on a long trip but her hat wasn't going anywhere.

Roger noticed her with surprise, took his hands out of his pockets and approached her, lifting his hat. He found himself dropping to one knee in front of her.

"Emily?" he spoke softly, as if they were in a hospital corridor, "Are you leaving?"

She nodded, "And time, too."

"Is she still there?"

"Ayah. She no longer mentions you."

"What does she do all day?"

"Smokes a great deal. Gets up late, retires late. Looks out the window a lot at the water and beyond. She seems strangely interested in what she calls the imminent danger. I think she's hoping a bulldozer will come into the parlor, drive her away."

"It's not imminent danger, it's eminent domain. It's much more powerful than a bulldozer, and it will force her to leave before a bulldozer ever gets near her property."

"It's not the ending that scares her; it's the starting over."

"I know," he said, slowly standing.

"At least I'm going home. Lord knows where you both will be."

The train sounded beyond the Great Quabbin Hill. It crawled in from Belchertown and heaved a sigh at the edge of the platform. Emily stood, picked up her suitcase, and watched expectantly as passengers stepped off the train. Roger turned to watch them. Dickie wore long trousers and an expression that openly revealed his sarcasm, his contempt, and childish sense of wonder.

"Um, here, Dickie, I'd like you to meet..." Roger said as he turned, but Emily was gone.

"Your girlfriend?" Dickie put his hands in his pockets.

"No, kid. Just somebody I was waiting with. A friend." He looked him over again. "All right, let's get you back to the hotel. I want you to remember one thing while you're here. You do what I tell you, and you keep your nose clean."

Dickie smirked, "Rawg, don't play the father figure. You're too pale and skinny."

Roger yanked his arm at the shoulder, "I mean it, kid. This is a break for you, in case you're too stupid to see it. But we have some pretty quick-fisted fellows on our crews. If you get cute with them, you'll end up in a hawspital."

"Since you ask, I haven't eaten since yesterday."

Roger pushed him away and exhaled a lifetime of resentment.

"Let's go."

CHAPTER 13

Dickie could eat and Dickie could talk. Roger felt his mistake immediately, but he had made a promise to his mother before she died, that he would look after his brother. Roger lost no time getting him a job on the project and a place to sleep with a family near Shaft 12.

"You'll be closer to your job. You won't have to walk as far, and I *cahn't* be spared to drive you."

Dickie smiled at him sideways.

"Sure, Rawg. Here's your hat, what's your hurry?"

A wagon approached far down the road ahead. Roger slowed the car out of respect for the man's horses. He felt in his stomach that it was Eli Vaughn.

"That man's getting to be my conscience," he muttered.

"What did you say?"

"Never mind what I said. Just you be polite to people hereabouts."

Eli slowed him team as well, so that it appeared the wagon and the car were meeting each other on purpose. Both men touched their hats.

"This is my younger brother, Dickie." Roger called. Eli nodded to the boy. Dickie sarcastically waved.

"Was that your daughter who just got married?" Roger continued doggedly.

"Yes, my oldest, Ida."

"Congratulations."

"Thank you," he nodded with enthusiasm he did not feel, "They're going to live in Athol," he added without thinking.

"That's fine." Roger said, "Nice town." They hurried each other away by their embarrassment and confusion. Yes, Athol was fine, they both thought. Athol was out of the Valley. Athol was in no danger. Nobody was going to come along and flood Athol. *Damn. What was I thinking? Why didn't I keep my mouth closed? Why do we keep running into each other?*

Roger barely kept himself from saying that Dickie had come to work on the reservoir. Eli barely kept himself from saying he was going to town to consult a lawyer.

This year, 1931, water from the nearby Ware River was diverted to the Wachusett Reservoir in the eastern part of the state through the new aqueduct. Like a line drawn to connect dots in a puzzle, the pipeline linked water sources from the upper plains of central Massachusetts down to metropolitan Boston, but the larger project of building the reservoir in the Swift River valley was only just getting under way.

The legislative work had taken exhaustive years. Planning for the removal of the Valley residents and preparing them for the move was another project in itself. The actual construction of the reservoir followed in the aftermath of so much preparation, almost as if it were an afterthought.

Attorney Barre Hurst was an old schoolmate from the time Eli had been in the Prescott schoolhouse. Hurst went to college. Then he came back to live in Enfield and practice law. No big city for him. No sir. He was a regular fellow. That was his reputation.

The engineers' and planners' work only paved the way for the laborers. They had proved, theoretically, that a reservoir could be built in this odd little place, but the actual moving of the earth was left to others. These others did not have the same vision as the engineers. They followed a blueprint, they studied a map, they went to work. It was a job to them in a time when jobs were miserably scarce. Some of the jobs were given to men from the Valley.

"They're just throwin' us a bo-won," one of them said, but some of the younger men in line for work didn't care if the State was throwing them a bone. It had nearly been a generation since the first news of this reservoir project hit them. They had heard about its coming since they were little boys. They wanted to have it over with so they could just go on to something else. Hopefully, something better.

Attorney Hurst replied to Eli's note promptly but wrote back that he could only spare him a moment on Sunday morning. On weekdays, he had his regular workload of deeds, wills and contracts. The weekends were for packing.

When the Ware River aqueduct was finished, eyes turned in anticipation to the west, to completing the final link with the Swift River Valley. Shaft 12, the last, most western section ended the aqueduct line at the edge of Quabbin Lake in Greenwich. Under the direction of the engineers, under their own convictions of progress and the hope that what they were doing was right, Valley men bore into their bedrock. They became used to the hydraulic equipment, and the dark and damp chill of the tunnel where they were shakily amused to find themselves over four hundred feet below the ground.

They became miners, young men whose entire lives had been spent out-of-doors, working the land. Now they burrowed beneath it, against the rock to build a great structure whose ultimate purpose would evict them.

Mr. Hurst, Esquire, answered the door himself and led Eli into his office across the hall from the dining room of his home. Boxes filled with books covered the floor. Hurst motioned Eli to clear a stack of them off the chair that he might sit down.

The Thirties was becoming a decade of great building projects throughout the nation. In some sections of the country, these projects provided badly needed employment, improved infrastructure in places where infrastructure did not even exist. In the Valley, the dirty subterranean workers fixed each other in the unaccustomed beam of their hat-lamps and regarded their newfound work as simply fate. Fate was not kind or forgiving. It just was.

Thirteen men would be killed in the construction of the Ware River portion of that dark aqueduct.

"Called by the Commonwealth, who giveth and taketh away..." but the man stopped his muttering in the line for water. Nobody was in the mood.

They cut the tunnel deeper and lined it with concrete. It was, at last, the physical link between Boston and the western lands that Boston envisioned in the vaguest terms, but always knew it owned.

"Back in February, as I'm sure you know, Eli," Hurst said, "The United States Supreme Court ruled in favor of Massachusetts over Connecticut's suit, claiming the construction of the reservoir interfering with the flow of the Swift River would affect manufacturing downstream. That's it in a nutshell. That's it, Eli. Massachusetts has every right to build a reservoir and build it here."

Valley men were not the only ones provided with work. Outsiders came to the Valley in numbers never seen. Many new accents were heard, though most of them were merely other typical New England accents.

"Set your mind to the future, Eli. Let the past lie. That's what I'm doing." Attorney Hurst waved his sweater sleeve over the room and motioned to evidence of his packing.

"Shame on you, Barre," he said, and showed himself out.

"Eli...Eli...."

"Shame on you. What a waste of education if knowing the law still means nothing."

"I'm not God, Eli!"

"You're not even a man," Eli called over his shoulder.

***

Other outsiders came too, but paradoxically, came here to live. The farms and homes that were bought by the overseers of the reservoir project, the MDWSC, rented the newly vacant places to temporary residents, until these spots could be prepared for demolition. A farm could be rented for only five dollars a month, and this gave some struggling families in what was being called the Depression a new chance, a new start at life, or at least a spot to rest safely for a little while.

Elaine Coffey observed new neighbors and smiled. There was still time.

Families arrived with children. The children were energetic and lively, captivated with the country while their tired parents dared hardly lift their eyes to the hills. Many came from the city, to rest and gain strength for the time when they would go back there.

The Holts moved away. The Vaughn children said goodbye to Nance, Charlie, and Jane with sober finality, but Mary did not say a word to her old school friend Eleanor, depressed at losing her only close woman friend, mostly because they were never really close. She had always meant to reach out more and try to build a badly needed friendship. There was only time for pleasantries, as if both women smiling over the fence unconsciously recognized the futility of it all.

Mary watched them load their truck from her bedroom window, behind the curtains. She watched them for twenty minutes. Finally, Eleanor Holt, putting her hands in her coat pockets, turned slightly to glance over her shoulder at the Vaughn farm. She would have been looking directly into Mary's eyes if she had known she was there.

Mary blushed, embarrassed behind the curtains, and went back to her mending.

The Holts were soon afterwards replaced by the Sullivans. They arrived from Ware and took the Holt farm over from the MDWSC with a ridiculously low rent in exchange for the sober understanding that their tenancy was temporary. The Sullivans did understand and were grateful.

"At least we won't have a vacant farm near us." Eli said too cheerfully.

Eli shook hands with Mr. Sullivan. They were Roman Catholic. Jenny liked to spy on the Sullivans to see if they did anything peculiar. Mostly they did not, which was a real disappointment. The only interesting thing about them was they were not especially good farmers, but it had been Mr. Sullivan's dream, and seeing as how it was only temporary, Mrs. Sullivan indulged him for once.

"He'd lost his job in the Ware factory closings," Eli told his family at Sunday dinner. "He thought the 'soul-grinding repetition of factory work' as he calls it was hard, wait till he knows the anguish of a dark sky that won't rain, or how big a small farm gets when there's only one man to do the work. Who doesn't even know what he's doing."

The Sullivans found a different world. They were used to Poles and French-Canadians and other Irish, first or second-generation immigrants whose ethnicity had sometimes put them at a disadvantage, and so they felt a common bond together when they were not fighting with each other.

The Sullivans were as interested in the Yankees as Jenny was of them, but neither side showed its hand. That would have been gauche. New Englanders, no matter what their ethnic origin, did not mind being occasionally rude, were even proud of the fact they could at times be very rude, but to give over one's dignity, to let down the standards of dignified behavior was repugnant.

Behind their dignified but aching curiosity, the Sullivans were one up on the Vaughns as far as transportation was concerned. Mr. Sullivan owned a Model A Ford, in which they all rode to the Catholic church in Dana every Sunday.

"The girl's name is Mary Margaret, and the two little boys are Charles John and Michael Francis," Jenny replied. Eli smiled as he sliced the last of the smoked ham from the previous autumn. No Depression here, he thought, satisfied. No sir, you're not the only lawyer, Barre Hurst.

"Eli?" he heard Mary say.

"What? What is it?"

"I said have done with it."

Eli was a neat and meticulous carver, and Mary smiled to watch him as she dashed back and forth from the sideboard with vegetables.

"It doesn't have to be a work of art, Eli," Mary muttered, "That's enough shaving, sit down and eat some of it."

"That's how they call each other, too," Harrison said.

"Well, they'll never forget who they are." Eli said, and with a flourish of his knife gestured to Jenny. "Init that right, Genevieve Sarah?"

Harrison began to sing "Genevieve, Sweet Genevieve" and Jenny glared at him.

"Ever wonder why there's no song with "Harrison" in it?"

Eli began to sing, "H-A-double R I, S, O, N spells HARRISON."

"That's not how the song goes."

"My name's Harry."

"Don't be spying on the Sullivans, now Jenny," Mary said, "and don't be asking them too many questions. It's not polite."

"Mary Margaret's twelve, she misses going to the movies at the Casino in Ware, and she hopes her father gets farming out'a his system soon." Jenny said, "I haven't asked her anything, she just likes to talk."

Eli looked at her over the rim of his cup.

"Did she ask anything about us?" Mary asked.

"Just our names and ages, and if we go to the school in the Village. She wears a little gold cross around her neck on a chain. Got it for her First Communion."

Harry asked, "Is it real gold? They must be rich!"

Jenny said, "She was going to join the Society of Mary or something like that at her old church and she's afraid she'll never get to do it now. What is that?"

"A club for people named Mary. Mama could join." Harrison said with a mouthful of bread. Eli roared.

After dinner, Jenny took Ella and Harrison for a walk. Mary watched them leave the yard. "Sundays are changing," she said.

Eli looked through yesterday's paper.

"When I was a girl they still had the day-long services they always had. A whole day of the Old Testament."

"Sermons applied like mortar with trowels."

"Stiff, polite visits with stiff, stern aunts."

Eli smiled. "Suppose you had to sit still in the parlor all day with your cross-stitch in your lap and listen to grown-up gossip without looking like you were listening."

"It wasn't always that bad. My father took us for walks. But these kids have the way of the wind."

"Let them. It's the least we can do for them."

"Y'mean the most." she frowned. "They play more with each other because their friends are leaving."

"Let 'em leave. They'll be sorry."

"How so?"

"You think this could happen in the city? Think Boston could just hop, skip and jump over to Worcester or Springfield and take over? All right, Springfield, everybody out! No. We need to show a little more fight around here."

"Dan Shays is long dead, Eli."

"We need lawyers, Mary. Real lawyers. That's what I'm saying. Legal ammunition."

"But he was exiled, first."

Eli glanced at her. "For God's sake, Mary, don't argue with me," he said, "I've got enough on my plate right now. Let's not fight each other."

"What are you up to, Eli?"

He stood, and because he was taller and stronger he did not need to say more. She watched him go to the barn.

***

Jenny led the walk to Quabbin Lake, only a mile or two from their home. The afternoon glistened, heavy with sunshine and humidity now it was the middle of July, and the pine and oak woods near the lake seemed like a tropical jungle no longer wearing the pastel colors of spring, but the deepest, most lush green.

The year before, an MDWSC photographer took aerial photographs of the Valley. The black and white photos, taken with a wide lens on a clear day, were like the blueprints of construction projects, a map of what needed to be done. They were also a revealing look at what had been.

Small, neat farms set on the hillsides looked upon shaggy forests, remote and rustic graveyards, churches and town buildings set squarely at dirt crossroads looking clean and quiet.

The Rabbit line cut across the Valley floor like a zipper that held everything together, though photographer Carter North had not yet seen such a thing as a zipper. That would belong to the future time to come. The photographs were already a part of the past, of the Olden Times. In them, it was summer, just a year ago. The land lay still and lush before August burnished the grass brown and late summer polished the silver lakes. Enfield curled around the southernmost tip of the Prescott ridge, between the Great Quabbin and the Little Quabbin hills like an infant in its mother's lap.

The homes at Greenwich Village looked like white squares in pale sunshine beneath the wide body of Mt. Zion. A photo of North Dana showed a remote community planted firmly in the vista of forests, where the giant trees stretched beyond the camera's range. Even Mt. Monadnock in New Hampshire could be seen from the plane, the day was so clear.

The photos displayed the orderliness of New England village life, the solitude of remote communities, and there seemed an ironic sense of permanence in the towns which would so soon be erased from the very ground they now stood upon, the ground itself to be shifted and changed. Only one thing in the series of photos was prophetic, if one looked very closely.

There were no people.

There were no animals to be seen, only the silent crops. There were no cars upon the winding colonial turnpike roads, no wagons or buggies. The railroad tracks were empty, and the yards behind the screens of poplar and oak were still. The pilot and photographer had managed to catch a lazy August day when the weather was clear and the people had somehow, amazingly, vanished.

Perhaps some, like Jenny and Harrison and Ella now a year later, were hiding from the sun under the arms of the trees by Quabbin Lake.

Signs of construction, like scratches at the back door, were encroaching ever nearer to the villages. Work on the aqueduct and what would be called shaft 12 was beginning, close to Quabbin Lake. Jenny did not know the design of the construction but was familiar by now with that vague paranoid sensation brought on by truck tire tracks in the road that revealed it was heavily used, and a mound of fresh earth piled by a fresh hole.

They took their shoes off by the edge of the lake and stepped with faces blissfully transformed, into the cool water.

"Better do that while you cahn. They don't like ya puttin' your dirty feet in a reservwah." the boy said. He was sitting under the trees to the left of them. Jenny pulled herself up at the sound of his yawning accent. A Bostonian.

The boy stood and approached them, he was her height exactly, and stocky, about sixteen years old.

Ella put her hand on Jenny's elbow, which anxiously telegraphed please don't talk to him, but Jenny ignored her sister's timid pawing and planted her feet wide apart in the water.

"Reservoir worker?" she asked, nodding to the slight gash on the east side of the lake just begun by the drilling equipment. It was not a question as much as it was an accusation, as if he had put it there.

He pulled the cigarette from behind his ear the way he'd seen the Cisco Kid do and lit it by scratching a wooden match on the side of his boot. He squinted and blew out the smoke.

"So far all they've got me doing is hauling water for the older fellows. Working the big machines, that's what I'd like. Climbed up on a shovel first day I came just to see what it was like, some son-of-a-bitch kicked me off."

Harrison smiled giddily into the water. Ella fingered Jenny's hand nervously, but Jenny only regarded him, tilting her head curiously in a way that showed off her strong, square jaw line and her deep-set eyes.

"Do you live around here?" he asked, taking her in.

"Greenwich Village."

"Yeah, I guess you people have all got to move, huh? That's something. My brother told me the mess over the cemeteries."

"How would you like somebody digging up your dead relatives?"

Dickie thought instantly of his recently deceased mother but shook it off. "Yeah, well, look at it their way, and first thing you know. Those dead bodies'ud leach into the drinking water...."

"All right!" Jenny interrupted him, "We don't have to hear it from you." She pulled Ella and Harrison out of the water that told them with severity to put on their shoes.

The boy watched her slip into her white ankle socks. "My name's Dick Lewis. What are yours?"

"None of your business," Jenny said.

He grinned, feigning insult, "Just trying to be friendly, you don't have to bite my head off."

"You can just leave us be."

"Hey, well, what did I say? Listen Blue Eyes, I'm just here to work, you don't know anything about me."

"I know y'got a mouth on you." Jenny hollered over her shoulder, which sent him laughing.

"A mouth? I think you're beautiful," he called after them, and chuckling, continued his walk along Quabbin Lake.

There were summer cottages, and diminutive docks with friendly rowboats. Dick Lewis stole a rowboat, and floated aimlessly for a while, like a leaf around the still green lake, drawing on his cigarette with practiced emphasis, thinking about those kids, about the girl.

He squinted at the hard glint of sunlight on the water and watched Elaine Coffey back out of her door and onto the porch with a suitcase. Clumsily she dropped it and nearly lost her hat locking the door. She seemed to laugh at herself and turned. She turned toward Dick and threw the key as hard as she could into the water. It plunked near the thin, dark ripple made by Dick's oar.

She caught herself being watched by the boy in the boat. She waved at him.

Dick Lewis sat up, startled, stiffly waved back. Was she trying to get his attention? No, she didn't want him. She turned away again and walked around to the front of the house to the taxi waiting for her.

Elaine was uncharacteristically quiet on the cab ride. She did not talk to the driver except to order him to stop and pull over when she saw Roger.

Elaine staggered out of the taxi, and walked unsteadily, but with determination to where Roger stood with Martha Atkinson in front of the manse. They both turned. Martha watched her with curiosity, and Roger watched with horror. She stumbled once but drew herself upright and continued where she was close enough to grasp Roger's arm. She shook it playfully, smiling.

"I've sold my house to the Commonwealth of Massachuz...chu-zits.." She said, grinning, "but the funny thing is, I haven't enough money to pay for that cab over there." She snickered, a hideous sound that made Roger want to gag.

"This is Mrs. Coffey," Roger said, as quietly as he could.

"This is Mrs. Coffey," she affirmed, "The car, the house, the taxes, the moving van, and the kitchen sink. Roger, dear, the funny thing is, if you don't help me out, that poor young man driving me all the way to Springfield is going to go without a tip. Or anything. See?"

It was apparent she had been drinking quite a bit. Martha, while trying to guess at her connection to Roger was also guessing about how to invite her in for coffee. Roger braved a glance at Martha and realized the same. He could not have that.

Quickly he pulled out his billfold and pushed a ten-dollar bill into her stomach. She released him, uncrinkled the money and examined it.

"This," she said, "should do." Then she smiled very broadly again and wagged her finger at Martha.

"He's irresistible, isn't he? A bit inexperienced, as you have no doubt discovered, but utterly irresistible." She kissed him.

She took a long look at Martha. She shook her head at Roger and stumbled back to the cab.

Roger stood frozen, looking away over the top of the church.

"I'm wondering if I should invite you into the house or what." Martha said after the cab pulled away, "I'm not going to ask you anything, if that's what you're thinking."

"No, I don't want to come in. I have to leave now."

"Goodbye, then." Courteously, she did not watch him leave. She felt it the least she could do for him.

Roger drove back to his room in Enfield. Elaine Coffey handed the driver the ten-dollar bill over the seat as he drove. That taken care of, she relaxed in the back seat and watched the Quabbin hills approach. She had taken a half a bottle of pills along with the Scotch and would have probably died somewhere between the Valley and Springfield, except her body slumped to the floor of the car. The taxi driver took her to the hospital, relieved that she was now someone else's problem.

CHAPTER 14

A few days later Roger Lewis drove to the work site near Shaft 12 and found Dickie waiting for him by the shed used as a site office. Dickie flashed that evil grin of his and waved. Roger motioned him over, not bothering to get out of the car.

"I figured you'd be visiting me." Dickie laughed.

"I'm here to tell you to knock it off. Your foreman doesn't need your fighting. Neither do I. We've got a lot of work to do, we don't need some spoiled jackass of a kid playing king of the hill. You read me?"

"Don't you even want to know if I got hurt?"

"I want to know when you're going to grow up."

The smile faded off Dick's face.

"It's plain your coming here wasn't such a good idea, was it? Just as much my fault for thinking it could work. I was a fool," Roger said into the rearview mirror.

Dick noticed the newspaper on the seat beside Roger. "Hey, that was something. I wanted to tell you," Dick nodded to the headline, "I think I saw that woman the day she tried to kill herself."

Roger looked at him. He would not look at the paper again. He spent all morning re-reading it. "Mrs. Coffey?"

"Yeah. I was down on the lake that day. I met some kids walking around the shore. One girl especially. Anyway, after they left I stole a rowboat...."

"Dickie..." Roger moaned.

"I just borrowed it. I put it back after. Jeez, Rawg, you're such an old woman. Anyway, I'm rowing around on the water near to this lady's cottage. I saw her come out all dressed up like she was going traveling. She had a suitcase. She flung something way out onto the lake. It fell into the water pretty close to me. I looked up. She saw me and waved to me, so I waved back. Then she walked around to the front of the house where I couldn't see her. She didn't look like a woman who was halfway to killing herself."

Roger did not answer.

"I might have been the last person she saw. Except the cab driver."

Roger started the engine. "Just take it easy, will you, please, Dick?"

"Sure. Yeah."

"We'll talk some more. Take care of yourself, all right?'

"I can take care of myself, all right."

"That's not what I mean." Roger pulled away, the rear tires kicking up a thin film of dust behind him. Dick waved the cloud away from his face, watching the car go.

Roger drove to Reverend Atkinson's manse. After a moment, Martha came out to him, still in her apron, a kerchief covering her head.

"It's hard to get my housecleaning done these days," she said, "I'm spending more time looking out the window for you."

"Do you? I'm sorry. A less rude man would knock on the door."

"You don't want to come in, do you?"

"No. If it wouldn't scandalize the neighbors, would you mind sitting in here with me for a minute?"

She went around to the passenger's side. He lifted the newspaper before she sat down upon it. She took it from him before he could hide it. "My brother got the paper yesterday. I already know. That cab driver is quite a hero."

"I'd like to tell you something you don't know. I had a relationship with that woman."

"That was kind of hard to miss."

"We broke it off. I broke it off, without much resistance from her. I met her shortly after I came to work here. She had a husband then. He was dying. She brought him back to her grandfather's cottage on the lake. It had been in her family since the '80's, I guess. That's what she said. After her husband died, we got to know each other."

"And you broke off the...relationship?"

"Yes. I just walked away from it, is more like it. Martha, I don't know how I became involved with her, except I guess she appealed to my vanity and I to hers. Wasn't even particularly romantic. We slept together. Even then, it was just an empty, only physical...and not even that...I'm ashamed of it. Even more ashamed that I walked away from her."

"Not sure what I'm supposed to say at this juncture."

"This is ungallant of me, I know. According to the rules, I'm supposed to just shut up about all this. I'm sorry." He shook his head, "She was so wrapped up in this place. She wanted to just stay put and let the world pass around her."

"You are also wrapped up in this place, sir."

"I know." He swallowed, rubbing his face. "I'll tell you how much I'm wrapped up in this place. The police asked for anyone who knew something about the woman, her family or friends, to step forward. I told my supervisor that I knew her, that she was depressed about losing her cottage, and I asked him for time off to go to Springfield and talk to the police. He said I shouldn't do it. He said the press would make a melodrama of it. It would be bad for the reservoir. So, I did nothing. Thank God some cousin of hers came forward to claim her. Thank God she's all right."

She smoothed the paper out on her lap, touching Elaine Coffey's photo, which had been taken by a professional photographer at the time of her engagement announcement, many years ago.

"Yes, thank God," she said, "I can see you're struggling, Roger. I don't have any ready-made answers for you. But, I want to give you something else to think about. As miserable as this woman, this Mrs. Coffey, was about giving up a comfortable place, a comforting past, everyone here has to. Many of these poor souls have little or nothing, except our towns."

Roger didn't answer. She got out of the car.

"Martha!" She came around to his driver's side window.

"I'm sorry I told you all this."

"Confession is good for the soul."

"Not for the one who's got to hear it."

She shrugged. "I know you better now." She tucked her hands behind her back and went into the house. For the first time he was glad he let someone know him better.

***

Going around to the back of Eli's house, John watched with amused empathy as his brother slapped at the spot near the barn with an old scythe where the mower could not reach. John approached Eli, measuring his steps against the rhythm of his brother's cutting. Eli looked up, pushed the soft cloth cap back from his head and set the sharp blade safely into the ground, leaning on the upturned handle as he nodded to John.

"Got y'self a good day," Eli said. John smiled and nodded. He was taking Eli's children to Springfield today on the Rabbit so they could go to a movie theater. They had never been to the movies.

They'd certainly never left the Valley, had no idea what movies or movie theaters, or anything else was really like. Doris had some claim to sophistication; she had visited Ida and Walter in Athol twice and slept on the couch overnight.

John had not been to Springfield since he came back to the Valley. He had passed through it in the night on the way to Palmer, that was all. He felt he must go specially to see it again.

Mary thought it was a good idea, and Eli agreed by not disagreeing. That the children should see something of the outside world even if it was just for the afternoon seemed more like an experiment than an outing.

John's purpose was twofold.

He had wanted to see Springfield again, to bring his life full-circle. He was afraid to go alone.

"Still hard at work, Eli?"

"Remember this?" he gestured to the scythe.

"Pa's."

Eli nodded.

"I guess Mary's still getting the children ready?"

"Why didn't you ever write y'father, or visit him?" Eli asked, watching John evenly, squinting from beneath the soiled brim of his cap.

"I was hoping you wouldn't stoop to that, Eli."

Eli reddened. "I haven't stooped to anything. I've done what I've had to and put up with what I shouldn't have."

John shrugged. "I just figured if I went away, you'd get the farm."

"That's not true. Don't put a heroic face on leaving, and don't play a hero before my kids."

"Afraid of what they might find out there, Eli? Like you're afraid?"

Eli pushed the scythe away from him and took a long step forward, pushing his hard palms into John's chest with a sound like a clap. Off balance, John fell clumsily on his back into the weeds.

Eli could see he'd hurt him. John coughed, allowed Eli to pull him up and silently retrieve his hat.

"Failure is nothing to be afraid of," John said, "It's even noble, in a way. Keeps you humble." He coughed again and spit phlegm into the weeds. "Listen, Eli," he said, "I didn't write much, but I kept the letters Papa sent me. He wrote over and over that the farm was my property. Fine. I never wanted it, but fine. I was talking to some of that gaggle of lawyers they've got to soak up this place. Lon may not have ownership after all. Do know if he's registered on the deed? Do you know if Pa formally made him his heir? Do you even know if the fool ever paid any taxes on the place? Or did you just walk away from it, in a mood, like usual? I might just have a right to that land."

"What for?" Eli asked coldly, wiping his cheek with his sleeve. "When have you ever been interested in hard work? You'd kill yourself." He half turned away from John and pretended to resume cutting the grass around the sun-baked barn wall.

John laughed, "You fool, I don't want to farm the place. I want to sell!" His eyes brightened for the first time since his return, or so it seemed to Eli who now gave him his direct attention.

"To sell?" Eli repeated with dull confusion. John shook his head and smiled the smile Eli was beginning to hate.

"To get cash! To leave! Eli, come on now! Don't be so slow! We have to leave here, at least you have a nice piece of property you can sell to the state, I have nothing! I could live on what I could sell that farm for! That's all I want, no getting rich, just being able to live."

"What about Lon?"

"Eli ...I'd...give some of it to him. I wouldn't just throw him out in the cold. But the boy's an idiot. He has no sense. I don't think he even knows what's going on here. I don't think he ever reads a newspaper or talks to anyone. Will you help me? Will you talk to him, ask him about the property, does he have proof of ownership...."

"You make me sick."

"Eli ..."

"It would be just like you to sell out."

"What in hell is that supposed to mean? Do you think you're not? You're selling out too, you idiot, sooner or later. Or do you think you're just going to sit here in your flowerbed while the bulldozers knock down the barn? What do you think you can do?"

"I can do plenty."

"You can't do shit, you moron. Eli, don't tell me you're not planning for the future. What's that going to do to your family? You'd better start thinking about those kids...."

"You keep your mouth off my kids. And you can stay away from them, too!"

"You already gave your permission for me to take them to Springfield today. Just because you're in a fit, don't take that away from them."

"Fine, take them today. Show them how wonderful the city is. They'll know the difference when they get back. Just like you did when you came back. You came back, didn't you John? You came back with nothing."

"That doesn't mean I was wrong for leaving."

Eli turned away. Mary watched from the kitchen window as he picked up his father's scythe and went into the barn.

***

For a moment on the train, John sat stiffly in his seat, drowsy with the heat of the summer and the rattling, rocking motion of the car. He tried not to think of Eli but pretended that the children sitting near him were his own. Ella sat to his left, alternately huddling in her seat with excitement and thrusting her nose to the window to see the river, or Enfield, or a truck, or a hill slide by. Doris and Jenny sat opposite them, Doris was alternately dignified as befit a sixteen-year-old and giddy as a child. John considered her, with her hand-me-down white gloves of her mother's, her stylish straw summer hat which was a gift from her sister Ida who knew about fashion being a married Athol lady now, and her round, country-girl's face. She looked like and was, someone who had eggs for breakfast, junket and Indian pudding for Sunday dinner desserts. If she were a city girl, she'd be practicing with makeup. She'd learn how to smoke, go to dinner dances, discover highballs. He smiled. She was a country girl who attended church suppers and picnics and piano recitals.

Jenny sat next to Ella, looking out the windows on both sides of the train because she was on the aisle seat. John wondered if she were as ambitious as Eli, had secret goals for herself the way he knew Eli had. She was a private girl. He wanted to crack her shell.

As the train jostled her head to bump into John's gaze, she smiled quite magnificently. He guessed that she was pleased with the trip, which she was. He did not guess that she was mostly tickled at the way Ella leaned against him and favored him with her giggles and her little girl's devotion. It touched Jenny very much. It also lifted a weight off her shoulders, a burden she would not admit.

Despite the engineer's assistant who spit out the window on turning bends, the Rabbit had its own kind of charm, though its hearty swaying was making Uncle John insidiously nauseous. Mr. Doane the conductor still eyed him as if he were an escaped criminal. That man ever going to retire?

Finally, they came into the long, flat yard at Springfield, to the platform that was above street level.

The city on the Connecticut River to the southwest was the largest city in the four western Massachusetts counties. It had grown more in John's absence. Though there were no skyscrapers here as he had seen in New York, still the downtown was all brick and stone and glass and steel, auto and train, trolley, bus and enough pedestrians to raise a small army. They were city people who shopped with energy and searched the signs of maniacal traffic for opportunities to cross. They were busy, confident people.

The Vaughn children stayed close together. Ella held her uncle's hand. They looked at their group reflection in the drugstore's plate-glass window.

Beyond the reflection, there were people inside. They sat at the lunch counter. There were young women by themselves, ladies with baby carriages, men in suits who strode with long, striped flannel legs. They spoke slightly different from the softer speech of the Valley, faster, a bit like Uncle John, though their clipped inflection reminded the Valley children they were still in western Massachusetts.

The children looked for signs of immigrant people of whom John had spoken. The army on the sidewalks gave little indication of their diversity. If John could have found the same Italian family, or German or Pole he had met years ago, he might notice the change in them now. There would be less shyness about their manner. They would be more at ease, more bold, more American. He might be disappointed, if he noticed. But he did not. He wanted things as he left them, and so saw them that way. He tugged on Ella's arm and led them off the sidewalk.

They went into the Capitol Theater on the corner of Main and Pynchon streets, which John had remembered as the site of the old Gilmore Opera house when he had first come to Springfield. Today they would watch a Warner Brothers film, something inappropriate for children, something with gangsters in it. John smiled wickedly. Time they had some fun.

The lobby was carpeted, the walls were of sculpted plaster and gilt decorated, like an ancient pagan temple. The seats were plush thrones. The floor sloped down into a huge, gilded cavern, with balconies and boxes, and Ella and Harrison vaguely wondered if there would be royalty sitting in them.

They gaped so foolishly that John suddenly felt the obscenity of this culture shock. He felt brutish. He whispered it was all right for them to eat their popcorn.

A gang of boys filed in from the far aisle. John noticed Harrison watching them. The kids talked loudly, as did everyone in this city, and fell into their seats with the confident tumble of people who knew what to expect next.

Just knowing what to expect was an advantage, Jenny thought, as she watched them.

The boys waited with impatience for the newsreel to end, then leaned forward over the backs of the empty seats in front of them to scrutinize the cartoon.

The city children were wise and impatient, but just as curious about the world and as vulnerable in it as any of the Valley children. They were just as susceptible to misfortune and disappointment. What gave them an edge?

They lived in the twentieth century. That was their edge. They did not live by the rigors of the nineteenth or by a code of behavior from the eighteenth. They belonged to the twentieth century. They owned its gifts, they were victims of its failures.

"Just like me," Jenny thought jealously, as she brought her doubtful glance from the boys in the dark back to the huge screen with its giant faces of platinum-blonde actresses speaking with nasal Midwest voices in a Hollywood scriptwriter's awkward imitation of New York City slang.

***

At Ligget's Drug Store, about a block down on Hillman and Main, their tiring uncle herded the Vaughn children in, and they tried to blend in with the people there.

Doris sipped her Coca-Cola in the trademark glass with the pretended sophistication of a debutante as she eyed the young waitress behind the counter enviously. That girl had a glamorous career.

Harrison and Ella chose orange soda because it was orange. They did not have soda to drink very often, except homemade root beer.

Jenny had root beer. Doris rolled her eyes in disgust at the wasted opportunity. Why root beer? She could have it at home anytime. It sat in the dark cellar in dusty bottles, with a raisin sealed in each one.

Root beer was like quilts and mustard plaster. It was old-time and therefore repugnant.

Jenny knew that. She only wanted to find out for herself which was better, her mother's handed-down recipe which was thick and syrupy and so root beer-y it could choke a person half to death, or this store-bought sweet, fizzy stuff.

Jenny frowned over the soda fountain glass. Both were fine. They were surely different, but she didn't see that either was superior to the other and she had a taste for both.

Her scientific experiment had failed, because it did not make up her mind.

She looked out the window at the traffic. Springfield was not the whole world. Neither, clearly, was the Valley. Why was there only room for one or the other?

She reached for a paper napkin in the metal thing where Uncle John had taken one and noticed again the girls perched next to her. One was dark haired and quiet, the other had wavy reddish-brown hair and an easy laugh. They were talking about boys they knew.

"Bethie, you have ice cream on the bridge of your nose." the dark one said, and fussily blotted the smudge between her friend's eyes. They were close to Jenny's age, well no, maybe younger. Perhaps they only seemed older. Jenny wondered if she had lived here, could they be her friends? Could she be as easy and unaffected with them as they were with each other?

Every friend she had ever known was transient and so her acquaintance with other people was brittle, tense, and unintentionally choked with unexpressed emotions.

"Of what are you thinking so seriously, Jenny?" Uncle John said.

She wanted to ask what he thought would happen to them, but Harrison and Ella only got upset at talk of the stupid reservoir. Unconsciously they equated what fragmented news they heard of the project with the biblical Flood. It was their own doom.

Jenny knew now, as she had not quite before, that her family would eventually move, and she began to resent the fact of this being kept from them.

"Hmm?" Uncle John said.

What could she say that would say it all, or even a part of it?

She smiled and shook her head.

"Seen Lon lately?" He glanced at the other children, and winked at Jenny, as if to tell her they shared a secret and he would not betray her. She felt uncomfortable and embarrassed, and that he knew this, and that, somehow, that was the point.

***

Mary held a design of lady's-slippers in her hand. Eli watched her hands as she touched the cloth square, looking closely at the stitches, running her index finger over the ridges of the thread, turning the square over, smoothing the face of it over her flat red palm. She looked at it critically.

"Jenny's quilt?" Eli asked. She nodded and turned to him.

"What do you think? I did roses and tulips for the older girls. Jenny strikes me as a wild thing."

"Guess she's one of the older girls now." Eli shrugged, smiling a little.

"Y'know, I'm not looking forward to a house full of people this time. I don't know what it is. I'm becoming frumpy and unsociable. I'm more isolated here than I ever was in Prescott." She caught his eye the moment she'd said it and dropped her glance.

"I didn't mean that for a criticism, Eli."

"That's all right. We're done with Prescott. At least, I thought we were. John wants the deed."

"I don't understand."

"Pa's farm. Lon's farm. John thinks the property was not made over to Lon legally, properly. He's hoping to find some way to get the place and sell it to the State."

There, that was plainly said. He wanted to mention it all week. He was afraid that by talking of selling the Prescott land, Mary would ask him why they didn't just sell this land. He didn't want to even think about it.

She said nothing. She draped the quilting square over the arm of the rocker and stood back from it, regarding it still.

"You're not satisfied with it?" he asked, nodded towards the piece.

"He's always thinking, isn't he?"

"Apparently." Eli said as he moved to the door, "He doesn't do much else. But, I should think I'd still have as much right to that land as him."

"Neither of you do. It's been Lon's responsibility for some time, now."

"Yes. Lon was responsible enough to own that farm and I wasn't."

"I don't think that was ever in your father's mind, Eli."

"I wonder if he was responsible enough to pay the property taxes. I could find out."

"Why? What does it matter, we've got our own farm to worry about."

"I'm not worried. And I'm not having anything taken away from me that's mine."

***

John Vaughn felt for the first time he was becoming dim. He gaped with amusement at Roger Lewis' animated discussion with Miss Atkinson outside the grocery. He had prided himself for an acute observer and judge of people. He wondered why he had not noticed.

So, the boy was silly over Miss Atkinson, who, with her Sunday missionary's zeal was obviously setting her cap for him. What a couple of fools.

He smiled from the door of his rooming house and stepped out onto the porch. The sun nearly knocked him over for a moment, even in the early afternoon it was still too early in the day for him.

"I'm dying," he thought to himself, but shook off the revelation when his lightheadedness disappeared. It was brief, and unimportant now.

Roger tugged at Miss Atkinson's elbow. "I'm not making light of this," he said, frowning at her harder, despite the fact that by now he'd learned she was impervious to glares.

"Dick doesn't need hard work, he needs you. You're an example to him whether you like it or not," she answered, glancing at his hand on her arm. She punctuated her argument with a light touch on his lapel. His face grew red and he blew a hard angry breath at the awning above them.

"What do you suggest I do about it?" he whispered, looking down into her calm gray eyes.

"I think you should rent yourself a house here and make a home for the boy. The home won't last, but your relationship might."

He rolled his eyes, but she could see him smile.

"Y'can't just shrug your brother off on a work crew and not take any part in his life."

"You are an irritating woman."

John Vaughn crossed the street toward them. He took his hat off to Miss Atkinson, who nodded briefly from over Roger Lewis' shoulder. Lewis turned and dismissed John Vaughn with an annoyed glance. Miss Atkinson felt she could not brave the suggestive grin Vaughn gave her. She quietly said goodbye. Lewis watched her walk away, surprised that she did not tease Vaughn as she always did him. He smiled but put his hands in his pockets and strode with pretended irritation back to the engineer's office in Mrs. Pratt's former parlor.

John Vaughn began to follow him delightedly, but with difficulty.

"Lewis," he said, "You shouldn't make a man of my years trot like a Morgan horse."

Lewis pulled up short.

"Did Smith fix your flat?"

"Who? Oh, George, yes, he's a good boy. So *gol-darn* resourceful ...." Vaughn grinned.

"Then see Carter for...."

"I've been meaning to ask you for some time, Roger, if you would come to Sunday dinner at my brother's house in Greenwich Village?" Vaughn enjoyed the irony of the name only he, who had frequented speakeasies in Greenwich Village, New York City, found in saying Green-witch Village and knowing what a shock it would be to anyone from Gren-itch.

Lewis stared at him.

"I had no idea you knew Miss Atkinson," Vaughn said. "She teaches the Sunday school at Greenwich Plains, did you know...?"

"Yes."

"Please bring her with you. Well?"

"Well, I don't know. Thank you for asking, though. I don't think your brother would appreciate strangers marching in on him...."

"Nonsense, he's been pressing me to bring a friend." He lied.

"Are we friends, Vaughn?" Roger Lewis tried not to look at him with outright disdain. It was a habit he was lately trying to break.

"We might as well be, Roger."

"I really don't...."

"Roger, my relatives are not hillbillies...."

"Who the hell said anything...."

"They will not shoot you because you are the enemy. That's what you're thinking, isn't it? Miss Atkinson isn't your enemy, is she? Well, my brother's family is much like Miss Atkinson, except perhaps they are better Christians."

"Don't goad me, Vaughn," Roger Lewis resumed his march to the office, "I know your way. I don't like it."

"It was a friendly invitation. Roger, you damned fool. You prefer to see this big pond you're building as some kind of sterile, scientific operation. I don't think you realize it displaces the people who have the misfortune to live here. You prefer to avoid that glaring fact."

Lewis stopped as one tortured and turned to him. "I know all about that glaring fact."

John Vaughn snorted. "You know? Roger, North's office is in my sister-in-law's birthplace. My brother used to work in that mill across the river. Hell, I used to skinny dip in this river. You can't avoid the fact that you are very much involved with the people hereabouts. You might as well get to know them better. I see you've already taken the initiative with Miss Atkinson."

"Shut your mouth...."

John Vaughn continued, not hearing him, "They are descended of patriots, Roger, deeply in tune with the rights of man and the common good, and all that bullshit. If you can make them believe that they are making a noble sacrifice, they're yours. Understand? Anyway, they don't understand eminent domain, they don't like it, but not one of them will be anything but civil to you."

"All right, we'll come."

"You can't just keep avoiding...what?"

"Thank your brother for the invitation. We'll be there."

"Oh."

"Sorry to cut short your speech. But you were boring."

"That's okay, I'll save it for Decoration Day."

"Thanks." Roger said, duty done, as he stepped towards the former Pratt house.

The younger man disappeared behind the slapping screen door. Bewildered at his success, John wondered if it was a sign that his luck was changing.

He saw Jenny's dust-kicking walk towards the store. She carried jars of preserves in a basket. Dick Lewis slapped the door open, a piece of licorice swinging from the corner of his mouth. He nearly knocked her down.

"Excuse me," Jenny said automatically, then looked up to him.

"My fault," he grinned, delighted that her look of disgust meant she remembered him.

"Yes," she said shortly, preparing to dodge past him to the door.

"Could you let me say I'm sorry? I never got the chance that day and I should have then."

"Thank you. Now if you'll get out'a the way."

"Oh, come on, don't be mad at me." Dick smiled, "I've got a big mouth and I'm not very smart so you should feel sorry for me."

"I feel sorry for anyone that has to live with you."

"Must be why my brother sent me to room with a family in Smith's Village, and I'm not sure they're too happy about it, either. Hey, do you know practically everybody there is named Smith?"

"Yes."

"The same thing with Doubleday Village. Practically everybody's a Doubleday. Isn't that weird? I'm dying to go to Puppyville and see what I find there."

In spite of herself Jenny smiled.

He reached for the door. "My brother brought me here to keep an eye on me after our mother died. We don't get along much. If it sounds like I'm fishing for an invitation to supper, I am."

"I'm sorry to hear about your mother." Jenny shifted the basket, "But I'm not taking any reservoir workers home to eat."

"What are you doing with these?" he touched the basket, "Are you selling them? What kind is it? Did you make this?"

"Yes. My mother made it. Mint. We have some in the back yard...."

"You walked from Greenwich Village?"

"Yes. My uncle...."

"You walked?" he took his cap off and slapped it on the railing, "Gawd, you must be fit as hell!"

"Y'like to move so I can go inside?" she glared at him.

"Oh, excuse my language." he laughed, "I forgot I had a mouth," he laughed out loud, covering his mouth with his dirty hand.

John Vaughn paused, watching the boy and girl, and thought how appropriate they looked. They were attracted to each other, their bodies knew it before their minds, and they made Roger and Miss Atkinson look ridiculous.

Were Lewis and Miss Atkinson flirting? Maybe he was wrong. Roger probably didn't know what a woman was for.

Jenny looked as though she could hit the boy, and John Vaughn hoped this was another boyfriend. Like some middle-aged men, sick and somewhat worn by life, he had the conviction that all young girls should be in love and that there was something wrong with them if they were not. He was pleased to find so much promise in Jenny. Her attraction to this boy might lessen her loyalty to Alonzo.

"I'm sorry," Dick choked, "Hey, no kidding, let me come in with you and watch you sell your stupid jelly."

"Why don't you go find someone else to make fun of?"

"I'm not making fun of you. I think you're very special. I never met a girl who let me have it like you do, Blue Eyes. You don't take any crap from anybody, do you?"

"Y'all right out there, Jenny?" a voice called from within the store.

"Yes, Mr. Paige ..." Jenny answered back. She lowered her voice in a parting shot, "I'm not sure what I mind most, your filthy language or your annoying accent."

"What accent?" he asked, truly astonished, and opened the door hesitatingly, "You're the one with the accent. I can hardly understand you unless you talk slow."

"HAH!" she said, stepping up into the store. "Listen to yourself!"

"Dickie!" Roger Lewis shouted from down the street. He whistled loudly and Jenny, Dick, and John Vaughn looked to him. He jerked his head sharply, indicating his wristwatch.

Dick Lewis rested the door gently against Jenny's right hip. "That's my brother. He's a pain. I won't tell you where."

"Thought y'were alone in the world."

"Would you believe I am?" he said sarcastically, flipping his cap roughly onto his closely-shaven head and he mouthed goodbye to her as he stepped briskly up the street, a little like his brother, John Vaughn thought. Jenny watched him go and went into the store. The store appeared not too unlike Miss Rebecca's store in Prescott, except it had no Miss Rebecca.

Vaughn sat on the step until she came out again, her basket lurching over her forearm from a pound of coffee and a can of salt. She nearly tripped over her uncle.

"I saw you from across the road, and just like that kid Lewis I couldn't believe you walked from Greenwich Village," he said, "I forgot we used to walk those distances all the time. I've gotten lazy."

"Mother says to remind you about Sunday."

He stood and took her basket. "I haven't forgotten. I'm bringing a surprise. Come over to the office."

"Where?" She hesitated, since he was involved in the Reservoir project. Like a family skeleton, they did not refer to it except in the vaguest, most polite terms. As they might refer to a relative's physical infirmity, they spoke of one's moral infirmity in a manner that showed they were protective, sympathetic, and ashamed.

"I've got to get home, Uncle John."

"I know. I'm going to drive you. My car is kept at the office, that's all. Don't worry, you won't have to talk to any steam shovel drivers."

When they were in the car driving on the eastern road to Greenwich, John Vaughn eyed her apologetically. "It's been a while since I drove. Don't worry though, I won't kill us. How do you know Roger Lewis' brother?"

"Dick Lewis? We ran into him one day over on the Quabbin Lake. Got a mouth on him."

John smiled, curling his lip back over his teeth and turning to check the side mirror to avoid chuckling. "Well, I guess you're going to be meeting all kinds of people from now on, Jenny-girl."

Jenny looked at him, suddenly smiling. "Hah, Lon calls me that. Funny you would."

"Or do you prefer 'Blue Eyes?'"

"*Uncle John…*"

"God, you blush easy. Wait till you have something to blush over. Hey, what have you heard from Lon lately? I haven't seen him since Ida's wedding. He doesn't come out of his hole, much, does he?"

"He's busy, Lon. If only the world would let him be."

"Well, it's not going to. You seem to know that. A lot better than your father does. Lon's a case. You know, I wanted to ask you…did you find out anything about his plans for that land? Jenny, I really need to know if he has proper title to that farm. I need your help."

"Uncle John, what's going to happen? Really?" She turned her face to him.

"I hope you don't think I'm a terrible man, Jenny, because I take the pictures," he shrugged, "I've made my home in the world. That alone has made me a kind of villain around here. But I'm harmless."

"I know."

"So is the world, mostly. You're going to have to not be afraid of it, Jenny. You have a lot of fun ahead of you. You've got to make up your mind to stop regretting what can't be helped."

"Then there's no right or wrong of it?"

"No. That's one thing the world's taught me."

"And coming home? What do I do about that? I know you don't think that's important...."

"In my way, I do. But you can get awfully stifled staying at home."

She looked at the road ahead. "Won't have to worry about that. Won't have a home soon."

"Oh yes you will. So, it won't be here. So, what? Your family will resettle...So will I, and so will Alonzo. Now, what about Alonzo...."

"When? Where? Even if we do, it won't be the same, nothing...schools, or church, or stores. You can't pack the whole town in a suitcase...."

"Then you leave it behind, child. At least you won't have to grow old in that town and see it change, see it get poor and mean. Or, see it grow and become rich. Hah, that'd be the worse conflict. What if the city came to you? What if they paved your roads and slapped up a few cafes and tenements, what if they brought bars and movies and neon signs? You'd only get the crime, the noise, the built-in loneliness of every city.

"Okay, so you can't stop them from tearing the town down. But if they never came here and left the place alone, you'd never be able to stop the town from changing in some way. If it thrived, you couldn't keep it from growing into something you'd eventually dislike. Someday, my Jenny, you'd sit on your porch, as old as I am, and wish for the Good Old Days, like all us old people do."

"I wish for the good old days now."

"At least this way you can keep it forever in your mind, the way it all is now. It will never change for you. In your heart you can always come back."

Jenny brooded out her passenger window.

"You can't believe Jenny, how damned strong memories can be. They can ruin your whole life."

"I don't like not being able to do anything about it."

"You're not helpless unless you let yourself be. But you have to be realistic. Lon is not realistic. Neither is your father. Your father hasn't mentioned any plan yet? Eli. He's a careful man, Jenny. That's always been his problem. He wants the moon, and he reaches for the plow."

"Do you want him to be like you?"

John slid his glance over her, from her knees, to her lap, to her breasts, to her determined jaw. "I won't defend myself, Jenny, if that's supposed to... not that I have much to apologize for, which is the same thing. I'll tell you the truth, Jenny, if you tell me the truth. My truth is...I've never been successful at anything, which is not so rare these days except some men have a great time trying. I haven't even tried. Not really, just halfhearted forays into...what I thought was exciting at the time. I'm as penny-ante as your dad, but at least I know it. Now you tell me something truthful."

"I don't know what you mean." she said, appalled at the sudden shaking of her voice.

"I mean just this. You're even more small potatoes than your father or me. At least I had guts enough to run away, and Eli had guts enough to push himself to Greenwich for another chance at God knows what. You have no plans. You haven't any dreams or ambitions. You're too big a girl not to, even in this place. You've set yourself up as some kind of mother hen to Ella, a lackey to your brother, who's just as lazy as you, I might add, and as some kind of tower of strength or Good Girl or damned if I know to your mother and father. You get a kick out of that, don't you? Wise up, kid, they don't need you. You're not as strong as you like to think you are, you're not as smart, and believe me, you are not as in charge as you think you are. Come on now, that's the truth, isn't it?"

Now Jenny knew why her voice had shaken and marveled both at the premonition, and her uncle's sudden ridicule.

She cleared her throat, but before she could respond her uncle threw a clever change of tactic. She began to understand that it was a tactic.

"You watch Dick Lewis. He'll give you a clue. I hope you and Dick get to be good friends," he said suddenly, "I think you'll see he's no Alonzo Vaughn."

Jenny was quiet.

"Did I hurt your feelings?" he smiled with too much sympathy.

"Don't worry about my feelings."

"You think you've got control of them, too. Too bad. I was thinking you were somebody, Jenny...."

If her uncle had touched her body wrongly she would have comprehended; she didn't understand this kind of assault. She turned her head to him to make him see she was not afraid. People only got hurt if they let themselves be.

"I was thinking you were somebody, too. I guess we're both wrong," she said.

He looked at her briefly then gave his attention back to the road. Driving was the best excuse in the world not to have to look at the person to whom you are talking.

"Despite what I've said, you know, I still think you're quite a fine young woman, Jenny. But if you grow up to marry Lon, you'll be the only farmwife with an ocean for a garden."

"You've got an imagination."

"I've also got eyes. Don't make a hero of Lon, Jenny. Being attracted to a man is no reason not to see his faults. Didn't your mother ever tell you that? No, of course not. Your mother never had that talk with you, did she? Well, I'll tell you the facts of life right now. Lon isn't any more immune to this situation than you are. He just thinks he is. The Commonwealth of Massachusetts is going to escort him out of the Valley. He's got no reason to moan about it either, because it's not his land to begin with. It's mine."

"What?"

"That farm is mine. It always was. I want you to tell him that. It'll be kinder coming from you, since you two are so, you know what I mean. He's your boyfriend, isn't he? Even if Mother and Father don't know. Your secret is safe with me, Jenny. Maybe you're the only one who can set him straight. It's in your hands."

CHAPTER 15

Eli tossed a weak smile at his children as they accepted the large box of chocolates Roger Lewis placed into Jenny's hands. Miss Atkinson beamed at them, with more vigor than she ever did in Sunday school, and led Roger to the table as if it were her home.

Jenny put the candy box on the sideboard as warily as if it held a dozen grenades. Harrison wouldn't have minded opening it now; Jenny wasn't sure they should ever open it. Their principles compromised, they came to the table.

John charmingly kissed Miss Atkinson on the cheek before he pulled out her chair for her. Everyone looked at him as if he were raving mad. He was only a little drunk. They reminded themselves to ignore it out of courtesy.

"Would you say the grace, Miss Atkinson?" Mary chirped over the potatoes. Martha Atkinson, still reeling from the kiss on the cheek looked up.

"Huh, what?"

"Uh, well…grace. I thought maybe…."

"Oh sure. Yeah, sure." Her minister brother always said the grace at home. If she ate alone, she never bothered. "Lord…thank you for these…the…food."

Harrison snickered. Eli raised his head to glare at him, but the boy knew enough not to look up, so Eli's glare was wasted.

After an interminable pause, Miss Atkinson helplessly wrapped it up. "Amen."

They all repeated Amen. Roger looked at her out of the corner of his eye. She was thoroughly flustered. He decided he loved her.

Eli carved the chicken. Mary began a smooth, only slightly rehearsed monologue on the weather. Roger took a deep breath and agreed as pleasantly as he could that it was a very warm September.

"You have some very fine children, here, Mr. Vaughn." Roger continued. Miss Atkinson looked at them across the table as if she just noticed them.

Eli was about to wave away the compliment, but John interrupted.

"They're being much too quiet," he said, "probably the combination of their Sunday school teacher and a representative of the reservoir is too much for them." He smirked. "It's as if God Almighty walked into the room with Satan in tow." Mary glared at him, which he saw, but it was still wasted because he didn't care.

"Well," Roger colored, "Martha has said often how much she enjoys teaching the Sunday school. Don't you?"

"Huh, what?" she answered.

"Sunday school and church are our whole upbringing here in the Valley, Roger." John said, "As small children we learn in church to Sit Still, to hold tight to our collection money, and especially not to sing louder than anybody else. This last is perhaps the worst offense. It implies showiness and conceit. Never mind if you've got a good voice." Roger smiled at him, a steel-like grin meant to endure everything from insult to inconvenience. He felt it was the mark of a gentleman, to cultivate such a polite barrier. John perceived this and laughed harder. He laughed until he began to choke. Eli looked over at him with only a little concern.

They ate as if they were on a mission, without appetite but full concentration.

"Well," Mary began again, "we're just…we're going to have Jenny's quilting soon. In another few weeks."

With help from Roger, who lightly kicked her ankle with his foot, Martha Atkinson realized this was her cue. "I am looking forward to it," she said as if beginning a recitation, "Are you excited Jenny?"

Roger looked over at Jenny and smiled encouragingly in what he felt a proper smile for young people.

"Yes. Yes, I am excited." Jenny answered like a robot in a voice that sounded like hers, but she didn't know from where it came. She met Roger's hyper-friendly gaze and bravely smiled back.

"Another country custom, Roger." John said. His plate was untouched.

Roger nodded. "It sounds very nice. Very old fashioned."

"Old fashioned." John repeated, "Yes it's very old fashioned. That's how it is here in the Valley. We are very old fashioned. But I'm afraid such things won't last for very long, will they, Roger? Not around here. When the reservoir is built, all these people will move away and the past will release its iron grip. Nothing like quilting bees will remain."

Eli looked over at Roger. Roger's smile had faded, but he was calm.

"I suppose that will depend on what they want to take with them and what they want to leave behind," he answered.

"They can't take their farms. Eli can't take his. I can't take mine."

"I didn't know you had a farm here, John." Roger said.

"My cousin works it right now. In Prescott."

Eli looked at him squarely and dinner was abandoned.

"No, John. It's not your farm."

"Eli…." Mary said, her voice low and soft, and warning.

"Eli means because I left for the city, I don't deserve it." John said. "But I won't bore you with old brotherly resentment. You know Roger, I, for one, harbor no resentment towards you. No, none at all. Y'see, all this old fashioned…," he waved his hand, "…it's basically as phony as scripture."

"John!" Mary said.

Eli roused himself, and said quietly, "That's enough, John."

"Remember those old popular songs when we were kids? About the peacefulness of the idyllic countryside? There's nothing idyllic about the country, not any more than the city. It depends, y'see, on what you prefer. What you're meant for. The country is pleasant, and it's pretty. Unless it's raining and you're six inches deep in mud and seven miles from home. The country is a freer place, unless you care what your neighbors think about you. And believe me, they think plenty. And a simple, happy, old-fashioned home life is difficult under blank, bitter poverty. Hard work is a virtue. Unless it kills you."

The speech took a lot out of him and he began to cough again. He staggered from the table and went to the kitchen, where he was very sick.

Eli stood and left the table without word and found John vomiting in the sink. He pushed John aside, pumped a bowl of water and pushed John's face into it. John pulled away, sputtered, wiping his face with his sleeve.

"You brought those people into my home," Eli said in a low voice, "I don't know them and I don't want them, but you brought them. Now you get out there and talk to them."

"Shut up, Eli. I don't feel well."

"Forget it. I don't want you talking to them anyway. You've said enough. You were always a smart-mouthed, mean tempered show off, John, and now you've behaved like a pig in front of my wife and children. If you ever show up drunk here again you'd better keep walking. 'Cause I'll wring your neck if you do."

He pushed John out the kitchen door to the back yard and let him be as sick as he wanted out there.

Eli cleaned the sink, washed his hands, and went back to the table. Roger stood. "Perhaps we should leave, Mr. Vaughn."

Eli looked at Mary. He would rather they left. He would rather they never came.

"You're welcome to stay, Mr. Lewis," Eli said, "I apologize for my brother."

"No need."

"Yes," Mary stood, "Please stay. We can't change the…well, circumstances, and we sure can't change John." She huffed lame laughter but it gurgled to death in her throat.

Miss Atkinson noticed the other three adults standing, put down her fork and stood at attention. "It's been such a lovely dinner," she announced.

Doris, Harrison, Jenny and Ella observed the adults standing in formation around the table. They looked at each other. They looked to Doris for leadership, but Uncle John being so demonstratively ill was beginning to work on her. She had a weak stomach.

Jenny took charge and made as though to stand herself, but Eli waved her down. She shrugged at Harrison.

"You and your family have been very kind, Mr. Vaughn," Roger said, "But I guess we're all pretty uncomfortable. I hope we all see each other again under more relaxed circumstances, sometime soon."

"Yes."

"If you'll take me to John, I'll offer him a ride back to Enfield."

"All right." Mary brought Miss Atkinson to the front porch. Eli brought Roger out the back.

John had passed out on the steps, the house pillowing his head.

"Fine picture, isn't he?" Eli muttered.

"I guess he's a bit of a rogue." Roger said, "He's a good photographer, though. A...a good worker."

"I'm glad for that at least." They each put an arm under John and hoisted him to his feet. John wasn't helping much, Eli slapped him hard across the face. Roger winced.

John roused himself. He pushed his face into Roger's shoulder, toppled, but was held up in their hug. In a moment he was steadier and could walk to the car as they held him by the arms.

When John had been packed into the back seat, Roger came to the porch for Miss Atkinson.

"Goodbye, Mrs. Vaughn, thank you very much." he said. It was more than Martha could bring herself to say.

"We're very sorry. Thank you for taking him home."

"That's all right."

They both quick-marched to the car and pulled away.

Eli and Mary stood quietly on the porch, watching the car get farther and farther away.

"I hope we never go through that again." Mary said.

"John sure fixed things, didn't he?"

"Yes. You were good, Eli. You did well. I know how mortified you were."

"So was Roger Lewis. He did well too."

She nodded. "He did, didn't he? He did very well."

They went back into the house. The three younger children were still seated at the table. Doris had removed herself to the bathroom where she was trying not to think about heaving.

"Doris doesn't feel good." Jenny said.

"What about the chocolates?" Harrison asked.

"Don't make yourself sick on them. Save some for Doris when she comes 'round." Eli said.

***

In a week, John returned to apologize. He had been on his way to photograph a shop in Dana, and he asked his driver to stop briefly at his brother's house. Eli was in the field, the children were at school. Only Mary accepted his apology on the front porch. He did not want to come in, as his driver was waiting.

Soon it was the third week of October, when the leaves glowed with their most magnificent dying colors. With the evergreens as a contrasting backdrop, the maples and the oaks, the cedars and the lindens ran riot with selective abandon.

The maples ran the most colorful, ranging in tones from deep red to pale gold. When the morning sun shone through their trembling leaves, they appeared luminous, an eerie, glowing force.

Nature transformed them a bit every day, so the artistry presented a slightly different picture each morning. Then suddenly the leaves were gone. Falling by ones and twos, then in awesome, noisy showers on a windy day. The Valley folk did not necessarily welcome winter, but they knew it was coming and so they anticipated it with a contrary excitement.

Jenny and Harrison would rake the leaves, and bank them against the foundation of the house to keep the cellar from freezing. Poor Harrison had a cord of firewood waiting for him to split as well.

Jenny breathed the fall air, tinged with the bitter scent of decay, and watched the bright leaves like little bright fans shiver in the warm southern breeze. It would go on like this forever, nothing, not even an edict could stop this. They could build right in the middle of it and around it, maybe, but surely, nature had its way eventually?

Today was her quilting bee.

Barely a few families kept up the custom in the Thirties. Mary had invited her mother and sisters, Ida, Cousin Eliza, Miss Atkinson, Miss Rebecca of course, and Doris. Ella was too young to take such a dignified role in the female community. Jenny worried that Ella might be hurt at this first break between them, but Ella tended to be shy in a crowd and was just as happy to be reading out in the yard.

Ella had finally done well in her arithmetic for once and won the honor of bringing a book home from school to read. She chose Bulwer's *The Last Days of Pompeii* which had been considered a potboiler over fifty years before and now was relegated to the schoolroom's meager library as a donation from some well-intentioned citizen who'd never read it himself.

The book was too depressing for Ella once she realized what it was about, and she shifted quickly to the safer if less satisfying *The Five Little Peppers and How They Grew*.

Eli had helped set up the quilting frame brought from Mrs. Pratt's in Belchertown. Eli brought back his mother-in-law and Hattie in the wagon, and though Mrs. Pratt, frail at seventy-one had not the strength to keep herself from being thrown about on the uncomfortable seat, she nevertheless was thrilled to be riding in a wagon again.

"You know, Eli," she chirped, "when Mr. Pratt was with us, we always kept a buggy. Do you remember it? He always kept it up so nice. But I sold it with the house, of course, years ago. I don't think I've ridden in a wagon since I was a girl and went for hay rides with the church Sabbath school scholars."

Walter drove Ida down in his company's truck, then continued on to Belchertown to make his delivery.

Mary was surprised to see him drive away without getting down to say hello. "Well, where is Walter going?"

Ida breezed in and dropped her coat on the back of a kitchen chair, like the daughter who always knows that her parents' house is still her home.

"Well, he's got to work, of course, Mother. He works on Saturday the same as everybody else, you know. He can't just stop and socialize like Dad can in the middle of his work."

Socialize? Where on earth did she come up with a word like that?

Ida's square was expertly cross-stitched with sunflowers. At first, she felt the quilting bee was a foolish idea. She had gotten used to a different world, and the homey quilting bee seemed archaic and silly to her now.

Ida would not have refused, however. She was still a child of the Valley enough to believe her parents' wishes still and would always require her obedience. Also, she recalled how she naively looked forward to her own quilting, and still had her quilt. She did not use it but put it away in her cedar chest from the catalogue. It would come in handy sometime, it would be right someday for a child, she thought.

Mary's party-planning made the house seem like someone else's home. Cookies and apple turnovers. Cream in a bowl and tiny glasses of cider.

Sakes. Jenny grit her teeth and accepted the honor of being the focus of a tradition, feeling silly and flattered and helplessly out of place.

The ladies arrived and Jenny, changed into her Sunday dress, greeted them at the door and thanked them for coming. She was taller than all of them, even Miss Rebecca, who entered the Vaughn house with her customary serenity, a wry smile offsetting stiffness.

Eli made himself scarce in the fields, and Harrison, after his morning chores, decided to climb Mt. Zion with a couple of the Berry boys. They were not present even in spirit, as Roger Lewis was. He pushed aside the curtain at his window and looked out on the quiet street in Enfield, thinking of what a quilting bee must be like.

The ladies sat companionably close, their cotton sleeves brushing each other as they fingered the material and worked steadily at their assigned seams. Like their men, the farmers who plowed straight furrows as their fathers taught them, the quilters' work had been handed down with similar diligence, order and austere method from their mothers. That artistry was involved they were only casually aware, for the purpose was not to create art for art's sake, but something useful. As they talked of children and other neighbors not present, they imagined Jenny's lean body and that of some man yet unknown, together and safe under this quilt. These women were genetically programmed to see to it that others were made warm and comfortable.

Had they known that fifty years later their handiwork would find itself auctioned in private sales and hung on museum walls, that other women would pursue the craft of quilt making as a painter works in oils, they would not have believed.

Jenny competently answered Miss Rebecca's polite questions on her schoolwork and kept the ladies supplied with tea, lemonade and cookies. She sat in and stitched a bit when one of the quilters needed to rest her eyes. Jenny sewed with her accustomed attention to detail, but she brooded over the patches of cloth, and their meaning, why they should all be here, and when were they leaving the Valley, and when would the flood happen, and considered the waxen face of Mary, looking less satisfied than she should be. Mary sat in her corner, listened to her mother's foot problems with effort, and seemed worn.

They did not speak much about the Reservoir. That was an unpleasant topic, and this was meant to be a pleasant occasion. Miss Atkinson found herself wanting very badly to broach the subject. She felt sure these ladies knew about her keeping company with Mr. Lewis. Blast, they would not ask her.

Mrs. Sullivan from next door felt the underside tracks of her thread with the tip of her middle finger. She had sewn for years, but never with a group. She searched her mind for topics of conversation but religion, politics, and the reservoir were out of bounds. These ladies were Protestant Republican Yankees whose families had lived here since the House of Hanover ruled England and ruled here. She was a Roman Catholic Democrat who arrived only because the Commonwealth already owned her farm and rented it to her cheaply until they were ready to flood the place.

"I thought it would never stop raining last night," she finally said. The ladies erupted in a chorus of agreement.

They had all worn their best, down to hats and gloves, had all toiled dutifully if not a bit competitively on their squares beforehand. To mention a missing family or a new rumor on the proposed baffle dam would be crude.

"Wind knocked down the last of our apples." Miss Atkinson offered.

Like Nero fiddling while Rome burned, Jenny thought.

Mary's sister Jane had the same thought from her corner. She looked at the women. They were a study.

Jenny's Aunt Jane, who had once impressed Eli with her new-fashioned femininity, was still a picture of a woman who knew what she was about and held nothing about her of vulnerability and equal hardness of these farmwives. Jane Pratt Davis, the Professor's wife, lived in a not too dissimilar house in Amherst, but in a community that was of the more typical if mythical New England variety: the semi-rural college town with a neat common, traditions which revolved around the student population, and a link to other educated communities around the nation and around the world.

Generic and tolerant villages, centered around a handful of multi-denominational (but always Protestant) churches, always attempting to sincerely cast off the old intolerances which formed the basis of their most revered traditions. These graceful towns adapted through time ever more gracefully, they did not need to be jerked into the twentieth century, and they would live long past it.

Jane Davis enjoyed her life as the wife of a professor. She attended academic social functions and settled herself as an important member of her social community. She mused ruefully, but still fondly on her Valley roots and watched her youngest sister attend her simple, unattractive company with thoughtfulness. She had chosen to share her life with a farmer and shared milking, mortgages, weather-murdered crops and moments of grateful harvest, as well as five children as dissimilar to each other as Jane and her sisters had been.

Jane and her husband had two sons, both graduate students in universities in New York State and in Pennsylvania. When they reunited at Christmas and on her birthday, something the boys' father insisted upon, they were a proper family, polite and formal with each other as a meeting of the Junior Class officers. She was satisfied with her family and knew that no life would have suited her more, yet she looked at the strain upon Mary's face; the bronzed and weathered face of Eli as he met her in the yard; the pseudo-sophisticate Ida; dramatic Doris; the staid, calm little farm boy Harrison; and the pale little Ella in the yard; and this one, this Jenny, who was so tall and straight, so simple and elegant as a cattail. Jane wondered if her own life was not as exciting and full as theirs, if her life would be more meaningful had she stayed in the Valley and faced the end with her own kind.

She and her husband had discussed it of course, as they had discussed everything from politics to faculty socials, and they spoke just as confidently and just as unemotionally about the destruction of the Valley towns. As she sewed, unaccustomed since many years at this handwork, she mused upon the craftwork of the Valley people, and thought perhaps her husband might be interested in organizing a field trip among his students about the vanishing Valley. Professor Tilton had taken his group of anthropology students into the Appalachian Mountains to collect folklore last year, something the board thought infinitely silly but the money had to be spent somehow. Perhaps her husband would be interested in a similar folk project on the Valley. Vanishing Americana and all that. Yes, that would be new. For at least a generation the shift to an urban, industrialized nation led concerned purists to predicting the downfall of the country, how Youth was soft, how the modern factory worker was demoralized, not like the noble farmer or Longfellow's smithy in days of yore.

Yes, there had been many essays of that sort, but nobody ever thought to look at what pastoral life remained. Here was a chance to actually watch it dissolve, like matter in a laboratory dish. Jane congratulated herself. *I should have been the professor*, she thought.

Her eyes swept briefly across the ladies before her and locked accidentally into Jenny's. Jenny was looking at her, studying her aunt's clothes, her makeup. Jane lifted her head and vainly allowed herself to be looked at, as she had when she was a girl and a young man passed. Jenny was more curious, and more critical. Jane suddenly pricked her finger and looked quickly back down at her work.

"Nice and sunny today," Mrs. Sullivan suggested, and the ladies erupted in cheerful agreement.

Jenny excused herself a moment and stepped out into the backyard, where the afternoon had begun to chill. The days were growing shorter and it seemed as if the tired old sun was pushing to get to bed.

Ella sat on the glider swing bundled in her coat, the book in her arms. Her cheeks were red and she stopped every so often to take another look at the trees.

Jenny plunked down on the seat beside her, her weight shifted the opposite end of the swing into the air and gently, lopsided, down again. She put her arm around Ella and hugged her briskly to shake off her quilting depression. Ella grinned sideways at her.

"Your quilt finished?"

"Pretty soon. Not soon enough. About as cheerful a ritual as speaking a piece over the dead, which is what everything feels like lately."

"Jenny!" Ella frowned, "I think a quilting bee is nice."

"Oh, it is, honey. I know it is. But we might as well go off to a corn husking or a barn building at Shaft 12. What's the point of it, Ellabella?"

"Don't talk like that Jenny. It's such a nice day. The blue jays have been talking to themselves. They think I don't see them."

"Remember when you used to talk to yourself?"

"I was little."

"You had an imaginary friend. Times I'd see you act out three or four people and I used to wonder which one was you."

"Did you laugh?"

"I mostly wished there were more other children so you wouldn't have to act out the whole scene yourself. Must have been a lot of work."

Jenny brushed Ella's bangs from her eyes. She thought of how Uncle John had behaved at dinner in front of Ella. She could not forgive him for that, either.

"Don't stay out here much longer," she said, "The sun'll beat you to the house. You'll get cold out here. Why don't y'come in now?"

"N-no."

"Come on," Jenny pulled her up by the arm, "I won't let anybody talk to you if I can help it. You can read in our room a while. They'll be leaving soon."

The only relatives Ella really felt at ease with were Uncle John, who could not come because he was a man, and Cousin Eliza, who was easy, comfortable and nonjudgmental as a stuffed animal. Eliza had not come today, but dejectedly sent her square in the mail. She could not arrange a ride to Greenwich Village from North Amherst today. Here was a sign of doom to her and to the others, who silently mused that this is what would happen to them. Family would scatter, like the dry leaves soon would, and they would keep in touch only through the mail, or through a telephone perhaps, those that might someday have them.

They sewed their seams, now along the finished edge of the quilt, farther apart from each other now that the quilt had been shaped and grown and stretched in the wooden frame. They had started working from the center and now they were along the perimeter, tired from talk, eyes dim with the sunset outside. Only the satisfaction of the quilt's progress before them was enough to keep them going the last hour.

CHAPTER 16

Ella wiped her sticky fingers with a rag kept in her small school desk for that purpose. Harrison performed the delicate operation of transferring the freshly glued paper chain, with sliding, damp-edged links, to the class tree. Miss Murphy supervised in between observations of the other children's handmade paper ornaments, smooth and comforting, equal in her gentle criticism and praise. They could have been drawing snowmen or pornographic pictures, all she cared was that it was neat and between the lines. They loved her.

The classroom had been noisier early in the day when they had closed their spellers and began their Christmas party. Now that the decoration of the windows and the tree was nearly complete, Miss Murphy extracted a wooden packing box made years before in the Swift River Box Company, from under her desk.

It was a kind of signal.

Miss Murphy walked up and down the rows of desks with the box crammed mightily under her large arm, and with assembly line precision, she handed out a Christmas cookie, a candy cane, and two new pencils to each child. For some of the children these things would be their only Christmas presents.

Refulgent under dim lantern light on a dark day against a dark desktop, the offerings were adored. The sugar cookie was shaped like a Christmas tree and topped with sugar Miss Murphy had dyed green with food coloring. The children noted the simple, irregular detail unique to their own, the golden edges which indicated Miss Murphy had watched them scrupulously and would not let them burn. The kids then traced the barber-pole design on the striped cane stick. They played with the pencils.

They knew Miss Murphy paid for these things with her own money, because that was the kind of person she was, and because they were used to being looked after by grownups whether they were their parents or not.

In her own insidious way, Miss Murphy was using her gifts as a teaching tool. Leading by example, by taking responsibility for Christmas in the face of her students' parents' poverty, she taught them that though gifts were scarce, generosity was not.

Evergreens were not scarce around here either, and it was their special symbol of abundance in the season of abundance. Why Daniel Shays' men in rebellion wore hemlock sprigs in their hats as a sign of liberty was probably because conifers were plentiful, and as good a symbol as anything.

The tree, at least, was not meager. They all would talk about it at home.

There had been a time when Christmas was not celebrated in the Valley, just as it was not celebrated anywhere in puritan New England, except in secret camps where debauched Colonial revelers made merry. Thanksgiving was the more important holiday. Gradually, over time, the desire to receive was greater than the impulse to give thanks.

By the 1930s, while children of struggling families pressed their noses to the fantastic train and doll displays of busy city department store windows, the rural children of New England celebrated Christmas much like their parents and grandparents. This was because of the solid, some would say insipid, drive of tradition, because stores and electric blinking Christmas lights were rare, because their towns were so remote, and because they were poor.

It was a strange kind of poverty. City folk out of a job went on breadlines and were desperate. They took work where they found it and sometimes moved from town to town in order to keep up with what they thought was something better just beyond. The rural poor were tied to their place, unless the bank manager removed them.

The Swift River Valley towns were even more rural than the rest of rural Massachusetts, partly because their geographic isolation left them alone, mainly now because of the Reservoir. Small improvements in infrastructure, roads, electricity, and services that occurred in other towns, even in the Depression, did not occur in the Valley, except as a prelude to what was necessary for construction of the Reservoir. Roads in the Valley were mainly dirt roads as they had been for centuries. A new paved highway would soon be created alongside the Valley, skirting its western edge, making travel to Athol and to Belchertown easier, but this was built for the Reservoir. Heavy equipment and new stonework would be seen along strategic areas in the Valley, but these were for the Reservoir. Men were working in the Valley, but mostly on the Reservoir. What had been "the Valley" was allowed to decay from inside.

In the most rural parts of the Swift River Valley, especially Prescott, which had no paved roads, never had telephones or electricity, the cash-poor lived. Not only did they live, but for as long as they were allowed to, they thrived. They knew how to do without.

Food was plain, simple, easily maintained in root cellars, smoke houses, ice houses and pantries rimmed with thyme and rosemary, bunches of herbs which were planted and managed to resist the severe winters and the severe summers year after year.

Christmas of 1931 was resurrected from carefully preserved rituals of the past. It may not have been joyous, but it came gently.

A cold snap before the holidays persuaded Eli and Mary to put off the annual visit to Mrs. Pratt's in Belchertown because it was so far to drive in an open wagon.

"There was a time," Eli mused over cocoa, "when five or ten miles even in the cold was nothing unusual, but things are sure different now. Such tests of fortitude don't seem necessary."

"It's just a sign of hard times, I suppose, Eli." Mary said from the window, "When people know something's wrong with the world, it's natural to grow fretful like a worried child and want to pamper yourself if you won't be pampered by others. By the times. The weather."

"By God?"

"I don't know what I mean."

"Well, I mean to pamper both me and my family, if no other person or kind force will do it."

"Let's wait and visit my mother next week. The children will have their vacation from school. Perhaps Walter could take us in his truck."

Eli sniffed, put on his coat and went to the barn.

There was little doing on the farm this time of year, and with the closing of Valley factories, there was less opportunity to work the winter months elsewhere. Eli had considered boarding by himself through the winter months in Athol or Amherst, some other town, some living town. But somewhat to Eli's amazement, there weren't always enough jobs in Athol either to support their own. It wasn't just the Valley then; there were hard times everywhere.

Perhaps Mary should be near her mother, now that Mrs. Pratt was older and even Hattie getting closer to retirement. Eli thought if something happened to him, he'd like Mary to be nearer her people.

If something happened to him? He paused, padding the horses' stalls with more hay from the loft above. That something would happen to him had not occurred to him before. He breathed deeply the warm, humid dankness of the barn to shake off the instant shiver of fear, the limp depression, a superstition evaded.

Where had it gone? The land of his dreams where he would be content and successful? It had not been the Prescott land his colonial forefathers cleared. It had not been here at his cousin's flatland farm, they wouldn't let it be. It was mostly in his mind, he thought, and he had failed to achieve it.

The barn door groaned and Harrison stood in the canyon of light. "Uncle John's here, Dad. Mother says to come in, if y'not real busy."

"No, Harry. I'm not busy. I'll be in."

Harrison paused at the coldness in his father's dark expression.

***

John Vaughn stamped his overshoes on the porch and had been settled in the Morris chair, shoes off, Eli's old sweater on him before Eli had tramped in from the outdoors.

"I know I'm not expected until dinnertime tomorrow," John said, made hearty up the Greenwich Plains road by sips of brandy from an obsolete and irrelevant hip flask, "But George was coming home this afternoon in the car, and I hate to drive in this."

"Good idea, John," Eli said woodenly, "Stay with us till Santa Claus comes...." He caught Mary's eye instantly and they both inwardly winced. They had avoided much discussion of Santa Claus this season. They had practically nothing to give to the children.

Mary had embroidered handkerchiefs for them all when the children were in bed and Eli slept soundly beside her. She knitted socks for Walter Doubleday, John, and Alonzo, who was expected tomorrow, as well as for Eli who did not expect a gift. He and Mary had agreed not to exchange gifts again this year, and he lived up to the bargain. Together, they put the oranges and nuts, and candy in the stockings, and a dime for each child.

Harrison wanted to buy Red Turner's arrowhead collection, an impressive and romantic archeological find in spite of its being kept in a shoebox under Red's bed.

John smiled, and wondered aloud if there wasn't a boy in the whole Valley that did not keep old arrowheads in his knickers, and where was the point? But no one laughed.

"Isn't funny how little we know about them, the Indians," John said, fumbling with damp cigarettes. "We know about legends and such, but I suppose most of those were made up, either by cowards coming home on a lonely farm road in the moonlight, or by liars and drunks. It's hard to really believe there was such life here once. Like those old stories about Lighthouse Hill, remember Eli? Now, could those really have been true?"

"Was there a lighthouse there once, Uncle John?" Harrison looked up from his fire-tending.

John Vaughn looked at Eli and winked, "No, son, there were these ladies," he batted his lashes, "and they all kept a house up there on the hill, back I think when your grandfather was just a boy, and the gentlemen, the rich gentlemen see, of the Valley and Amherst and other such worldly places I suppose, would come to visit them."

Mary stepped in from the kitchen, wiping her hands on her dishtowel, her brow knitted. She looked to Eli for confirmation, but he seemed only to watch Harrison push new logs into the fire.

"You see," John merrily continued, "there are some sections of big cities they call the Red-Light District, and aldermen frown on them even while they spend time in these places, and it is from the word "light" in the phrase that we have quaintly gotten the term lighthouse, because you see we were too poor to have a whole section of town for these..." John waved his hand and caught Mary's eye. Sweet Mary, as innocent as when she wore braids. He looked over to Eli, who was like a stone.

"Well," John said, "Some stories are legends, and some really happened, and we will never ever know which is which. Someday, children, this whole Valley will be a legend, and some people will wonder if it ever really existed."

This they all understood, down to Ella, who fingered her sleeve quietly.

"Once," Eli said, still looking into the fire, "There was a little girl, even younger than Ella." He looked at Ella and told the story only to her.

"She lived in the Valley years and years ago, when there was no Prescott, no Greenwich, no Dana, and no Enfield. There was no Rabbit train. This place was called Narragansett Township 4 when it was opened to soldiers who'd fought for the King in the French and Indian wars. It was their reward.

"But the Indians around here, the Nipmucs, called the land Quabbin. You've heard of the Bear's Den. Remember, I told you that Uncle John and I explored it when we were boys? North New Salem. Well, before it was New Salem, during King Philip's War when all the tribes in the area fought with the English settlers and scalped them and took some of them prisoner, a little girl was taken by the Indians. They didn't kill her, or hurt her, they might have ransomed her, I suppose, but there was nobody left to ransom her to. They were kind to her, and she lived with them until King Philip himself came to gather more tribes to join him against the English. He was a crafty leader, a ruthless chief. His name was Metacomet, really, but they called him King Philip."

Eli licked his dry lips and his eyes darted to his other children. Jenny watched Ella, with that reserved smile.

"His men had burned Deerfield, and Springfield, and thousands more Indians joined him to attack other settlements on the frontier. This was all the frontier then.

"King Philip came to these Indians' camp and he saw the white child and told the Indians here to put her to death. He wanted no captives, no whites left. But one Indian woman had taken this little child to her heart, and she hid the girl, nobody knew she'd done it. Well, after King Philip went on his way with another troop of braves, the Indian village was quiet. The husband of the Indian woman who hid the child knew nothing about what his wife did. He was a great hunter who stayed behind and didn't follow King Philip.

"He went to the place called Bear's Den to hunt. Climbing up the ledge he looked into the cave where the bears were and got ready to kill or be killed.

He stood up and raised his weapon, ready to get himself a bear...but there she was sitting among the bears. The little white girl, where his wife had hidden her. The bears didn't hurt her, and the Indians didn't hurt her. Seemed like everyone wanted to take care of this little child. The hunter took the girl back with him, and he and his wife adopted her. King Philip's War died down after a while, and this little child lived happily with her Indian parents."

Ella smiled, satisfied with a happy ending. John watched her face and sipped his quietly laced coffee.

"That's an old story. Eli, I remember how we went looking for arrowheads and bear bones to prove it was true."

"Did you find anything?" Harrison asked.

"Well, I'll tell you…" John began.

"No," Eli said.

John thought about the presents in the pocket of his wet overcoat. He had intended to present them grandly after supper, a real Christmas Eve celebration because he knew that his brother was not able to give them a grand Christmas this year, if he ever had been able. He decided to wait until they were asleep and put the things in their stockings. The presents would be from Santa Claus instead, if they really still believed in him. John looked at Eli and thought possibly they did.

***

Alonzo arrived in his wagon for suppertime and entered the house with the bashfulness of a small boy. He wore a clean flannel shirt buttoned at the neck and bore the look of someone who could not shake off the outdoors as he tried to shake the snow off his boots.

Quiet and thoughtful, he looked as strong and hearty as any young man whose way of life brought him healthy exercise and solitude, but he seemed empty inside.

He's already forgotten what it's like to be with people, Mary thought with horror.

Eli noticed it too. John only noticed with amused detachment how handsome Alonzo was, how hot he was for Jenny, and how Jenny was so unaccountably attracted to a fool like that.

John tried to compare Dickie Lewis, the little thug from Boston, with this Alonzo. Physically, John found himself taking Jenny's side with Lon. After all, the giant baboon could certainly give her a lot in that department, if he was a Vaughn. *Vaughn, hell, he's twenty-six and sees a woman probably every three months and then she's the minister's old mother.*

Does Jenny know that? Does she see something else? He wondered who was better for her and then caught himself. What did it matter who was better and who could say?

165

He admired Alonzo's independence and stubbornness. Alonzo had a lack of easy charm, a lack of wit, but nobody could tell him what to do. Like his forebears, John thought this was the true measure of a man. Unlike his forebears who were righteous men, he thought a sober mien, a serious attitude to work and religious belief had nothing to do with it, yet Alonzo had all these qualities as well. He was serious, he was hard-working, and he was a devout God-fearing man though he never went to services.

John was not aware of these other qualities, because he was unobservant of what did not interest him.

"Christmas is a-coming, the goose is gettin' fat,
Please put a penny in the old man's hat.
If you haven't got a penny, Then a ha'pn'y will do,
If you haven't got a hay-pun-ney, May God bless you...."

Ella and Harrison sang in thin children's voices. John and Eli stared into the fire, seduced and drained, while Alonzo peeked out the curtains at the snow, and Jenny watched them all contentedly.

As his gift, Alonzo brought the tree. Harrison helped him drag it in off the porch after supper.

Eli rose only a moment, then dropped back into his chair. He was inclined to help, but either sense or sudden mental fatigue or both kept him as an observer. The children wrestled with the tree and cleared the furniture and did all the work. John sat and watched with less strain, and no intention to help, a hot drink now in his hand. They all saw that Alonzo was a child again, and he lifted Ella on his shoulders to put the star on top.

Ella and Harrison were sent to bed. Jenny, Doris and her mother made molasses candy in the kitchen, as Jenny peeked into the living room more often than she should at John, Eli, and Alonzo sitting apart from each other, saying nothing.

It was a powder keg, as both Jenny and her mother knew, but neither let on that the other knew. Eli marveled that he actually enjoyed the suspense, now that he had nothing to lose.

In the end, John bunked with Harrison, Alonzo slept on the couch, successfully separated.

Jenny brought her new maiden's quilt to cover Alonzo, draped it over his body, a gesture which unsettled her parents more than a possible fight between John and Alonzo.

***

On Christmas morning, sunlight dazzled and danced off the crusty snow and made John's head hurt to look out the window. He laced his morning coffee not so secretly under the shocked gaze of his sister-in-law.

"Should you do that?" she muttered in dull-witted manner, a pancake turner in her hand.

John smiled at her. "Your pancakes are burning."

The children were surprised as John had meant them to be, pleased with the Big Little Books and puzzles he had brought them, and for Doris it was a charm bracelet, for Jenny, a ring with her birthstone.

It made them feel rich and elegant. Jenny stepped into the kitchen and leaned over John. Hugging him stiffly from behind she kissed his rough, sallow cheek and felt a traitor, even more angry that he wouldn't appease her anger by acknowledging it. He felt the muscles on her upper arms tighten.

"Thank you, Uncle John," she whispered roughly.

John stole a quick glance over his shoulder at the children in the other room and was about to scoff and talk about Santa Claus when Jenny's embarrassed expression to her mother told him not to be a fool. He grabbed her reluctant hand and slipped the ring on her finger. "A beautiful young lady should have nice things."

Mary watched them from the stove. She abused breakfast in the pan, gripped by one of her red, aged hands, stood resting her weight on one leg, and nearly cried from envy and something inside her that was gone.

After breakfast, John had presented her with gloves, which she thought peculiarly appropriate, and Eli with a can of pipe tobacco. John accepted his socks with equanimity, and Eli puzzled over his.

Late in the afternoon, Alonzo prepared to leave.

You're a coward, John Vaughn, he thought to himself. He wanted to ask Alonzo about the deed. He wanted to blurt it out, openly, and damn the ruffled feathers, damn the lack of tact, damn the always silent, iron-bound code of behavior which still stifled him even though he had lived outside the Valley for years.

He caught Eli looking at him, with a hint of malice. *He knows. He knows what I'm thinking,* John thought. *He's daring me to say something.*

But what wrath awaited him if he did, John could only guess. Eli's anger? Alonzo's fist? Or just the look of disapproval from Mary and the children's turning their heads away to avoid seeing a grownup embarrass himself, again.

Damn them all.

When Alonzo went out to hitch his horses for the trip home and refused help, but asked Jenny to carry out his parcel of jellies and bread Mary had wrapped for him, John smiled at the Christmas tree. Yes, that young fool wanted to be alone with Jenny. Poor dumb kids. Groping in the dark. Literally.

Maybe Eli didn't deserve that kind of trouble, but so what?

Funny tree. Decorated only with paper chains and homemade ornaments, John thought it the saddest thing he'd ever seen. He recalled the shapely, almost elegant trees in hotel lobbies, and the more dowdy annual forest of Christmas trees crippled by wooden cross-stands, all dewy under the pale glare of a string of electric bulbs, sold on city lots, each to be dragged home to apartments and hung with colored electric bulbs and glass balls. He wondered if the children would suspect him of lying if he told them this.

Alonzo cinched the girth and patted the mare's rump absently, watching over her back as Jenny stepped out the door in her woolen coat.

He took the bundle and set it under the seat, then took off his rough gloves and grasped Jenny's hands. She wore no mittens. She had long, thin fingers, and he rubbed them as if trying to start a fire with sticks and blew on them to warm them. "Where'd you get this ring?"

"Oh, Uncle John gave it to me."

"He gave you a ring? I wish'd I had something for you."

"You brought our tree."

He kissed her palms. He kissed her lips, only a brief, gentle touch. Clutching her hands as if he expected her to start, he was pleasantly surprised by the warmth in her eyes. She tenderly kissed his lips again, and then his cold cheek as he trembled.

"Off y'go, Lon." she whispered in her low, laughing voice, "Sun is already on the other side of the ridge. Don't be caught in the dark."

"Will y'come to me soon?" he asked. She nodded.

"I'd like to talk to you about something serious, Lon. But not now. I don't want to ruin this."

"How could you ruin it? What's the matter?"

"It's about moving away."

His eyes grew wide, "You're not moving?!"

"No, no. At least — they've not said anything. I was wondering what your plans are?"

"My plans are to stay right where I am."

"But Lon...."

"Shh. You do something for me, will you?"

She nodded.

"You keep a sharp eye on that uncle of yours. You tell me what he's up to. I don't trust him."

"Why?"

"Nothing you need to worry about. If he says anything about my farm, I want you to tell me, okay?"

He kissed her again. "I love you," he said, pulling away from the kiss. From the corner of his eye, he noticed a face in the window but he did not look towards it. Instead he filled his lungs with the frosty twilight and climbed onto the seat of his wagon. "I'll be waiting for you, Jenny-girl."

"Bye, Lon!" she called out as he pulled out of the yard, "Merry Christmas...."

He waved his arm and headed up to Prescott. Jenny stood in the yard a moment and watched the Christmas star. It was really Venus, the first pinpoint on the darkening sky to rend the pattern of day and create a new one. This star always appeared on the western horizon at twilight, but she had pretended since she was small that this was the Star the wise men followed to find the Baby.

She saw her uncle push away the curtain at the window, and she put her hands in her pockets and went back into the house because there was nowhere else she could go. Not yet.

Eli came to John at the window. John dropped the curtain quickly and smiled.

"No need to spy on her." Eli said.

"I guess you think you have that situation under control, too, do you Eli?"

"There isn't any situation. You didn't ask him about the deed to his land."

"I already created one scene in your house Eli, and I apologized for it. I won't do it again."

Eli sneered. "That's not why you kept your big mouth shut. Afraid he'll kill you?"

"The day I'm afraid of that imbecile I might as well be in my grave."

"It's not your land, John. I went to the county courthouse."

"You left the Valley all by yourself? You're getting brave."

"Your father did not put your name on the deed when you became twenty-one, and there was no will. You and I had an equal share according to the laws of this state…."

"Huh, the laws of this state be damned. The laws of this state are what's taking it away…."

"And Lon has homesteader's rights."

"What? That's ridiculous…."

Eli raised his eyebrows. "But, he's never paid property taxes. The town never bothered to go after him because they figured it was going to be the MDWSC's headache. So, the property goes to whoever pays those back taxes, before the state gets wise and grabs it for free."

"I see. Always careful, Eli. Always scheming. So, what are your plans?"

"What are yours?"

Jenny came in, stomping snow off her boots. John and Eli turned to watch her.

***

The brisk, throat-catching cold snap of Christmas became afterwards a long, wet winter. Few complained, as if sensing the dismal grayness was but another test. Few looked for cardinals to cheer them, as if it were no use.

With effort, John Vaughn slid the plate into the camera so that it snapped in. He pulled his hands back and blew on them. They felt as if they were on fire from touching the cold metal.

He felt suddenly faint, but he resisted the temptation to lean on the tripod. Professional to the point of sacrificing himself rather than the shot, he fell backwards in the snow instead. George Smith opened his eyes wide and rushed from the car where he'd been taking notes on the building.

He clumsily lifted John up out of the snow by his armpits and dragged him to sit upon the running board. John neatly turned his head and vomited.

"Oh Lord, Mister Vaughn, can I take y'home?"

John wiped his mouth on the sleeve of his topcoat and threw his head back with a clunk to rest against the car. "Get the shot, George."

"Sure?"

"Get the goddamn shot, George." John muttered placidly. George approached the tripod, took that careful, motherly look through the lens that photographers must do a few extra times to make sure they are seeing what they are seeing, and caught George Vaughn's farmstead on film. Now immortalized, the scruffy, sagging, empty house could be bulldozed.

John and his assistant kept careful notes on each building they photographed, labeling them by the names of their former owners, the assigned identification number, the date the picture was taken and the location of the site. In MDWSC archives, the building would always be known as R-010-1, George Vaughn House, Prescott, 2/29/32. This information, with a simple diagram of its proximity to the road and the nearest landmark would be included on the archival photo.

Documentation of the Valley's destruction was thorough. It amazed some locals that the State would take such care to verify the existence of what it would obliterate in a few years and they felt it was morbid.

George, who knew nothing about photography except the Brownie his Uncle Conrad used to fool with at picnics, was becoming a good shot. John Vaughn was generous with his knowledge. He genuinely liked the young man and besides, he knew he needed help. He relied not only upon George's muscles to carry the equipment up a knoll or stand in cold weather assembling the camera while John waited in a nearby store or home or the car but was depending more and more on George's ability to take good shots.

George worried about Vaughn, his bad periods, his illness. He would not have called Vaughn an alcoholic but knew this was his problem. George was polite to the point of ignoring unpleasantness, but he wasn't stupid. He had comforted himself with the thought that it was none of his business.

This time he was scared. John was obviously very ill, pale and feverish.

"I hate this place," John muttered to the sky, "Oh, how I hate this place!"

"I'm taking you home now, Mister Vaughn...."

"I am home. Son of a bitch. Look across the field, on the other side of those trees. That's where I was born! I'm so close, and I'm afraid to go there." To George's horror, Vaughn began to cry. John's shoulders buckled with noiseless sobbing, and George sat down heavily on the running board with him.

"Easy now..." George whispered and did not know where to touch him.

"Oh God, God, Papa ..." John's wet, bloodless face was quickly buried in George's arm. George patted his head with a cold bare hand.

Behind him he heard the measured slosh of the steps of a large animal in the wet snow. Alonzo rode between the properties, emerging from the ground fog like the ghost of one of his colonial ancestors. He rode with no saddle, only a plain dark blanket on the back of the large draft horse.

His rugged red face was speckled with the hard, black growth of a week-old beard, and he carried a rifle bent in the crook of his arm. George, who had carried rifles and ridden horses himself was none the less startled at Alonzo's appearance. "Oh my..." he mumbled, standing respectfully with the intention to run if need be.

Alonzo stopped the horse in front of the car. He glanced down upon John. "Y'not taking any pictures of my place."

John lifted his wet face. George looked from John to Alonzo, waiting for direction. He sat down again.

"Mister Vaughn's not himself," George announced apologetically, "I guess we're through here today."

John sniffed some woolen fibers off George's coat arm and wiped his mouth with his own. Belatedly, he came to George's rescue. "Alonzo?" he said, "George, this is my young cousin, my second cousin, Sh...sla...slonzo Vaughn. He now owns MY land. He *thinks*. But he's got no deed. He owns shit."

"Loosin' y' New York City accent, John? Take care, or y'll sound like us again."

"Give it up," John growled, "you can't win. You don't even really own this filthy place, do you? And you know it."

"Y'friend's raving," Alonzo said to George. George looked away.

John continued, "My father had no more notion of legal wills and ... property ... he was a man with a grudge... He left this land to me. To his eldest son. I have the rights of an eldest son. Where are we George?"

George looked horror-stricken. He whispered, "We're still right here, Mr. Vaughn."

"I mean with the schedule, you idiot."

"Oh. We've got the Berry store to shoot," George whispered.

"Good. Get me there...."

"I think I should take y'home...."

"Get me to the store. You can do the shot. I'll wait inside. Alonzo, does Miss Rebecca still run the store?"

"They're leaving soon." Alonzo said, "Why don't you at least have the decency to wait 'til they're gone?"

John met Alonzo's disgusted gaze. "No winter work, boy?" John asked, "Staying home with the ghosts? You look like a hermit."

Alonzo bristled, shifting, then smiled, "If that's what they'll have me be, fine."

"Will you plant again in spring?"

"None of your business."

"Alonzo, you are an idiot."

"Don't know what y'talking about, you drunken wreck. I don't want to know."

"Think of somebody other than yourself...."

"The two of you should be ashamed."

George looked off in a different direction, wishing he were over there.

"What about Jenny?" John asked.

"Could ja help me get him in the car, and we'll be outa here?" George asked Alonzo, hopeful that he wouldn't kill them both. At the mention of Jenny's name, Alonzo slid down from the animal's back, deliberately, and pulled John roughly to his feet. George leaped up and heaved open the passenger door.

"What *about* Jenny?" Alonzo dropped John onto the seat.

"What?"

"Jenny! What about her?"

"Jenny loves you, you stupid bastard," John muttered, continually rubbing his face as if to clear his mind of confusion, scrub away his headache, to obliterate the weakness. "She's crazy about you. God knows why a smart, gorgeous girl like that wants a worthless, dumb ox like you when she could have anybody—Dick Lewis for starters. Now, that kid's got guts."

Alonzo tucked John's legs neatly into the car while George scrambled for the equipment.

"Suppose I come down and carry Jenny off one night," Alonzo mused, "Carry her up to Prescott where she belongs."

"Can't even prove it's yours, I know it," John mumbled, "Eli told me. I'll get my land! George! Where the hell is he?"

As George threw himself into the driver's seat, Alonzo pushed himself away from the large black car and pulled himself up upon his horse. He and the horse stood like an equestrian statue, calmly waiting for the car to leave around the turn. George watched in the rear-view mirror as Alonzo stared at the spot in the snow where the tripod had stood, as if the piece of ground were contaminated.

At the Berry's store, which was empty of goods, George pulled John Vaughn through the door. Even in his delirium John noticed the absence of the merchant's jingling bells and looked around in suspense. He always remembered the bells above the door.

Miss Rebecca, behind the old counter still, cleaning meticulously the bare shelves behind her as if preparing for a new tenant, came quickly to them. George caught his breath and began to speak the explanation he had rehearsed in the car but Miss Rebecca seemed not to notice him. She lifted John's arm around her thin shoulders and walked him to the back room. George warmed himself a moment by the Franklin stove, stole curious glances towards the back room, and stepped back out into the damp cold to shoot the store. Like a professional, he took his time and was as fussy as possible.

Miss Rebecca placed John on the narrow bed, covering him with the quilt that had been made for her years ago.

Fifty-seven years old now, with streaks of iron gray woven into the severe dark knot of maiden hair on the top of her fine head, she still looked ten, fifteen years younger than her age, as she always would the older she became. Age which clearly showed upon her was due more to her inner sense of amused resignation at her fate than to the delicate lines etched around her warm brown eyes, or the loose skin at her slender neck, or the inevitable thickening of her waist. When John looked up at her, revived by the warmth of her quilt and the coolness of her touch, she was still Rebecca to him, a mysterious older woman who knew what he was about.

What she was to John she had never been, nor would ever be, to anyone else. For this reason, she rinsed a cloth and dabbed his sickly face, about which there was no mystery. It revealed the bare truth of his forty-six years. She removed his thin shoes and set them to dry. He rinsed his mouth, and took some water, and pulled away fretfully for a moment.

"Rebecca ..." he whispered, and wavered. She watched him with her even gaze, accepting, without opinion, with an interest that was still reserved. She waited. When it seemed too much for him, she placed her thin gentle hands upon his shoulders.

"No matter, John. No matter, my dear boy."

He opened his eyes again and traced the outline of her as she sat over him. The quilt smelled of her, and he turned his head to the slender hand upon his shoulder and nuzzled it.

She smiled at the boy he once was: charming, arrogant, restless. Gone for good. She smiled behind sudden, angry tears.

She put her lips to his cheek, and when he turned his wooden head to her, she brushed his lips.

Even without the bell, Miss Rebecca knew when the door opened. She welcomed George to the stove and asked if his work was through. He nodded.

"I think I'd better take Mister Vaughn home...."

"I think y'd better take him to the *huspital.*" she said simply. George blew a breath of frustration, followed by a shiver.

"He's really bad, ain't he?"

"Well, I think they can help him there better than his landlady could do for him, and a lot better than he could do for himself. Shall I go with you?"

He looked doubtfully at his raw, red hands a moment, then lifted his face and nodded gratefully.

"Take us to the Mary Lane Huspital in Ware, then," Miss Rebecca said, "You can tell his boss what news there is on the way back."

"Yes ma'am. By the way, I'm George Smith, from Smith's Village."

She smiled her wry, lonely benediction. "How do y'do? I'm Miss Rebecca Berry, of right here."

John looked around in a lucid moment at the bare walls of the empty room. He fingered the quilt and remembered. He said in what he thought was a loud voice:

"Watch out for Jenny. He's crazy. He's just crazy enough to kidnap her." It was the voice of a small child, and it went unheard. Miss Rebecca and George pulled him from his sweet warmth, walked and dragged him back out to the cold and to the damp, musty car. He sat cradled in Miss Rebecca's arms in the back seat while George steadied his hands on the jumping steering wheel and plowed the car down the ridge, out of the Valley, onto the unfamiliar paved roads, out to Ware.

Miss Rebecca's first trip out of the Valley. She thought of that.

"Y'should have some mittens, or gloves." Miss Rebecca said to George absently, caressing John's hair.

"Yes, ma'am, I know. That's what my ma always says."

Miss Rebecca smiled, enjoying with her usual sense of latent irony the warmth from John's body against hers, and the indulgent glance at the back of George's head, his hair that needed combing, his crooked cap. Her husband and her son, as long as the ride lasted.

CHAPTER 17

Spring came in through the back door, they said, as if it had wanted to avoid notice. Things began to grow again. The nightmare shadow on the wall became nothing but the wallpaper in the morning.

In the spring of 1932, Eli Vaughn bought a truck. He was forty-five years old. Prepared by two lessons from his son-in-law Walter, Eli drove the truck home from Palmer, where he bought it. Second-hand, it was a 1928 Ford truck and cost him several months' wages if he had a regular weekly salary. Being a farmer, he did not have a regular salary.

Buying the truck was perhaps the first thing he'd ever done without actually knowing why he did it, certainly the first thing he'd ever done without weighing the odds so carefully as to torture a man less sure about his judgment.

Mary did not know what to think of the loud, exhaust-belching truck with the consumptive rattle as it pulled into the yard with Eli waving his cap from the window, trying not to steer into the barn.

Eli honked the tenor horn and the children clambered upon the running boards.

Momentarily flushed and pleased with his triumph, Eli shook off the surprised and delighted reception of his three younger children.

He stepped up to the porch, removed his hat, and briskly kissed Mary's cheek.

"I think I understand," she said. "You've realized you can't buy the Prescott farm for back taxes, so you've gone and bought this instead. I'm at last beginning to know how you think, Eli Vaughn."

Eli swallowed, and said with sudden emotion, and great difficulty, "There's still the mortgage on this place. Even if I could get another loan to pay the taxes, the only way I could profit would be to sell the Prescott farm, pay the loan, and keep the remainder."

"And selling that land once having bought it was never the point."

"No." He never wanted to sell. To own it, oh, to own it for himself. And bought land, too, not left to him by default. It was still beyond his grasp, just as it always was.

Lon had already sent a state appraiser packing. That's what they'd heard. Could he do it, too, when the time came? It was coming. Eli wiped his face with his sleeve.

It was the time again of lilacs, sweet and unbearably poignant. They also tore at the heart. Lilacs were not native to New England but had been brought over from Europe a few generations back. These Valley lilacs were huddled in neat yards, ignorant of their progenitors, placid and adapting to their new soil. They could grow as high as trees, and multiplied from the roots with amazing heartiness, yet they were not wild things. They would never be wild things. One would never find them in the scruffy woods; they were tame and would never stray beyond the neat fence of a proper little yard.

Out beyond in the meadows, in the straggling strips of woods bordering properties or huddled in untenable designs of the land, there were other flowers, wildflowers native to the place which still stubbornly managed to propagate despite the plow, flowers that stood unforgiving time in some young girl's scrapbook, pressed to dusty nothingness, yet whose scent lingered on the very page. But lilacs. They were beloved for their tameness, their symmetrical cones of sentimental lavender in a sentimental age, their heartiness in the environment of the yard, their vulnerability beyond the fence. One had to both admire and forgive them. Their softness and their scent seemed to embody the elusiveness of the brief New England seasons. According to them, it was spring again. So, Alonzo planted again, as had Eli, as had many Valley farmers, including the newcomers, the renters like the Sullivans.

"No, not *that* way" was becoming a joke between the two families, now that the spying stage of their relationship was over. Eli gave a hand to Sullivan, who in turn gave Eli another pair of hands. Still, there was something inside made both families withhold themselves a little from each other. Like military families which are accustomed to brief friendships and an unknown destiny in an as-yet-to be named place, the renters and the Valley folk assumed a good-natured and thoroughly temporary acquaintance which would have puzzled their forebears.

The children sensed it. They imitated their parents. The population of children, as well as adults, dwindled in the 1930s, and the kids became like solitary travelers in a busy station. They were uncertain of their destiny and of how long it would take them to get there. They only knew they could not stay in the station forever.

Pulled apart from friendships that had been established for them by families even before their birth, these children now looked to schoolmates outside the Valley, or, if they were lucky, to a large family of brothers and sisters to be their friends. Others grew lonely without these and became as restless as their worried parents, as sullen as their resentful and bitter grandparents.

Doris graduated from Belchertown High School this spring and looked to Ida for an example. Ida lived quite happily beyond the Valley in her Athol apartment, with the radio to listen to while she ironed, magazines on the coffee table. They bought the table on time payments with the couch. In a sense, though they were not sitting right there in her apartment, it seemed to Doris that Ida also owned W.T. Grants, and the A & P, and Woolworth's. She certainly marched into these stores as if she owned them. Ordered herself a frappe without so much as a by your leave. Was it because she was Mrs. Walter Doubleday? Doris did not know. Ida surely wasn't Valley folk anymore.

Armed with her shorthand and typing courses learned at high school, Doris accepted an unexpected offer from her Aunt Hattie. Hattie, like Doris, may have had no man who wanted her, but she had something else almost as impressive. She had connections, and she got Doris a job as a clerk in a manufacturing plant.

Feeling more superior than she ever before had a right to, Doris announced her plans to her family and requested permission to live in Belchertown with Aunt Hattie and Grandmother Pratt while she advanced on her career.

In his new second-hand truck Eli drove her to Belchertown to get settled in her new room and start work on Monday. They all went along to see Doris off on her adventure and to visit Grandmother Pratt.

Eli, who Mary noted still had the ability to say the proper things, leaned over Mrs. Pratt's arm and said very clearly and from the chest.

"Remember how I came to you as a young man, Mother Pratt? And you took me in. Well, now I send you my girl." He patted her arm, and she grinned.

"Oh, aren't you nice, Eli." she beamed, and Mary laughed, her mother at last completely won over.

In the spring, the new cemetery for the Valley folk in Ware was dedicated and called "Quabbin Park Cemetery." The name "Quabbin" was, of course, a reference to the Enfield hills of that name, and a reference to the area's Indian history before the establishment of Narragansett Township 4, before any of the towns had materialized. Some thought it was a fitting geographical name to choose, others thought how ironic it was that the label on the cemetery of reinterred corpses should echo another extinct era in their timeline.

Mrs. Pratt spoke of visiting the new site of Mr. Pratt's grave when it opened to the public. "I'll be joining him there," she said into her lap. Hattie said Mother was tired and pulled her along to her simple bedroom on the first floor.

Eli and Mary were silent in the parlor, no longer interested in tea or gingerbread. Eli thought about his parents' new graves in that new place, about all his ancestors removed from the Prescott Hill graveyard. He had given his permission for the graves to be moved. The town clerk made up the permits. Eli felt a traitor. His father would hate him. All his ancestors would probably hate him.

Nathaniel was not his ancestor. Nathaniel was his younger brother who died from playing with fireworks when he was a boy. Eli did not remember his face.

He glanced about Hattie's parlor.

John remembered Nathaniel. He had spoken about him, a few times, nostalgically, sadly. John used to ride Nathaniel on his back because he was the oldest and Nate was the baby. Eli came in between. Eli had never ridden Nathaniel on his back. He distanced himself from Nathaniel, did not want him tagging along, did not want his opinion on clouds or stars. Did not recall now the color of his eyes.

Eli wiped his face with the back of his hand. The bell tolled three times because Nathaniel was a child. Once for a man, twice for a woman, three for a child.

He shouldn't have been playing with those firecrackers. Somebody should have been watching him.

I should have been watching him.

Eli was not sure he could ever visit the new cemetery.

Most of the Valley folk would visit the new cemetery as curiously as they might a new store, but with more timidity and with greater sadness than they ever felt in the old colonial graveyards that had absorbed the grief of centuries.

Perhaps we are growing old, they thought. *We never used to think of things like that.*

"We never used to have the State come tell us where we shall be buried," one old man angrily mumbled, echoing the unspoken, even unformed sentiments of the others.

It was also the spring Jenny began to look to her own future. Her parents' silence depressed and disappointed her. They could not be relied upon. They were cowards.

Jenny's teachers in Belchertown High School noticed an unexpected spark of intelligence in Doris Vaughn's younger sister. Some of her teachers began to encourage her.

They knew they shouldn't have, after all, it was hard times, and her family lived in one of the doomed towns being taken by the state, and surely her farmer father would have no money to send this girl along to college.

It was irresponsible of them, they felt, to encourage her beyond her place in life. With guilt they did it anyway.

Jenny watched Doris unpack in her new room upstairs in Grandmother Pratt's house while Harrison and Ella explored the neighborhood.

"I'll be earning $12.15 a week," Doris said, "I'm going to buy a radio like Ida's, first thing. I'll have it right up here in my room."

Jenny watched her unpack the clothes and carnival souvenirs from the paper bag she saved from the Athol Woolworth's.

"Second thing I'm getting is a real suitcase. Just glad nobody saw me with this paper bag. I'm going to travel all over like a tourist. Ida says she'll take me to Old Orchard Beach in Maine when she and Walter go sometime."

Jenny was not listening, heard half of what Doris told her. She struggled with her own dilemma. She wanted very much to confess to Doris that her teachers were talking about college.

Ridiculous. But still, they were supposed to know what they were talking about. They were part of the trinity of authority in her life, her parents, her church, her teachers. The teachers were the only ones *not* to lead by example, but to feed her facts remote from her life, giving her invisible dimension.

"With my money I get I'll buy you younger children presents. Don't worry about that."

She said nothing to Doris.

Jenny walked home from the bus by herself on Monday. She stopped by the village school before going home. The children were just being dismissed. Harrison ran off with some boys and Ella came to her.

"I came to visit Miss Murphy, Ella. Could you go on home? I just have to talk to her for a little bit."

"Can I wait?"

"Oh, all right, if you want to."

Miss Murphy tied up her satchel. She looked up and smiled at Jenny and came to her for a hug. Jenny bent down to embrace her, ruffled at this un-teacher-like behavior.

"How are you, Jenny?"

"Fine, Miss Murphy. How are you?"

"I'm always fine. I wouldn't have it any other way."

"I was wondering if I could get your opinion on something."

"Go ahead."

"Some of my teachers have been telling me I should apply to college."

Miss Murphy did not answer. She looked out the window.

"It's flattering, but I know it's not possible," Jenny said, watching her.

Miss Murphy sighed and sat down behind her desk.

"I guess I should forget it."

"Jenny, wait. Don't leave yet." Miss Murphy said, "It is possible. It's not practical, and it's not easy, but it is possible. It would mean a lot of work and worry. It would mean anxiety to finish what you start, and it would affect your whole family, not just you."

"I just don't know much about it."

"I'll tell you Jenny, I've seen many children come into my classroom and go out into the world. I'm tired of helping them to settle for what's best. For once I'd like to have the courage to tell one of them to reach for the moon. So, I'm telling you. I think you should want more. I think it's good to want more."

"What should I do?"

"Think carefully about what you want to do, and what you want to study, what you want your life to be. When you're ready, I'll help you find a way to get there. I promise you that."

"So…it's really all up to *me*, then?"

Miss Murphy smiled at her fear, her awe, and her humility. "Yes. Isn't that something?"

***

It was in the spring that Uncle John, after nearly a month in the hospital, returned to Eli's house to live. At first it was a temporary arrangement, a couple weeks to rest and a few hesitant walks in the damp, fresh backyard before going back to work. Mary fussed over him in her no-nonsense, efficient way. It was eventually accepted more than decided that John Vaughn should stay permanently.

Eli regarded it as a wry victory. If only his parents could see. John came back to him. He would not return to his parents, but he returned to him.

John feared to be anywhere alone. Something slipped askew in his pretend bravado, and John Vaughn would never be quite himself again. He aged quickly in the way very aged people desire comfort, warmth, and not too many decisions to make.

"He likes the attention he's getting," Eli muttered to Mary in the kitchen.

"Of course, he does, who wouldn't?"

"Sometimes I have the feeling he's become my father. He's an old man, Mary."

On sunny afternoons John sat out on the front porch facing the southern sky, bundled in his sweater, his tie neatly knotted under his sagging chin. He did not recall much about his illness, which had developed into pneumonia, only that he regained consciousness in the hospital after two days.

He was a quiet, dutiful patient, a quiet houseguest, and Eli doubted whether or not he still had gained consciousness.

Jenny watched him, brought him tea without speaking to him, waited for him to pump her about Lon's plans, but he did not. He only looked at her with sad, rheumy eyes. Only once did he say something curious, suspicious.

"If you were my daughter…if you were mine…." He shook his head emphatically, disgustedly, as if he felt he had made his point.

It was the spring Miss Rebecca left the Swift River Valley for the second time in her life; this time it was forever. She mused only that it had been a long time coming.

Those who remembered her were discreetly and distantly sympathetic when they heard her brother was taking her away. She wouldn't be able to cope, poor thing, they said.

Miss Rebecca accepted her fate as squarely as she accepted a room off the kitchen in her brother's new house in Amherst. Not quite of retirement age, she considered taking a job at first, but came to realize that with few jobs for younger people there was little chance of her obtaining one. Perhaps it wasn't fair anyway. Besides, no job here would be the niche she had in the Prescott Hill store. That had not been a job to her as much as it was a purpose, her role in the quiet community, which like her proprietary brother, seemed always to hold her back.

She accepted that, too. Not timid, or lazy, yet she saw from an early age what the Lord seemed to expect from her, and she was dutiful.

With similar obedience, she arranged her samplers, her personal things, and her maiden quilt in her new corner of the world. She would make do. Her brother's irritable gallantry in bringing his older sister into his marriage, into his new house, into his new life because it was his responsibility as a male Berry to take care of her, was due really more to the fact that he needed her. Her stoic application to mundane situations was his bedrock. Miss Rebecca realized it even if he didn't, and this made up for a lot.

Placing his long-suffering sister next to his long-suffering wife like heavy bookends to support his life, he went to work in the real estate office, pleased with himself at last.

Miss Rebecca did miss the Valley. Not a farm girl, but still a country woman, the summer goldenrod along the shaggy ridge meant a great deal to her, and she surreptitiously collected lady's slippers and Queen Anne's lace when nobody noticed. She pressed them in her Bible, which was her only book, but discarded the dry things afterwards, scraping crunchy petals out of Leviticus as if the idea had been blasphemy.

Once, as a young woman on a clear, late July day under a deepest blue sky, she stood upon the ridge looking over the blue hills toward the east. She glanced around her a moment to make certain she was alone. Satisfied, she quickly unbuttoned the top three buttons of her shirtwaist, released her long, straight black hair from its bondage, slipped a fan of goldenrod behind her ear, stuck a stalk of wild grass between her teeth, put her hands upon her slim, boyish hips, and let the breeze make love to her. She kept her heavy, thick glasses on, because without them she couldn't see, which was not romantic, but it was practical. Both the romantic and the practical fought within Miss Rebecca to win out; that was the only real struggle in her otherwise clear conscience.

She learned diplomacy early, not only with fussy older people whose praise she was never to win, but with herself. She cleverly compromised, using the practical like a shield, so she could keep the romantic to herself.

Now she watched the passing roadside from the car window on the trip to Amherst, partly to enjoy the unaccustomed view, and partly as if memorizing the way back home, so that she could find it again by herself.

Other than all this, and the growing sand pile outside the tunnel at Shaft 12 in Greenwich Village, it was a spring much like any other.

CHAPTER 18

After the lilacs came the roses, the lilies of the valley, iris and yarrow. Soon vines of morning glories would tangle themselves over everything they touched. Annuals were planted, one more season. What would happen to the perennials? The very word meant enduring.

Summer arrived and the river valley humidity returned. Children splashed in Pottapaug Pond, and Walker's Mill Pond, and Greenwich Lake. The Vaughn children said goodbye to the Sullivan children.

Mr. Sullivan had grown tired of his dream and Mrs. Sullivan tactfully suggested a produce market in Holyoke that a friend of her cousin's owned. He could get a job with regular hours to keep him out of trouble and still be around vegetables. Sullivan didn't see the correlation but conceded the Greenwich farm wouldn't be here forever anyway and they might as well move now.

Mary sent Jenny over with a bouquet of zinnias. "My mother says good luck, and it was nice to have you for neighbors."

Mrs. Sullivan took the fist of flowers with awkwardness and surprise. She touched Jenny's shoulder. "Well, isn't this nice? Well, thank your mother for me, Jenny." She looked towards the Vaughn home, and then let her eyes wander over their own rented farm on which they were unable to make a living.

"It must have been really nice here once, in the olden days," she offered.

Jenny did not answer, was in fact busy for days afterwards still trying to think of one.

While the Sullivans moved hopefully to Holyoke.

Holyoke, the industrial city of cavernous brick mills and brick tenements, and rows of stagnant, green canals westward on the Connecticut River, also contained a rather large Irish Catholic population. Mrs. Sullivan hoped to get her children back into parochial school among their own kind. She liked her Greenwich neighbors, they were good people she confessed to her husband, but the thought of the coming destruction and the natives' unspoken, seeming denial of it depressed her. When their overloaded automobile rumbled through South Hadley and approached the bridge over the Connecticut River to Holyoke, Mrs. Sullivan felt as if she was leaving a sick room. Her sympathy was genuine but the relief that it was not her was exhilarating, and the ethereal beauty of the landscape she left was not as comforting as the solid picture of a brick city. Holyoke was more beautiful to her.

There was another inducement to their exodus. A New Hampshire innkeeper who heard of bargains to be had came to the Valley to seek a suitable building for his new dining room extension.

In the Sullivan house, labeled on the official photo John Vaughn and George Smith took as the Cy Holt Farm, as if the Sullivan era had never occurred, the New Hampshire man found not only a suitable hunk of dining room, but a whole new wing for his expansion. A classic of New England colonial structure, though anyone not with an architect's eye and heart for the detail of colonial carpentry would say it was just an old house.

His contractor arrived and hauled his purchase away.

The Vaughns were fascinated to see one of the house movings up close, and anxious that this very graphic demonstration should happen so near. There were really very few house movings, most buildings were just destroyed.

That Shaft 12 excavation nearby was a sign of the immense engineering work being done of course, but the little house made an even bigger impact on them.

Mary slowly pulled her wash in, dropping the shirts and sheets laconically into the basket as she eyed the busy men with their ropes and jacks, treading on the flowers around the foundation. Jenny and Ella stood by their mother with propriety, also plucking laundry from the line to cover their curiosity. Harrison and Eli, being males, could stand upon the property line and gaze unabashed and somewhat admiringly at the trick.

Suddenly, Grandmother and Grandfather Holt drove up in a strange car. Cy Holt, their son, whose wife had gone to school with Mary, drove the car and hid behind the brim of his hat in the driver's seat watching his parents step out. He fingered the dash dials as if to look busy and nodded briefly to Eli. The Vaughn children looked for Nance, Charlie, and Jane, but they had not come.

Old Mr. and Mrs. Holt had resented their son's churlish early selling out and would give him no peace until he allowed this last visit. The old man knew the house moving would be today, and he had a certain dramatic flair which might have put him on the stage had he been less successful a farmer. With a hand trowel, he uprooted a clump of yellow irises near the left foot of the supervisor. Embarrassed, the crew chief excused himself and went to have slug of coffee from his thermos in the cab of his truck.

The old man took his time, making a great effort, scooping up as much of Greenwich as his handkerchief would hold. Mrs. Holt stood back, not brave enough to approach the heavy equipment. She said that she could get a better look at her house from the road. After only a moment, she turned in quiet tears to the car and would not look again.

Helpless disappointment tore her lined, sensitive face, and her round, pale blue eyes fitfully gave in to anguished tears.

Jenny watched, more captivated and horror-stricken by the old woman's childlike expression of helpless heartbreaking than by the sight of the house being moved. Jenny burst into tears. Mary looked at her and dropped her hand upon her daughter's shoulder, shaking her awkwardly, shocked by this weird behavior. "Stop it, Jenny. What's the matter?"

Ella jumped and stared at them, devastated to see Jenny so strange and inconsolable, fearful at what to do, what was her place, watching her mother grow angry to control her own nervousness.

Jenny shook off her mother and ran, like someone who knew how to run, with her shoulders hunched and her arms working from the shoulder to make her get where she was going.

Eli only noticed in amusement that she ran like a boy, and asked Mary where Jenny was off to.

Jenny herself didn't know, but after a while dropped her frantic, bleary-eyed charge to a more enduring pace. She slowed to a jog and kept it up like a stoic marathon runner until she had reached Quabbin Lake. Dick Lewis stopped her.

He threw himself against her, otherwise she would not be stopped, and pulled her off the road. She struggled, frightened in his grasp, then angrily recognized him.

She pushed him scornfully away, and breathing heavily, leaned over to cough. She swallowed and wiped her tear-streaked face with her small, useless regulation ladies' handkerchief, and lowered herself to the grass.

Dick watched her. Then he quietly sat down beside her. "Something's wrong?"

"Shut up."

"I was coming to see you, Blue Eyes. I wondered how you were."

"You can stop calling me that."

She caught her breath, and drew her knees up, making sure her dress covered her.

"So, what is it?" he asked, frowning at her covered knees.

"House moving."

"Your house?"

"No, fool," she muttered, irritated now. "Right next door."

"Oh."

"Wish I didn't live here. I wish I came from the city or someplace where I wouldn't care."

"They'd care. Nobody likes to get pushed around."

"You don't care. You don't want to go back home to...."

"Scituate."

"Sitchoo-it," she echoed. "Sounds like a swear-word."

That broke him up.

"Is it an Indian word?"

"Damned if ...I don't know."

"What it's like? Is it near the ocean?"

"That's right."

"Never been to the ocean. What's it like?" She hurriedly brushed errant tears with her fingers while he watched. She knew he was excited to be with her; he knew that she was embarrassed to cry in front of others.

"That depends on what kind of mood I'm in. Usually I'm glad it's behind me."

"Leaving because you want to is different."

"Yah. I'd like to see new places. I'd like to join the Navy and see the world, like they say. Except I don't like being bossed around."

"Don't y'ever want to have a home?"

"Probably when I get to be old, yeah."

He waved his hand, gesturing to the road, to the hills behind them, to Greenwich beyond. "I'm sorry about all this," he said. "I like working on the reservoir. Sorry to have to say that, but it's true. It's a better job than I thought it would be. Even living with my brother is better than I thought it would be."

"I thought you were living with a family in Smith's Village."

"Rawg moved out of the hotel to a rented house there in Enfield, and he asked me to move in. Got my own room; how's that for high living?" She didn't answer.

"Look, come with me for a little walk," he tugged her elbow and she shook him off.

"What for?"

"I want to show you something." He laughed at her expression, "You prissyface. I want to show you my work. Have you ever seen the construction up close? Bet you haven't."

"I don't care to." she pulled herself up.

"Chicken."

She turned, swiped her arm and slapped him across the face as hard as she could. He stumbled but would not let himself fall, and straightened, with surprise and a red mark on his face.

"You got me good, didn't you?" Dick said it softly, without a trace of anger. That small thing captivated her. She searched his gray eyes and could not think of a reply, a remark, an apology.

"It's best to face things, Jenny. I learned that when I was still a little kid. It doesn't make things any better, but it gets you ready for them."

She marveled that it sounded, even in his atrocious accent, like the first sensible thing anybody had said to her in a long time. It was how she had always felt, as if she had always been guarding against something. Maybe this was it, and maybe she could be ready for it.

She tucked her stinging hand into the other one behind her back and eyed him impatiently and nodded. She fell in step with him when he turned. They walked apart down the road towards Shaft 12. Her sense of dread led the way.

Other furtive inspections had taken place when the work crews went back to their lodgings. The shaft, the baffle dams and spillways were visited with curiosity, fascination, and dread by the remaining families. A few shot photos less precise than John Vaughn's, made mediocre by imperfect light, too careless posing, and shaking hands.

Jenny would not have thought of taking a picture of the shaft entrance, even one with her standing in front. Almost as if by regulation most photos of the landscape or architecture of the Valley had somebody planted in front of it. A pretty backdrop was the only purpose a cornfield or front porch served. The person in knickers, the running board of the Ford, the radio on the table would identify the subject and give it perspective much later that an ordinary hillside or pond lacked. After all, an ordinary hillside or pond was timeless, could not identify an era.

Unless of course the hillside or pond was shortly to disappear.

The tunnel, the baffle dam needed no such lending of chronological perspective; the subject standing alone by itself was its own chronologer, occasion and reason for being. The people in the photo, fighting for balance on the slope of riprap, were pointless.

Dick and Jenny came near to the site, a muddy battlefield, heavy machinery parked randomly about like a herd at rest.

There was no movement from the makeshift office-shack, none from distant outbuildings of former cottages. Dick seemed to have no suspicions they would be disturbed and clamped his rough hand on the crusty blade of the bulldozer and pointed to the shaft. It didn't look like a grand construction project yet, just sort of a mess.

"You should see the guys come out of there," Dick said, "all covered with dirt. All over their faces, just their eyes bugging out, the only white spots. Did you grow up here?"

"Partly here and partly in Prescott. That's where we're from."

"This is my brother's dream. I wonder what he'll do when it's over."

She drew a sharp breath and looked up at the dwindling light in the sky. "When it's over."

"Guess you think it's the end of the world, don't you?"

"I don't know. Yes." She hugged herself.

"Well it's not the end of the world. People say that over everything... the Depression, anything. Do you know, in the year 999, all the people in Europe, and all throughout the Christian world people gave up deeds to their lands, and money and jewels because they thought the world was going to end? Just because they couldn't imagine counting to a thousand? People went to church on December 31st, the last day of the year, what they thought was the last day ever, and waited for Judgment Day. The bells rang, everybody fell down on their knees. Nothing happened. So, it's midnight and the year 1,000. They were so relieved they started building all sorts of cathedrals to give thanks. Judgment Day had to be postponed."

She looked at him incredulously. "You read?"

He rolled his eyes and slapped his hat on his knee. "Thank you very much, yes I do. Jeez, what do you think of me anyway? Do you read?"

"Yes, but I don't know history like that. My grandfather left us some books, Shakespeare and science. Poetry. I know lots of poetry."

"I hate poetry. Look, my mother used to think the world was ending every time we got a new border that drank or was divorced. We had a lady once who smoked cigarettes and made money in dance contests. My mother said it was like the Fall of Rome. Still took her money, though. I figure nothing can be the end of the world as long as somebody else can make a buck off it."

"You had a boardinghouse? That must have been interesting."

"Why? Mostly it was just me sleeping in the front parlor on a cot because Mother thought I didn't need a room or a bed of my own. I've got both, now. Rawg may be a pain..." he looked at her and finished mashing a cigarette with which he'd been playing, to oblivion. "My father left home years ago, just left one day. I don't even remember him. Mother was pretty hard to get along with after that, real moody and, well, she had troubles. I guess I didn't make things easy for her. Rawg sent us money. He's not such a bad guy."

"He seemed very nice. I mean when he came to dinner with Miss Atkinson."

"Rawg came to dinner at your house?"

"Yes, didn't you know?"

"He comes and goes. I know he's been seeing Martha Atkinson a lot. Huh. I thought you didn't take reservoir workers to your house to eat."

"I didn't take him, my uncle did."

"Oh, is your last name Vaughn? I think I met your father once."

"How close was your house from the ocean?"

"High tide or low tide?"

"That close?" She smiled a little, and cocked her head towards the construction site, as if seeing the ocean there.

"Sure," he looked her over good now that she had taken her eyes off him. "My mother grew up in that house. Everything was nicer in the olden days. That's what they always say. Hey, you have Egypt Road and Egypt Brook in Prescott? Well, in Scituate we have a section of the town called Egypt, and an Egypt Beach...."

"Hah, Egypt Beach...."

"And an Egypt Beach Road...oh, and something else. I've never told anybody this, so you have to keep quiet. Y'know that "Old Oaken Bucket" song? The well is in Scituate. No kidding. We've got an Old Oaken Bucket Pond, where the well is, and an Old Oaken Bucket Road. D'you see? D'you see why I don't want to go back there?"

She laughed.

"If you don't believe me, I'll take you there some day if you want."

"I'm sorry for that." She gestured to his cheek, without touching it, suddenly looking so stricken that he took his cap off in agitation and swiped a hand through his blond hair. It was longer than when she had last seen him, slightly curling now and losing that close-shaved haircut made him look less like an inmate. A thin shadow of rosy sunburn colored his face and neck, more vivid on his pug nose.

"That's all right. I guess this didn't help much. I'll take you home," he said, and paused as if the thought just occurred to him, and wordlessly offered her a cigarette, and just as silently stuffed the pack away when she shook her head. Now he could tug on her arm briskly, as if it were businesslike, and she could let him guide her unnecessarily around a puddle as they began the march home.

"Thanks. You don't have to walk me home."

"I am sorry about all this, and I admit I like the work, but I won't do it if you don't want me to."

"It'll be built with or without y'help, Dick."

"I know. But, I don't want to have any part of it, if it's gonna make you feel badly at me."

"I don't care what you do. Can't see you throwing a job away for no reason."

"See what I mean, as long as somebody makes a buck off it, it can't be the end of the world."

"Just the one you knew. Maybe this did sort of help."

"Yeah? Good. I like you and I don't want you to think I'm a thug."

"I don't think you're a thug."

"You thought I don't read."

She laughed. He reached for her, but she pulled back with such a splintering of emotions in those eyes of hers and mostly something leaden inside that he nearly choked when he said, "Fine…but don't count me out."

She started a new pace somewhere between marching and running.

"I'm still walking you home."

"No, you're not."

He charged after her and ran alongside. "I said I'm walking you home, I'm walking you home! Slow down, you're in better shape than me."

They trotted in tandem, a yard or two apart.

The Holts left like the bereaved from funeral, and the Vaughns went indoors to maintain in discreet sympathy and to recover from what they had just seen.

Alonzo rode into the yard from the back fields, not taking the road almost as if he knew he would meet with the harbinger there. Dropping from his mount, the slow, surefooted and massive draft horse he was somehow becoming to resemble, he saw Jenny walk into the yard.

She giggled, "Get lost, you pest!"

"We're not to the door, yet."

It was someone he didn't know. He had that accent.

"The old oaken bucket…the iron-bound bucket…the moss-covered bucket at that hung in the well…." Jenny was singing and trying to walk in front of the boy, while he was trying to step in front of her and they took turns taking the lead.

"Stop it, stop it, stop it…!" the boy giddily shrieked, which made Jenny laugh more.

They both stopped when Alonzo called sharply, "Jenny!"

The boy put his hands on his hips. Looking at the house he said to her, "I know where we can go tomorrow," he puffed. She stopped and turned to him for a moment, whether to catch her breath or to acknowledge this last, Alonzo didn't know. They were both red-faced and out of breath.

Alonzo met them at the front porch.

"What do y'want?" Alonzo said to Dick Lewis. He was struck at once that Lewis and Jenny were the same age. Dick met Alonzo's glare with calmness.

"He's come to talk to Uncle John," Jenny said.

Though he did not remove his eyes from Alonzo's, Dick marveled at how quickly she lied.

Eli stepped laconically out onto the porch, hearing voices.

"'Lo, Lon, didn't hear y'come up," Eli said, watching his daughter and the boy who stood beside her in the yard.

"'Lo, Eli," Alonzo said, "Know this kid?"

"Take it easy, Lon," Eli said, "Where y'been, Jenny?"

"Out walking. This is Dick Lewis. He's come to speak to Uncle John."

Dick Lewis. Alonzo knew the name. He had brooded about it since John mentioned it.

"Would'ja like to come in, Dick?" Eli said.

"No, sir," Dick said calmly into Alonzo's face, "I'd just like to give Mr. Vaughn a message, but if he's not home...."

"He's home, son. Let me call him." He put his head briefly into the screen door, whispering something to Mary.

"Well," Jenny said, hesitant and feeling foolish, "See you, Dick. Late with my chores...."

"How 'bout I come by next Sunday afternoon and we go for a walk?" Dick said it in Alonzo's direction, and braced himself as Alonzo fell off the porch and landed against him, shoving him to the ground.

"You're not going anywhere with her."

"I didn't ask you."

It was only an instant. Eli pulled himself away from the screen door and grabbed Alonzo from the back, Dick scrambled from his knees and charged at Alonzo, throwing his shoulder into Alonzo's stomach.

Eli stepped between them and John came cautiously out onto the porch saying, "Stop it! Stop it, now!"

Dick stepped back, instantly composed. Alonzo took a moment longer, and finally mumbled a ragged "Excuse me," to the older men and put a hand on Jenny's shoulder to lead her into the house.

She stood firm, but said to him gently, "I've got chores, Lon. I'll be in in a minute." She threw a backward, quizzical glance at Dick, and walked around the house to the barn.

Eli put a hand on Alonzo's shoulder and silently turned him to the house. John wiped his face with his handkerchief and waited for Dick to give him his attention.

"What did you want to tell me?" John asked. "Did Roger have a message for me?"

"He says hi."

***

"Be careful here, Lon," Eli said to him as they sat, tense and worn out in the dim living room. "You can tell anyone you want t'go to blazes on your farm, but not here. I don't want trouble with the State people."

"You can get into trouble being timid with these people, too, Eli."

Jenny entered. Alonzo stood. "I want to court Jenny. I'm asking your permission. Now you know how it is."

Mary looked at him doubtfully, hushed Ella's noisy table setting and folded her arms over her stomach. Eli exchanged glances with her—the sort of glances shared by married couples where volumes of feelings and emotional half-logic can be compressed in the glint of an eye.

They admired Alonzo's hardworking stubbornness, as long as it had nothing to do with them.

He dared them to refuse, to be sarcastic, to hurt his feelings.

They pitied his comic formality. No one asked permission to court anymore. No one "courted" anymore, they went on dates until they either decided to get married or else decided not to.

Eli licked his lips and stood. "Thanks for being so plain about it, Lon," Eli said, "But Jenny's too young to think about that just now." Yes, too young. That's good.

"She's only sixteen. You know that. I want her to finish high school. Y'understand, Lon."

Alonzo looked down upon them without flinching, and graciously nodded. It was acceptable, in part.

"Then may I take her...."

"When high school's through, I'm going to college..." Jenny interrupted.

"I think that's a good idea, Jenny," Uncle John said from the Morris chair. She glanced at him, as if to brush him off and not seek his support. *Nuts to him.*

"I think we're about ready to eat, aren't we, dear? Lon, stay to supper, will you?"

"Thanks," Alonzo waved them away, dismissing John with a warning look of disgust, "I've got t'get back. I'll be around, Jenny. We can talk about this some better time. I wanted y'to know how I feel. So now you know how it is."

He was hurt at the smooth dismissal of his proposal and would have been happier if Eli had gotten angry and thrown him off the property. Then he would have an excuse to come back for Jenny. They could elope. That would be fine. This was too calm, too polite.

That is the problem with us, he thought, as he rode back up to his Prescott farm in the afternoon shadows, *all the blood and thunder has been bred out of us. We're so damned accepting and proud and stiff and closed up. No wonder outsiders can walk all over us.*

Alonzo knew only stilted, simplistic history from the schoolhouse. He knew that the men who came to settle here were adventurers, dissidents, zealous, fanatical fighters and seekers of freedom and fortune. Like a fire whose embers have died down, New England was now no longer the rugged outpost of outcasts and self-proclaimed saints, the touchstone of American thought and character, but a quaint, cozy, home-and-hearth caricature of itself. Like a Longfellow ballad it was rhythmic, measured, sedate, and orderly, and obsolete.

It did not occur to Alonzo that Jenny had not accepted him, only that her father had the normal objections. It also did not occur to Jenny that she had not accepted him.

Eli sat down to supper feeling sick. Alonzo had acted with bravado over his land, and that was fine. That was his business. Every man had a right to make an ass of himself. Eli wished he had brought up the subject of back taxes not being paid. That would have taken care of the fool.

But Jenny was not Alonzo's property. What was he thinking? What were they both thinking? He looked at Jenny. She paid very close attention to her food. What was she hatching? His children ate their supper, his wife wiped the rim of the milk pitcher. He caught John's eye. They said nothing.

Well, as it should be. Eli took a deep breath and smoothed his napkin over his lap. It was all right not to say anything. It was most acceptable. Eli had grown up in a society where not to curb expressions of feelings was unmanly, and unwomanly. It was proper not to expose oneself emotionally. He looked at Jenny. He wondered how she had been encouraging Alonzo. That big ox certainly never had an idea on his own.

Jenny fought the quick blush on her tanned cheek unsuccessfully and busied herself smashing carrots with her fork gently and methodically. Mary stole glances at her daughter over her own food. Mary, caught between admiration for Jenny's unexpected handling of so vigorous a man, and her foolishness at letting him get so close to her, yet wondered even more if she were really serious about college.

No, it was just a ruse, teasing a man who was clearly in a position to be teased. Alonzo had accepted it more or less graciously because he was a willing victim of courtship. They were playing out a game, and the poor fool was trapped by its rules. Now, if he were Jenny's husband, she would never be able to handle him.

College. It was ridiculous, of course. They had no money for college. Nobody did, not now. She was naïve to the ways of the world. That other world out there.

John also watched Jenny. Where had she gotten the notion? John wondered if the Lewis boy had anything to do with it. Roger was college-educated. Perhaps Roger intended to send Dick, too. Maybe that's where Jenny was getting her ideas.

There was no money, so that would end it.

Ella, usually less in command of herself and allowed to be as the youngest, knew Jenny would not mind her questions. Though Ella had learned to be quiet at the dinner table, she slid into bed that night with the satisfaction that Jenny would share the event and give her interpretation on the world.

They had always talked a little before falling asleep, nothing talk about friends and what would they do if they were rich, but tonight Jenny didn't notice her. She lay on her side, her back to Ella. Her eyes grew wet watching the night stars out the window.

Ella stretched herself under the gathering warmth of the familiar ritual. Her body relaxed and she grew limp, and her legs explored the space that was hers.

She touched her forehead to the back of Jenny's neck and wrote her name in block letters on Jenny's flannel back, but her sister was not playing the game with her.

"Jen, are you going to college?"

Jenny did not answer. Her throat hurt.

"What did Lon mean?" Ella stroked Jenny's arm and could feel the tension in her.

Jenny swallowed, "I shouldn't have said that about college. That was stupid, stupid. Go to sleep now, Ella."

"Don't marry *Lon*, Jenny."

"Not marrying anybody tonight. Go to sleep."

"I mean really."

"Ella, please. Cut it out."

Ella pulled slowly away, in drowsy disappointment. "Don't be mad, Jenny."

Jenny swiped the covers off herself and leapt away from the bed, striding to the far wall for no reason. She threw her glance out the window. She had revealed her dream, and thereby let her guard down. "Sick of all of you. Wish I was a thousand miles from here, by myself."

Jenny sat down on the foot of the bed, too tired now to pace.

She would not face Ella's hurt expression. She could imagine it and that was enough. Jenny had always tried to explore safe footsteps for Ella to follow and control her easy path, like the first soldier through a minefield. Control was satisfying, but exhausting, and it was harder and harder to find. She did not know where she was going now.

"I'm tired." she murmured to her lap, "I'm just tired, Ella."

Sometime after she heard the sound of Ella's even breathing in sleep, Jenny realized that she had been sitting there, stiffly, a long time.

Jenny crawled to the pillow. She could not defend Alonzo to Ella. She could not even explain to herself. Something stirred, always. She did not know what it was, but the unnamed feeling complicated her desire for him.

Lord, what now? It was more of a demand on herself than a prayer and interrupted by the memory of the hard look in Alonzo's dark eyes, by the rough fresh growth of beard on his handsome face. It was an adult face, full of moods and longings, not impish like Dick's. He was not like Dick at all. Alonzo already knew so much about Jenny. That was a comforting thing. It was half the distance of being loved.

Jenny looked out the window. Uncle John had crawled out a window when he was young, to run away, to make his future. She slipped out of bed again to touch the cool windowpane, staring at the blackness outside.

CHAPTER 19

"Jenny...." Eli said over his shoulder as she passed him in the barn.

He pulled his hat brim lower and peered at her from underneath it. She swung an empty milk pail, touching it against her hip.

"You know this nonsense with Lon..." he gestured with his shoulders as if to both describe and settle the matter.

She did not want to talk to her father.

"Yut, I know." she said, and stepped out into the warm sunlight.

"Jenny, I'm not through...wait." She stopped, her back to him. "I'm glad you didn't...I'm glad you let Lon's words pass."

Jenny turned. "I didn't know he was going to say that."

"I'm glad of that, too. He's confused about some things, our Lon. Especially about that farm. State's going to get him for back taxes if he doesn't...."

"State's going to get all of us."

"What?"

"State's going to fill the town up with water. Haven't you thought about that?"

"That...matter isn't over, Jenny. Don't worry...."

"I'm not worried. Not anymore."

"This isn't what I wanted to talk about." Eli rubbed his forehead. "Jenny, I'm running out of time to talk to you. You're growing up. I want you to use your head about things...."

"Which college are you choosing?" John emerged in the doorway, throwing his arm around her waist. She writhed involuntarily, like a tremor. John, rebuffed and repentant, stiffly put his hands behind him.

Eli turned back to his work. Jenny waited a moment, then walked away.

"She's a pretty girl." John offered, not waiting for her father to agree. "Too pretty for Lon, though."

"Shut up, John!" Eli threw his hat to the ground.

John started.

A car pulled into the yard.

"Oh, there's, there's Smith. We're shooting right down the road today, would'ja believe?"

George Smith carried John Vaughn's camera over to the abandoned farm, and John wandered around the tall grass in his shirtsleeves while George loaded the film plate.

On this warm, late summer day, the light was perfect. The light was so perfect.

John stepped up to the tripod, hunched into the camera, placed his eyeball to the lens and stuck his tongue out of the side of his mouth. Inevitably a moment of epiphany, only another moment of epiphany, one of many he beheld behind the lens, where things were always clearer. The empty house framed by an outbuilding, a bit of sky, and the shaggy field beyond. He clicked the shutter, straightened himself slowly, deliberately and with satisfaction, and waved to George to remove the plate and set up again. Then John took a cigar from his vest pocket and walked around the property as he performed the slow business of lighting the cigar.

He walked around to the back, brooding thoughtfully on the detail of the barn and the land. Where last year lay a productive field, now only a vast lot remained, where encrusted lumpy furrows sprouted wild grass. Two or three bastard stalks of corn stood withering in the grass, the struggling orphan progeny of former crops.

"I would have made one lousy farmer, Papa."

All the myriad shadows fell in waves, as orderly as a woman smoothing down a sheet to make a bed. It had been a hot summer, but the dog days were past and western Massachusetts was breathing its first hint of September. In another month, the earth would begin to cool. For now, everything was simple, static, and seemingly permanent.

Standing knee-deep in the grass, with the warm wind fluttering its tufted tops, making his shirtsleeves billow, John vaguely felt for a moment as he did on his father's farm in Prescott when he was a young man. His father's vigorous, irritable, energetic way of working his land, his mother's proud gloom. Did they know? Did they foresee this somehow?

"There are no bays in the western half of the Bay State." he said aloud, "Just rivers. Just rivers that give life and take it away."

He took the flask from his pocket. The liquid was warm from being pressed to his flank. The warmth on his back seemed to beckon for his attention, so he turned to the warm sun in the giant sky.

He recalled nothing more. Not George's frantic calling, not Dr. Wendell's cool touch, not the roughshod ride to Ware, or the hospital. He did not hear his own mumbling and was completely unaware of Eli's awkward kiss upon his forehead.

"Give this to Nathaniel." Eli whispered.

Around that time, the new Quabbin Park Cemetery was open for business, as they said. John Vaughn was buried next to Nathaniel's new grave. Eli gave his permission.

The new cemetery lay neat and orderly. It felt strange to see familiar headstones standing in a different place, in a different pattern, creating an eerie kind of disorientation. Here were the new graves of his parents, marked by their old headstones. Here was Nathaniel's second grave.

The winding road and trees, the orderliness gave the cemetery the effect of a small suburban neighborhood, it had not yet reached that feeling of comfortable maturity, as if all the sorrows of the world had been put to rest here and the souls of these dead were at peace with God. It was new, that was all, Eli thought. *In fifty years, it will seem more fitting than it does now. It's just new to us, that's all.*

He talked to himself in his mind to calm his childish anxiety. Funny, no church next to the cemetery. There would be no bells tolling the news to the town. One for a man.

Reverend Atkinson read the service at the gravesite. He was very busy these days, as much for his own sake as for his flock's, writing to communities outside to find another pulpit. He mourned the passing of his town as the passing of his own special place in it, and it seemed to the mourners that his feeling for John Vaughn, though he met him only a few times, must have been true and deep.

Arriving late was his sister, Miss Atkinson, and Roger Lewis. Eyes turned slyly to the newcomer, saw meaning in his presence, in his escorting of Miss Atkinson, and accepted both.

Lewis felt uncomfortable, but he was by self-design a man of duty who aspired to noblesse oblige and saw attending funerals of subordinates as the first step to this state of grace. Miss Atkinson, for her part, attended most Greenwich funerals her brother performed and was glad to finally have a beau to go with her.

She called him her beau. They had argued in the car all the way from Greenwich about whether "Tecumseh" was really General Sherman's middle name or only a nickname. Roger called her aggravating, said she was no authority on historical figures or anything else.

She glanced down and marveled how small and white her hand was in his. He had large hands. Large, warm hands.

Roger found himself asking more questions about Greenwich and the other towns. Being brought up in an aura of gossip all her life, Miss Atkinson was able to supply him with colorful information. He realized, painfully, that it was just the sort of place where he would like to settle down. The order, the quiet, the slow but real sense of purpose that had pervaded each day here matched his own need for a controlled environment.

The State chose the name for the Reservoir this year and called it Quabbin Reservoir. In years to come people in the surrounding area would simply call it The Quabbin, in much the same way as the early Indians must have referred to *the place of many waters.* The Quabbin. It was a name of strength and dignity.

It was the name of the Great Quabbin Hill and the Little Quabbin Hill and Quabbin Lake, so it was not unfamiliar to the Swift River Valley residents. A part of the Swift River would remain, but the Swift River Valley was a name that would in years to come be recalled by fewer and fewer people as the "Survivors," as they would come to be known, died out. Quabbin would resurface after hundreds of years as the land's identity, not only of the manmade reservoir, but of the region. The Quabbin Park Cemetery was only the first placard. In fifty years, there would be "Quabbin" stores, "Quabbin" manufacturers, "Quabbin" plumbers, car dealerships, but so far nobody has thought of the Quabbin Burger.

The name Quabbin sounded familiar, yet still unfamiliar, like the pattern of the new cemetery. They would still call the place the Swift River Valley even while the buildings were removed and their neighbors leaving, even when the construction of the Reservoir grew to such obvious magnitude that the Valley ceased to look like it had, they still called it the Valley. To them the construction work was the Reservoir.

Alonzo did not come to the funeral. Like a hypochondriac who morbidly worries about infection, Alonzo wanted nothing to do with connections to the Reservoir. John Vaughn was connected with the Reservoir, and so were the men he felt would surely show up at the funeral, and he did not want to risk contamination.

Alonzo had imagined a kind of state funeral for John Vaughn, but there were no flocks of construction men at the service in an honor guard, only Roger and George Smith, who looked lost without his boss. He twisted his cap in his hands and stood near Roger and Miss Atkinson.

How funny, Roger thought, how funny that Smith is an outsider like me. He is from the Valley, yet he has become an outsider like me.

They had begun, even before they knew it, to separate into a caste system. There were the Men from the State, of course, but they were not so foreign now, one got used to them. There were the renters who came to live from other towns, there were the ones who left early, and lastly the ones who stayed or said they would stay until the end. The young, the old, all with different perspectives. What had been a fairly homogenous community crumbled into mere aspects of what it had been.

Another faction would soon join these, the men called "Woodpeckers." They were like lumberjacks, assigned the awesome task of clearing the Valley floor of vegetation once most of the homes were removed. The young men who performed this work were mainly outsiders from the eastern part of the state, but some were locals. "Woodpecker" was considered a derogatory term, but as the gentle name implied, criticism was tempered by the feeling that it wasn't their fault either.

They were men and boys without jobs, who hoped to learn skills, to find a future, to earn some money. The Valley men and boys had that much in common with them. The few businesses that remained in the Valley in the middle 1930s catered mostly to the laborers' and woodpeckers' needs. The stores, the soda fountain in the drugstore, and the family homes which took in boarders were all for their use.

It was at the cemetery where Jenny made her decision. Uncle John was a traveled man, she would call him an urbane man because he was the closest thing she'd ever seen to it. A man who had seen and done much, yet only to end up back here. While he lived, his parents mourned him as a man who never came home. At last he came home to find nothing left for him.

All right then, Uncle John. I'm not going to be like my father and nothing like you. Watch me do more than you ever did.

And I should have made up with you.

In a fit of unaccustomed self-centered zeal, Jenny took a job in Haskell's store in Enfield and told her parents about it afterward, explaining that it was to earn her way through college. She would sell supplies to the woodpeckers.

Eli stood, put his hands in his pockets, glared at his daughter for a brief second and went outside to split and stack firewood. Mary lowered herself to a kitchen chair and scrutinized Jenny more closely.

They were surprised. They were angry at her boldness, annoyed that she should think of such an impossible thing as college, be so troublesome as to take herself so seriously, and mostly hurt that they could not provide her future for her as parents were supposed to do.

Jenny sat stiffly before the kitchen table, wondering what to do if her parents never spoke to her again.

"You've got two years of high school yet." Mary said.

"That's why I've got to start earning money now."

"What do you think you're going to do, be a doctor or something?"

"I have two years to figure that out."

"Watch your tongue, now. Don't you want to get married?"

Jenny turned her head to her mother. "Do you want me to marry Lon?"

"I didn't mean Lon particularly. I must say, your Grandfather Pratt would be pleased. He had high hopes for us girls. Jenny, he was a dear man, but he wasn't practical always. He had his head in the clouds and he wasn't very practical all the time."

Mary stood and retrieved an envelope from the pocket of Eli's coat that was hung on the back of a chair. "Came last week. It's addressed to you, but we opened it." She handed it to Jenny.

"Insurance company?"

Mary nodded. "It seems John had gotten a policy for himself a while ago. Put your name to it. He gave it to Mr. Lewis to hold for him, and asked Mr. Lewis to take care of it, when the time came. They're sending you three thousand dollars, young lady."

Jenny read the letter and the envelope a second time and placed them before her mother. "Why?"

"Because that's how life insurance works, you foolish... I don't know how he ever kept up the premiums, he never seemed very careful about money." Mary muttered at the envelope.

"I don't want it. I know Dad must still owe for the hospital or the funeral. I hope you'll take this."

"I don't know what he was thinking of, this kind of money for a young girl... this is more than your father earns for us in three years...."

"Is it?" Jenny immediately felt her heart pounding. Like many children who never saw more than fifty cents at one time in her life, the idea of many dollars, thousands of them, was beyond her comprehension. She knew they all worked for a living off the land, but cash in a bank was only a vague idea.

"Well, I don't want it ...."

"It was just his way to pull a joke like this...."

"I don't want it! I don't want it!" Her eyes welled, and there were more tears in the sound of her voice.

Mary looked at her, wondering why she never really noticed her before.

"Mom, when are we leaving? Why don't you *do* something?"

"Do you want to leave?" Mary threw the question at her like a dare, knowing Jenny was ever too cautious, and too proud, to take dares. Mary shook her head and huffed a short laugh.

Mary wanted to touch Jenny's face the way she would feel for a fever when she was a little girl, but she kept her hands tightly in her lap because she had no excuse to touch her daughter except for the urge to do it. They listened to the thud-song of the wood chopping outside.

She began to wipe the table needlessly with a soft wet, gray rag that had been a shirt of Eli's. She thought of that every time she used it. "Well, if y'want to work at the store, it's all right with me. Now's as good a time as any for you to learn to make your way. No sense throwing a good job away, despite an insurance check."

Jenny went to her room without a word, accepting that no gift ever came without chastisement. She meant to put both to good advantage.

Mary stepped outside. Eli wore the scowl she recognized.

"She says we can have John's money for the bills," Mary said, leaning on the fence post.

"You told her? It's not such a fortune that it won't go pretty quick," he mumbled to the ax handle.

"It is to her."

"John was a great one...it was just another quirk of his...."

"He did us a great favor. It was for us as much as Jenny."

"You know why he didn't name me on his policy? Because he knew I'd buy the old place with it. His place."

"And do what with it?"

He did not answer.

"Are y'going to keep the watch and not give it to Harrison?"

Eli looked at her evenly and fingered the pocket watch which had been his father's, given to John, and now left by John's instructions to his nephew Harrison.

"Oh, Eli," Mary came to him and suddenly slipped her arms around his waist and kissed his damp shoulder.

"I'm going to miss him. You're going to miss John, too."

"John..." he scoffed, "What was he ever about?"

"He made you what you are, y'know."

"Is that right? Thought I made me what I am. Well, just what in blazes am I? I don't even know. All I know is my mother and father would be mourning him proper right now; they surely did it all his adult life. Wished they could have lived to see him come back here. Wished they could have seen him then."

"The state appraiser came by today while you were on the milk run. I told them you'd be here tomorrow."

"That's what you told him, hey?"

***

They divided the insurance benefit and gave Jenny half, which was still much more than enough to see her through college. The only one she mentioned was the Massachusetts State College in Amherst.

She talked about her new job only a little more. She told them what she sold, to whom she sold it. She did not mention that Dick Lewis stopped by daily to see her.

He acted neither sarcastically playful as usual nor stiff and courtly like Lon, which perturbed Jenny because she knew everyone must have a secret purpose. He did not ask her for dates, but he asked her questions about herself until she told him to mind his own business more than once. He retaliated by telling her about himself and telling her more than she wanted to know about the progress on the Quabbin Reservoir.

"I'm sorry I missed your uncle's funeral. I had to work. I'm joining the Civilian Conservation Corps in a couple weeks," he added.

"Why? Isn't there enough work here?"

"I meant what I said that day. I don't want to work on the Reservoir if it bothers you."

202

"I wish you'd do what you want and leave me out of it. I don't care what you do."

"Well, I'm stupid enough to care. I hate leaving you here. You're going to get hammered by every house that gets torn down or neighbor that moves."

"Oh, shut up," she brushed her hand through her hair. She thought about the old woman's shaking hands that touched her throat, her face, and covered her eyes. Jenny took a deep breath.

"I also hate to leave you with your cousin. Jenny, I get the idea you don't know...."

"Lon?"

"I don't know how you feel about him. As you say so often, that's your business. Guys like him trip me off, I guess."

"Guys like you trip him off. So?"

"Well, I want you to know. If you don't already. He's following you."

Jenny jerked around, "Where?"

"Not now, but he has been before. When you leave the bus stop after school to come to work, he's there behind the mill. He waits outside the store sometimes for a long time. Sometimes he waits until you leave and he follows you up the Greenwich Road. Once I followed him until he saw you go into your house. Then he waited for about a half hour, then he went away."

"So, you're following him? That's swell."

"Only to see what he was up to. It's a weird thing for somebody to do, don't you think? You ought to be careful of him."

"I've known Lon since I was a baby. Lon...."

Dick said, "You're not a baby anymore. He's figured that out."

"I think you'd better just be careful yourself."

"All right, cool off. I'm leaving. At least you know now. It's always better to know, Jenny. I think you agree with me on that. We're more alike than you think. We're not the kind that can pretend. We'd rather know where we stand, even if we're standing in mud." He watched for her reaction to this. She only looked disapprovingly at the ground. "Anyway, what you do about it is your business. Like I said, I'm leaving for C's in a couple days."

"How long will you be gone?"

"Depends on if I like it. My hitch is supposed to be six months. If it's good, I'll sign on again. If it's not, I'll sneak out the first week."

"Don't get into trouble. Being told what to do isn't the same as being bossed around. I think it's time you realized that. Don't be a jerk, just because you want to be your own man."

He was quiet. His eyes never left her. "I'm gonna write to you, and I hope you write back. You might not be here when I get out. None of this might be here when I get out."

"Goodbye and get lost."

"Just keep your eyes peeled for him, okay?"

***

Alonzo looked over the western view from the ridge. At the base of the Pelham hills he watched the tiny men move the earth. There was no blasting of rock today, only the silent ant-like diligence of a swarm.

Deliberately keeping himself uninformed about the Quabbin Reservoir, he did not know that they were building a highway. It would by-pass the Valley from Belchertown to New Salem and Athol. Skirting the Valley's edge, it was the first major indicator of the Valley's future nonexistence. He did not know that it would be named the Daniel Shays Highway, but had he known he would have smiled at the Commonwealth's rare show of humor.

They had meant it to be a tribute, of course. They did not see that by taking the name of a man venerated for his disobedience to the Commonwealth and stamping it on a project which those Westerners believed to be a punishment was a further insult to that man and to them. It took more sensitivity than Beacon Hill ever had to see the sarcasm.

They could not have chosen a more fitting name. The new highway led away from the Valley. Shays had never returned from his exile, either.

Alonzo sat upon his horse, disdainful and proud, close to the site of Shays' old farm. The construction men, far on the other side of the Western Branch of the Swift River were stupid slaves, dirt scratchers. He pitied them and rode on.

Now there were only two other families living in Prescott. Alonzo hardly saw them, himself a virtual hermit. His farm, though it was small, had become too much for him to work alone. He hadn't realized his own depression took a huge part in pulling him away. More and more, he pulled the old draft horse away from his chores and rode aimlessly about the ridge.

He planted very little now, mostly hay for the stock. That alone was an enormous effort to harvest by himself when it came in. There was no one close to help him, and he did not ask for help.

Alone on his rides a new idea occurred to him. He found irony, contradiction in the changing landscape. It seemed that the reservoir workers (surveyors, woodpeckers, appraisers, they were all the same to him), were encroaching nearer and nearer, and that he could not ride far now without encountering some bold and ugly evidence of the new world they were creating. Its tenacious fingers threatened to choke him, and there were days he felt physically sick from it.

He also noticed on the farms which had been deserted the wild grass grew without shame on the neat yards and gardens, a tiny crop of baby pines and oaks speckled the fields and dirt roads like a nursery.

Once his orderly farmer's eye would have looked at this havoc of nature with scorn, but Alonzo was less a farmer these days. He felt more like a Pioneer. His aloneness made him feel special. Alonzo watched the timid rebirth of wilderness with approval. Nature, in New England's long history, had always been something to be conquered. Perhaps not now, Alonzo thought. Perhaps nature was there to shelter. Perhaps it was here to shelter him.

The weeds and shoots did not shelter much yet on bare, sunny hillsides that had been cleared of their virgin forest two centuries ago, they only made it look unkempt. Alonzo didn't see that.

It came to him then that he was like the first Vaughns who came west on the rugged trip from the Bay Colony, an eighty-odd mile trip on horses and foot which had taken days. It seemed more than ever this was his land, that he felt kinship with it, that he belonged here. He felt suddenly comforted, confident, and did not mourn the Reservoir anymore. It could not touch him here. He would not worry about it anymore.

With an eagerness that belied his too-worn face, he made simple plans again. He could live very well on truck, on what he could raise in chickens and pigs, keep a few cows for milk, and hunt and fish.

He looked about him at the shabby farm and was pleased. The first thing to do was sell off at least half of the stock. He would live as a pioneer in the years to come, needing little, owing nothing to anyone. Jenny would like that. She was independent, like him.

He took his pencil and tore a page from the farm account book he no longer kept balanced. He wrote to James and Calvin, and his father. They would probably be glad to take the stock.

It had been months since Alonzo had seen any members of his family. Though North Amherst was not a far distance, it might as well have been a thousand miles. It was a place of large, flat farms, of trucks and motorized tractors with heavy iron wheels, of gas pumps and Coca-Cola and diners with radios on the counter. Alonzo was ashamed of them, and they were ashamed of him.

But when they responded, he was happy to see James and Calvin walk into the yard. He had started at the rumble of their truck but smiled when he recognized them. Then he came out in the open.

They shook hands, they strolled and spoke in low, reserved tones, saying much in very few words. Anyone who did not know better would think that the three young men were complete strangers.

"Selling out, Lon? Will y'move soon?" Calvin said, and James nervously caught his eye.

As the youngest, James always felt like a little boy around Alonzo. To show Alonzo he meant nothing confrontational about it, Calvin did not look at him when he said this. He looked calmly at the horizon and breathed deeply as if he truly appreciated the Prescott air.

Alonzo lowered his mood, cautiously, looking right at Calvin. "D'you want to buy my cows or not?"

Calvin put his hands in his pockets. "Yes, of course, we do, Lon. I just wanted you to know that we miss having your ugly face around and we'd like y'to help us out on our place if you ever did feel like picking up and starting over. Dad's getting old. Y'know how it is."

Calvin felt winded after his careful speech, but Alonzo relaxed. James wandered away to pet a cow.

"How's Mother?" Alonzo asked.

"We've got some bread in the car she made us take for you. She thinks about you a great deal."

They agreed on the sale, and arranged that Calvin, James, their father and whoever else they could find would drive the small herd to North Amherst at the end of the week.

"What'cha gonna do with all your money, Lon?" Calvin slapped his back.

"Jenny and I have plans for this old place."

"Jenny? Eli's Jenny?" Calvin asked, "Well, gosh Lon, we didn't know. She's a grand girl. Best of luck to you." He shook Alonzo's hand vigorously and looked into his brother's eyes.

When James and Calvin drove away, Calvin turned the truck toward Greenwich.

James said, "Are we going to Eli's? I didn't think of that. Guess we could use more help to move the herd."

Calvin pulled the truck over to the side of the road. "James, I think he's crazy."

"Well. Y'know Lon. He was always one to have his own way...."

"No, I mean I think he's crazy. I was afraid of what to say to him. Did you see the look in his eyes? Wonder if he's really going to marry Jenny? How old would she be about now? Wonder if it's true?"

"We can ask Eli...."

"How do we go about that?" Calvin slapped his hands on the steering wheel. "Damn, I was glad to take the cattle, I thought he was finally coming to his senses, but he just wants to re-trench himself up there. Wish I knew what to do."

"The place looked a little ragged."

"Lives like a gol-darned hermit." Calvin sputtered, putting the truck into gear.

"You know what? I think maybe we could call Doc Wendell. He knows how to handle people. Remember that old story about when Joe Alden got drunk over his daughter gettin' in a family way, and nearly burned the town down...."

"Yut, I remember talk about that. Doc settled him down, and also got six fellows to confess to fathering the child and got his fee six times around. I heard one of them boys was John Vaughn."

"That was just a rumor."

"Still, very enterprising, that old Doc."

"Girl, too."

"Well, I won't say about that. Anyway, he gave all that money to the young mother. He set things up pretty well. Oh, he's crafty...."

"Well, I'm saying Doc was the only person to quiet Joe. Wouldn't even listen to his wife. Doc's seen everybody born and die around here. I think Lon would listen to him, and Doc's too old for him to punch."

"That's a good point. All right. We can't handle him, that's certain. We'll always be his little brothers," James said.

***

The contrast of Eli's farm to Alonzo's was glaring, yet a similar forlornness remained. Eli's yard was green and neat, the grounds were tidy with clusters of flowers planted as a border along the porch and like lace doilies around the base of a tree. The fields beyond thrived, and the barn stood firm and did not sag, and was even painted. The farm did not hide among overgrown grass and bushes, teetering off a hillside. It lay flat in the sunshine, with the wash blowing carelessly on the lines.

The children were at school. Calvin and James wandered into the barn and watched Eli sharpen his father's old adze on a millstone with the mechanical dullness of a man who was either thinking deeply or trying not to think at all.

He stood with a brief smile and shook hands with the boys, indicating the porch. Calvin and James had never studied the amenities as closely as Eli had, and preferred to shuffle around the dark barn to talk.

James took hold of the pitchfork and ground it into the dirt, leaning on the tool in apprehension. Calvin took off his hat and picked at the frayed brim.

"Friday we're driving a herd from Lon's place to ours. He sold half his stock to us." Calvin said. "We could use your help if you can spare the time, Eli."

Eli opened his eyes wide. "Lon selling out? My word."

"No, Eli," Calvin continued, "He's just selling some of his stock for cash. He wants to reduce his operation (Calvin had learned the word as a synonym for farm), re-trench, sort of. He's as stubborn as ever."

"You should see his place, Eli," James piped up, "It's a poor sight. Cut down on his planting, scrub growing all over yard. House looks like it's about to fall down."

"Well, Eli, we're a little worried," Calvin said, "He...um...I'm worried about him, I'll tell you plainly. He acts like the Reservoir is never going to come. He's living like a hermit. His clothes are all...carries his gun all the time. Cuts out in the middle of the day to go fishing. Lord, Eli, I'm worried."

"If he could only see our farm," James said, "No backhouse, that's for sure. Electricity, we've got a radio, electric washer and stove. Coal delivered, regularly. People are having it rough now, sure, but it's still so much better on the outside than it is here. Lord, Eli, but it's better. You'll be moving soon, and you'll see."

Eli stiffened. Sheepishly he listened, feeling like a bug in a jar with talk about the outside. He found himself half-sympathizing with Alonzo for being pitied and treated behind his back like a stupid country cousin.

"Live-in maid to muck out the barn?" Eli muttered.

"Eli," Calvin continued, "We need to get a hold of Doc Wendell. We thought maybe he could talk to Lon. We need help. What do you think?"

Eli lifted his head. "Doc's livin' in Ludlow now. Boys, he's over seventy years old."

"Is he retired?" Calvin asked, scornful in his disbelief, "Not him."

"Well, he's about as retired as people will let him be. What do you think he can do?"

"Lon's acting crazy. We need somebody to talk to him." James said.

"He's crazy because he didn't sell out when you did?" Eli said, "Well look around you, the Valley's full of crazy people. Lord and you pity us for not having y'father's foresight. For all I care, Lon can stay up there shooting rabbits till he drops. For all I know, he's got the right idea."

"Maybe Jenny won't like that kind of life."

"What do you mean?"

"Lon's getting his home ready for her. He gave me the impression they were to be married. Or something."

Hours later Eli still heard Calvin saying it.

***

A car drove up in front of the house, then another. The man in the first car was a stranger with a briefcase, the second man from the other car was Roger Lewis. Still in the road, he removed his hat when he saw Eli on the porch steps.

The first man was smiling, tugging at the waistline of his trousers below a big belly, and nodding to Eli.

"Eli Vaughn," Roger said in a soft voice, "this is Eben Clough."

"How do you do, Mr. Vaughn," Clough thrust out his large paw, "I'm happy to meet you. I'm an appraiser for the MDWSC on this stretch around here, and Mr. Lewis kindly offered to show me out. Is this a convenient time?"

"No, it's not."

"Oh, well…when should I call again?"

"It's never going to be a good time. Get out."

"Eli…" Roger said. He had not used his first name before. It sounded strange in Roger's accent.

"Roger," he returned, "I don't know why you brought this man here. My brother is dead. You have no further business with my family."

"Mr. Lewis didn't bring me here today, Mr. Vaughn," Clough answered affably, "We ran into each other by chance in Enfield and I told him where I was bound for. He asked to come along. I assumed it was an occasion for you to visit."

"Mr. Clough is doing his job…Eli. I thought…I might make it easier for you."

"You thought."

"Just to smooth things over."

"I'm not selling this farm."

"In point of fact, Mr. Vaughn," Clough answered, "you are. I'm only here to get the best price for both you and the state. I can come back at a more convenient time, but I will come back. You know, sir, I've been turned away before. Times I've been received like the Grim Reaper. I've also been received like Santa Claus, the man with the money and the promise of the future. It all depends on how you look at it, Mr. Vaughn. No matter what happens to your farm, life goes on for your family. You can make it hard or you can make it easy."

"I have nothing to say to you except get out."

Clough rubbed his chin. "All right, Mr. Vaughn. I'll say good day to you. Please think about what I said. I'll be back."

"Wait, Clough…" Roger called. "Wait by the car, will you?"

"You can leave too, Roger." Eli turned to go into the house.

"Wait," Roger repeated to Clough. He walked up the porch and put his hand on Eli's shoulder. Eli threw it off, faced him with rage and prepared to hit him. Roger watched the workings of his expression and stood calmly waiting for Eli to sort it out.

"I know you're not ready to talk," Roger said softly, "so don't. Just let this man take his pad and pencil around the place and do his figuring. He can get back to you with details later. I'll show him out when he's through. Let me do this for you Eli."

"I'm not selling."

"God help you, Eli."

Yes, he thought, God help me.

Mary opened the screen door with a slow creak. She nodded to Roger. He stepped backward off the porch, motioned to Clough, and led him around to the barn to commence with his appraisal. Eli and Mary watched them.

"It's the end of the world." Eli said, gravel in his voice. "Mary, keep me from shooting them."

She put her hand tentatively on his back, and began to rub in slow circles, not knowing if it was the right thing to do. "Let's go into the house." she said.

"No."

"Please, Eli."

"No."

"Well," she swallowed, "what else did James and Calvin have to say? They didn't stay long."

"Calvin and James said something else, which I didn't tell you. It's about Jenny. They have...the impression that Lon intends to marry her."

"What...did they say?"

"If they don't mean marry, I don't want to think about what they do mean. They said he's fixing up his house for her, that he's going to live with her up there. He thinks. Now you tell me, what has that stupid girl been doing...."

"Oh Eli, be sensible! Jenny hasn't been doing anything. She hardly sees him, except when we do. Unless he drops in at that store...."

"Unless he drops in at that store. Exactly right. I want you to talk to her, I want you to find out what sort of plan she's hatching...."

"Oh Eli, I can't believe she's planning anything. She's only mentioned college, and she doesn't talk much about that either."

"Unless that was just to throw us off...."

"Eli, listen to yourself. Jenny's not deceitful. We can be grateful for that. I know she's not. Either those boys were mistaken, or Lon's taken some sick fancy into his head."

"I don't even want to think about that."

"No, you'd rather think y'daughter's been luring him."

"I want you to talk to her."

"You talk to her."

"YOU talk to her."

"If you don't do something soon...."

"If you don't do something soon, Eli, it'll be too late. And you know I'm not talking about Jenny. No miracle, no loss of state money, no sudden lack of interest in Boston, nobody saying in the statehouse, 'you know, this reservoir thing wasn't such a good idea. Let's give it up.' None of that's going to happen."

Jenny listened from her window, watching Mr. Lewis stroll behind the fat man. She frowned, her chin balanced on her fist, planted on the warped windowsill. Yes, no miracles about to happen here.

Poor Lon. He wasn't like her father. He wouldn't think twice about shooting Mr. Clough.

He needed her. She was the only one in the whole blasted family to see things clearly. She would see to Lon, first. Uncle John was right about that. Only she could handle him.

CHAPTER 20

Roger Lewis dropped his hat on the kitchen table, took a bottle of beer from the icebox, and walked into Dick's room.

"I was going to leave you a note. Pretty dumb." Dick turned to Roger, "Can you believe I almost left a note on your pillow?" He started to laugh, "Gawd."

"You're leaving?" Roger asked. "Oh, I forgot. You wanted to join the Civilian Conservation Corps, didn't you?"

"I already did."

"Don't you like working on the Reservoir? It'll amount to the same thing. Clearing brush...planting later on...."

"Cutting trees and planting more. They could make up their minds. Anyway, I think it's time I went out on my own."

"You've been on your own since you were ten," Roger scoffed, "Nobody could ever tell you...."

"That's not what I mean. I mean you've gotten me jobs, there wasn't ever really a time where Mother or you couldn't bail me out if I got in trouble. Or bawl me out."

"That's what I'm here for."

"The hell it is. No, that's not your job, or it never shoulda been. Just because Dad walked out doesn't mean I should have been your problem. Anyway, I appreciate your help, Rawg, but I'm tired of being Peck's Bad Boy and somebody's little brother. I heard you can get your high school diploma in the CCC. I think I'm gonna try for that. Besides, I'm damn sick of tearing up somebody's little world."

"I don't want to hear it like that," Roger pulled the keychain with the bottle opener on it from his pocket. "I've had a pretty disagreeable day, all in all." He took a long drink.

"Trouble on the project?" Dick continued packing.

"It's not a project, Dick. It's a place." Roger sat on the edge of the bed. "So, it's really a place, after all. I've spent quite a few years here with the wrong idea. Dead wrong."

"You sound like you're dead drunk."

"Dead tired. I had to make a man face the inevitable today. I think I've finally faced it myself."

"Well, I've had enough of this place."

"Don't try too hard to dislike the place. That doesn't work."

"You're talking about the Valley, not the reservoir, aren't you?"

"The Valley." Roger smiled, "Yes, the Valley. For as long as it is the Valley. Y'know a place has an effect on a man, somehow. A woman, too. Makes them who they are. Their thinking, the way they see things. I'm thinking we have a lot of Scituate in us, pal. We're both so damned pragmatic."

While Dick wondered about the word "pragmatic" and what it could mean, he thought immediately of Jenny. Instead he said, "Are you going to marry Martha Atkinson?"

Roger looked at him. He took another drink and did not answer.

"I know somebody who looks out her window each day and looks around her yard as if it were for the last time." Dick said. "Every day she does that."

Roger glanced at his brother's profile.

"I wonder they don't all crack up." Dick muttered aloud.

"Do you mean Jenny Vaughn?" Roger asked, "I was with her father today. I went out with the appraiser."

"Oh hell."

"Yeah."

Dick put his hands on his hips and stared a moment out the window.

"Nothing you can do, kid." Roger stood, "Except let me drop you at the station."

***

Eli heaved a coil of rope into the back of the truck.

Alonzo's cows were on a straight path out to another pasture. They had no choice in the matter; they were being driven. They didn't care.

Eli had milked his own stock and drove them to pasture out back, beneath Mt. Zion.

The farm was just about holding its own again. They were late on a loan payment for the used equipment he'd bought from Sam. Eli wasn't worried about it; the insurance money would pay it all off. He felt he earned it. Investment demanded return, and he thought he'd spent enough of himself on John.

Stop it, stop thinking about him.

Mary came from the house with a basket. Eli took it from her and placed it in the truck bed.

"Harrison coming?"

"He's on his way."

"I shouldn't let him come on the drive. He didn't get up this morning to help me."

"It'll be good for him." Mary answered. "You did promise."

"The outside world is a mess," Eli muttered. "The outside world has hit rock bottom, just like the Valley. He won't learn much."

"So, it's traitorous for Harrison to want a radio, for Jenny to go to college, for Ida to live it up with her two-sided toaster and moving pictures in Athol, for Doris to sock money away for nothing but stockings, hats and magazines?" Mary said. "Oh Eli. Helpless indecision. That's what's eating you. Eli, it's time to leave. Let's go." Mary crossed her arms over her aproned bosom.

Eli straightened himself and looked at her over his shoulder and under the brim of his hat as if he were ready for a knife-fight. "That what y'think, hey?"

"I don't care where. It doesn't matter."

"Right now, up and leave? Fine, I'll start the truck."

Mary pulled her gaze away and fired it over the back field. "Time we got on with it, Eli, that's all." She sighed.

"Figure out how to do that without losing what we've got?" he said, placing his rough, dirty hands on the hips of his spattered brown trousers. "All the effort it took for us to move here. Sakes."

"We had a choice then, we don't now. Tomorrow or the next day, but surely not never. We can't stay. It's all going. Everything we know is dying. When you told me about Lon, I suddenly realized the water isn't here yet, but we've been choking on the idea of it. Dear, we're here drowning without it! Lon, he's the least of our problems."

"Lon," Eli snorted a laugh and took his hat off to play with it, "If we don't have enough problems. Fool."

"Fool now. But we both had a sick feeling then, didn't we? Sweet, foolish boy was evil himself then, wasn't he?"

"So, you want to take Jenny away?"

"Remember when you asked me to marry you?"

He looked at her quizzically, "Did you think me as big a fool as Lon?"

"No."

"Now that I recall, we did fight about it, didn't we?"

"I felt you were using me as a next step in your life, like you weren't wooing me as much as offering me a business deal, to your advantage. It was just the way you put it."

"Oh, sakes. I'm sorry, Mary. Young men are foolish."

"But Lon isn't half the man you were and are."

"Jenny didn't fight with him the way you fought with me. She didn't say a word, except about college. Where did that come from?"

"I don't know, but she's a lot like you. She thinks about things a long time before she says them. I can't see her at Lon's place."

Eli shook his head. "Lon's place. I remember when it was our place. Well. Y'never did want to be a farmwife, did you?"

"That's what I am." Mary replied.

"That's what y'are."

"I don't care what y'do for a living, Eli Vaughn, I want you to do it someplace else now. The children should be settled close to their school. We should all be settled, and we're not. I swear, Eli, if you don't start looking for a new home for us out of here, and I mean tomorrow, I'm taking the children to my mother's. That's the only choice you've got."

"Don't y'talk to me like that...."

"If we wait, in another year or two Harry'll be working on the Reservoir," she said.

She walked away, pausing only to watch Jenny emerge from the house to return the egg basket to the barn. Mary looked him in the eye and turned back to the house. Eli glared at his daughter. "What is this between you and Lon?"

"Lon?"

"You are not going to marry him."

Jenny colored. "I don't think he was serious. He never proposed to me, y'know. Not really."

"You don't think he was serious? How empty-headed can you be? I'm telling you he was serious and I'm telling you it's not going to happen, so just forget it and stay away from him."

"I haven't been near him!"

"Don't you raise your voice to me! From everything I hear ...."

"About what! Has Dick said anything to you? Well you can forget about him, he's crazy."

"Who's Dick?"

"Well then, wherever you got the idea, it's not true!"

"I said who is Dick?"

"You know him...he came to the door, that day. Mr. Lewis' brother," she edged away.

"Lewis? Yes. If I had known how much Lewis was going to be involved with us I'd have never have given him a ride home that first day. He probably would have walked to New Hampshire by now."

"What?"

"I don't know about Dick but you can just as well stay away from him, too. You are too independent for your own good, y'always have been. It's about time you were taken down a peg. You stick to school and this farm, and for the time being just forget about everything else. We have enough on our plates without you."

They allowed themselves one last long hard look at each other to embellish their anger, and Jenny left the barn. As she passed by her mother in the kitchen, Mary announced from over her shoulder,

"Don't mind his anger, Jenny. It's a good thing, for now. You don't know this, but anger has been the thing to push him for nearly every important step that man's taken in his life. He's got another important decision in front of him now and he's got to build up a good head of steam to do it."

"When have I ever been any trouble to you?" It was not so much a question as an accusation, and Jenny's own head of steam was building up, her words like hot lead.

Mary did not comment but turned her back to Jenny to end the conversation. Mary made lunches to take in the truck with quick competence and relief. They might move bag and baggage without any words between them if it came to that, but at least they would leave, and not leave with that sick despair so common now with the others.

***

Roger Lewis stepped out of the church and paused by the oak tree, lit a cigarette and waited for Miss Atkinson to follow out of the church. As the organist, she usually emerged last, after everything was put away and tidied.

Jenny noticed Roger Lewis and nodded to him. He straightened up and nodded back, lifting his hat for a brief second. She waved, and turned to the younger girl, the small, fair child and spoke low, breathless words that Roger could not hear.

The blonde girl shook her head but Jenny put her gloved hands on the girl's shoulders and spoke firmly.

Miss Atkinson finally came out of the church, an ornament in chiffon, smooth and unruffled from another performance, and Roger took her arm. They went to his car, for they were to have dinner and spend the afternoon in Springfield. He opened the car door for her. Reverend Atkinson watched them go. He wished he could have invited himself along. He was more miserable about looking for a new post in far-off New York or Pennsylvania than his sister knew.

"Please go home by yourself Ella," Jenny repeated, "It'll be all right. I just have something to do. We're not having a dinner today, Mom said there'll only be sandwiches, and the men took theirs already in a bag. She won't miss me; just tell her I'm going into Enfield. Well, no, don't tell her that."

"Where are you going?"

"I don't want to tell you. It'll be all right, but I don't want them to know until I come back. It's kind of a surprise, and I don't want y'to have to tell them a lie for me, so just say you don't know where I went, that I said it was a surprise and I'd tell you later."

"I don't want to do that, Jenny, tell me where you're going," Ella pleaded miserably with her, "Why can't y'just tell me? I won't tell. Please Jenny, this isn't nice. I know where you're going, and you'd better not. If you're going to Lon, I'll tell."

"Ella, go home. I mean it. Right now. If you say anything, I'll never speak to you again. You get home. It'll be all right, I just can't tell you right now, that's all. Don't you be a burden to me now, I've had enough of that. I can't take any more of that."

Jenny shook off Ella's grasp and gave her one last stern look as one would give a dog he wanted to stay put. Then she strode away towards the road to Enfield. Ella did not go home immediately but stood, stubbornly and sorrowfully on the spot, determined to watch Jenny until she disappeared. Jenny walked faster, and broke into a run to shake off the guilt of Ella's unblinking stare.

She did not go to Enfield but ran through back fields and backyards once she was out of sight to reach the Prescott road. She crossed the tracks of the Rabbit Run carefully in her Sunday shoes, and marched up the hill to Prescott.

The back of summer had been broken, which is to say there would be no more heat waves this year. There is a period in late July when temperatures can soar to the upper nineties and last for five and six days at a time. This becomes unbearable for New Englanders who are used to weather changes each day, sometimes several changes in a single day. Whether it is the heat or the monotony which is the most torture is up to the individual. Certainly, the notorious humidity in the river valleys makes even breathing difficult.

But not today. The air was warm and dry, all that was behind them now. All the sweet scents of the maturing fields and woodlands traveled on the lovely breeze. Summer could be enticing now that it was getting ready to leave.

***

"Harrison, where do y'think we should move?" Eli asked from the side of his mouth. Harrison pulled his arm in from the passenger window. He wished the truck could go faster.

"Bill's going to Peters-ham," he offered, shocked that his father brought this subject up, but proud that he brought it up with him, man-to-man.

"Any particular reason?"

"His father's brother has orchards. Mr. Thatcher's going in with him. Bill's going to work, too."

"Well, guess that settles Bill. You are not lucky enough to have relatives outside the Valley, except for your sister in Athol and y'grandmother here. And there's my cousins in North Amherst. Guess we're really spreading out, after all. We'll be all over the world, soon.

"Would y'like to live in Athol? Go to work in a shop or factory? Or d'you want t'be a farmer?"

"I don't know."

"Y'don't know." Eli kept his eyes on the road, "Well, suppose that's not unusual. But, when I was your age I knew what I wanted. Yut. Knew what I wanted. And it didn't happen, and it still ain't happening. Orchards, like Bill Thatcher's uncle. I was never able t'do it." His voice shook and Harrison was appalled to see his father's moist eyes.

"All that work, all that work over land we weren't *even* going to get to *keep*."

***

Eli arrived at his family's old farm but did not get to speak to Alonzo, did not even get a look at him through the truck window. Calvin rode up on horseback and directed him to take the rear in his truck.

"Isn't Lon coming?"

Calvin scoffed, "He said the stock's mine now, it's my job to take them. Cash and carry. Won't leave his precious land. Damn him to hell. Let's go."

Doctor Wendell was to stay with Alonzo and talk to him. Alonzo seemed not to know what to do with the doctor when the old man invited himself for a visit. As the others departed with the stock, Alonzo fidgeted around the barn attending to milking and separating and feeding the chickens while the old man followed him, keeping up a stream of conversation like a neglected child.

Doctor Wendell tired. At last he said, "Lon, your people are worried about you."

Alonzo did not answer but began to work on the old cultivator as if it needed something, a finishing touch.

"Lon, please leave while y'can. You're young and strong, not an old man like me with the best of him left behind in this dear old Valley. Y'can make your mark anywhere. Need people around you. Everyone needs people around him. Do you know the worse thing y'can do to a man is put him in solitary confinement? Well, it's true. You're doing terrible things to y'self, son. You're going to be living here like an old ghost in a graveyard soon...."

"The graveyards," Alonzo said with a sneer, "are empty."

***

Jenny felt more sure now, having shaken off her anger at her father, and her mother, and Ella. She felt more confident and easy the deeper she went into Prescott, the higher she climbed. She was coming home.

A black Ford ragtop crept carefully around the curve, its tires grinding on the dirt, spewing pebbles to the side of the road. The car was Doctor Wendell's pet, his reward, he'd often said, for a lifetime of midnight calls in a bone-shaking buggy.

"It's Jenny Vaughn, isn't it?" Doctor Wendell called to her. She approached the car and he grasped her wrist as if he'd wanted to take her pulse. He pumped her hand.

"Yes sir." Jenny said, "How are you, Dr. Wendell?"

"I am old man, Jenny," he said, with a wheeze for a laugh. "But, not so old I can't appreciate a sight like you on a day like this. You're not headed up to see Alonzo, are you?"

"Well...sort of. Yes." Lying to Doc Wendell would be like lying to God.

"Hope you have better luck conversing with that boy than I do. Might as well be a fence post. His family's worried about him. See if you can talk some sense to him. Get him to give up that place."

"I'll sure try."

"No matter, I suppose. State'll convince him with greater powers of persuasion than we've got. How are you doing these days?"

"Fine."

"Still in Greenwich Village?"

"Yes, sir."

"Well." He drummed his fingers on the wheel. "The future will take care of itself. You take care of yourself, Jenny."

"Yes, sir. Bye."

He waved and pulled away, continuing his slow crawl back to the outside world. Lon was right to be stubborn. She stopped still on the dirt road and watched a small dust devil swirl ahead and die in a weak breeze. No. Being right was irrelevant; he could not win. That was reality. Even Dr. Wendell wasn't fighting it.

It was too beautiful a day to be unhappy. The deep, wet, earthy smell of the woods comforted her with the idea that the land was old; it would go on forever, no matter who owned it, no matter what they did with it. Yes. That was the reality, too.

Like other hill towns, Prescott was remote, proud, sullen, dignified, and jealous of its own view. The exodus of people had been more severe here than in the other towns, and it had always been the poorest. Weeds began to carpet the dirt road. Oak saplings grew bold and came out into the open.

They seemed relieved, as if they had been set free, as if they ruled the ridge now that the people were gone.

This is what Alonzo must be feeling. Jenny smiled. No one could understand Lon's feeling for Prescott like she did. Nobody else could persuade him to leave the place, despite that strong feeling, and resign himself to a new happiness, if such a thing as happiness was out there.

She did not know that Alonzo followed her from the woods. Because of the purpose in her walk, because of her Sunday dress, he knew she was coming to him.

He marveled at her. At seventeen, his Jenny had left the little girl somewhere along the way. She was womanly, despite her rugged attitude as she pounded the rising dirt road in her good shoes. He watched her.

At twenty-eight, Alonzo seemed virile, strong in a way her father was not and Harrison never would be. He wore the mystic strength of a soldier of the Dark Ages, a Crusader, an adventurer who enjoys testing the limits of his capacity to give and receive pain. Like one of the nameless men of history whose memories are not left to us, but who built worlds out of belief and blood. Jenny had created many such scenarios for him. He had begun to create them for himself.

In reality he had no strategy, only a stubborn belief in himself. Except when he looked at her. Lord, her careless, sweet loveliness.

A mistake in his tracking, and she sensed his presence. Jenny turned, searched the small thin trees which had grown pathetically between the cold rocks in the stone fencing. Caught, Alonzo emerged from the shadows, shy and embarrassed.

She had always known this humble, diffident side of him, even without ever before seeing it. She smiled in recognition and reached for his hand, pleased and deeply touched.

"Did you know I was coming to see you?" She bumped her shoulder against his arm as they walked, strolling the rest of the way, testing each other's company, saying little. She spoke in low tones, almost motherly to soothe him, and he nodded slightly, or smiled.

"Between the Reservoir and the Depression, seems the like the Lord has forgotten us. Or we forgot Him." she said, fingering his hand, "The ancient Hebrews never seemed to forget Him the way we have. We're good and lost, aren't we Lon? Sometimes I wish Bible study was more like a newspaper and less a fable. I'd like to find out how people made do and less about angels."

Her deep-set eyes glanced lightly on all the uneven impressions in the dirt road. She squeezed his hand.

"They don't seem to know that they're taking away our identity, when they take our towns. So much for the tributes of long ago kings, right? Looks like the towns were ours only at the pleasure of the Commonwealth after all. I always wondered about the 'wealth' part of that word.

"If it had been a war or an earthquake, it'd still be terrible, but it's because some fellows we don't know voted on it without our say, before we knew what was happening. That's what gnaws at us."

Alonzo smiled at the lazy drift of her hem, and she noticed, pleased, but kept walking to help her talk.

"That's sort of why I want to go to college. I want to find out about all this, how things really work, and how to make do in a world I never knew anything about. Nothing more to lose, is there? I was hoping I could get you to take on the world, too, out in the open, with me. Not to hole yourself up here. You can do it, Lon. You can do anything. But not here, not anymore. Sometimes I think this place is a dream, something we all made up."

Alonzo's eye caught a tuft of Queen Anne's lace. He released Jenny's hand to fish the clump from the tall grass. As they walked, he threaded out the strands of weeds, and tossed away two sprigs of goldenrod.

"You've got to decide what *you* think, Lon, and not wait for anybody to tell you what to do. That sort of thing isn't for us."

She glanced at his dark profile, but he was quiet.

"Don't know how much you've seen of the construction," she said, "making scars all over the place. It hurts.

"But y'know Lon, I don't think it's all bad. I think good will come of it, if they're careful. I don't just mean for Boston or jobs. Nobody ever paid much attention to this part of the state before. We have so much that's good here. We have to share it now."

She stopped a moment, as rigid as a retriever and stared blankly into the dark canopy of trees over the road ahead. "Please make this all not so terrible. I need you to be strong."

Picked through and plumped, Alonzo handed his bride her bouquet.

He flushed, awed and humbled by her. Something he had wished for, something he had planned for actually happened.

The yard glowed bright with sunlight, alive with the muted sounds of distant birds, hidden animals and tiny flying things dancing in the air.

He smiled suddenly, secretly. She grew up. He had waited for her. That was all he had to do. It was so simple.

She would want to see the house. A woman would want to see her house first. Her kitchen, her parlor, her rooms. He would give it all to her. She had been a child here, he remembered. How right it was she should go away and come back a woman. Like a fairy tale. Like something God had planned for him.

He held the screen door open for her and guided her up the step, placing his large, rough hand against the small of her back.

Jenny looked around, calling dim memories from her childhood. She looked around with amusement at the sagging house whose neither exterior nor interior had changed in fifty years, then checked herself in case she should hurt Alonzo by her condescension. She remembered she was not superior to him because she now lived in a nicer house, because they owned a truck. That was how some people lived in the Valley and how many left it. They developed an ugly, self-satisfied revulsion to cover their aching hearts.

In this manner they reviled all they had been taught from infancy to revere: workless, reverent Sundays, courtesy between men and women bordering on formality and distance, hard work, simple, spare lives, and the rewards of fireflies, rainbows, and gentleness.

For some, when Massachusetts denied them what they believed was their birthright, then they themselves denied who they were. It felt less painful than being hurt because one was too proud or too helpless to change.

Jenny stepped into the dim, stale and dirty parlor. An expert would have called the table by the window and the highboy in the corner valuable antiques, but Jenny and Alonzo were ignorant of this.

She walked with careful deliberateness, and smiled with encouragement when Alonzo lifted a tattered, yellowed, dusty curtain so she could see the side yard. The grass stood tall, and the road in front of the house nearly gleamed in the harsh sun, the ruts bone-dry gashes in the hard earth.

Jenny noticed the psalm needlepoint her Grandmother Vaughn had made before she was born. She made it when her own boys were small and here it still hung above the old settle, brown with dust and ragged where threads had pulled loose. Mary Vaughn hadn't wanted to bring that thing to the new house, but it didn't matter because Grandfather would not part with it anyway.

"What d'you suppose she was like, Grandmother Vaughn? Being here, I can see why it's so tough for you, Lon," she said, slowly and absently reached to fish for the hatpin which held her straw hat in place. "The past is set in stone here."

She struggled with her knot of hair, Alonzo quickly came to her rescue. He took her hands and dropped them neatly to her sides, while he examined the hat and the placement of the hatpin with the thoroughness of a mechanic about to take on a job, the adoration of a disciple examining a holy and precious thing.

He drew the hatpin slowly from her crown, and lifted the warm straw hat from her head, catching strands of her dark hair in its weaved brim. It excited him to touch her hair.

Her back to him, she smiled to herself, then turned and snaked her arms around his waist.

"I hope you never change, Lon. So many people have turned themselves inside out over this. I'll help you, if you let me. You've just got to make up your mind to do it, and I'll help any way you say."

He touched her face with joy and smiled. He put her hat on the table by the window and took her elbow. Very gently he led her through the house.

He realized with amusement he felt more pride in her than he did in the silly walls and rooms. She was really what the house needed, the adornment to his house and to his life. At last, everything seemed to fit into place.

He thanked the Lord for his good fortune but could barely trust himself to believe in it. He had felt that he had been only dreaming for such a long time, and it made him despair. He didn't want to dream anymore. He wanted something real at last. Here was someone very real, someone so grounded, just like him.

He brought her to their bedroom, with infinite tenderness sat her upon the edge of the worn patchwork quilt his mother had made him and sat down beside her. He welcomed her, his sad heart filled with gratitude that felt almost too much to bear.

"I don't want to overstep my bounds," she said, almost in a whisper, "but I know about your problem with the back taxes. I have money, Lon. I have an inheritance from my Uncle John. I'm using it for college, but I still have enough to cover the taxes. It's for you, Lon. I want you to have it. From what I understand, what you can get for selling this place to the state will be far more. Then you will have something to start over."

A wide, slow smile. He touched his forehead to hers, still grinning. He held her with gentleness. He put his lips to hers, slowly, letting her respond as she wanted, and when her breasts touched against him he felt her heart through her thin summer dress.

Jenny happily responded, but felt slow and clumsy, even if Alonzo did not seem to notice. He whispered half-formed thoughts in beautiful quick breaths and called her his beloved wife.

She gripped his belt, slipped her fingertips underneath the waistband of his pants. She left light scratches on his hips, heard herself saying his name, and was instantly aware. Moved to know she wanted him, and how much, she listened to his breathing.

"Lon," she murmured and dragged her heavy hands to his face. He lifted himself slightly to look at her, his face glistening with dampness, his expression intense. That he could be intense surprised her, a lack of control that made her interested and curious.

Eyes never leaving her, he pulled himself off her until he was kneeling on the bed. He lifted her so he could reach around to her back, and kissing her neck he whispered as he unbuttoned the back of her dress.

"I can. Let me."

Wonderful chaos. He touched her throat, gently dragging his fingertips to the base of her neck, down her chest.

"I've been waiting forever." He murmured the words into her shoulder, "and now we have forever."

She gently covered his hands with her hands, as if to guide him, and at the same time, to follow him, to explore with him.

"I'll keep you safe here with me forever." He said it so sweetly, and she almost answered, "Yes," but instead heard herself through deep breaths absently replying,

"Forever? We don't have forever."

"We have forever," he smiled and turned her around, kissing her as he lowered her gently onto her back.

"You don't mean here?"

"Right here, my Jenny-girl. Right here is all we need. Us, and our kids, and we won't need nothing else."

"Lon, stop. Wait a minute. I don't understand...you mean live in this house? What about the reserv— "

He put his hand over her mouth and kissed her forehead.

"Shhh. You and me, right here, forever. Tell me you love me."

He pulled his hand from her mouth and placed his mouth against hers, a long, hard kiss that left them both breathless, but when he finally pulled away, she only stared at him, searching his face.

"We don't have forever here, Lon. That's why I came to talk to you. I wanted to help you see...."

"Shh. We have forever."

"We don't even have the rest of the afternoon. You've made a mistake if you think I can pretend. I can't. Not even for a little while." She searched his face, looking for him in his expression of need and desire, and joy.

"I love you."

"You can't love me someplace else?" She tried to laugh. "Be reasonable, dear." It was no use. There was something about his eyes, his intensity, that made him seem to be in a place where she could not reach him.

Jenny rubbed her face on his muscular arm holding her, then rolled away from him, sat on the edge of bed, and slipped her dress back up over her shoulders. She put her hand on his shoulder to steady herself and stood up. She leaned into him on liquid legs, hoping another moment would clear the pulse in her body, just as her mind was already focusing.

"This is where you belong, Jenny. This is where we both belong."

"No, Lon," she said, mainly for something to say, to give her time. The bright sunlight slid into the room at an afternoon angle, yet the room still seemed dim, the contrast of white beaming on the dusty film on the sill caught her attention. It was disturbing. She looked at Lon.

"This is too much," she whispered, "this is too much for me." She pushed herself away and leaned against the wall and rubbed her forehead. She looked at him guiltily and shook her head sadly. "And not really enough. I want more, and I'll never have it here. I'm sorry."

He smiled from beneath moist and glowing eyes and pulled off his shirt.

Jenny glanced absently for her missing shoe. Alonzo swung his legs over the side of the bed and began to untie the laces of his boots. He kicked her shoe accidentally noticed it and picked it up. He examined it for a moment, then placed it on the floor, neatly lining it up with the bed. Satisfied, he removed his boots.

She glanced at the dirty windowsill again, then gazed more closely at the beam of light which distracted and distressed her. It held a haze of dust, tiny floating debris which must surely have been everywhere in the room but could only be seen in the painfully bright sunlight.

Dear God, this is too much for right now. We don't even have right now. He doesn't know that. I don't want to pretend this. And if pretending is all it's ever going to be…but, oh, Father in heaven, I feel so beautiful and so loved….

Jenny pulled herself up straight. She had been praying to a sunbeam. She felt she had never really prayed before. This was the first time. There were tears in her eyes.

"Lon, I'm so sorry. We're stopping now. You know that. I wanted this too. I never knew how much. But that's not enough. Not when you're like this. This is a mistake. I don't know you. You're lost. Or, I'm lost. Forgive me." Her voice was low and trembling, it so moved him that he did not listen to her words, only the emotion of her soft, low voice.

She took a hesitant step toward him, and briefly touched the dark damp hair on his forehead.

"Find yourself another home, *please*. I'm sorry. I meant it about the back taxes. All this ignoring what's going to happen has got to stop. It's all become just a big, stupid game of pretend for you, and for my father. I love you both, but you're both dead wrong."

She pulled her eyes away from him and turned from the room. He sat still a moment, stiffened, puzzled to see her walk down the hall. He followed her.

"Jenny?" he called.

"It's got to stop, Lon. We have to wake up."

She walked past her bouquet of Queen Anne's lace resting on the rough table in the kitchen, and out the back-screen door. Lulled by the warmth of the afternoon, yet she roused herself stubbornly and slowly felt steadier. The pleasing flush diminished and she stirred a breeze with her walk which chilled her perspiration. Had she really felt all that, made him feel it, and had she really prayed?

Better to walk faster, think about it later when her throat stopped hurting and she didn't feel like crying.

Alonzo stepped out of the house.

"Jenny?" His legs were stiff, he walked woodenly towards her, "Jenny, where are you going?"

"Home, I guess."

"This is your home. It always was. Jenny, you're my wife, y'belong here now…."

"Stop it, Lon."

"Jenny are you afraid of me? You can't be. It'll be all right. You don't have to be afraid. I love you, you're my dear wife...Don't you love me?"

She turned and stopped. "It's got nothing to do with...Lon, I'm not your wife ...shouldn't pretend. I can't live a fantasy, Lon. That's not the kind of person I am. Look at this place. It's a wreck, and you want to keep it forever. You can't. I've seen my father eaten up by a life-long pipe dream, and my uncle falling apart over one in his last days. And now you're so steadfast to pretend the world is going to side step you. Well, that won't be me, Lon. That's not for me. I'm different. I have to face things. I have to know where I stand." Odd, that she would think of Dick right now.

"Jenny?!" his astonished face tore her. "Jenny? You can't leave!"

She turned and walked away, "My offer to help you still stands, if you really want my help. I'm sorry, but I don't come with it. I didn't come here to play house with you."

"Jenny! Come here!" The voice was angry now. She knew now. She stopped again, and swallowed the sick dread, and she was sure.

She turned so she could see his eyes. Slowly, she removed her remaining shoe. He watched her, frustrated, excited, puzzled. She slipped trembling hands under the hem of her dress, lifted it up and her slip, groping for the garter on her thigh. Facing him, she removed one stocking, then the other, as he watched. She bunched them in her hand.

Then she bolted.

"Jenny!" He followed her, both galloping barefoot into the ragged corn. She had meant to plow her way down the steep bank at the edge of the fallow field beyond, down to the Egypt Road and make her way back to Greenwich, but he cut her off as a dog circles and herds sheep, driving her confusedly to different directions by shifting his own. She tore into the line of trees which separated his farm from the abandoned land his father George had once owned.

The waist-high weeds which blossomed in spiny eruptions on George Vaughn's old farm cut her legs as she scrambled through them. In splintering flashbacks of memory, Jenny remembered slopes and thickets from her childhood, she recalled the feel of the land beneath her pounding feet and though the ground was rough she knew how to run. Old hiding places leaped from memory, and she stalled Alonzo for minutes at a time in these pockets of earth, while he gasped for breath and called her name.

Once, behind thin fingers of young maple trees protruding courageously from the very rocks in the stone wall, he got very close to her. She hunched down, fitting her lean body lithe and submissive against the cold stones and a gnarled old trunk. She remembered the hiding and seeking games of her childhood, the absurd excitement it felt to be almost tagged. She opened her mouth very wide so as to swallow quantities of silent breaths. She drew the muscles of her torso in to stifle her panting and listened with all her body to the stumbling footsteps near her.

He paused and listened to the breeze. He called her name in anguish, and for a tortured moment, she nearly answered. Closing her eyes, she touched her damp forehead to the rough, cold wall and prayed again, this time to the ancient stones.

Then he saw her.

***

On their way to Springfield, Roger Lewis and Miss Atkinson stopped in Greenwich Plains to pick up a sewing pattern from her friend Mildred and also to show off Roger. Here on the road to Enfield, Ella caught up with them.

As they were waving goodbye in front of the house and climbing into the car, Ella ran to them, hysterically shouting that her sister was going to get herself in trouble with a dangerous man. Miss Atkinson patted the child and shrugged amusement at Roger. Beaus were supposed to take interruption with good nature, particularly if they involved children. Roger did not look amused, or even annoyed.

"Let's see what this is about." he said and opened the back car door and motioned Ella to get in. He opened Miss Atkinson's door for her but forgot to return her smile as she lifted her skirts, partly for him.

"For a man who never likes to be involved, you sure seem to get involved with the Vaughns." Martha smirked.

"More than they would like, I'm sure. I'm a changed man. You changed me."

He drove to the Enfield depot. Dick was there waiting for the Rabbit train, which just huffed to a stop. He picked up his bundle, was about to board under the disapproving glare of Conductor Doane, when he heard Roger call his name. Roger jumped onto the platform, motioned for him to follow, and paced a step forward and back like a dog trying to get his master's attention. Roger ran halfway to the car and pointed to it.

Roger shouted, "Get in!"

Dick took his hands out of his pockets and looked curiously at his brother.

"Jenny Vaughn!" Roger shouted.

Dick leapt off the wooden platform, tossed his small duffel into the back seat at Ella and climbed in. He exchanged a head-snapping nod with Miss Atkinson as Roger floored the accelerator. Suddenly noticing Ella, Dick roughly put his arm around the child.

"Tell me, what is it?"

Ella gulped directions up the Prescott road with uncertain memory and an anxiety-inspired attack of the hiccups. She wished her father or Harrison was here, they would know the way better.

Roger knew the land only as a grid on a map, but it all suddenly served him. He recognized landmarks he had studied for years from engineering reports and photos. How interesting the real land was, alive and three-dimensional, he chided himself for stupidity. And yet he recognized it all. He knew this place.

"I know where I'm going."

***

Jenny eluded Alonzo twice in the abandoned fields. His anger fought with his anxiety. She was the only thing that mattered. He saw her again and would not be teased anymore.

There, towards the graveyard ahead he chased her, and caught her.

"They can take my neighbors. They can take my town. They can take my farm. But I will have you. Jenny, you're all I have left, and by God, I will have you!"

More brutal than he realized, he fell upon her with a hard tackle, crumpling her to the ground.

***

"There!" Ella pointed wildly, hiccupping at Roger, "Jenny's over there!"

"Remember what I said, now," Miss Atkinson said smoothly, "try holding your breath but you count to ten at the same...."

"Oh, for God's sake Martha, let the girl hiccup!" Roger barked.

From the car they spotted Jenny and Alonzo at the former cemetery near the former site of the former town meeting house.

The heavy car stopped with a wrench, and Roger and Dick scrambled out. Miss Atkinson whispered anxiously to Ella, "Stay here, dear."

Dick galloped over the warped and rutted ground, now empty of graves or markers. Alonzo noticed him through bleary eyes and stood sharply, yanking Jenny to him.

"Get out!" he yelled and Dick stopped quick. Hunched like a boxer out of breath, he stood helpless, waiting for a cue from Alonzo or Jenny.

Jenny was white, dazed, with a scrape on her head and the breath knocked out of her. With Alonzo's arm thrust through her tousled hair and firmly across her collarbone, she listened and gasped and looked for meaning in Dick's being suddenly here.

Roger remembered the hunting rifle in the trunk of his friend's car and clumsily trotted over with it in his arms. Later he shamefully remembered wondering if it gave him authority. He aimed it at Alonzo, whom he had never seen before.

"Let her go," he shouted, and Dick turned in surprise to see his brother with a gun. Like Jenny, he plunged helplessly into dream-like confusion, not sure of what was really happening and doubting his own perception of it. He looked from Roger to Jenny and back again.

Alonzo clutched Jenny before him as a shield, pulled her body to him, and kissed her hair.

"Get out." he said wearily over her head.

"Let her go now." Roger said in a calm, even voice.

"Love you my Jenny-girl," Alonzo whispered to the back of her head. "I'll love you forever. Do you know that?"

"I don't...believe you...anymore." Her words were mere gasps, but he heard.

Ella climbed out of the big car and walked, teary-eyed and trembling, into the war-torn looking graveyard, past Roger, past Dick who tried to grab her but missed, and stood a few yards away from Alonzo and Jenny.

Miss Atkinson, alone in the car, mumbled "Damn."

"Jenny come home," Ella called in her thin voice. Jenny looked at her, concentrated on her and would not let herself feel Alonzo's touch.

He kissed Jenny's hair again.

"Hi, Lon."

"Hello, Ella."

She smiled, and brought her glance back to her sister, watching his hands grope her. "Come on now, Jenny."

Alonzo looked beyond Ella to the boy who was Jenny's friend and the man with the gun. Damn them all to hell. He hadn't brought his gun, he wished he'd brought his gun.

He was more distracted by Ella. Standing stiffly in a clump of weeds, she held out her arms, waiting for Jenny to come.

"Jenny has to come home with me, Lon. Mother needs her. It'll be all right. Okay?"

"She is home."

"It'll be all right. You can let her go, Lon. Everything's all right. Okay?"

"All right...okay," he echoed finally, and his arms relaxed as he released his grasp. His hands sifted the folds of her light dress. With tears he watched her stumble on scratched and bleeding legs to her sister. Ella wrapped her thin arms around Jenny's waist and supported her like a crutch.

"It's all right," Ella murmured to comfort her, "Just a little farther. You can do it."

Dick wanted to lift her and carry her the rest of the way, to get out of this place quickly. He looked from Alonzo to Roger. Roger motioned him away to the car. Dick obeyed him.

Jenny whispered hoarsely into Ella's hair, "You're a pretty tough kid, aren't you?"

Alonzo, without shoes or shirt or gun or hope, dropped to the cool, disheveled earth and cried. Roger lowered the rifle, which had not been loaded.

"I'm sorry." Roger whispered to him. "I'm really sorry."

***

Eli had driven back to Prescott after he had finished helping to move the herd. It was nearly twilight when he arrived at the house, his boyhood home. There were no lights.

"You stay in the truck," he told Harrison. He stepped in the back door.

"Lon!"

He glanced quickly into the front room, his parents' room that had been the room he shared with Mary when he first brought her here.

"Lon!"

He pumped the handle at the kitchen sink until cold water spurted out from the earth below, and he splashed the water onto his face, wiping it over his neck, drinking from his hand. As the trickled slowed, he listened for any sound around him, but could hear only the crickets begin their evening chorus outside.

He stepped briefly into the dark parlor, looking at the old furniture, his mother's needlework on the wall. He stepped into his parents' old room. The bedclothes were rumpled on Lon's bed, and Lon's boots were beside the bed.

He did not notice Jenny's straw hat on the parlor table.

Eli stepped out into the yard. Deepening shadows made him feel unaccountably anxious, such as he had never felt before here.

"Lon!"

It would be too dark to see soon. Lon was not answering or Lon was not here, but either way it would have to wait until daylight.

Eli got back into his truck and turned on the headlights and drove as carefully as he could down the ridge back to Greenwich.

"Somebody's here," Harrison said, pointing to the car parked in front of the house.

"It's Roger Lewis' car. Could this day get any worse?"

Roger and Miss Atkinson sat in the parlor with Ella, and Roger stood when Eli entered.

"We brought Jenny home," Roger said. He nodded toward the kitchen. Mary was dabbing scratches on Jenny's face with a washcloth.

"My gosh, what happened?"

Jenny took the washcloth from her mother, and with gentleness, kissed her mother's cheek. She turned to her father and gave him a hug. Eli put his arms around her and looked to Mary with a stricken expression for some quick explanation. Mary's eyes filled. Jenny pulled away from her father, and called into the parlor,

She said, "Mr. Lewis, could you please ask Mr. Clough to come back here? I'm going to pay some back taxes and buy my grandfather's farm in Prescott. I'd like him to come up and appraise it for me, so I can sell it to the state."

She turned, and looked back at Eli, gently, with sympathy but with firmness.

"My father will want to talk to him, too, about this farm. We're ready to sell now."

End of Part III

PART IV
1935 - 1938

CHAPTER 21

The Acts of 1927 could have been one of those documents which every local patriot kept in a desk drawer or in a frame on the wall, like those yellowed copies of the Declaration and the Constitution, and the Thanksgiving proclamation. It had an even more personal and direct influence on the lives of the people living in the Swift River Valley towns in the 1930s than any of those other more famous documents. No one wanted a copy.

Perhaps the crisp language of the Acts of 1927 kept its victims from wholly understanding it. Proclamations had used to be flowery, giving free reign to the imagination, which made them good for reading on Decoration Day. This document which proclaimed their doom was sparse, general and almost vague. It left them reading between the lines and finding nothing to grasp. What were they looking for? A justification? Or verbiage which might hide an apology? Or some footnote on their noble sacrifice? It was noble, wasn't it? At the very least it was a sacrifice. They hoped that would be understood.

One family who left their Greenwich home for good learned the full measure of sacrifice when they settled in a section of Chicopee once called the Tobacco Plains for its stretches of commercial broadleaf tobacco plantations. In the late 1930s this land was sold by the City of Chicopee to the United States for an Army Air Corps base. Westover Field sent that particular family on its way again.

"This is the last time," the father mumbled as he hoisted the kitchen table onto the roof of the car, "they can build the next public works project around me."

Back in the Valley, those who had not yet left had much to consider, but few choices.

After 1935, things began to move quickly. Dana's population, which had been decreasing steadily, was now down to 387 people, while unobserved and relinquished, Prescott's population dropped to eighteen. Prescott had been doomed for a generation, but Dana's citizens were not given the official word whether their town would be required as well until nearly the very end. There was debate about the extension of necessary watershed land, and it was decided that since the Quabbin was to be such a large and important water resource all efforts should be made to safeguard the quality of the water. The engineers were determined to create a large protective ecosystem, though the word was not commonly used then.

The Dana townsfolk who stayed were hopeful until the final disappointment, and those who left previously were spared the suspense. Greenwich and Enfield, which up to this time had lost inhabitants slowly, often replaced by the transient renters, now began to face the inevitable.

The last active factory in the Valley, the Swift River Box Company, was shut down this year. The abandonment of the local railroad forced the old factory to move its production from North Dana to Athol.

That poky little train service which epitomized the isolation and yet strong sense of community binding the four towns together was discontinued. In June the last ride on the old Rabbit Run was taken by about one hundred who wanted to say they'd done it. Old Mr. Doane was called out from retirement to yell, "Ull…Booo-wud!" It was all he would venture to say about the whole matter.

Then the tracks were pried up.

It was the year Mr. X. H. Goodnough died. He was the originator of the Reservoir project, author of the first proposals, a visionary in what might have been an improbable engineering feat. The work on the Quabbin Reservoir continued, and the following year the contract was awarded for the building of the main embankment to what would later be called the Winsor Dam after chief engineer Frank Winsor. The names of these two important men, Goodnough and Winsor, were bestowed as memorials on the two main structures which would hold back the man-made sea they had created but would not live to see.

The Winsor Dam and the Goodnough Dike were works of applied imagination. Cement caissons were sunk deep into the earth, and men would work inside their cores under air pressure not unlike that experienced by deep-sea divers.

The core wall rose, as one town observer noted, like one of the ancient pyramids from the hands of many men. But it was really due to hydraulics. The wall rose from the core sunk into the earth, attached to bedrock. The concrete face was cuddled by stone and riprap, while an earthen embankment nestled against the dam on the dry side. The Winsor Dam rose in Enfield between the Great Quabbin Hill and the Belchertown line, past the point where the three branches of the Swift River became one. On the other side of the hill, where tributaries of the Middle and East branches ran down through Greenwich, erupting into small lakes like rivulets on a pane, the water would be trapped by the Goodnough Dike in Enfield near the Ware line. The land, the Valley itself was a perfect, natural cup.

Rock ledges were blasted, and spillways, baffle dams, aqueducts were created around the remaining valley residents like a fortress, where they were threatened from the inside.

People began to leave in droves, as if it would be too late to leave and they might be trapped if they waited any longer. Though the railroad was gone, the Daniel Shays Highway aided their exodus. A long, smooth, winding, efficient ribbon of macadam such as they had never seen in town, the memorial to their outlaw rebel ancestor by-passed the Valley on its western side, from Belchertown up through Pelham, Shutesbury, New Salem and into Athol.

Dismantling of houses quickened, and many sections of homes were to be moved to other areas. The bell from the Greenwich Congregational church was sold to a Catholic church in the nearby village of Bondsville. The Coldbrook Baptist church of Greenwich was reassembled in the town of Greenfield by the Connecticut River. Most of the buildings, however, were simply destroyed. These spared remnants were unique survivors. The people were beginning to feel that way themselves, as echoed in the local press. They were called the Survivors in the sudden flutter of interest displayed by the outside world.

Some stayed to work on jobs with the Reservoir construction. Jobs came as a godsend in days like these, though one young man named Adam who was employed as a water boy began to doubt this as his partner lowered him in a metal barrel down the thin, dark hole to the caisson deep in the earth to retrieve spring water. He prayed each time in the dark until he rose again to the sunlight, each time swearing it'd be the last. Once back on the surface, his job was to bring the cold water by the dipperful to each dusty man in the trenches, who put down his shovel and rinsed his filmy mouth, passing it on to the next man.

Despite the opportunity for employment most of the work was done by outsiders. These included the woodpeckers.

The woodpeckers were assigned the awesome task of clearing the valley floor of all vegetation to a height reckoned ten feet above where the flood line would be. With axes, saws, bulldozers and tractors they cleared all life. Underneath the tangled mass of crops, flower gardens, trees and orchards and groves, they revealed a new face upon the Valley. It was bare, rocky, violently naked. It showed no history and no future.

The last generation of children began to celebrate the end of the last school day ever, the last grammar school graduation class in town. Miss Murphy taught "In Flanders Fields" for the last Decoration Day ceremonies, and then thought about her future. The school board was making plans to distribute desks and books to other towns which could use them. Nobody was going to distribute her anyplace. She had to find a job. Her serenity was shaken for the first time in twenty years.

It was the end of the church of various denominations, which had been founded by a pioneer community cherishing their freedom, prayerful that their boldness in settling so far into the woods would not destroy them, and always asking for God's mercy.

"And the children of Israel went up in orderly ranks out of the land of Egypt...." their descendents read in Exodus. Others, less able or likely to proselytize, cringed at "Remove not the ancient landmark, which thy fathers have set ..." as they watched their churches fall. Other kinds of landmarks fell too, like the old Eagle House in Dana, and Enfield's grand Swift River Hotel.

"By the rivers of Babylon, there we sat down,
yea, we wept when we remembered Zion...."

They would always remember Mt. Zion, and all the hilltops that became islands.

Farmers reaped their last harvests in the autumn of 1937. No more planting would be allowed by the Commonwealth.

Eli Vaughn reaped his third harvest that fall at his new farm in Belchertown. It was thirty acres and little by little, he worked to transform it from subsistence farming to commercial fruit crops.

He never let himself feel as if his Belchertown farm would always be his home, as if it really belonged to him. Life would not play such tricks on his ego again. Permanence was at last shaken from his psyche. In his weary mind he became a transient and did not feel safe enough to set markers and lay cornerstones, not even a wooden sign. They meant nothing. All life was temporary.

"Unless this was meant to be." Mary remarked in another strange new kitchen. Eli looked absently at her.

"Destiny." she said, "Or, or pre-destination. What would your mother have thought?"

Eli's eyes lit up, and he lowered his chin to his coffee cup. He smiled grimly. Mother would have had a handle on all this.

But it was the next generation, it was for Harrison that Eli focused himself. He had left the decision to settle there to Harrison, and then worked for his son's benefit alone. Eli had always needed to apply himself to one goal, one clear purpose. It was the only way he could apply himself at all. He did not dare consider the possibility of Harrison's wanting another occupation, or another home. Harrison dared not consider what would happen at home if he did. Resigned, he took up his father's burden.

If Harrison thought of pre-destination at all it was not in reference to the Quabbin Reservoir, but to himself and his few remaining friends. They had grown up knowing their communities were destined for extinction, had come of age in the worst Depression of modern times. Though they did not know it now, they were to spend the remaining years of youth left to them in a catastrophic world war in which many of them would be killed.

They endured all this better than their sentimental, fearful and lonely parents. They had to; whatever was left of the Swift River Valley was left only in them.

Jenny Vaughn had not considered this yet. She was more preoccupied with surviving herself than keeping the memory of her town alive. In autumn of 1937 she was in her junior year at the Massachusetts State College in Amherst.

Founded as an agricultural college in a part of the state where agriculture ruled the local economy for three hundred years, the "Aggie" as the school was sometimes called was developing into a broader-based school just as New England had been attempting since the turn of the century to develop a broader-based economy. Balance was the key to survival, and balance was ever elusive.

Jenny pursued her Bachelor's in economics, having discovered an interest in this science that complimented her ant-like energy for order and accomplishment. Economics, it seemed to her, was a factor in their losing the Valley, the trauma which created the decade of her teen years, and reasons for what would stimulate the future, if there was to be a future at all.

She lived at her Aunt Jane's house in Amherst, near the college where her husband still taught. Their boys were grown and gone, and Jenny was like the daughter they never had; and never would have had if they'd had her, Mary smugly told her husband.

Dick Lewis had completed his high school equivalency in the CCC and began college prep courses on his free time. His brother Roger wanted to send him to college, and Dick gave in. As soon as his last CCC hitch was up in the late spring he agreed to begin courses at the Massachusetts State College at Amherst in engineering.

While he was in the CCC he wrote to Jenny as he said he would. He told her about life in the camp, his visits to local New Hampshire towns, and of playing baseball against the town team in Contoocook and hitting the first home run of his life. He sent her a picture of himself in his CCC uniform.

At the time he had been loading picks into the back of a truck, his shirt draped across the side mirror on the driver's door when his pal Benny asked him to take a picture for him. Benny offered to take Dick's picture in return, and Dick put his shirt back on, made himself presentable and stood with his hands in his pockets next to a two-foot conifer tree. Benny pulled the box brownie from his face and grinned at Dick.

"What, is this for your mother?"

"Just take the picture."

In return he received a photo of Jenny, taken in the sun-filled garden at the home of her Aunt Jane and Uncle Robert. Uncle Robert took the photo and glowered in his displeased professor look to discover that his bumbling technique revealed only a cock-eyed angle of her face and shoulders, with broken sunlight streaking her hair, leaving the right side of her face darkened. Because of the long ordeal of posing and her doubtfulness of Uncle Robert's picture taking abilities, as well as the sudden memory of Uncle John taking her photograph one day in the backyard of the Greenwich Village farm, her smile had faded slightly and there played a wariness in her clear steady eyes which looked directly into the camera. Dick thought it appropriate to her nature and laughed in the delight of recognition.

"Do you still hate taking orders and being bossed around?" she wrote, and described her classes, her aunt and uncle, and the rally bonfire. They did not write to each other about the Valley, or the Depression, or Hitler, or of the future at all.

Dick had wanted to ask about Alonzo but didn't. He knew only that Jenny had taken part of her inheritance from her Uncle John to pay the back taxes on the Prescott farm, and in doing so, bought it.

***

Everything in the house was as she had last seen it. She decided to keep the old highboy.

She gasped at the sight of her straw hat on the table. Her shoe in the yard.

When Mr. Clough arrived to appraise the property, she strolled with him through her grandparents' house and all around the grounds with stoic, dignified propriety which impressed Eben Clough.

In deference to her being mistress of the land, he asked a few polite questions on its history, which she capably answered, about her family's arrival in Narragansett Township 4 after King Philip's War, about her family's personal involvement in Shays' Rebellion, about the stone walls which each successive generation maintained, about the sturdy row of rock maples her great-grandfather planted for syrup.

"This place has been in your family for some two-hundred years?" He whistled.

"Granted to us by a king, and taken away from us by democracy," she teased him.

He sat at her kitchen table, drank her lemonade, and made his notes under her watchful eye. He made vague compliments about her land as he scribbled. She sold it at a profit.

"The last Vaughn ever to own that land," Eli marveled.

"And the one who sold out." Jenny ruefully reminded him, yet accepting that burden, too.

He looked at her. She was nearly as tall as himself. She had her mother's eyes and something of his own mother in her. She was smart, and no matter where she stood, her feet were on the ground, despite the burdens they imposed her, and the ones she would always create for herself.

He put his arm around her. "But for a short time, at least, you owned the promised land." His eyes filled, and for reasons she was only beginning to understand, so did hers.

Nothing was heard from Alonzo after that day. It was rumored he lived on the ridge still, as wild as a rabbit, carrying on a surreptitious, guerrilla life by night and hiding among the soapstone cliffs by day. Not very likely of course, but no one knew and in the end, it was just another improbable story in what had been for them a long, bizarre decade.

***

The remaining residents were given the order to evacuate by June, 1938.

They felt the irony then, as if now that they were given a definite date they felt a sense of direction. Like the end point on a timeline which gave definition to an era, it seemed as if the evacuation notice gave their lives sudden meaning though they had foundered for over a decade. They would leave with ceremony.

There was the tidy business of final meetings, final women's club meetings, including the coincidentally named ladies' Quabbin Club of Enfield. There were the final Grange meetings. In February of 1938 the final town meeting of Greenwich was held ending 225 years of town government. Among the voters attending were former residents who had since moved to other towns. Eli Vaughn and his wife Mary did not attend. It seemed to Eli as if his friends were rushing down a great river towards a waterfall. Now that he and his family were safe away from it, he did not want to look.

In March, the final town meeting in Dana was held. Roger Lewis brought his wife Martha and her brother Reverend Atkinson who traveled from his new church in Vermont. Their family had originally come from Dana.

They conducted the meeting solemnly, and defiantly in the dim hall. Roger gave the remaining seat to his wife, and he stood in back of her, leaning against the whitewashed wall, his arms folded, watching the proceedings with interest.

Voters present conscientiously, belligerently, elected town officers for the coming year, though the town's existence was scheduled to end in a month. Dana would surrender its charter free of debt. This mattered to them. Roger Lewis smiled with helpless pleasure at their dignity and thought with pride how his children would inherit their mother's Dana heritage somehow.

Town meeting was as sacred a New England custom as Thanksgiving, in part because it was also communal despite the treasured self-identity of *independent* thought and actions. It was a man's birthright, much later, a woman's. It imparted responsibility, and the taking up of responsibility engendered nobility.

Twenty-six turned out to the final Enfield town meeting in a sleet storm. In March, the remaining unbought land in the Swift River Valley was taken by eminent domain. Those who had refused to sell since the beginning had no choice now. Eminent domain was the opposite of town meeting, it paid no homage to democracy and was yet more powerful, an historical display of government omnipotence.

The people were all monetarily compensated for their losses.

The official date for the disincorporation of the towns in the Swift River Valley was scheduled for April 28th, 1938. On the night of April 27th, a Farewell Ball was held. The event was chaired by officials of the four towns.

Again, Eli had not wanted to go, but Mary this time insisted.

"Do you want to go for the kids' sake, or yourself?" Eli asked her, "They don't care that much."

"I'm doing this for my mother and father."

Ida and Walter came down from Athol, leaving their little son Water, Jr. with a babysitter, another unheard-of innovation in Ida's long history of them. Doris came with her new beau Charlie. However influential she found her capable Aunt Hattie, Doris did not want to follow her footsteps into spinsterhood. Hattie had been left alone except for Doris after the death of Mrs. Pratt, and typically, Hattie stayed home this evening. Harrison, who was seeing a Belchertown girl did not care if he attended, but it seemed like this was going to be one of those family things, so he asked the girl and she thought it would be fun.

Jenny asked Dick Lewis, now her schoolmate in Amherst, to come.

"This is for you folks. I'm an outsider, Jenny."

"So will we all be the day after."

Roger and Martha Lewis would attend, of course. Roger was becoming a well-known face at many of these last events, and no one seemed to bear him the grudge he feared. He and Martha were in the process of buying a house in Belchertown, not far from Eli Vaughn's place.

A crowd of three hundred was expected, but over one thousand came home that night to buy their fifty-cent tickets, including amused but sympathetic members of the local press, who insisted on calling them

"Survivors." They at last were beginning to feel more like survivors, and less like the damned.

A line of cars snaked along the inadequate remaining road in a dusty parade beginning early in the day, long before the scheduled 8:00 p.m. start of the event. It was to be held in the old Enfield brick town hall, one of the few buildings left for miles. The Grange, such as what was left of the organization, offered box dinners, and the volunteer firemen doggedly served beer from the basement of the town hall. No argument needed now about being "dry" or not.

The Vaughns drove in their truck with the Lewis car behind. Dick and Jenny rode with his brother and sister-in-law, and Jenny gaped out the car window at the barren Valley floor.

There were no trees, no landmarks or buildings, only a lingering ribbon of road and the desolate plain following the torn old railroad bed and a finger of the Swift River which flowed down from an equally barren Greenwich. It seemed to Jenny that the face of the moon could not be so uninhabitable.

Night came and discreet darkness covered with propriety the naked scene.

Roger opened the door for the ladies as they entered the Town Hall. He patted Jenny's shoulder for their mutual reassurance.

Bodies jostling from the bandstand to the balcony. The small orchestra played modern dance tunes and the younger set thought perhaps they might enjoy themselves after all. Their parents and grandparents shook hands, wiped at tears, and tried to remember everything that had ever happened to them in this place. Their fear was no longer over leaving; it now was about forgetting.

They ate and drank. Dr. Wendell, who seemed almost ironically revived by the shattering experience, led the Grand March. The crowd looked to him and thought to themselves, yes, we'll be all right.

He had delivered most of them to the world they knew. He had set bones, treated illness, gave them Necco wafers when they were children. He held the hands of the dying, held confidences and secrets. No single man in the entire Valley was as important. They treasured him. They wished they could tell him how much. Instead, for years afterwards they told their children and grandchildren.

Just before midnight, he stopped the orchestra with the slightest tremor of his weakened old hands. He drew himself up, though fragile with age, and summoned all the dignity and proportion in him as the hall grew quiet. He looked at them, almost sternly, as if warning them to mind themselves, and said in a clear baritone voice,

"Ladies and Gentlemen...Goodbye." Then he nodded silently to them, a New Englander's both welcome and farewell. A spare movement of economy, it required little energy, expressing only acknowledgment, which was everything. They wanted only to be acknowledged.

Eli, hand shaking, eyes blurred, tugged his grandfather's watch from his vest pocket. His family pulled closer to him to watch over his arm as the second hand swept past midnight.

Dana, Massachusetts, was gone.

Enfield, Massachusetts, was gone.

Greenwich, Massachusetts, was gone.

Prescott, Massachusetts, was gone.

Author's note: X.H. Goodnough and Frank Winsor were instrumental in the Quabbin Reservoir project. All other characters in this novel are fictional.

**

Also by the author:

Fiction:

The Double V Mysteries series:

Cadmium Yellow, Blood Red (No. 1)
Speak Out Before You Die (No. 2)
Dismount and Murder (No. 3)
Whitewash in the Berkshires (No. 4)
Murder at the Summer Theater (No. 5.)

Other fiction:

Meet Me in Nuthatch
The Current Rate of Exchange
Beside the Still Waters
Myths of the Modern Man
Collected Shorts

Non-fiction books:

Ann Blyth: Actress. Singer. Star.
Comedy and Tragedy on the Mountain: 70 Years of Summer Theatre on Mt. Tom,
    Holyoke, Massachusetts
States of Mind: New England
The Ames Manufacturing Company of Chicopee, Massachusetts
Hollywood Fights Fascism
Movies in Our Time: Hollywood Mirrors and Mimics the Twentieth Century
Classic Films and the American Conscience
Calamity Jane in the Movies

ABOUT THE AUTHOR

Jacqueline T. Lynch's novels, short stories, and non-fiction books on New England history and film criticism are available from many online shops as eBooks, audiobook, and paperback. She is also a playwright whose plays have been produced around the United States and in Europe, and has published articles and short fiction in regional and national publications. She writes *Another Old Movie Blog* on classic films, and the syndicated newspaper column *Silver Screen, Golden Memories*. For more on Jacqueline T. Lynch's book and projects, and to receive newsletter updates and special offers, please see: www.jacquelinetlynch.com.

Made in the USA
Monee, IL
18 August 2021

75977912R10134